Shaun Hutson is a ... fiction and has writt... pseudonyms. He v... authors taking part in the BBCs *End of Story* competition and has appeared in his first film. He lives and writes in Buckinghamshire with his wife and daughter and two pairs of Michelle Pfeiffer's shoes.

For more details on Shaun Hutson and his books visit www.shaunhutson.com

SHAUN HUTSON OMNIBUS

Erebus
&
Victims

Shaun Hutson

sphere

SPHERE

First published in Great Britain in 2007 by Sphere

Sphere
An imprint of
Little, Brown Book Group
Brettenham House
Lancaster Place
London WC2E 7EN

A Member of the Hachette Livre Group of Companies

www.littlebrown.co.uk

Erebus

Dedication

To Peter Williams
Make mine a de-caffeinated with honey

Acknowledgements

To everyone who helped with this book, thank you. On the research side, I would like to thank Mr Peter Milton. Regarding the actual writing, many thanks to Niki, who helped me even more than usual. Thanks also to Bob Tanner who, at the beginning, gave me the kick up the backside I so richly deserved. And I am grateful to everyone at W. H. Allen concerned with the production and distribution of this book.

Shaun Hutson

Erebus (er-u-bus): 1. A region beyond Hades; the abode of the Dead.

2. The Greek God of darkness, born of chaos.

PART ONE

'The motions of his spirit are dull as night,
And his affections dark as Erebus . . .'
    – *The Merchant of Venice*; Act V; scene 1

'Shame on the night.
For places I've been
And what I've seen . . .'
    – Ronnie James Dio

PART ONE

One

The gravel of the driveway crunched loudly beneath the wheels of the Rolls Royce as Terence Bristow brought the vehicle to a halt.

He switched off the engine and glanced across to the passenger seat where his wife, Laura, sat. They exchanged smiles and clambered out of the car. The drive from their home some eight miles from Wakely, to the stables, had taken less than fifteen minutes and they had passed just two vehicles on the way.

It was still early and Laura pulled her white mink jacket tighter around her in an effort to ward off the slight chill in the air. Fingers of mist drew patterns across the grass which surrounded the complex of white-washed buildings. She wasn't normally up so early in the morning, and, glancing down, she saw that the hands of her solid gold Cartier watch had barely reached 7.06 a.m.

Bristow rubbed his hands together, smiling as he saw the senior stud-groom approaching from one of the stables. They exchanged pleasantries and proceeded up a narrow path towards another building.

'How are things today?' asked Bristow.

'Fine, Mr Bristow,' said John Peters, scratching at his left ear. 'We had the foal out in the paddock yesterday. He's feeding well and he looks strong.'

Bristow nodded approvingly. The foal had been late, born just two days ago. A May foal. Something of a

3

rarity in the world of racing but, Bristow reasoned, the animal would be worth millions. Sired, as it had been, by Regal Gent, winner of both the English and Irish Derbies the previous year. After the second win, Bristow had decided to put the animal out to stud. Now, as he leant on the gate of the box and looked in, he smiled contentedly.

The smell of fresh straw was strong in his nostrils and, inside the box, one young studman was busily turning the yellow strands over with a small pitchfork. Another lad, a rotund, red-faced youth in his teens, was brushing the tail of the mare which stood quietly before him. Bristow's eyes strayed to the foal and he was suitably satisfied by the sleek sheen of both animals' coats. The mare was a bay, a large animal perhaps eighteen or nineteen hands and she seemed to dwarf the foal which nuzzled her flanks.

'A winner if ever I saw one,' said Bristow reaching across to grip his wife's hand.

Laura was looking at the mare which had begun to move its head back and forth somewhat agitatedly.

'She's lathering up a little, isn't she?' Laura said, noticing some flecks of sweat around the animal's neck.

The studman brushing the mare's tail merely continued with his task. He stepped back, accidentally treading in some droppings. His companion held back a chuckle and continued turning the straw. But, as he looked up, he too saw that the bay was beginning to sweat. She continued to swing her head back and forth for a moment longer then she suddenly froze. But her ears were pricked, her nostrils flared wide and, as he watched, her eyes seemed to roll in the sockets. She snorted loudly.

With lightning speed, the mare lashed out with her offside hind leg, driving her hoof back savagely, catching the younger studman in the solar plexus. There was a sickening thud, accompanied by the strident cracking of bone as several ribs splintered under the impact and he was propelled backward by the blow, crashing into the far wall of the box. In the twelve foot square area all hell suddenly seemed to break loose.

'What's wrong with her?' Bristow shouted at Peters who was already slipping the catch on the door in an effort to get inside the enclosure but, as he saw the mare rear up, he slowed his pace.

The first studman dropped his fork and pressed himself against the wall, heart hammering against his ribs. He glanced at the mare and then at his companion who was slumped against the rear wall, blood dribbling over his lips. He had no means of restraining the mare for she wore no harness of any kind. The foal took a couple of nervous steps back, whinneying softly.

'For God's sake do something,' Bristow demanded as he watched the mare turn its attention to the foal.

The larger animal struck swiftly, its head snaking forward cobra-like to strike at the bewildered foal. Powerful teeth were clamped together like a vice and the mare bit hard, twisting its head for a second, tearing a large lump of flesh and muscle free. The bite was a lethal one for it severed one of the foal's carotid arteries. Blood exploded from the savage wound with the force of a high pressure hose, spraying the horrified onlookers.

Laura Bristow screamed as the crimson fluid splattered across her face and body, turning her white mink the colour of poppies. Bristow himself could only watch mesmerised as the mare reared high in the air before bringing both front hooves crashing down onto the smaller animal's back, smashing its spine. The foal crumpled beneath the onslaught, its legs collapsing under it. The little animal raised its head as if soliciting help but a piledriver blow from the mare caught it above the right eye. The sharp edge of the hoof shaved away a portion of the skull and tore the glistening orb from

5

the socket. Still attached by the optic nerve, it dangled like some bloodied table tennis ball from the gaping hole in its head.

The first studman took his chance and ran for the unlatched door. The mare struck at him but missed and the youth vaulted the partition, rolling over in the gravel on the other side.

'Get some help! Hurry!' shouted Peters and the lad scrambled to his feet.

Laura had fainted but Bristow himself could only stand and stare, as if entranced by the horrendous tableau before him. He failed to notice that Peters had turned away and was shouting to several other men nearby, motioning for them to join him.

The foal was already dead and the mare stood over the body, her mad eyes fixing Bristow in a challenging stare. The air was thick with the stench of blood and excrement, the only sounds now the low snorting of the horse and the moans of pain from the injured studman.

Bristow heard voices drawing closer. He felt his stomach begin to churn and then, as he took one last look at the foal, he bent double and retched until there was nothing left in his stomach.

Two

The mist hung thickly around the hills and hollows which surrounded the town of Wakely. But, as a watery sun began to haul itself across the sky, those shreds of

6

condensation began to disperse, as if a veil were being drawn back to reveal the small town.

It stood amidst a patchwork of woods and fields, some of the many farms which dotted its outskirts clung to the sides of the low hills. Others, like the town itself, seemed to be hiding away in shallow valleys.

The closest town to it, about twenty minutes drive along the main road which bisected the countryside, was Arkham. The two places could not have been more different. The latter being a thriving, bustling centre of industry and commerce whilst Wakely depended largely on its livestock and arable farming. The economy of the whole place seemed to revolve around the dozen or so farms nearby. The land rewarded the efforts of those who toiled on it. The soil was rich in minerals and, other than a disastrous failed harvest back in 1964, no one in Wakely could remember when nature had denied them full bounty.

The town itself was a curious amalgam of ancient and modern. In the high street, one or two half-timbered houses sat almost reluctantly alongside red brick shops and small offices. The town was regarded affectionately by its older inhabitants, sometimes reviled by the younger members of the community due to its lack of leisure amenities. But for a bingo hall and a twice weekly disco (held in the small youth club) Wakely offered little in the way of entertainment. Days were spent at work, nights in front of the television or at one of the six pubs. Once more the clash of chronology showed itself in the architecture of the pubs themselves. There were those which still burned real fires in their grates in winter and refused the intrusion of a juke-box, whilst others sported pool tables and drinking was done to the accompaniment of pop music and the electronic bleeping of Space Invaders.

The town seemed to represent a polarisation of styles

and opinions but its inhabitants were united by one thing. Their reliance on the land.

Butchers bought local livestock at the weekly market. The numerous grocers purchased their goods from those farmers who maintained arable lands. Even bakeries made their own flour from wheat and corn supplied locally. Outsiders came to buy, naturally, but the town seemed to guard its yields jealously and buyers from anywhere other than Wakely itself usually went home with little or nothing.

But, if the produce of the surrounding countryside was something to be horded, friendship was not. Isolated it might have been but Wakely's inhabitants were not imbued with the coldness which sometimes afflicts residents of isolated communities. Nonetheless, it remained a town in hiding. Nestled within its cocoon of hills, trees and fields Wakely and its residents survived admirably without the help or hindrance of outsiders.

In the stillness of the morning, sounds of men at work were already beginning to fill the air. Those who worked on the farms had been on the go since before the break of dawn and now, as the sun burned away the last wraith-like vestiges of mist, Wakely began to come to life.

Three

Ken Hargreaves put down his slice of cake and grunted irritably.

'Do you have to do that at the bloody table?' he

rasped, looking across at his companion who was busily inspecting the contents of one nostril on the end of his finger.

Nick Daley apologised and returned to his cup of tea instead. At just twenty-nine he was almost twenty years younger than his thick-set colleague opposite. Ken Hargreaves took one more fleeting look at the younger man then stuffed what was left of the cake into his mouth, his attention shifting to the newspaper spread out before him. All around other men chatted, smoked, drank tea or coffee and ate. Some with hearty appetites, others more perfunctorily. Hargreaves saw this same ritual every day and had done for the past thirty-two years.

In the canteen of Wakely abattoir men discovered whether they really *were* hungry or not. Of the younger men, Daley amongst them, few ate with such gusto as Hargreaves and his older workmates. He, himself, had just demolished three rashers of bacon and two eggs before his cake. Daley had prodded at a piece of apple pie, more interested in gazing round about him than eating. Or, Hargreaves reasoned, somewhat reluctant to fill his stomach, imagining the sight he would shortly be witnessing.

The only thing which Hargreaves had not been able to get used to in all his years at the place was the smell. He expected it to smell like a charnel house downstairs because that was what it was. The stench of blood and excrement was almost palpable, such was its intensity. But, even now, in the light, air-conditioned canteen, that smell still followed him – the smell of death which clung to him after work like a second skin, resistant to even the strongest soaps, unremovable by countless showers and baths. His clothes were washed every night yet still that pungent odour seemed to permeate the very fibres as an ever-present reminder of the job he did.

9

Wakely abattoir employed just over fifty men engaged in tasks ranging from the unloading of livestock, the inspecting of those animals for disease, preparation of the carcasses and, naturally, killing. That was the job which Hargreaves performed. As many as 500 animals a day passed through the slaughterhouse, arriving in twos and threes, brought by individual farmers. Some arrived in the huge two-tier trucks which could hold as many as eighty pigs.

Hargreaves had been given the task of showing young Daley the ropes and, as he glanced up periodically from his paper, he could see that the younger man was nervous. He had only worked at the slaughterhouse for two days and it was to be his first time in the killing room, nicknamed 'the carcass cave' by the men who worked in it. In five minutes' time, when the hands on the wall clock crawled round to 10.15 a.m., he would follow Hargreaves down to the pens where the various livestock were waiting to be despatched. Already he looked pale and the older man smiled to himself, wondering if Daley would be like the last youngster they'd assigned to him. The youth had watched fascinated as Hargreaves had loaded the humane killer then, as it was pressed to the cow's head he had keeled over, falling face down in the sea of crimson which swam ankle deep on the floor of the killing room. No one had seen him since.

'If you think you're going to throw up, go outside and do it,' said Hargreaves, glancing up at Daley.

The younger man swallowed hard.

'What?'

'If you want to puke,' Hargreaves expanded. 'Don't do it in the meat room.'

Daley nodded, a thin film of perspiration sheathing his forehead as he saw Hargreaves down the last of his tea and get to his feet. He motioned for his younger companion to follow.

They left the canteen and headed down a flight of stairs which brought them into a long corridor, sealed at the far end by a heavy steel door. Hargreaves opened it and ushered Daley through. They emerged onto a high walkway which ran around the cavernous interior of the meat room. The slatted metal cat-walk had a handrail and Daley leant against this in order to look down into the pens below. Tethered there were up to two dozen bullocks, some standing still, others pawing the blood-soaked floor in bewilderment. The stench was unbelievable. Despite six powerful extractor fans which hummed loudly inside the large room, the smell still drifted up in invisible tendrils, causing Daley to recoil slightly. A large set of double doors to his right were open and he could see two men pulling away the carcass of a dead bullock, a large hook driven through its nose. He swallowed hard as he saw that the body was still twitching. The lowing of the cattle seemed to bounce off the walls, rolling around inside Daley's head like slowly breaking waves.

'Put these on,' said Hargreaves, handing the younger man a pair of what looked like waders. They fastened by a strap at his thigh and he saw that the older man also wore a pair. When both were suitably attired, Hargreaves led the way down another flight of steps to the floor of the room. Daley saw the blood lap around his ankles and he gritted his teeth as a portion of bone floated past on the sea of gore, bound for one of the many drains which dotted the concrete floor. One or two had already become clogged with pieces of animal debris and excrement and Hargreaves decided that the place would have to be hosed down before he started on the next group of animals. However, he intended to dispose of the bullocks first.

Near to the animal pens was a wide, stainless steel-topped bench. On top of it lay an assortment of tools. Daley noticed a small sledgehammer, a couple of saws and what looked like a large air pistol. It was that particular device which Hargreaves picked up. It had a vicious looking metal bolt extending from it, protruding about an inch from the end of the barrel.

'The humane killer,' Hargreaves announced, holding up the weapon. He then crossed to the nearest of the pens and approached a bullock which was licking the metal struts of the enclosure, apparently unconcerned by the presence of the two men. Hargreaves leant forward, pressed the bolt to the animal's forehead and pulled the trigger.

There was a loud thud. The implement bucked in the older man's hand as the bolt slammed into the bullocks's skull then quickly retracted, bringing with it a sizeable lump of bone. The animal let out a low grunt then dropped as if pole-axed. Streams of blood erupted from the hole in its forehead. The sphincter muscle gave out and, as the bullock underwent its death-throes, Daley heard the rapid splattering of excrement in the sea of red fluid beneath. He blenched, gripped the pen with both hands and coughed.

Hargreaves watched him for a second, noticing that his skin had taken on a pale, yellowish tinge.

A blast of coppery-smelling fumes swept over them both and, almost immediately, the two men from the double doors to the right emerged and headed for the dead bullock. They nodded a greeting to Hargreaves who exchanged brief words with one of them. Both men were sweating profusely.

'There's eighty pigs coming in at eleven, Ken,' said the first man. 'If you can shift this lot,' he made a sweeping gesture towards the penned bullocks, 'I'd be grateful.'

Hargreaves nodded.

Daley was still gazing down at the body of the dead animal.

'First time in here, is it?' asked the man with the meat hook.

The youngster could only nod.

Hargreaves suppressed a grin as he saw the first man squat down beside the dead bullock. He pulled back the animal's lips and bared its teeth, turning the head in Daley's direction.

'Say cheese,' said the first man, grinning.

Hargreaves and the other two cracked out laughing but Daley didn't see the joke. He merely watched in silence as the carcass was dragged away.

'You all right?' Hargreaves asked him.

The younger man nodded although the gesture was a mechanical one. He could feel his stomach somersaulting.

They moved to the next pen.

The animal inside it was still but it watched the slaughterer with rheumy eyes that seemed to hide a glint of fear. Fear? Anger? Realization? He had often wondered, during his years in the abattoir, whether the animals actually knew what was going to happen to them. Did this particular bullock somehow understand what was about to take place?

He steadied the humane killer in his hand and took a step closer.

Suddenly the animal lunged forward, slamming itself into the metal pen. The impact shook the small enclosure, causing the two bullocks next to it to spring into action as well. There wasn't much room inside the pen for it to gather momentum but, nonetheless, the bullock still managed to attain sufficient impetus to bend the top two struts of the enclosure.

'Jesus,' muttered Hargreaves, stepping back for a second.

The steer let out a low rumbling bellow and launched itself at the frame once more.

Daley saw the gate buckling.

13

The other two bullocks by now were also slamming repeatedly against their pens and Hargreaves realized that he must act quickly. He stepped forward and lowered the bolt. However, the animal brought its head up sharply and knocked the device from the slaughterer's hand. It flew into the air, disappearing beneath the tide of crimson.

'Christ,' he growled. Then turning to Daley.

'Get the other one – it's on the workbench.'

Daley was frozen for long seconds but the sight of the pen gate bending spurred him on. He waded through the blood, nearly slipping once, and snatched up the second of the bolt-loaded killers.

'Hurry,' shouted Hargreaves.

The first bullock let out a booming roar and drove its way through the battered metal of the pen.

Rivets, screws and pieces of aluminium exploded into the air, showering the two men who raised their hands to shield their faces. The large animal skidded on the slippery floor but then regained its footing and turned on its would-be executioners. Hargreaves managed to leap aside, blood spraying up in a crimson wave as he went sprawling in the mess, but Daley was too slow.

The bullock hit him in the stomach with its left horn, driving him up against the metal work-bench, the lethal stubby protuberance gouging his skin. He screamed in agony as he felt his stomach wall give way beneath the unbearable pressure. The stench of the bullock mingled with the powerful odour of his own viscera as the crushing impact first mangled the lower part of his ribcage to a pulp, rupturing both lungs, then tore open his belly, releasing a tangle of intestines.

'Oh my God,' gasped Hargreaves, rolling over. He was lying less than two feet from the maddened bullock and its victim, his hand still firmly clamped around the humane killer. Daley's screams filled his ears like the cries of the damned, echoing off the walls.

14

The slaughterer dragged himself to his feet and pressed the bolt to the bullock's side.

With a roar of rage and pain it backed off, the hole in its left shoulder gradually growing bigger as the flesh seemed to rip like tearing material. A mess of entrails began to bulge from the riven hide. The beast snorted, blood spilling from its nostrils. It tried to turn but staggered and fell as its bolt-blasted shoulder gave out. Hargreaves leapt back, hearing the sound of tearing metal from behind him.

The other two bullocks had broken free.

The meat room had become a madhouse, a deafening cacophony of bellows, roars and screams, both human and animal. Hargreaves found his breath coming in gasps and he looked around desperately for a means of escape. There was an alarm bell on the far wall. Whether he could reach it or not was another matter.

The second bullock spun round and headed towards him, stumbling momentarily, giving him precious seconds. But, the waders slowed Hargreaves down. In his mind's eye he could see the bullock. Head lowered, charging towards him, ready to grind him into the ground beneath its crushing weight.

The alarm looked a hundred miles away.

'What the fuck is happening?'

He heard the shout of surprise and horror as the first of the men with meat hooks appeared and looked in upon the scene of carnage. He barely had time to shout a warning to them and they slammed the metal doors, dropping the locking bar in place as the third bullock smashed into it. Then they stood helpless, listening to the unholy commotion from inside the meat room itself.

Hargreaves reached the alarm and smashed the glass with one bloodied fist, the strident shriek of the siren immediately joining the fierce bellowing of the maddened cattle. There was no more sound from Daley.

Hargreaves turned.

15

The bullock slammed into him, shattering his pelvis, destroying kidneys and liver in the fearful impact. He felt as if his internal organs were being forced upwards first into his chest and then into his throat. What was, in fact, filling his throat was a mixture of blood and bile which, seconds later, gushed from his mouth like water from a broken dam. As the animal backed off, the slaughterer slumped to his knees and found himself gazing into the burning eyes. The beast fixed him in an insane stare, eyeballs bulging madly in red rimmed sockets, thick streamers of saliva hanging from its mouth.

The bullock drew back a foot or so then butted him again, pushing him down into the ocean of blood, pressing hard on his chest until the sternum collapsed and his body seemed to fold in upon itself.

A moment before he lost consciousness he heard footsteps above him on the metal cat-walk, the metallic rattle as a shotgun cartridge was chambered and, a second later, the deafening blast as the weapon was fired. The bullock was hit just behind the left eye, most of its head exploding, showering Hargreaves with a confetti of bone, blood and brain. The creature lowed and its legs buckled as a second discharge tore a hole in its side the size of a football.

The body collapsed beside the fallen man.

Hargreaves could only lie motionless as footsteps drew nearer. He heard shouts then another thunderous gunshot this time close to him.

Then he heard nothing at all.

Four

The light breeze set the curtains billowing, fluttering like the membranous wings of giant moths. The cool air was welcome because the room was stifling.

Vic Tyler lay on his back watching as the curtains danced softly at the bidding of the wind. A single bead of perspiration trickled from his forehead and he wiped it away with the back of his hand. Beneath him the sheets felt damp, a legacy of the warm night, and he shifted uncomfortably, finally swinging himself upright. Perched on the edge of the bed he sat motionless, head lowered, inhaling deeply in an effort to draw some sweet fresh air from the atmosphere of musty stale sweat and freshly laundered linen.

Outside the window birds sang in the clutch of willows which bent and sagged in the bright sunlight. Despite the fact that it was still relatively early, the burning orb in the cloudless sky blazed with savage intensity. Tyler glanced at the clock on the dressing table and saw that it was 10.30 a.m.

He muttered something to himself and ran a hand through his short brown hair. He'd overslept, or rather he'd been allowed to oversleep. If his father had still been alive . . .

The thought trailed off and Tyler swallowed hard, getting to his feet. He padded out of the bedroom across the landing to the bathroom where he switched on the shower, testing the water. He studied his reflection in the mirror, satisfied with what he saw. Tyler stood about six foot two, his body thick with muscle. At thirty-two he was in reasonably good shape for a man who had spent the last six years of his life working behind a desk. The transformation had not been easy for him. Born and brought up on a farm in Wakely, the farm to which he had now been forced to return, Tyler had always known and loved the freedom of the countryside. The city made him feel like a prisoner, an outsider. He had felt like a child, thrust into a strange environment.

At his father's suggestion he had left the farm just after his eighteenth birthday to attend agricultural college. Jack Tyler had seen the wisdom of allowing his son to learn that there was more to farming than driving a tractor and shovelling manure. Tyler himself had left with mixed feelings. Nevertheless, he settled to his new task. However, when his mother died three years later, he had been devastated.

He had returned to Wakely for the funeral and considered whether or not he should even contemplate making the trip back to college but his father persuaded him. He returned and completed the course, but the death of his mother was something which obsessed him. Guilt began to loom large in his mind. Would it have been any different if *he'd* been there? The spectre of that guilt still plagued him. From college he had moved on to work for the Ministry of Agriculture itself. He was good at his job, he earned an excellent salary and he had his own flat in Bayswater. He had friends too. Tyler was a likeable man, always quick to smile, ever ready with a warm handshake and a pleasant word. There had been a succession of girls, mostly one night stands but that was sufficient for him. It was how he wanted it. Yet still he felt a curious ambivalence towards the city. He welcomed what it gave him but he hated it for what it was. And he missed the country.

On hearing of his father's death his actions had been instantaneous. He had handed in his notice, packed his belongings into every available suitcase and carrier he could find and headed back to Wakely, leaving London and his memories behind him.

Now he stood beneath the shower, eyes closed, his mind full of thoughts and ideas yet somehow able to appraise the situation clearly and rationally. He was back where he belonged. Back in Wakely on the farm which had been his home for so many years and which, he promised himself, would remain so until his own death. There was a savage irony to the entire scenario which Tyler was not slow to consider. His father had originally sent him off to college and now, with Jack's death, he was home once more.

The last of the Tylers, he mused to himself. He smiled thinly but the gesture faded rapidly, as if washed from his face by the swiftly flowing water. He was back where he belonged but God alone knew that he would have given anything for it to be under different circumstances.

He turned off the shower and stood for long moments, watching the last of the water swirl away down the plughole. Then, he stepped out, wrapped a towel around himself and began drying his hair.

From the bathroom window he could see the red bulk of the Massey-Ferguson moving slowly across one of the fields to the North of the farm. It was driven by Russell Jenkins, one of two farmhands who Jack had employed. The other, Jim Harrison, was feeding the livestock elsewhere. Both men were in their forties and had worked for the family for as long as Tyler could remember.

Both had been present at yesterday's funeral.

Indeed, Tyler had been surprised at the number of people who had turned up. It had seemed as if the whole of Wakely had come to stand at his father's graveside. Each one of them carrying their individual memories of the man. Tyler had been both grateful and moved by their gesture. The townspeople had welcomed him back amongst them as if he had never been away. The place seemed to radiate cordiality, the homecoming only soured by the circumstances which necessitated it.

Tyler dried himself thoroughly then wandered back into the bedroom where he pulled on a pair of jeans and some old wellingtons. There was a crack in one of the toes and Tyler muttered irritably. There had been several violent thunderstorms recently and the earth of the farm was caught in a curious kind of limbo. Some parts were cracked and parched, others were like a quagmire. From the humidity in the air, Tyler had every reason to believe that they were in for another storm that night.

He went downstairs and, unable to face anything cooked, devoured six rounds of toast which he washed down with several large mugs of tea. Formica cupboards and stainless steel glinted in the rays of the sun which streamed through the open windows. The farm might be old and traditional on the outside but its amenities were strictly modern. The only concession to a bygone, less hectic and mechanised age were a couple of antiques housed in the sitting room: a full size man-trap which hung over the fire place and the rusted blade of a horse-drawn plough. Both had been put there by his father.

His father.

He exhaled deeply then got to his feet, wandering out of the house into the yard itself.

He winced momentarily, shielding his eyes from the glare, but then he relaxed, drawing in a deep breath which smelt of wet grass, hay and manure. The smell had a welcome familiarity about it and Tyler smiled as he headed towards the pig-sty which stood near to the farm's main gate. There was a barn close by which housed the sows and boars but the sty was used for weaners and it was obviously well populated judging by the noise which was coming from inside.

Tyler saw Jim Harrison standing amongst the hungry piglets, his gloved hand dispensing meal to them.

'Morning, Jim,' said Tyler, approaching the sty.

The farmhand looked up, the sun glinting on his bald head.

He nodded at Tyler, momentarily stopping his task.

'Me and Russ thought it best to let you sleep in, Mr Tyler,' said the bald man. 'With all what's happened, like.' He swallowed hard, as if embarrassed.

Tyler nodded.

'I appreciate it but I've got to get used to being up at dawn again now I'm here to stay.'

'Well, the work's underway anyhow, Mr Tyler.'

'Thanks. And you can drop the *Mr* Tyler bit too, Jim. Call me Vic.'

Harrison smiled, mischievously.

'OK,' he paused. 'Vic.'

Tyler peered into the sty and ran an appraising eye over the pigs inside.

'I thought we just used this sty for weaners,' he said, puzzled, looking at the size of the pigs rummaging around for the food which Harrison dropped.

'We do.'

'*These* are weaners?' asked Tyler, almost incredulously. 'But the bloody things are twice the size they should be. You're trying to tell me that these pigs are only ten weeks old?'

'We found it hard to believe at first,' Harrison told him. 'But it's the same with all the animals fed on that new meal.'

Tyler frowned, looking first at Harrison and then at the pigs again. One of them raised its head, nostrils flared, small eyes fixing him in a glassy stare.

'Your father,' Harrison said, dropping his gaze as he spoke, 'he bought some new multi-purpose feed a few weeks back. The fellow who sold it to him said it would increase growth in livestock.'

Tyler nodded approvingly.

'What about the milk yield from the cows, has it affected that?' he wanted to know.

The farm hand shook his head.

'Where did my father get this feed?' asked Tyler.

'There's a new company just outside town,' Harrison said, struggling to remember the name. 'But I'm buggered if I can remember what they're called.' Harrison shrugged. 'Anyway, they make and sell the stuff.'

Tyler nodded.

'Well, it obviously works. We should get a better price for the stock at market.'

'Most of the farms around here are using it,' Harrison added. He tossed what was left of the meal into a small trough then unlatched the sty and eased himself out. He lingered for a moment then wiped his head, leaving a dark smear on his bald dome.

'If it's all right with you, Mr Ty . . . sorry, Vic, I'll get on with my other jobs.'

'Right, I'll be along to help in a minute,' Tyler said, listening as Harrison picked his way across the muddy yard, his boots squelching in the thick ooze.

The younger man leant on the wall of the sty and gazed in at the weaners gathered around the trough. As he had first noticed, for their age, most of the animals inside the enclosure were twice their normal size. It looked as though he was going to make a sizeable profit at the market in two days' time.

Tyler stroked his chin thoughtfully.

He wondered how big the weaners would be when they had finished growing.

Five

The first low rumblings of thunder rolled across the bruised sky, banks of blue-black cloud giving it a mottled appearance. The first silent forks of lightning pushed their way tentatively across the darkened heavens.

The lights in the laboratory flickered once then regained their initial brilliance. The banks of fluorescents in the ceiling reflected off the work tops in the large room. The animals in the rows of cages scurried back and forth nervously as the storm drew nearer.

Geoffrey Anderson crossed to the lab door and peered through the meshed glass panel near the top then, still not fully satisfied that he was alone, he pushed the door open a fraction and peered out. The corridor on either side of him was deserted, the floor sparkling as if someone had been over it with a gigantic buffing machine. The white walls reflected the glow from the strip lights overhead making it seem brighter in the corridor and Anderson felt suddenly conspicuous. But he was satisfied that he was alone.

The clock behind him ticked noisily in the silence, the hands having crawled around to 10.15 p.m. Apart from the rhythmic sound of the timepiece the only disturbance in the solitude was the distant thunder and the agitated squeaking of the animals.

Anderson locked the door behind him, flicked off the lights and stood silently for long seconds. There was a film of perspiration clinging to his face which he hurriedly wiped off with the sleeve of his white overall. As he looked down, the red and silver V C, the logo worn by all Vanderburg employees, seemed to wink at him. He swallowed hard then moved across to the wall phone, looking over his shoulder once more towards the meshed window.

His hand was shaking slightly as he began to dial.

The staccato clatter of typewriter keys sounded like machine-gun fire in the confines of the small office and Jo Ward sighed as she read and re-read the piece she had just finished. There was something not quite right about it but she couldn't put her finger on what it was. To hell with it, she thought, at least she'd make the deadline with time to spare. The stories didn't have to go to press until eleven in order for them to reach the morning edition of the *Arkham Comet*. Elsewhere in the office things were at various stages of organized pandemonium as other reporters rushed to complete their assignments, some hampered by the fact that their typewriting dexterity had not yet extended to more than one finger.

The phone on Jo's desk rang and she picked it up.

'*Arkham Comet*,' she said, her American accent sounding as strong now as it had been when she had first come to work for the paper six months ago.

'I want to speak to Joanna Ward,' the voice at the other end said, breathlessly. It sounded as if the man had been running.

'Speaking. Who is this?' she wanted to know.

'There isn't much time. My name is Anderson. Geoffrey Anderson, I've spoken to you before.'

Jo ran a hand through her chestnut hair, brushing two or three long strands from her forehead.

'Oh, the guy who works at Vanderburg Chemicals,' she said, finally recognizing his voice. She had, indeed, spoken to him before but his voice sounded different this time. There was a strong note of urgency in it, fear even.

'I have to meet you,' he said. 'Tonight.'

Jo reached for a pencil and began drawing irregular shapes on the pad before her. She glanced briefly at her watch.

'It's getting late, Mr Anderson, surely we could discuss it tomorrow or . . .'

He cut her short.

'No.' He almost shouted the word at her. 'It must be tonight.' She could hear him breathing hard.

'Whereabouts?' she wanted to know. 'A pub maybe, there's . . .'

Again he interrupted.

'No. Nowhere where there are people. What I have to say . . .'

The sentence trailed off and, for long seconds, Jo thought that the phone had gone dead. Outside there was a loud growl of thunder.

'Mr Anderson,' she said.

Silence then a burst of static.

'Mr Anderson, are you still there?'

'Yes.' His voice was lower but still strained. 'There's a lay-by on the main road between Wakely and Arkham, it's near an old roadside café. The place is deserted now. Meet me there at eleven-thirty.'

She scribbled something on her pad.

'Hello,' he babbled. 'Did you hear me?'

'Yeah, I got it. Eleven-thirty. I'll see you then.'

'Don't tell anyone,' he gasped. 'I . . .'

The line went dead.

Jo flicked the cradle but there was just the steady hum of static. Finally she put down the receiver, replacing it slowly as if she expected it to burst into life once more. Whatever it was that Anderson wanted he was certainly in a hurry to tell her. She chewed the end of her pencil thoughtfully then glanced down at the location she had scribbled on the pad. A lay-by in the middle of nowhere – what the hell would he want to meet her there for? She wondered if the guy was some kind of creep, maybe he was going to try and jump her the minute he got her alone. She shook her head. He didn't sound like that sort of person. He *did* sound frightened however.

25

She got to her feet, slipped the notepad into her handbag and headed for the door.

Outside, the storm was drawing closer.

Geoffrey Anderson drew in a deep breath, held it a second then opened the door of the darkened lab. The corridor outside was still empty, all the doors leading down to the lifts tightly locked. He had removed his white coat and stood now in his two-piece suit, his tie undone. He felt as if it were strangling him and, when he swallowed, the muscles of his throat seemed to be swollen. He wiped a hand across his face, salty drops of perspiration stinging his eyes. Overhead, the strip lights buzzed like indolent bluebottles and Anderson paused momentarily as he heard the distant thunder growl menacingly.

He locked the lab door and began walking along the corridor, his shoes beating out an urgent tattoo in the preternatural silence of the deserted building.

Anderson turned a corner and found himself at the lifts. He jabbed the button which would take him to the ground floor, shuffling impatiently as the car rose. His eyes were fixed on the glowing white numbers which lit up as it passed each floor.

It stopped at 3 and his heart missed a beat, the breath frozen in his lungs, but when the lift finally arrived it was empty. He stepped in and rode down to the ground floor.

The reception area of Vanderburg Chemicals was vast, large enough to hold a football pitch. Doors and corridors led off from this carpeted central chamber like the tunnels in a termite nest. At the far end were six sets of reinforced glass double doors. Rain was already coursing down them as the deluge outside began and now bright forks of lightning tore through the blanket of clouds. There were just three lights burning in the reception area, the shadows in the corners seeming

26

thicker, conspiratorial. As if they were hiding something.

Anderson walked quickly towards the exit, his feet now cushioned by the carpet. In the dull light its normal orange colour reminded him of congealed blood.

He reached the doors and paused for a second. His car a blue Ford Granada, was parked on the other side of the car park. There were other vehicles out there and he counted six large Scania lorries, each one with a tanker attached. The black tankers bore the familiar red and silver logo of Vanderburg Chemicals, the two letters joined together at the curve of the C.

Rain was beating heavily against the glass doors of the main building and, every so often, Anderson would shield his eyes as the sky exploded into a patchwork of searing lightning which left an afterburn on his retina.

There were one or two lights still glowing in windows on the East side of the building and Anderson wondered who could still be working at 10.45. He just hoped they hadn't seen him.

The large sheds to his right were silent, huge black leering shapes, they seemed to grow from the night itself. These were the warehouses and manufacturing buildings where hundreds of tons of the new Vanderburg multi-purpose feed were stored and created using a formula which Anderson himself had worked on. Beyond them stood the well-lit living quarters used by all but a handful of Vanderburg's employees.

There was movement behind him.

He spun round, the breath catching in his throat. In the abyss of the large reception area he could see nothing. The shadows seemed to grow darker, the lightning momentarily abating as if even the elements were combining to conceal the source of the sound from him.

It came again.

A soft, swishing sound, close to him.

A particularly vehement crack of lightning suddenly

27

lit the entire area, bathing it for precious seconds in cold blue light and, in that light, Anderson saw what was making the noise.

Someone had forgotten to close a window and the broad leaves of a rubber plant were swatting the glass nearby. He smiled thinly, a whisper of relief escaping him.

He almost laughed aloud at his own foolishness. He was, he told himself, becoming paranoid. Nevertheless, his heart would not stop pounding.

There was a loud ring as the lift purred into action.

Someone was descending.

Anderson moved quickly, pushing open the exit doors, ignoring the rain which drenched him. He ran across the tarmac to his car, fumbling in his jacket pocket for his keys as the heavens exploded in a deafening symphony of power above him. He jammed the key in the lock and slid, gratefully, behind the wheel. For long moments he sat there, his breath coming in gasps, head bowed. Then, he pulled the handkerchief from his pocket and mopped his face as best he could. His breathing began to slow down somewhat. Anderson inserted the key in the ignition and gripped the wheel, glancing down at the clock on the dashboard as he did so.

It was almost 10.59.

He prepared to start the engine.

The dark shape rose from the back of the Granada as if it had materialized from the blackness itself. Something cold and thin was looped around Anderson's neck and it was a second or two before he realized what was going on. He was slammed back in his seat as the wire was pulled tight.

He tried to grip the lethal strand, to ease the mounting pressure on his oesophagus, but the more he struggled, the tighter it was pulled. A second tug nearly hauled him over the back of the seat and now the cheese wire began to cut through his flesh, through his windpipe. Jets of blood sprayed the windscreen as veins and arteries were cut. Anderson's eyes bulged in their sockets and his attempt at a scream came out as a liquid gurgle. Blood poured down the front of his shirt as his body began to go into an uncontrollable spasm.

The dark shape in the back seat made no sound but merely pulled harder on the wire, wrenching Anderson several inches up from his seat.

His bladder gave out and a dark stain spread rapidly across his crotch, mingling with the blood which was puddling on the mock leather beneath him. His eyes rolled upwards in their sockets, bulging like swollen boiled eggs, as he felt the tide of unconciousness roll over him. There was a sound in his ears like that of the sea. A great pounding, churning noise which blotted out everything else.

The sound of fluid excretion signalled his death but Anderson's executioner pulled the wire tight against the dead man's spinal cord. Only the bone prevented Anderson from being decapitated.

The car smelt like a slaughterhouse.

The dark shape in the back sat perfectly still for long seconds just gazing at the body of Anderson.

Outside the rain lashed the car unmercifully. Inside, blood trickled down the windscreen like crimson tears.

Jo Ward wiped the condensation from her windscreen and peered through the lashing rain which slammed against the glass. The wiper blades seemed unable to clear the torrents and she wondered if she was going to have to stop.

The road between Wakely and Arkham was badly lit, framed as it was on both sides by trees. They bent and bowed beneath the driving rain, spidery branches reaching down towards the slowly moving Chevette. The headlamps cut a swathe through the blackness but still Jo found visibility was down to about fifty feet. The dull orange glare of the sodium lamps were like pools across the road, islands of light in a sea of darkness.

Why the hell did Anderson have to pick a place like this to meet her? she thought.

She caught sight of the disused transport cafe from her side window. Just beyond it, shrouded by trees, was the lay-by which Anderson had spoken of.

Jo eased the Chevette along the last few tortuous yards of slick tarmac then drew to a halt, the car facing Wakely. She wondered whether or not to switch off her headlamps. Surely he would find her anyway? She decided to leave just the side lights burning. A rolling crack of thunder seemed to shake the car and Jo shuddered involuntarily. She reached for her handbag and pulled out a pack of cigarettes, easing the window down slightly to let the smoke out but rain poured in too freely and she hastily wound it up again. The car began to fill with a blue haze.

Jo smiled thinly to herself. It was like breathing New York air. The smile faded rapidly. Even the thought of that dirty city sent a shudder through her. She'd been born and brought up on Manhattan's East Side, overlooking the slimy brown tongue which was the East river. Some days, she and her friends would stand on the Queensboro bridge and look down at the small boats and tugs which moved along that aquatic thoroughfare. Jo often wondered where the boats were heading, her curiosity more usually extending to the men who worked on them as well. Were they going home to loving wives? To endless rows? Had some of them even got homes to go to? All through her early years Jo's interest in other people had been something which amused and surprised those who knew her. Not least her parents. Her father worked for a cab company while her mother cleaned rooms at the Hotel Roosevelt, less than three blocks from where they lived.

Jo began her own working life at the hotel, earning enough money to support herself while she pursued a faltering career as a freelance journalist. Her interest in people and her curiosity seemed to find a pefect outlet in the articles she wrote. Forever probing and searching for something, she would work an eight hour day at the Roosevelt then begin anew when she got back to her home at night. But journalism was her real love and, as the years passed and her payment cheques totalled just 1,500 dollars, she began to despair of ever making a real breakthrough into the profession she craved so much to be a part of.

Then she met Tony.

Tony Hagen was a guest at the Roosevelt when he first met Jo. Immediately impressed by his appearance and looks she was at first taken aback by his advances. She was a very attractive girl and she was aware of that fact but they came from such vastly different ends of the social spectrum that contact seemed impossible. However, as she got to know him better she found that the fancy suits and expensive jewellery came from an unexpected source. Hagen worked for Alberto Scalise, great grandson of one of Al Capone's top trigger men and then head of the largest of New York's five families.

31

The temptation was too great for her. She slept with Hagen, she used him, remembering each little piece of information he let slip until she had enough material for an article which she managed to sell to *The New York Times*. They wanted more and they were willing to pay a high price. The opportunity was irresistible.

After the third article appeared she was offered a job on the paper which she took immediately. However, Hagen became more evasive, frightened even. He warned her off, telling her not to write anything else about Scalise but Jo had always been stubborn.

She continued seeing Hagen who, she realized, had fallen in love with her despite the dangers to himself. But she could prise no more information out of him. Or so it seemed.

When he asked her to marry him she agreed and Hagen once more allowed his tongue to flap.

The next story she wrote made the front page.

Within two days it was all over.

They had been sitting in a bar on Lexington Avenue when two men walked in who Hagen instantly recognized.

Now, as Jo sat in the Chevette sucking hard on her cigarette she could still see the scene, printed indelibly on her mind. The first of the men had been carrying a coat over his right arm, the second merely stood in the doorway. Hagen had turned to face them, the beer glass still mid-way between his mouth and the bar top. The first man had let the coat slide away to reveal what he held beneath. Jo had recognized it as a .45 automatic. The man had fired three times.

The first shot caught Hagen in the face, shattering the beer glass before ploughing into his chin, blasting away most of his bottom jaw. The second shot hit him in the chest and lifted him off his feet. The third blew a fist-sized hole through his left shoulder, the impact

32

spinning him round. He dropped to his knees, the screams of the customers ringing loud in his ears.

Jo had thrown herself over the bar, pulling her legs up and shielding her head as more slugs ploughed into the thick wood, blasting long shards away. She heard the hammer slam down on an empty chamber and she took her chance. Leaping to her feet she pushed past the terrified barman and scrambled for the rear exit.

Neither of the men followed her.

Naturally, the incident itself made front page news but Jo had been shaken nonetheless, and then when someone blew the windscreen of her Lincoln away with a shotgun as she was driving home one evening, it was the last straw.

She left America and came to London where she found freelance work relatively easily, but London seemed too central. Too exposed. She moved to Arkham and had worked on the *Arkham Comet* for six months.

She ground out the cigarette in the ashtray and lit up another, glancing at her watch as she did so.

11.48 p.m.

Where in the hell was Anderson?

No other vehicles had passed by, coming from or going to Wakely. She drummed on the wheel irritably and peered out into the storm blasted night.

Away to her left stood the old transport café, now a hollow shell. The only thing moving was a rusty old sign which swayed and rocked precariously as it was buffeted by the wind. The large windows which had once formed the front of the dining area had been smashed and scores of stones lay in the forecourt. There was even the wreck of a Volkswagen rusting in what used to be the car park. The entire, decaying complex was cloaked in blackness, illuminated only occasionally by the bursts of lightning which ripped across the rain-sodden sky.

Jo ran both hands through her hair and glanced at herself in the rear-view mirror. Considering some of the things she had been through in her life she looked remarkably fresh for her twenty-eight years. There wasn't a worry line to be seen and the almost perfect curve of her skin was broken only by a small scar near her right eye – the legacy of that night in the bar on Lexington Avenue. She wore little or no make-up, except for some eye-liner. Even in the darkness of the car, those twin green orbs seemed to glow like jade beacons. She wore a pair of jeans, cut off at the bottom, the material slightly frayed, and a dark blue sweatshirt accentuated her breasts.

She was in the process of lighting another cigarette when she heard the loud drone of a car engine.

Seconds later, powerful headlights cut through the night, shining brightly in her face for fleeting moments as the car drove past.

'Goddamit,' she muttered as the vehicle disappeared in the direction of Arkham.

Jo looked at her watch again. It was almost 12.15. After another five minutes she intended leaving. She'd stop at the first phone she came across and ring Anderson's home. Maybe the stupid son of a bitch had forgotten. Jo quickly dismissed the thought. He had sounded too anxious on the phone, too distraught. He needed to see her and she believed him. Perhaps his car had broken down. She quickly ran through a list of reasons why he hadn't turned up then looked at her watch once again. Three more minutes and she was going.

She snapped her fingers. She'd noticed a phone box on the forecourt of the deserted transport cafe. If it was still working she could ring from there. She had his number at Vanderburg too in case something had prevented him leaving. Jo decided to ring there first.

She twisted the key in the ignition and started the

engine, swinging the Chevette around, heading back towards the night shrouded derelict cafe. She pulled into the kerb and pushed open her door. Leaving the engine idling she sprinted the twenty yards to the phone box.

In the Stygian gloom of the rain-soaked woods something moved.

Something large.

Across the other side of the road, hidden by the impenetrable blackness and the stifling confines of the trees, a portion of the night seemed to detach itself and find animation. The shape moved slowly through the trees, watching as Jo first stopped her car and then clambered out to scuttle to the phone box. She could be seen quite clearly because the lightning now lashed the sky with increasing rapidity, casting a cold bluish glow over the landscape.

The shape watched intently as Jo lifted the receiver, then, like a shadow, it seemed to spread as it approached the roadside.

There was a particularly vehement explosion across the heavens and the shape paused, ducking down behind some bushes.

Jo's car was just ten yards away.

The box smelt fusty and Jo wiped the dirty receiver on her jeans when she lifted it, relieved to hear the steady purring which signalled that it was still in working order. She fumbled in the pocket of her jeans for some change and pulled out a handful of ten pence pieces which she laid on the metal shelf beside her. She dialled Vanderburg Chemicals.

Behind her, the wind whistled mournfully through the smashed windows of the deserted café. A sign proclaiming

HOT MEALS SERVED HERE

hung crookedly, one end of it having come loose. It slapped against the wall of the main building beating out an intermittent rhythm.

The ringing tone sounded and Jo prepared to push one of the coins into the slot.

It continued to ring.

No one answered.

She let it ring fifteen times then put the receiver back down and pulled a piece of paper from her coat pocket which had Anderson's home number on it. She dialled once more. This time it rang just three times before it was picked up. Hearing the rapid pips, Jo pushed her money in.

'Mr Anderson?' she said.

Silence.

'Mr Anderson. Hello.'

Just a low hiss of static. Nothing more.

'Do I have the right number?' she asked.

There was a thunderous explosion of lightning which caused the receiver to crackle alarmingly. It was so loud that Jo held it away from her ear for a second. When she listened again, the line was dead. She put the receiver down angrily.

'Shit,' she muttered, scooping up what was left of the change and shoving it back into her pocket. She paused in the phone box for a moment, preparing herself for the dash through the rain to the car. Then she pushed open the door and scurried across to the waiting Chevette. Was Anderson playing some kind of game with her? she wondered. If so, why? She exhaled deeply and reached into her purse, pulling out her diary. Jo reached back to flick on the car light, puzzled to find that it didn't come on when she touched the switch. She sat in darkness for a second before turning slightly in her chair to see why it hadn't come on.

The bulb was missing.

Not just blown, the entire bracket which held the light, including screws, was gone.

She frowned. It had been fine before she got out of the car . . .

It had been removed. Torn out.

But by whom she wondered? her heart unaccountably beating that little bit quicker. She put the Chevette in gear and stepped on the accelerator, anxious to get away from this place, to get home. However, her curiosity was aroused and she was already determined to visit Anderson the following day.

The light and bracket from inside the Chevette lay on the roadside until a foot came down slowly and deliberately on them, grinding them into splinters. The dark shape watched as the tail lights of Jo's car disappeared around a bend then, as stealthily as it had come, the shape dissolved back into the trees and became as one with the night once more.

Seven

Ronald Faber barely heard the alarm. As he woke he reached out instinctively to switch it off but the clock had already run down. Instead he lay beneath the sheets his eyes crusted shut as if someone had sealed the lids during the night. He raised both hands to his face and murmured something to himself. The sheets beneath him were sodden with perspiration and, as he swung himself upright, he swept some matted strands from his forehead. His breathing was shallow, asthmatic almost, and when his body was suddenly racked by a powerful spasm of coughing he gripped his chest in alarm. It certainly wasn't smoker's cough. He hadn't touched the damned weed in any form in all of his forty-two years.

The spasm passed and he got slowly to his feet, a strange gnawing pain in the pit of his stomach. He rubbed his mountainous belly gently as he crossed to the window and looked out.

Sunlight blazed brightly through the chink in the curtains and Faber closed his eyes tight once again, recoiling from the blistering heat and brightness. Below him, the main street of Wakely was starting to come to life as early morning shoppers moved about and some of the other businesses opened their doors for the beginning of another trading day.

Faber knew that he too must have his shop open at nine o'clock, just as he had done every day for the last twenty years. As sole owner and proprietor of Faber Menswear he prided himself on not having missed a single day through illness or anything else. But, today, he would have given anything not to have to go down into the shop and work.

He was a big man, perhaps twenty stone, and the dressing gown which he pulled on barely met around his ample stomach. His black hair was plastered to his head by perspiration and, when he tried to swallow, it seemed as if his throat had seized up. His mouth was dry, his tongue felt as if it had been turned to chalk.

He passed slowly into the bathroom and gazed at himself in the mirror, a little disturbed at what he saw.

His skin was milk white, not just on his face but all over his body. And it had a uniformity to it, there didn't seem to be one part of him that had any colour. Even the dark mole which stood out so prominently on his chin appeared to have been drained. He raised one

38

hand to his cheek and rubbed gently at the skin, his eyes narrowing as some pieces of flesh came away. He looked as though he'd been exposed to the sun for a great length of time but for the deathly pallor of his skin. The flesh around his nails was cracked and split, the nails themselves broken. His lips were swollen, puffy and thick and when he opened his mouth, a strangled cry escaped him.

As he pulled his dressing gown open he saw that the skin on his chest was coming away in great coils. Like some kind of obscene sloughing he looked like a man in transition, shedding one skin for another. And, everywhere was the bloodless colour of his flesh.

He splashed his face with water, quivering slightly when he stepped back and saw that there were fragments of skin floating on the surface of the water.

'Oh God,' he muttered, his words strained.

He turned to the toilet and began urinating.

As the first spurts of blood jetted from his penis and spattered the white porcelain of the lavatory bowl, Ronald Faber fought back a scream.

The water began to turn a dark red colour as the thick fluid continued gushing forth. It was as if his bladder were filled with red ink. His eyes bulged in horror as the bowl seemed to fill with the crimson liquid then the coppery odour reached his nostrils and he realized that his urine wasn't merely the *colour* of blood.

It was blood.

At that point he did scream.

Eight

From its exterior it could well have been a concentration camp. All it lacked were the machine-gun nests.

The complex of buildings which made up Vanderburg Chemicals stood in the middle of thirty acres of country-side about a mile or so off the main Wakely-Arkham road. The entire collection of monolithic structures was enclosed by a wire fence fully twelve feet high. A daunting enough prospect as it was, topped by several lengths of barbed wire, the fence also bore a sign. Stencilled in large red letters, it proclaimed:

DANGER ELECTRIFIED FENCE

Beneath that, as if any would-be interloper should be foolish enough to ignore the warning, another, smaller, sign read:

THESE PREMISES ARE PATROLLED
BY GUARD DOGS

Jo Ward pushed her sunglasses back onto her nose and ran an appraising eye over the array of fortifications before her. She was driving parallel to the high fence, looking alternately through her windscreen and open side window. A cool breeze wafted into the car and for that she was thankful. High above her the sun had already risen in the cloudless sky, its powerful rays bathing the countryside beneath. Jo drove slowly, the Chevette bumping over the uneven road.

So, she thought, this is where Geoffrey Anderson works. She turned the name over in her mind, wondering just what the hell he'd been playing at the previous night. Two or three things still puzzled her about the events surrounding the mystery. She had recognized the click on the other end of the phone as she'd reached Anderson's house. It had been an answering machine switching itself on. But, she reasoned, why no message? What good was a goddam answering phone without a tape in it? Secondly, the light bracket which had been taken. She glanced up at the place where it had been. Taken. That was something of an understatement. It had been ripped out, by hand too from the look of it. Jo pressed her foot down on the accelerator a little harder. The sooner she saw Anderson the better. Besides, she was anxious to find out what he had to tell her.

After another minute's drive she found herself approaching a set of gates. They were topped with barbed wire like the fence but both stood open and only a narrow yellow barrier separated her from the long driveway which led up to the Vanderburg complex. Jo took off her sunglasses, ran a hand through her hair and pulled up at the barrier. She banged her hooter twice, trying to illicit some response from the blue uniformed men seated in a yellow Porta-cabin to the left of the barrier. They were drinking tea and chatting but one finally sauntered out, brushing the sleeve of his uniform as he approached. Jo caught sight of the red and silver VC on his breast pocket as he drew closer.

'Good morning,' said Jo.

'Morning, Miss,' said the guard, eyeing first the car and then Jo, his attention drawn momentarily to the valley between her breasts, visible in the vee of her white blouse.

'I have an appointment with a Mr Anderson,' Jo told him.

'Who are you?' the guard wanted to know.

She told him her name.

'What do you want to see him for?' the man asked, his eyes now turned on Jo's face.

The lie was ready on her tongue.

'I represent a company which is interested in amalga-

41

mating with Vanderburg. Mr Anderson told me he could introduce me to the right people.'

The guard licked his lips, gazing once more at Jo's breasts. His brow furrowed. She hoped he wouldn't notice how tightly she was gripping the steering wheel. The plastic felt clammy beneath her sweaty palms.

She played her trump card.

'Call him – you must have a phone in there,' she motioned towards the yellow cabin.

The guard took a step back.

Jo felt her heart beating faster. He had called her bluff; now she had to hope it worked.

'What was the name of your company?' he asked.

'That's really between Mr Anderson and myself,' she told him. She pushed open her door and stepped out. 'Look, let me call him.'

The guard appreciated the chance to see her standing upright and he nodded approvingly as she walked towards him. He held up a hand to halt her.

'OK, we'll let you through,' he said.

Jo slid back behind the wheel, her whole body shaking in a mixture of anxiety and triumph. The barrier was raised and she drove through, smiling at the guard as she passed. She watched him in the rear-view mirror for a moment, relieved when he didn't go back into the cabin. He might just decide to alert the main building while she was on her way up the drive. The macadamized surface was wide enough to accommodate four or more cars driving abreast of each other and, a moment later, Jo saw why.

A huge Scania rolled towards her from the opposite direction, the sun glinting off its metal tanker. The juggernaut sped past and she felt the Chevette tugged momentarily into the larger vehicle's slip-stream. The large lorry rumbled away towards the main gate.

She finally reached the maze of buildings and pulled up before the main block. There were numerous other cars parked outside. She spotted a Jensen, even a Porsche, amongst the lesser vehicles. Her own car she left right outside the six sets of double doors which led into the main reception area.

It was cool inside the cavernous arena, a welcome change from the heat outside and Jo felt the perspiration chill on her skin. Two large fans, set near the doors, rotated full circle, ensuring that the whole reception was kept at a comfortable temperature. Her high heels sank into the thick carpet as she approached a desk behind which sat a girl of about her own age. She was dressed in a dark blue skirt and jacket which reminded Jo of an Air Hostess. The only difference was the familiar VC on the breast pocket. The girl wore a name tag on her lapel which identified her as Julie.

She gave her perfect practised smile as Jo approached the desk.

'Good morning,' said Jo. 'I'd like to see Geoffrey Anderson please.'

'Do you have an appointment?' asked Julie, the smile apparently bolted to her face for it didn't fade even when she spoke.

'He's expecting me.'

'Who shall I say is here?'

'My name's Joanna Ward.'

Julie flicked a switch on the console before her, reaching for a small set of earphones as she did so. There was a loud bleeping, rather like an overloud pager.

'There's a Miss Joanna Ward in reception,' said Julie, into a mouthpiece, the smile still not slipping. 'She says she wants to see Mr Anderson.'

There was a moment's silence, mutterings at the other end of the line and Julie listened. Jo took the opportunity to glance around. There were a number of people moving about in and around the reception area, coming and going through the corridors which led off, spoke-like from the central chamber. Some were in pairs, others alone. All wore the dark blue uniform of Vanderburg or white coats, some even had overalls on. Two young men, both in their early twenties, passed by and cast approving looks at Jo. Even their overalls bore the red and silver VC. The reception smelt of carpet cleaner and polish. The drone of muzak added a background to the chatter of typewriters and the almost constant purring of lift doors as people came and went.

'Someone will be down in a moment,' said Julie, flicking the switch on her console to 'Off'. 'Would you like a cup of coffee?'

Jo availed herself of the offer then went to sit down in one of the soft leather chairs near the lifts. She had hardly seated herself when a tall, white-haired man in a three piece suit emerged from the lift nearest to her. His shoes, she noticed, were in need of cleaning. He headed straight towards her, as if he'd known her for years but, she reasoned, considering she was the only person in sight not sporting a Vanderburg logo, it was safe for him to assume she was a visitor.

She got to her feet as he drew closer.

'Miss Ward,' he said, smiling. He extended a hand which was dotted with liver spots but there was a warmth in his handshake. Jo looked at him carefully. He was in his fifties, perhaps older but his blue eyes twinkled with a radiance which belied his years. His skin was wrinkled, a double chin wobbling fluidly as he shook her hand.

'What can I do for you?' he asked.

'You're not the guy I spoke to last night,' she said. He smiled.

'No. My name is Glendenning. Martin Glendenning.'

'I wanted to see Geoffrey Anderson.'

'So I understand.' He motioned her towards a door on the left and she began walking towards it. When he opened it, she found herself in an office. It was a small room, the desk and filing cabinets making it seem over-crowded. He invited her to sit down, taking up position himself on the other side of the desk. The room was obviously sound proof because Jo could no longer hear the muzak from the reception area once Glendenning closed the door.

'As I was saying,' he began. 'I realize that it was Mr Anderson you wanted to see. Might I ask in what connection?'

'I'm a journalist,' she told him. 'He rang me last night and said he wanted to speak to me.'

'Really,' said Glendenning, his smile fading slightly. 'How did you manage to get past the security men at the gate? They have instructions not to let members of the press in.'

'Something to hide?' said Jo, grinning.

Glendenning chuckled.

'I wish it were that exciting here, Miss Ward,' he said. 'No, it's nothing like that but we're a new company and our backers are somewhat shy of publicity.'

'Who are your backers?' she asked.

He smiled.

'Do journalists always leave the office in the morning with the intention of finding a story?'

'We do our best.'

Glendenning nodded. He rested his elbows on the desk and propped his chin on his hands.

'Well, Miss Ward, I'm afraid there seems to have been some kind of misunderstanding. Mr Anderson doesn't work here any more. In fact he moved on some time ago.'

'He spoke to me from here last night,' Jo protested.

'That's impossible. Besides there is no record of a call, all phone messages are monitored you see.'

'You mean the phones are bugged?' said Jo, flatly.

'Not in the sense you mean,' Glendenning told her. 'It's just part of security procedure.'

45

Jo exhaled in exasperation.

'He called me about eleven last night, maybe a little earlier.'

Glendenning shook his head.

'Most of our employees leave the main building at seven,' he said. 'It's extremely unlikely that anyone would be working at such a late hour in any case. Besides, as I said, Mr Anderson has not worked at Vanderburg for some time.'

'What do you call some time?' Jo demanded.

The older man shrugged.

'Weeks.'

The American shook her head.

'If you'll excuse the expression, Mr Glendenning, someone's been shafted and I get the impression it's me. Some guy calls me last night, says his name's Anderson. I know the man's voice for God's sake. He says he has to meet me. Now you tell me he's been gone for weeks.'

'I'm sorry I can't be more helpful, Miss Ward,' Glendenning said, getting to his feet. He walked to the door and opened it, a gesture which was unmistakable. Jo rose and walked past him into the reception area.

'You never did tell me how you got past the Security men,' the older man asked her, smiling.

'I lied to them,' said Jo. 'All part of the job.'

He chuckled and they exchanged pleasant farewells. Glendenning closed the door behind her and, only then, did his smile dissolve into a frown.

'Left weeks ago, my ass,' Jo rasped, fumbling for the pack of Marlboro. She lit one and sucked hard on it. On the seat beside her was a piece of paper.

It bore the address of Geoffrey Anderson.

One way or another she was going to find out where he was.

Nine

The cow tried to rise but then dropped forward onto its spindly front legs. It raised its head and snorted in pain, its body lathered in thick white sweat. A Friesian, it was virtually all white due to the creamy coating of fluid it exuded. The barn smelt of damp straw, mingling with the fusty odour of cattle and the more pungent stench of excrement. The cow twitched its tail frenziedly as if trying to brush away some non-existent flies and, as he watched, Tyler saw blood trickling from both its anus and also from the gaping opening to its womb.

'Did you call the vet?' he asked, agitatedly, looking round at Russell Jenkins who was carrying a bucket of hot water and some cloths.

'He said he should be here in ten minutes,' Jenkins replied setting the bucket down.

Tyler looked back to the cow.

'I hope to God she lasts that long,' he murmured.

The animal had managed to lift itself up onto its forelegs once again and stood swaying uncertainly, its eyes bulging in pain. Its stomach and much of its hind quarters appeared grossly swollen and, as he watched, Tyler could see rapid undulations beneath the skin. The calf was a large one and it was due to be dropped very soon. Tyler crossed to the cow and laid his hand on its muzzle, disturbed to see that there was blood coming from its nostrils too. The animal was bleeding internally.

'Come on, Hawley, for Christ sake,' he rasped under his breath.

'Is there anything more we can do?' asked Russell Jenkins, watching as the cow's hind legs buckled as if unable to bear the immense weight they were supporting. Tyler coaxed the animal into lying down but it seemed unable to do so adequately. The huge protuberances in its hindquarters making this almost impossible. It was as if someone had inflated the creature with a high pressure pump. The undulations became more rapid, more violent and the cow tossed its head about spraying Tyler with the foam like perspiration.

From outside the barn, both men heard a car pull up. A door slammed and Jenkins ran across to see who it was.

Dan Hawley walked in carrying a large black bag which he swiftly opened, pulling out a stethoscope.

'Get her up if you can,' he said, tugging off his tie, hurriedly unfastening his shirt. He crossed to the stricken cow and pressed the stethoscope to its ribs. The heart beat was faint. He moved down and tried to locate the calf's upper-body. There was no sound but the animal was obviously still alive because Hawley could see the frantic movements inside the cow itself. He pulled off his shirt, quickly washed his hands in the bucket of hot water then approached the rear end of the cow which was now on its feet, partially supported by Tyler and Jenkins.

'What the hell is wrong with her?' asked Tyler, perspiration coursing down his face.

'The calf's stuck lengthways by the looks of it,' Hawley told him. 'I'll have to right it.' He steadied himself. 'Hold her tight,' he said. Ignoring the vile odour which was coming from the groaning beast, Hawley slid first one then two dripping hands into the bleeding orifice before him, feeling for the calf's head. He found the feet, the fore-legs he guessed.

'Give me some rope, quick,' he snapped, withdrawing his hands, both of which were dripping crimson.

Tyler scuttled across to the other side of the barn and snatched up a piece of stout hemp, almost knocking a pitchfork over in the process. He cursed and threw the rope to Hawley.

48

'Why didn't you call me earlier, Vic?' asked the vet.

'Because things didn't start to get bad until about twenty minutes ago,' Tyler told him.

'Here,' said Hawley. 'You'll have to help me, we're going to have to pull the calf free.' He plunged his hands back inside the cow's riven uterine passage and tried to loop the rope around the forelegs of the calf. He cursed as he attempted to complete the difficult task, sweat running off him in salty rivulets. He was a thick set man, powerfully built but he showed remarkable dexterity when dealing with animals, and now Tyler saw a slight grin spread across his face as he succeeded in fastening the rope around the calf's legs. He gripped it hard and Tyler did likewise.

'Hold her head,' the vet told Jenkins.

The cow let out a bellow of pain which sent shivers through all three men – a low rumbling ululation the like of which Tyler had never heard before. Jenkins stepped back in surprise.

'Hold her, dammit,' snarled Hawley but, a second later, he too stepped back as he saw blood begin to pour even more rapidly from her gaping median vagina.

'Oh Christ, the Müllerian duct has ruptured,' the vet rasped. 'The bloody thing could bleed to death.'

'Is there anything you can do?' Tyler demanded.

'We can at least save the calf,' Hawley told him.

The cow bellowed once more, even more loudly this time. The sound seemed to thunder from the very walls themselves then, as that roaring sound of agony subsided, another very different noise took its place.

There was a sound like tearing fabric and the cow's side began to split open. Blood burst from the gash and, a second later, what looked like a hoof tore through the rent.

Tyler stepped back in horror and, even Hawley could only stand transfixed as part of the cow's rump seemed first to be sucked in and then to rapidly bulge, the

49

flesh straining to the point where it became shiny, as if pushed from the inside by some impossible force.

There was a rasping sound and the skin broke. Blood and excrement sprayed upwards in an obscene fountain and, from the ruins of the cow's hindquarters, a head appeared. It rose on a long, snake-like neck. It was the head of the calf, but no calf any of them had ever seen before, and it gazed defiantly at them for long seconds. Then the rear end of the cow literally exploded as the calf tore itself free.

Tyler and Hawley recoiled, splattered with blood, watching as the calf, which they could now see was huge, struggled to free itself from the torn body of its mother. Pieces of cow and calf became momentarily as one and it was as if the men were witnessing some monstrous kind of binary fission as one animal became two. Like the nuclei of two cells, the animals separated, the cow going into spasm as the calf continued to tear itself free. It burst from the torn remnants of its mother, lumps of the allanta chorium hanging from it, the membranous sack sticking to it like grotesque streamers of translucent flesh.

'What the fuck is it?' gasped Jenkins, looking at the calf which now stood upright.

The creature was at least four feet high at the shoulder. A living nightmare. A patchwork of life. Bumps and growths seemed to cover it, leaving not one square of skin unaffected. Its head was heavy, weighed down by what appeared to be a large tumescent protuberance on one side. Tyler noticed with horror that this additional growth had an eye and for fleeting seconds he thought the monstrosity had two heads. It stood perfectly still, watching them, blood and pieces of internal tissue dripping from its gore soaked hide. Then it moved towards Jenkins.

The calf opened its mouth to reveal a set of powerful

teeth and Jenkins pressed himself back against the wall of the barn.

Tyler leapt to one side, grabbing the pitchfork, lowering the two prongs at the deformed calf.

'Don't touch it,' screamed Hawley, as the abomination spun round to face him, lips drawn back in a grimace of rage. It uttered a low sound in its throat, a noise which gradually grew in volume, impossibly loud for a creature of its size.

Tyler gritted his teeth and thrust the pitchfork forward, driving it into the chest of the calf, ignoring the fresh gouts of blood which sprayed him. He wrenched the weapon free and struck again, this time piercing the calf's side, pushing deeper until he caused it to topple over. He leant on the fork with all his strength, holding the creature down as it bucked and twisted frantically, trying to escape the twin prongs which pinned it to the floor like a butterfly to a board. The calf raised its head and tried to bite him but Tyler merely stepped back a foot or two, tore the fork free then rammed it through the dying monstrosity's head. One of the prongs punctured an eye on the way and, amidst the cracking of bone, the thing writhed one last time then was still.

Panting, Tyler staggered away, looking down with digust at the calf and what was left of the cow. Blood had sprayed everywhere and the barn reeked of the coppery smelling substance.

'What is it?' Jenkins asked once more, looking down at the body.

Hawley knelt beside the dead calf.

'It's a mutation of some kind,' he said. The vet turned to look at Tyler. 'I'll have to do an autopsy.'

Tyler nodded, wiping some blood from his face.

'What the fuck would make it grow like that?' he said, his voice a hoarse whisper.

51

'I won't know that until I've done the autopsy,' Hawley told him.

'Call me as soon as you've got any information,' said the farmer.

'I'll need something to put it in,' the vet told him.

'Russell,' Tyler hooked a thumb towards the other barn and Jenkins scuttled out to fetch something in which to wrap the monster.

'I've never seen anything like this in my life,' Hawley confessed, prodding the calf with his index finger. 'Mutations yes, but never as advanced as this.'

'Could the growths be tumours?' said Tyler.

'I doubt it, not as large as this, especially the one on the head.' The vet looked at the bulge with its extra eye. 'What about the bull that serviced this cow. Is *it* all right?'

'I told you, Dan, there was nothing out of the ordinary until about thirty minutes ago when the cow started bleeding. I thought it was an ovarian rupture like you did but . . . not this.'

'I'll need to examine the cow as well, chances are there was some kind of genetic fault with either the bull or the cow – some kind of change in the DNA, perhaps a translocation of chromosomes.' He exhaled deeply. 'I won't be able to say until I've given them both a thorough going over.'

The two men stood in silence for long seconds, their gaze fixed on the mutation at their feet.

'Have you had any other breeding problems?' Hawley asked.

Tyler caught the note of concern in his voice.

'No, why do you ask?'

'Just curious,' said the vet.

'I *have* got weaners and lambs that are twice the size they should be for their age,' Tyler said.

'You're not the only one, Vic,' said Hawley, flatly.

'You know Stuart Nichols over in Western Orchard farm and old Ben Thurston? So have they.'

Tyler looked puzzled.

'But no mutations?' he said.

Hawley shook his head.

Both of them returned their gaze to the deformed calf, its third eye fixing them in a glassy stare.

Tyler exhaled deeply, the blood starting to congeal on his hands.

'What the hell is going on?'

Ten

The multi-coloured awnings which adorned the stalls of Wakely market flapped in the wind. The central square of the town was awash with colour. It resembled the palette of a mad artist, greens, blues, reds and all manner of stripes alongside each other in bright rows.

Jo drove slowly past, glancing over at the market. The clock on the council building across the square struck eleven, trading was in full swing. Why then, Jo wondered, were there so few people around? She had been in Wakely on market day before and had always found it practically impossible to walk around the central square let alone drive. But today was different. People moved about quietly and few voices were raised for there was no need to shout. Everything had a calmness about it and a serenity which was almost unnerving.

Anxious for some fresh air, Jo stopped the car and

got out. She had parked next to a large fruit van and two men were unloading it, one of them struggling across to a nearby stall with crates of oranges. The man seemed to be managing without too much trouble but, half-way to the stall, he sagged and dropped the crate which promptly burst open. Jaffas went rolling in all directions like huge orange marbles.

'Oh sod it,' grunted the man and began picking them up.

His companion chuckled, jumped down from the van and they set about gathering the dropped fruit.

Jo ran an appraising eye over them. Both men were in their early twenties, stripped to the waist, one of them with dark hair that reached his shoulders. Yet what struck her as most odd was the colour of their skin. Considering it had been so hot during the past few weeks and these men were obviously from one of the farms around Wakely, both were milk white. There wasn't the slightest trace of sun tan on either of them which was something Jo found surprising. She walked past, aware that the one with the long hair was gazing at her legs.

'Morning,' he said, cheerfully, looking up at her.

Jo smiled, even more aware of her own smoothly tanned skin as she looked into the pale face of the farm hand. His eyes were narrowed against the sun as he looked at her, his glance shifting furtively from her face to her breasts.

'I thought you were supposed to sell your goods,' she said, motioning towards the oranges. 'Not throw them around.'

The two men finished gathering up the fruit and succeeded in placing it amongst the other produce. The stall seemed unusually well stocked.

'Business not too good?' Jo asked.

'There aren't that many people around today,' said the one with the long hair.

54

Jo scanned the first aisle, flanked on both sides by stalls selling everything from wet fish to brass antiques. It stretched for at least a hundred yards ahead of her yet there were barely two dozen people in it. They seemed, some of them, to be moving in slow motion, as if every step were an effort.

'I thought it was usually busy in town on market days,' she said.

'It is,' the first man said, touching his cheek. Jo frowned, noticing how sunken his features were, the dark rings beneath both eyes which looked as though someone had smudged soot there. She put it down to a rough night.

'Can we interest you in anything, love?' said the second man brandishing a cucumber before him. Both he and his companion laughed.

Jo grinned.

'Maybe some other time,' she said and wandered off.

The town square of Wakely was cobbled and she found that she had to walk slowly for fear of overbalancing in her high heels. As she passed up the aisle, glancing at each stall, she noticed again just how quiet it was, even in the centre of the market. A few people chatted animatedly and every so often a peal of laughter would ring out but, in the main, the shoppers and traders were subdued.

Jo paused at a stall which sold miniature glass animals. All of them, she guessed, made by the proprietor. He was sitting at the rear of the stall reading a tatty paperback, his face hidden from view. The journalist looked at him, studying his hands which were large, comfortably enclosing the book. She frowned slightly.

The fingernails of his left hand were long and pointed, the skin of the cuticles cracked and raw. The nails of the other hand were the same, the index finger particularly long to the point where it had begun to curve over.

Jo picked up one of the glass animals, an elephant sitting up balancing a ball on its trunk, and inspected it.

'Need any help, lady?' said the man, his voice low.

The American looked up and, once again, found herself looking into a face the colour of sour cream. Only this time the man's lips were cracked too, as if he'd been exposed to the sun for a long time. Yet he had no colour. His cheek bones were high, the skin looking as if it had been stretched over them. She saw that it was peeling in places, just small fragments which flaked off as he rubbed his chin.

'These models are very nice,' she said, replacing the elephant.

'All my own work,' said the man, proudly.

'I was saying to some guys back there, it's not very busy for market day,' said Jo.

The man shook his head.

'It might buck up a bit later on,' he explained. 'The livestock market is held this afternoon.'

Jo nodded.

'Nice talking to you. I like your models very much,' she told him as she walked away.

The man returned to his paperback.

It must have taken Jo thirty minutes to walk up and down all six aisles of Wakely market and she found that she managed it without the customary barging and bumping which usually occurred on this, the town's busiest day of the week. She headed back to her car, passing the fruit stall where the man with the long hair winked at her and smiled. She returned the gesture, noticing that he too had long, hooked fingernails on at least four of the spindly digits. Her initial surprise and curiosity had diminished somewhat and, by the time she slid back behind the wheel of the Chevette, her mind had returned to more important things.

She glanced down at the piece of paper beside her which bore Geoffrey Anderson's address.

Jo started the engine and drove off. She wriggled uncomfortably in her seat at first. The sun, pouring through the windows, had turned the plastic seats of the car into a hot plate which seared her legs and even burned her backside through the thin material of her skirt. As she drove, she rolled her head back and forth in an effort to release some of the tension which was gnawing at her shoulders.

Anderson's house stood amidst a large expanse of garden, separated from his neighbours on both sides by a high wooden fence. The grass, Jo noticed as she got out of the car, looked short, freshly mown even. The man she sought might indeed have left Vanderburg Chemicals but he certainly hadn't left Wakely. The garden looked immaculate. She approached the front gate, inhaling a heady mixture of blossom from the trees and the numerous fragrances of flowers growing in abundance in all the gardens before her.

There was a sign on the gate which read: 'Avalon'.

She double checked her piece of paper, although it was a formality. This was definitely Anderson's house. Jo walked briskly up the path, noticing as she did so that the curtains at the front of the house were drawn – doubtless to keep out the scorching sun. She knocked on the door and waited.

There was no answer. No sounds of movement from inside.

She tried again.

Still nothing.

She pushed open the letter box and tried to peer into the gloom inside the hall. It was like looking into a pit. She could see nothing. Jo followed the path around to the back of the house where she banged on the rear door. Once again she noticed that the curtains, both upstairs and down, were drawn. The American tapped on the kitchen window with her car keys and still she received no answer. She wandered down the garden to a large shed, surprised to find it unlocked. It smelt fusty inside, an odour of damp wood and earth. The windows were dirty, the tools inside caked with dried mud.

Jo walked back to the house, around to the front and along to the house next door.

The curtains there were drawn too.

She banged the front door twice, stepping back to look up at the red brick dwelling.

She waited for five minutes but there was no answer.

She was becoming increasingly irritable by now and walked back the way she had come, to the house which stood on the other side of Anderson's.

She almost breathed a sigh of relief when she saw a woman, a little older than herself, emerge from the front door, a plastic bucket in one hand, a wash leather in the other.

'Excuse me,' Jo called.

The woman looked up as the journalist walked up the path towards her.

'Sorry to intrude,' said the American. 'I won't keep you a minute.'

'If you're a Jehovah's Witness I'm afraid I'm busy,' said the woman, taking a step back.

Jo smiled.

She held out her hands.

'No Bible, see.'

The woman smiled, running a hand through her tousled blonde hair. She was a trifle on the plump side, the jeans she wore just that little bit too tight around the thighs. Her face was aglow, her ruddy complexion making it look as though someone had scrubbed her cheeks with a wire brush.

Jo could hear the sound of a record player from inside the house.

'I'm sorry to stop you working,' said Jo. 'I won't take up a minute of your time.'

'Who are you?' the woman wanted to know.

'I'm a journalist, my name's Joanna Ward. I work for the *Arkham Comet*.'

The woman nodded.

'I'm looking for the guy who lives next door, Geoffrey Anderson. I wondered if you'd seen him.'

'You're American, aren't you?' the woman said, smiling as if she'd just made some earth-shattering discovery.

Jo nodded.

'About Mr Anderson,' she persisted, 'I wondered if you'd be able to tell me anything about him.'

'Is he in trouble?' asked the woman almost excitedly.

'No, it's nothing like that. *Have* you seen him lately?'

'Not since Sunday, he was out there cutting his grass,' the woman told her. 'A nice man. He kept himself to himself but there's nothing wrong with that is there?'

Sunday, Jo thought. 'He was here two days ago?'

'Yes.'

'But you haven't seen him since?'

'No. You could probably contact him at work. I think he's got something to do with that new chemical place.'

Jo fumbled in her pocket and produced a card.

'Look, if you see him, could you call me on that number, please.'

'I can't really tell you much about him,' said the woman, apologetically. She ran her eyes over the card which Jo had given her.

'Do you know if he finished working for Vanderburg Chemicals recently?' Jo enquired.

'He's worked for them since they started.'

'So he hasn't left or been fired in the last three or four days?'

'Not as far as I know.'

Jo nodded.

'Thanks very much, you've been a great help.' She turned and headed back to her car.

The woman looked at the card once more then pushed it into her back pocket. By the time she had done that, Jo had driven off.

Eleven

'I reckon you must be using the wrong soap, Jack. You've frightened all the bloody customers away.'

A chorus of laughter and cheers greeted Stuart Nichols' remark. He downed what was left in his cider glass and ordered another round, pushing the other empty glasses towards the barman. Nichols was a big man, a year or two older than Tyler. He ran a farm to the west of Wakely, a large holding on which he kept a herd of more than two hundred cattle. He and his wife, Bet, had lived there for the past twelve years.

'It's not me,' Jack Vernon told him. 'It's you lot, come trooping in here with your sodding great boots covered in cow shit.'

The group of men gathered around the bar of 'The Black Swan' laughed.

'That's a fine way to talk to your best customers,' said Tyler, taking a hefty swig from the fresh pint which Vernon handed to him.

'It is quiet in here though,' said Reg Gentry, looking around the bar. He chewed thoughtfully on the stem of his pipe and scratched his face, careful to avoid the nasty scar on his left cheek. He'd been kicked in the face by a pony when he was eleven. It had broken his jaw in four places and cost him five teeth as well as leaving him with the scar.

As he sat on the bar stool he glanced up at the light above him and winced slightly.

'I bet you don't know where you are, now you're back doing some real work again, Vic,' said Nichols, taking a hefty swallow from his pint pot.

'Well, it beats sitting on your arse behind a desk I'll say that,' Tyler told him.

'How are you settling in?' asked Ben Thurston.

'Fine thanks, Ben,' said the younger man warmly. 'It's great to be able to breathe clean air again.' He chuckled.

Tyler had always reserved a certain affection for Thurston. The man was in his early sixties, the oldest of the landowners around Wakely. He and his three sons ran a fifty acre farm to the North. Thurston had intended to retire when he reached his sixtieth birthday but, with the passing on of his wife, that had not transpired. He reminded Tyler of his own father in many ways; his dogged determination, sharp business mind and other, less noticeable features further endeared him to the younger man.

Nichols took another swig of his pint, wiping his mouth with the back of his hand.

'One of my sows gave birth to a litter,' he said. 'About two days ago and every one of the little buggers was dead. All seven of them. I can't understand it.'

'Dan Hawley told me you'd been having trouble with your weaners,' said Tyler, wondering whether or not to mention the incident with the calf.

'When did you see Dan?' asked Nichols.

'This morning, about three hours ago,' Tyler told him. He decided *not* to mention the deformed animal. 'I said to him that my weaners were twice the size they should

61

be and he mentioned that you and Ben too were getting the same results.'

'I'm not complaining,' said Thurston. 'With the stock as big as it is we should all get better prices.'

'Bloody right,' echoed Nichols. 'I'll be asking more than usual I'll tell you that.'

'Bred a super-pig have you, Stuart?' asked Jack Vernon, grinning.

'You could say that,' Nichols told him, smugly, then he laughed.

'It's been the same with my lambs,' Thurston added. 'Only three weeks old but some of them are as big as collies.'

'What do you think's causing it?' said Reg Gentry.

'I couldn't give a sod what's causing it,' Stuart Nichols told him. 'All I know is my profits are going to rise.'

Tyler was the first to notice Jo when she walked into the bar. She strode past the farmers, smiled softly at them and ordered herself a drink.

'If there's any more like that come in today, profits won't be the only thing rising,' Nichols said, lecherously. He watched as Jo seated herself on a stool at the far end of the bar, hitching her skirt up until it was well above her knee, revealing her slim tanned thigh. She took a notepad from her handbag and began scribbling something down.

'I've not seen her around before,' Gentry said.

Tyler didn't speak. He had his eyes fixed firmly but discreetly on Jo, watching her over the rim of his glass.

'I believe we were talking about livestock,' said Ben Thurston, smiling.

The other men seemed to come out of their trance, their eyes turning away from Jo who could see them out of her eye corner. She smiled to herself and continued writing.

'What about you, Vic?' said Nichols. 'You're the one

with the brains, you went to college. What do you think's causing the accelerated growth?'

Tyler shrugged.

'It's difficult to say. My farmhands were telling me about some new multi-purpose feed they'd been using.'

Nichols nodded.

'That stuff from Vanderburg or whatever the hell it's called?' he asked.

'I don't know the name of it,' Tyler said.

'It's from Vanderburg Chemicals,' the other farmer continued. 'The bloke who sold it to me said it would increase growth.'

Jo sat up at the mention of the word Vanderburg. She swung round on her stool and faced the men.

'Pardon me,' she said. 'Don't think I'm eavesdropping but I did hear one of you mention Vanderburg Chemicals, didn't I?'

The men were a little taken aback by her accent but Tyler broke the sudden silence, hesitantly at first perhaps but thankful for the opportunity to converse with such an attractive young woman.

'Yes you did,' he said. 'Do you know something about them?'

'Not as much as I'd like too,' said Jo. She picked up her drink and walked over to the group of men. Thurston offered her his stool.

'You're a Yank, aren't you?' said Nichols.

'I'm an *American*, yes.'

'What are you doing here?' asked Gentry.

'I work for the *Arkham Comet*. I'm just covering a local story,' she said.

'Anything interesting?' asked Nichols.

Jo shook her head.

'Not really.' She sipped at her drink. 'Are you all in town for the cattle market?'

Tyler nodded.

'Was that an educated guess?' he asked, smiling at her.

'I've been to it before,' she told him.

Jo looked deep into his blue eyes and could almost feel the warmth there. She afforded herself a quick inspection of this tall, hard-faced man dressed in jeans, boots and a check shirt. His face was pleasantly tanned, the material of his shirt unable to conceal the powerful body beneath.

'To be accurate,' said Thurston, 'it's a livestock market.'

Jo shrugged.

'Whatever it is I was surprised there weren't more people around.'

'So were we,' Nichols told her. He eyed the newcomer up and down, noticing that her full breasts were unfettered by a bra, the twin peaks of her nipples dark beneath the fabric. 'What's a Yank doing working for the *Arkham Comet*?'

'It's a living,' she told him.

Gentry looked at his watch. The hands were approaching 1.00 p.m. He downed what was left in his glass and got to his feet.

'If we don't get a move on we'll miss the bloody market,' he said and the other men also finished their drinks. Tyler hesitated.

'Want to come along?' he asked her. 'You can see how we yokels spend the day.'

He smiled at her and Jo responded. Tyler found himself drawn to those twinkling green eyes of hers, hypnotized by them.

'I have to make a phone call first,' she told him.

He nodded.

'Jack, the lady would like to borrow your phone,' he said.

The barman smiled and ushered Jo towards the end of the bar where, from beneath the counter, he produced a phone and set it down before her. Tyler watched her as she jabbed at the numbers, drumming agitatedly on the bar top as she waited for the receiver to be lifted at the other end. When it finally was, she recognized the voice.

'It's Jo Ward,' she babbled. 'Put me through to Doug Clark, please.'

Another moment's silence at the other end then she heard the familiar voice of the editor.

He wanted to know where she was.

'I'm in Wakely,' Jo said and then, before he could ask why, 'Listen, Doug, this could be important.' She told him about the phone call of the previous night, about her visit to Vanderburg Chemicals, of Glendenning's lie about Anderson and of that particular man's disappearance. 'I think Anderson is still in Wakely. I have to find him.'

He asked how long it would take her.

'That's impossible to say but, whatever it was he wanted to talk about must have been pretty goddam important. I have to stay here until I find him.'

Clark suggested that her imagination might be getting the better of her.

'For Christ's sake,' she blurted, 'you know me better than that. Besides, when I asked Glendenning who Vanderburg's backers were he changed the subject. I'm sure Anderson knows something worth knowing and I want to hear it.'

She hung up and rejoined Tyler.

'Do you want to follow my truck in your car?' he asked her.

'What's wrong with me riding in the cab with you?' she wanted to know.

Tyler smiled.

'Fair enough, if you don't mind the twelve cattle and sixteen pigs in the back. It doesn't exactly smell like a rose garden in there.'

65

He led her out to the waiting truck, a large van that looked like a container lorry, its sides painted white. He opened the passenger side door and helped her up onto the running platform. From there she scrambled into the cab.

'You weren't joking, were you?' she said, wrinkling her nose.

Tyler chuckled and scuttled around to the driver's side where he hauled himself up and started the engine, the smell of diesel mingling with the odour of livestock.

'I did warn you,' he said and, this time, they both laughed.

Twelve

The livestock market was held in a maze of yards and sheds on the main road leading out of Wakely. It always attracted a sizeable gathering of people: buyers, live-stock breeders and interested onlookers. It was, like the other market in the town square, something of an event for Wakely's inhabitants and also those who made the trip from outside the town be it for business purposes or just plain curiosity.

The trucks and vans which carried the animals were parked in a large tarmac area to the rear of two corru-gated iron sheds. From there, the animals were herded through a series of pens and enclosures, separating them into varying sizes, breeds and species.

Some of the farmers were under contract to the various butchers, restaurants or hotels in and around the town so business was done briskly. It was just a matter of deciding on a price. The livestock would then be herded back into their respective transporters and driven straight to the abattoir for slaughtering. The whole process took less than a day from arrival at the market to delivery of the prepared carcasses to the appointed destination.

Those animals belonging to farmers not under contract were open for auction to anyone who cared to pay the right price for them. Tyler's stock came into this latter category but he felt confident about making a healthy price on all his stock. Some of the animals were occasionally bought by other farmers. Particularly dairy cattle and pigs. One or two of the small-holders specialized in one type of livestock, so bidding for what was termed 'independent stock' was also their privilege.

Jo lit up a cigarette and offered the pack to Tyler.

He declined.

'I don't smoke.'

Jo lit one and blew out a funnel of the bluish haze.

'Does this place always smell as bad as this?' she asked, waving a hand in front of her as if to drive away the odour of animal excretion and damp straw.

Tyler grinned.

'Country air is good for you. You've lived in towns too long.'

'I intend staying in towns if the country smells as bad as this.'

They were standing beside a small enclosure which housed a sow and six piglets. Tyler ran an interested eye over the smaller creatures, at once impressed and puzzled by their exaggerated size. The largest was at least twelve inches high at the shoulder. Nevertheless they had, as he'd expected, brought him an excellent price and he'd already negotiated a deal for the litter with a buyer from a restaurant in Arkham. He watched as the animals moved agitatedly around the sow, one or two trying to reach her swollen teats in order to feed. The sow herself grunted and moved around the pen as if attempting to keep away from her hungry offspring.

'Look, mum.'

The shout startled Tyler and he turned to see a small boy, about twelve, clambering onto the metal struts of the enclosure, leaning over to get a better look at the animals inside. His mother, who had two other younger children with her, trudged wearily over to her son and joined him at Tyler's side.

The farmer looked at the little group and then at Jo who smiled, as the boy began to make grunting noises like the pig.

The sow had finally stopped her agitated pacings and remained still long enough for one or two of the piglets to begin feeding. They were swiftly joined by the others, all jostling one another in an effort to reach the milk secreting glands.

'They're sucking her tits,' said the boy loudly, laughing raucously.

'*Teats*,' said his mother, slapping him on the back of the head, looking around to see if anyone else had heard. She looked at Tyler and coloured slightly. He smiled.

The piglets were becoming more excited and Tyler could hear a series of low grunts coming from the sow. A grunt that suddenly turned into a bellow of pain.

One of the litter had gripped a teat in its mouth and, with a powerful twist of its neck, wrung the swollen appendage off.

Blood jetted from the gash, splattering the other animals.

It was like a signal for them.

Almost as one, they began gnawing and tearing at the teats, ripping them free, swallowing them, the mixture of milk and blood cascading from their jaws. Then, as the sow toppled over they moved in frenziedly

68

upon her, almost burrowing into the soft flesh of her underbelly, seeking out the vital organs inside.

Tyler began to clamber over the rail as he saw two of them use their trotters to gouge a cleft in the bloodied flesh. A foul-smelling flux of viscera erupted from the wound and the piglets squealed excitedly, devouring the bulging intestines which presented themselves, bursting forth from the sow's mutilated stomach. She tried to rise, to shake off the cannabalistic horde but it was no good.

The boy on the fence had turned the colour of rancid butter, his sisters screaming hysterically, his mother trying to drag all three of the children away.

Tyler grabbed one of the piglets and pulled it off. He hurled the animal to one side, horrified when it rolled over and then came at him, trying to bite his leg. He kicked it hard in the face, the blow momentarily felling it.

Jo saw two men nearby, dressed in dark green overalls, one of them carrying a small sledgehammer. She called to them, one eye still fixed on Tyler who was trying to save the dying sow.

The men in the overalls were stockmen, employees of the livestock market and both came running when they heard the commotion. The one carrying the hammer vaulted the rail, heading for the nearest piglet.

'Kill them,' shouted Tyler, driving his foot into the side of another of the litter.

The stockman needed no second bidding. He brought the hammer down on the head of the nearest piglet and killed it with that one crushing blow.

The sow was trying to crawl away, her intestines dragging in the straw like bulging bloodied party streamers. Jo gripped the rail tight, the cigarette stuck to her bottom lip. She watched as the squealing piglets were despatched, each one killed by a blow of the sledge-hammer. Except for the last which Tyler himself finished off. Sliding his sheath knife across its throat he dropped the writhing body to the ground and watched as it quivered violently. Blood jetted from the slashed throat.

'What happened?' asked the stockman with the hammer.

Tyler told him.

'I've heard of sows eating piglets before,' said the man. 'But not the other way around. What the hell caused it?'

'How should I know?' snapped Tyler, irritably. He looked down at the sow. The animal was dead, sprawled amongst her dead litter. One of the stockman hurried off to get something in which to conceal the carcasses.

Jo merely stood gazing at the scene of carnage. She looked at Tyler who was shaking his head slowly, trying to wipe some blood from his hands.

The stockman returned with a number of sacks, one of which Tyler took from him. He bent and lifted the nearest dead piglet by the ears, tossing it into the hessian bag then he clambered back over the fence, clutching his grisly acquisition in one gore-soaked hand.

'Come on,' he said to Jo, walking briskly towards the car park and his waiting truck.

'Where are we going?' she asked, hurrying to keep up with him.

'To see about this,' he told her, holding up the sack.

They were back in town in less than ten minutes.

Thirteen

Dan Hawley's veterinary surgery stood in a quiet, residential area of Wakely about two minutes' drive from the centre of the town. A large, detached house with white-washed walls and a spacious garden, it looked more like a rest home than a place of work. Hawley worked alone, helped out during the day by his receptionist, Mandy Potter, a lively girl in her early thirties who, because of the enormous glasses she wore, reminded Tyler of a barn owl.

The house had a sign outside with Hawley's name and credentials engraved on it and, on either side of the front door, two large stone dogs stood sentinel. It was a garish touch which never failed to amuse Tyler but, as he pulled the truck into Hawley's driveway, the last thing he felt like doing was laughing.

Jo followed him as he got down from the cab, clutching the sack and its bloodied load. He had hardly spoken during the drive from the livestock market and his face was set in tense lines as he approached the front door of the surgery. He walked into the reception and found that there were perhaps half a dozen other people waiting inside.

Dogs began to howl and bark at him. An elderly man who was balancing a parrot in a cage on his knee coughed as the bird began squawking, sending feathers and sand in all directions.

The smell from the sack which Tyler held began to fill the waiting room.

'Hello, Mr Tyler,' said Mandy, eyeing the sack curiously.

'Is Dan in there?' Tyler asked, motioning towards a green door to his right which led into the surgery proper.

'Yes, he is but . . .'

The farmer spun round and headed for the green door, Jo right behind him.

Mandy got to her feet, pushing her glasses back on her nose.

'You can't go in there yet,' she protested, but already Tyler was pushing his way in, leaving Mandy to cope with the complaints of the other visitors.

'Knock before you come in for Christ's sake,' said Hawley, without looking up. He was hunched over his desk writing something in a large red book. The vet turned when he heard the door slam.

'Vic, what the hell do you want?' he asked, his gaze quickly shifting to Jo.

Hawley got to his feet, watching as Tyler upended the sack and dumped the dead piglet on the stainless steel work top nearest to him.

'First calves, now weaners,' said Tyler angrily. 'Six of the fucking things, from the same litter, have just torn one of my sows to shreds.'

Hawley frowned and moved over to look at the still body of the piglet.

'It was like they were crazy, rabid or something,' said Jo.

The vet momentarily transferred his gaze from the dead pig to Jo. Tyler made hurried introductions then all three of them returned their attention to the carcass before them.

'What exactly happened?' asked Hawley, pulling on a pair of rubber gloves and reaching for a probe.

Tyler told him.

The vet nodded almost imperceptibly, using the probe to open the jaws of the piglet. A thick slush of blood and bile oozed from the open mouth and puddled beneath the piglet's head.

'What about that calf?' asked Tyler. 'Have you had the chance to examine it yet?'

Hawley shook his head.

'As soon as I find anything I'll let you know. No doubt you're expecting there to be some kind of link between the calf and this weaner?'

'Yes,' said Tyler. 'Perhaps some kind of genetic defect that's peculiar to both of them.'

'It's unlikely, Vic.'

'Then what's your bloody answer, Dan?'

'I haven't get one yet. I wish to Christ I had. Deformed calves, still-born litters, weaners that tear their own mother to pieces, baby animals that are growing at four times the rate they should be. I can't come up with answers to problems like those in a couple of hours.'

'How long has this been going on?' Jo asked.

Hawley shrugged.

'Well, for one thing, we don't even know if any of the incidents are related.'

'Don't tell me that these things are coincidence,' Tyler snapped.

'I didn't say they were,' Hawley muttered. 'But you can't put your finger on a calendar and say "it started then".'

'But when *would* you say the incidents began?' Jo asked again.

'Four, five weeks ago,' Hawley told her.

Jo nodded, her eyes flicking around the large surgery as the vet returned to the animal before him. The room was large, with a table and what looked like two operating tables inside. Powerful arc lamps on adjustable arms were arranged over each one. Rows of filing cabinets filled one wall and above those hung Hawley's certificates of practice. The other three walls were covered with shelves. Medicines, tonics and pills of all descriptions were contained there and, as Jo looked more carefully she saw that there was a larger jar containing some amber coloured fluid.

Floating in it was a small dog, which, on closer

inspection, she noticed had just three legs and no eyes. The journalist shuddered involuntarily.

'Like I said, Vic, I can't tell you anything until I've done autopsies on the animals. You'll just have to wait for my call.' Hawley pulled off his rubber gloves, muttering to himself as some skin flaked off in the process. He rubbed the back of his hand gently, more flesh peeling away to reveal a raw area beneath.

Jo looked at the hand and then at the vet's face which was pale, dark rings beneath his eyes. He turned off the light over the table, massaging his temple as he did so.

'I *will* get back to you,' he said again.

They all exchanged brief farewells and Hawley showed them to the door. As he walked back inside the surgery he took a last look at the dead piglet and pulled a sheet over it.

'What do *you* think is going on?' said Jo, studying Tyler's profile.

'I wish I knew,' he said.

Tyler drove slowly through the narrow streets of Wakely, heading back towards the pub where Jo had parked her car.

'For a quiet town this place sure has its share of mysteries,' she said, smiling.

Tyler nodded.

'It seems like we both have problems,' she said. 'You need answers, so do I, I have to find Geoffrey Anderson.'

'What's so special about this bloke anyway?' asked Tyler.

'Well, between you and me, I think he knows something that someone doesn't want him to talk about.'

'Like what?'

'If I knew that I wouldn't have a problem would I?'

'Ask a silly question . . .' Tyler let the sentence trail off.

'Look, you've lived in this place for most of your life. You know the people, you know the places.'

'You're asking me to help you find Geoffrey Anderson?'

'Right.'

Tyler brought the truck to a halt alongside Jo's Chevette. He switched off his engine and looked across at her.

'Look, Jo, I don't know anything about Anderson. I don't even know much about you.'

'We can soon put that right,' she said. 'How about dinner tonight?'

Tyler grinned, finally chuckling aloud.

'What's so funny?' Jo wanted to know.

'It's the first time any woman has asked me to dinner.'

'So, is it a date?'

'How could I refuse? What time?'

She checked her watch and saw that it was almost 3.45 p.m.

'I've got to go back to Arkham and pick up some stuff, then I'll check into a hotel here. I need to be in town. If Anderson's in Wakely and I'm damn sure he is, I mean to find him.'

'And dinner?'

'How about eight-thirty?'

He nodded, watching her as she jumped down from the cab.

'Eight-thirty in the hotel, I'll meet you in the bar,' she nodded in the direction of 'The King George', one of two hotels which overlooked the main square of the town.

Tyler nodded.

He watched her as she crossed to her car, started the engine and drove off. Then he himself turned the key

75

in his ignition and the big truck roared into life. He swung it around, squinting up at the burnished sun as he did so.

By 4.00 he was back at the farm.

Fourteen

The late afternoon sunlight crept like an intruder through the chinks in the venetian blinds. Vera Duggan stood at the sink peering at the partially hidden glowing orb which still burned brightly in the cloudless sky. As she watched it she felt her skin begin to tingle and her eyes begin to water. Vera looked away, moving across to one of the yellow painted cupboards on the wall by the fridge. She moved slowly. Arthritis had eaten deep into her joints and now, at sixty-eight, there were times when she could hardly move her hands. Ordinarily the sun eased the tightness in her joints but, for the past two or three weeks, it had been having the opposite effect. She felt stiff all over and she had been forced to retrieve the thick walking stick which she had discarded ten years before.

It had belonged to her husband, now dead for more than fifteen years. But his slippers were still in the same place in the hall, his photo still on the wall. He had looked so handsome in his uniform. Arthur Duggan of the King's Own Yorkshire Rifles. He had been wounded at Amiens in 1917. Gassed at Passchendaele. It had been that which had brought on his bronchitis. The same complaint which had taken him from her those fifteen years ago. Since then she had lived alone but for her succession of cats. Her sons rarely visited her but she didn't really miss them. One was an engineer, the other a plasterer. They took turns to look after her at Christmas but, other than that, she hardly saw them from one year to the next.

She hobbled to the pantry and retrieved a tin opener, working it with difficulty around the lip of the tin until she finally managed to open it. She scooped out the contents with a fork, pushing them into a bowl which bore the name 'Beth'. The cat finished preening itself and looked up, smelling its food.

'Come on,' said Vera, holding the bowl before her.

The cat, impatient for its food, leapt up onto the table and pawed at her hand.

'Get off,' Vera told it.

The cat continued trying to reach the food.

'Get down, now,' she snarled.

The cat hissed and tried once again to reach the dish of food, only this time it scratched Vera's hand. The claws cut easily through her thin flesh and she yelped, dropping the bowl, looking down at the four gashes on the back of her hand. The cat remained standing on the table, looking at her as if it realized that it had done wrong. It meowed and jumped down off the table, eagerly devouring the spilt food.

Vera muttered something under her breath and raised the walking stick above her head, steadying herself against the table.

With a grunt she brought it crashing down again.

There was a strength and ferocity to the blow which belied her years and condition for, so powerful was the impact, she heard the crack of bone as the walking stick connected with the cat's head. It screeched and tried to run but the blow had stunned it and, as Vera struck again, blood burst from its skull. The animal fell forward and Vera drove the end of the stout stick into its side, pressing down until she heard the breaking of ribs. The cat rasped, blood spilling from its mouth. The sight of the blood seemed to inflame Vera even more for she brought the walking stick down once more on the creature's head. This time the force was enough to rend bone and a gobbet of grey and red brain matter welled up through the smashed skull.

Still Vera continued beating at it until the kitchen floor was spattered with blood. Only when the cat was completely motionless did she sink to her knees, hands in the mess of grey and crimson. She was panting from the effort but there was a crooked smile on her face and, as she gazed at the dead animal, she began to salivate madly until streamers of sputum hung from her false teeth.

She shielded her eyes from the sun and began to laugh.

Fifteen

Despite the approach of evening, the sun still remained dominant in the sky. Now bleeding some of its colour into the heavens it retained its heat and Jo wiped a bead of perspiration from her forehead as she parked the Chevette in the car park beside 'The King George'. It had taken her just over an hour to drive back to her home in Arkham and pick up a few clothes.

Now she checked that the vehicle was securely locked up and walked around to the main entrance of the hotel.

Ivy grew thickly all over the old stonework, so thick in places it seemed that if it were cut down the entire building would collapse. The dining room was as yet in darkness, the only lights burning were those in the reception.

It was cool inside the hotel and Jo welcomed the respite for the cloying humidity in the air was making her feel uncomfortable. She smiled to herself, realizing that she must already have been away from New York too long. Out there residents learned to cope with eighty per cent humidity during the summer. But, the heat had unpleasant side-effects. Jo knew that the murder rate rose by almost double during those dog-days.

Now she carried her suitcase up to the reception desk and scanned the place for a member of staff. The hotel smelt of polish and new wood and, from somewhere nearby, there was a tempting aroma of food. Jo rubbed her stomach as she heard it rumble. There were two old pikes crossed on the wall over the open fire place behind her and on either side were metal pots which looked like witches' cauldrons. The entire place was panelled in dark oak, the beams, from the look of the tiny holes in them, being genuine.

Jo spotted a bell and shook it.

She looked around to see if anyone was going to respond. There didn't seem to be any guests or staff about.

The man rose from behind the desk, a tall fellow who towered over Jo.

'Can I help you?'

She spun round, shocked at the sudden sound.

'Damn,' she gasped, her hand going to her throat. 'Where did you come from?'

'Sorry if I startled you, Miss,' the man said, apologetically. 'I was down behind the desk, I didn't hear you come in.'

79

Jo nodded, regaining her breath.

'I'd like a room please. For a week.' She gave him her name and address. When she filled in the confirmation form she charged it to the *Arkham Comet*.

He turned and selected a key.

'Number 24,' he told her. 'On the second floor.' When he spoke, his voice was low and rasping, his teeth reducing the sounds he made to harsh whispers. His teeth looked huge, to the point where he had difficulty closing his mouth.

Jo nodded, looking more closely at the man. The badge on his lapel read 'Mark Bates'. He was in his late thirties, although it was virtually impossible to guess his age accurately. His skin was pale, shrivelled around the eyes and lip corners, sunken around the cheeks. It was peeling in places, particularly on the backs of his hands which, she noticed, bore the long, hooked nails she had seen earlier in the day on other Wakely residents. But his most striking features were his eyes. The irises glowed with an unnatural brilliance, quite in contrast to the yellowish, vein-infested whites.

Jo picked up her case.

'There aren't any porters,' said Bates. 'But I can help you with that.' He nodded towards the case.

'No that's fine. Thanks anyway,' Jo said.

She'd got as far as the lifts when he called her back.

'You forgot your key,' he informed her, walking out from behind the desk.

Jo smiled.

'One of these days I'll forget my name,' she said, reaching out to take it from him.

For a second she almost gasped aloud but she clenched her teeth together, the breath caught in her throat.

She could see it. There before her. The key was in his hand but she hesitated.

She looked at Bates and then down again.

There was hair growing on the palm of his hand.

Sixteen

'There's no one else for me to see is there, Mandy?' Dan Hawley asked, peering out from inside the surgery.

The receptionist was sitting at her desk glancing at *Cosmopolitan*. She put the magazine down and ran a finger through the list of names in the appointment book.

'No, Mr Hawley,' she said. 'But Stuart Nichols rang about half an hour ago and asked if you could go out to his farm tomorrow.'

'Did he say what was wrong?'

'Something about his lambs losing wool.'

Hawley nodded. He pulled off his rubber gloves and balled them up, pushing them into a pocket in his apron.

'You can drop the formalities now, Mandy,' he said.

She smiled and got to her feet.

The vet pulled her close, their mouths meeting, tongues probing urgently. She snaked her arms up around his neck, eager to prolong the sensation. When, finally, they did separate Mandy found that her glasses were misted over. She removed them, laying them on the desk behind her. Hawley brushed a speck of dust from her long lashes then kissed her softly on the end of the nose.

'If you're going to call me Mr Hawley during working hours,' he said. 'Perhaps I ought to call you Miss Potter.'

She chuckled.

'I don't know why we bother keeping up the pretence, Dan, everyone in Wakely knows what's going on between us.'

'You make it sound like something from a Barbara Cartland novel,' Hawley said, brushing a strand of hair from her forehead.

81

'You know what I mean.'

'People in Wakely are what you might call traditionalists. They have their standards and they expect everyone to conform to them. But they turn a blind eye when what they see starts to offend their moral sensibilities.'

'Very philosophical,' she said.

'And very true,' he added, kissing her again.

They had lived together for nearly a year in the vet's house. Prior to that, Mandy had been married to a plumber named Andy. There had been two children from the marriage, both boys. With Andy, she had endured a secure and steady way of life. He was a dependable, even predictable man. But that had not been enough for Mandy. She deplored his lack of ambition, his willingness to settle for what life gave him rather than taking it with both hands. And, over the years, she had seen her children being moulded into the same shape as their father. Neither of the boys had any desire to leave Wakely or the surroundings they had grown up in. At thirteen and eleven, she could see them as mirrors of their father and she began to resent them for it.

Hawley had been everything she had always hoped to find in a man.

She'd met him quite by chance. One day, taking the family dog along for its distemper shot, she had encountered the thick set, dark-haired man who was to become her lover.

Hawley had been in partnership with an older man for some time and, eager to have his own practice, he had often thought of leaving Wakely and setting up somewhere else. The problem had been solved for him when his partner had been killed in a car crash some eighteen months earlier. The practice had automatically come to him and since taking over he had expanded it until he alone now served Wakely and all areas for thirty miles round about.

She had found him so easy going on that first meeting. Mandy relaxed in his company until it felt as if she had known him all her life and, before she left the surgery, he asked her to have dinner with him one night.

She had agreed, thinking for days beforehand of an excuse which would not arouse her husband's insane jealousy and suspicion. She had gone to Hawley's house where he had cooked them a lavish meal and, afterwards, as if it were the most natural thing in the world, they had gone to bed together. Through him she had found her true self, discovering passions which she had thought dormant, finding others she never knew she possessed. He helped her shed her inhibitions until *she* became the teacher. Revelling in her newly awakened sexuality, overcome by Hawley's own expertise, she became insatiable. They were fused together by a ferocity of feeling which surprised them both.

She had found it easy to leave Andy and the two boys. At least, she had in the emotional sense. When he found out where she had gone he turned up at the house carrying a crow bar and he broke every window he could until, that night, Hawley had emerged to face him. The two men had exchanged blows, the vet sustaining a hairline fracture of the left tibia from a blow with the metal bar but he had left Andy with a broken nose and two fewer teeth.

It had been Hawley's suggestion that Mandy become his receptionist. At first she had been reluctant, realizing how quickly word of what had happened would spread around Wakely. However, she agreed eventually and, after the first few weeks of knowing looks and sly remarks, she had come to accept and enjoy her new way of life.

She didn't intend to contest the divorce case. She

didn't want anything from Andy and she certainly didn't wish for custody of the children. She had all she wanted with Hawley.

The cuckoo clock on the wall above the desk signalled its presence by screeching six times.

Mandy touched Hawley's cheek, tutting when some skin came off. Small flakes of it stuck under her nails.

'You look pale, Dan, are you feeling OK?' she asked, noticing also that his lips were swollen and cracked.

'I'm a bit tired, nothing more,' he told her.

'Then don't you think it's time you packed up?' She began undoing her white overall. 'I'll go and get dinner ready.' He ran an appreciative eye over the figure previously concealed by the overall. She was blessed with large but firm breasts, her figure narrowing slightly at the waist before filling out again into a well rounded bottom. Her stomach was flat, her legs long and slender.

'Are you going to eat some proper food tonight?' Hawley asked her, smiling.

Mandy feigned irritation.

'And what's that supposed to mean?'

'It means, when are you coming off that bloody stupid diet?'

'A fish and fruit diet is good for you. I've already lost three pounds in the last two weeks.'

He slapped her backside.

'From where?' he japed.

Mandy stuck her tongue out at him.

'I won't be long,' Hawley said. 'I've got something to do first.'

She hesitated.

'I promise,' he said and headed back into the surgery. Mandy disappeared into what were the living quarters of the house.

Hawley crossed to the work top nearest him and slipped on a fresh pair of rubber gloves. Then, slowly,

84

he pulled back the sheet which covered the remains of the piglet brought in by Tyler that afternoon. The vet pulled one of the arc lamps over and flicked it on, wincing at the powerful light. He closed his eyes for a moment, a sharp pain jabbing at his temples, and when he finally opened his eyes it was as narrow slits. The light felt hot on his skin.

He reached for a scalpel and steadied his hand then, with consummate skill, be began to cut a hole in the pig's skull.

Jesus, the light was bright. His eyes were almost watering now, making it difficult to concentrate. He put down the scalpel and blinked hard. His eyes felt gritty, as if he'd gone for too long without sleep.

The lamp felt even hotter on his skin.

He took a small saw and set about opening the cranium of the piglet, finally exposing the brain. This done, he cut two thin sections, small enough to fit on a microscope slide. He carried them across to the magnifying instrument and slid one beneath the powerful lens.

'Now,' he murmured to himself, relieved to be out of the rays of the arc light. 'Let's see what we've got.'

Seventeen

The bar of 'The King George' was empty but for Tyler, the barman and a couple of other people. The barman, dressed in white shirt and jacket and a pair of black trousers which had gone shiny around the backside, was busy cleaning glasses. Hardly for the rush of business, Tyler mused.

He pulled self-conciously at the top button of his shirt, anxious to loosen his tie a little. He had got out of the habit of wearing one and it was beginning to feel a little uncomfortable. Nevertheless, he had made a special effort for this night. As soon as he'd returned to the farm he'd taken his blue suit from the wardrobe where it had hung since his father's funeral and pressed it over, careful not to burn it. Then he'd showered, shaved and dressed, discovering that he'd been too early, so he drove into Wakely anyway and had a pint or two at 'The Black Knight' enduring the warmly sarcastic comments of his friends who had only once seen him in a suit.

Now he sat glancing alternately at the clock in the corner and his own watch.

It was 8.30 p.m.

With the timing of an actress who has just received her cue, Jo emerged from one of the lifts to the right. Tyler smiled at her across the darkened bar, immediately impressed by her appearance.

Her thick hair had been recently washed and allowed to dry naturally, making it look shaggy. She wore little make-up, the near perfect bone structure of her face making her features glow in the dull light. She wore a black dress, slashed across one shoulder and also up as far as the thigh. The curve of her tanned legs was accentuated by the silver high heels which she wore.

'Hi,' she beamed, seating herself beside him.

'Hello,' he said, smiling at her. 'What will you have to drink?'

She asked for a vodka and lime and, when the barman had poured it, heaping the glass with ice first, she sipped slowly at it, regarding Tyler over the rim.

'So, you hung up your wellington boots for the night, huh?'

86

'Yes, ma'am,' he said, saluting. He raised his glass. 'Cheers.'

'Here's to secrets,' she said and smiled that radiant smile once more.

Tyler nodded.

'Secrets,' he muttered. 'I still don't know what it is you're looking for, apart from this bloke called Anderson.'

Jo sighed.

'Maybe I don't either. Doug said it was just my suspicious mind.'

'Who's Doug?'

'Doug Clark. My editor and . . . friend.'

'What's that supposed to mean?'

'We had a thing going for a time. Notice I use the past tense.'

'Serious?'

'It would have been if I'd let it go that far. He wanted it to. I didn't.'

'So you split up.'

She ran the tip of her index finger around the rim of her glass.

'There was never too much there to begin with,' she told him. 'It wasn't long after I came to Arkham. I was lonely I guess. If it hadn't been Doug it would've been someone else.'

'And now you're not lonely anymore is that it?' he asked.

'Hey, you ask a lot of questions. I think you're in the wrong job. You should be a private detective.'

'Just curious.'

'What about you? Any sordid truths to tell?'

'I should be so lucky.'

They both laughed.

At nine they got up and walked through into the dining room. But for one man alone in a corner the place was devoid of people. They ordered, the menu

87

brought to them by a thin waitress whose face looked like a skull in the dim light. Jo frowned.

'I'll tell you one thing I've noticed,' she said. 'There seem to be a hell of a lot of people in this town who need some sun. Did you see that waitress? She looked anaemic.'

Tyler scratched his chin thoughtfully.

'Now you come to mention it I *have* noticed. Perhaps it's a virus of some kind.'

The first course arrived and they began eating. Both had prawn cocktail.

'So, how did you come to be a farmer?' Jo asked him.

'My father died, not long ago, left me to look after the place.'

'I'm sorry.'

'That's OK.' He smiled at her, mesmerized once more by her raw beauty, her mixture of sensuality and pure animal magnetism. She reminded Tyler of a caged beast, forever on the move, her questions probing, her manner relaxed and yet possessing a certain urgency. 'I'd been brought up on the land, it's what I know best.'

'I didn't even see anything green until I was seven and that was Central Park.' She laughed, sardonically. 'Muggers parade. Do you know that one in three families in New York have had someone amongst them mugged? That's a lot of people.'

'It's a lot of muggers.'

'They tell us to feel sorry for minority groups. You know, Negroes, Chicanos, Puerto Ricans. The underprivileged.' She shook her head. 'The underprivileged are beating our goddam brains out.'

'It's the same in some parts of Britain. I used to live in London. That's going the same way, you can't walk the streets in some areas without getting attacked. It's the political situation as much as anything, if people can't get money by working, then they'll nick it. No jobs, no money, no future.' He stuffed a spoonful of prawns into his mouth.

'Some of the city cynicism rubbed off on you,' she said.

'Perhaps. Why did you leave America?'

She told him about Tony, about the stories in the papers, about the murder, about the attempt on her own life.

'Christ,' he muttered when she'd finished. 'It must be quite boring living in Arkham after what you've seen.'

'I'd rather be bored and *alive*,' she told him and they both laughed. 'Anyhow, it's fine here for me. There's no pressure on me now like there used to be.'

The waitress returned and took away the empty dishes.

'You said your father was dead,' Jo said, softly. 'You haven't told me about your mother.'

Tyler lowered his gaze momentarily, staring into the bottom of his glass as if seeking an explanation of some kind.

'She died when I was twenty-one. A heart attack.'

Jo sensed she'd struck a wrong chord in his emotions.

'I still blame myself for her death in a way,' Tyler continued. 'She never wanted me to go away to college. It was all my father's idea. I knew that whatever I did I'd end up hurting one of them. It turned out to be my mother. She never did forgive me for going.'

'You shouldn't feel guilty about her death,' said Jo.

'I've come to terms with it now but it was difficult in the beginning.'

The main course arrived. Tyler had fish. Jo had chicken.

'Why not steak?' she asked, smiling, grateful for the opportunity to change the subject.

'I work with meat, so I don't feel like eating it too,'

he explained. 'I haven't touched meat or poultry for years.'

He re-filled Jo's wine glass. Then, he watched, amused, as she cut up her food, switched hands and began picking up the pieces, holding her fork in her right hand.

'Have you heard anything about this Anderson bloke?' he asked.

Jo sighed.

'No, but I know he had something important to tell me. I know he sounded frightened when I spoke to him on the phone.' She paused to swallow. 'And, what's more, I also know that the people he worked for lied to me about him. I'm sure he's around here somewhere, it's just a matter of finding him.'

'He could have left the country.'

'He had no reason to, besides, one of his neighbours saw him two days ago.'

'There's probably a perfectly simple explanation for it.'

'Terrific. If there is then I'm happy but I'd like to know one way or the other, you know what I mean?'

'And how do you intend doing that?'

'By breaking into his house.'

Tyler looked at her carefully across the table.

'What the hell will that solve?' he asked. 'You're a reporter not a bloody copper, you can't just go around breaking into people's houses.'

'Got any better suggestions?'

'And you want me to help you?'

She nodded.

'When do we do it?' His tone had lost some of its surprise.

'Tonight.'

'Fair enough.' He couldn't resist a smile. 'I reckon the Mafia should have tried to recruit you, not kill you.'

They both laughed.

90

Jo found herself gazing deep into the blue pools that were Tyler's eyes. Like twin circlets of June sky they seemed to glow with a radiance which she found both sensitive and arousing. As she ate she looked closely at him, the chiselled features, the broad shoulders, and she felt a stirring within her. She was drawn not just to his physical appearance but also by his easy manner. Christ, she was hot for him. It was as simple as that.

Tyler himself found his gaze drawn to her. She looked like something from an erotic dream, sitting opposite him with one tanned shoulder bare, the hair cascading over it. The tips of her nipples nudging the material of the dress. When she moved her foot he felt one of her legs brush against his and a feeling much akin to an electric shock ran up his spine. He watched her eating, fascinated and attracted by the way she licked her pouting lips after each mouthful. He saw the pink tip of her tongue flick forward, snake-like before disappearing back inside that moist orifice.

'You said you had some problems of your own,' said Jo over coffee.

The farmer nodded, as if reluctant to talk about them.

'It's the animals,' he said, finally. 'Well, you saw what happened at the market today with the weaners.'

The American shuddered at the recollection.

'It's not just that, it's other things and not only on *my* farm either. Those fellows you saw me with this afternoon in the pub, each one of them has been having problems with his stock.'

Jo rubbed her stomach and pulled a face, remembering the chicken she'd eaten.

'Thank God it seems confined to the bigger animals. Cattle, sheep and pigs and it's mainly affecting the young.'

'You say "it", what do you think it is?'

He shrugged.

'I don't know, I'm just hoping that Dan Hawley can come up with some answers.'

Jo sipped at her coffee and considered the farmer's troubled expression. He had his hands clasped on the table before him.

Putting her cup down, she reached forward and gently squeezed Tyler's arm.

He looked up, a little surprised then responded by pressing her slim hand between his. Their eyes locked.

'A town full of secrets,' he whispered.

She nodded almost imperceptibly, enjoying the contact with him. The strength in those hands.

'Maybe we won't like the answers we find,' she murmured.

They regarded each other a moment longer, as if disturbed by her words. Tyler finally managed to look away from those hypnotic green orbs of hers, the pupils now dilated.

He paid the bill and they left.

A cool breeze had sprung up and Jo shivered as they walked to her car. Above them, dark clouds conspired to blot out the watery moon. She shuddered as she slid behind the wheel, taking a glance at Tyler as she started the engine.

She guided the Chevette out into the road. The drive to Geoffrey Anderson's house should take about ten minutes.

It was almost 10.48 p.m.

Eighteen

The ticking of the wall clock sounded deafening in the silence of the kitchen. There was no other sound and the dull green luminosity of the clock hands was the only thing which was able to infiltrate the totality of the darkness. The room, in fact the entire house, was swamped in a gloom as impenetrable as pitch. All curtains were drawn, as they had been for the last two days. Not even the sodium glare of the street lamps outside was able to penetrate the abyss.

But, inside the home of Geoffrey Anderson, there was movement.

The darkness may have been almost palpable but there was a part of it which seemed to move independently of the rest. It was no shadow for there was no light to cast one. As if a piece of the gloom had gained form, the shape moved effortlessly through the black house. It walked slowly, noiselessly, completely at one with the cloying funereal surroundings.

It moved through the kitchen, opening the fridge door. There was a pool of water near the door, a spillage from the melted ice inside. The shape pulled out drawers and rummaged through them but all with an economy of movement which caused little sound.

It passed through into the sitting room, discovering a bureau. This it inspected more thoroughly, pulling open the cupboards and drawers but discovering nothing. Still it made no sound and even its breathing was muted and low, scarcely audible.

The shape froze in mid-stride as it heard a car drive past. It stood for long seconds then, satisfied that it would not be disturbed, it headed for the door which led to the hall.

The stairs creaked slightly as it ascended. Four closed

doors confronted it as it reached the landing and it moved towards the closest one.

It was open and the shape entered quickly.

Outside a car pulled up, the powerful headlamps cutting through the blackness.

The shape moved cautiously to the window and pulled the curtain back slightly, gazing out. It looked down upon the two people who had clambered out of the car and who, it now saw, were coming towards the house.

It watched as they approached then it let the curtain go and retreated back into the gloom.

There were sounds of movement from outside the house but, hidden within, surrounded by the cocoon of blackness, the shape waited.

Tyler closed the car door behind him and ran an appraising eye up and down the street. But for the odd light burning in sitting rooms or bedrooms, the tree-lined thoroughfare was in darkness broken only by the dull glow of the street lamps. A moth fluttered lazily around one of them, its wings skittering against the housing.

Jo pulled a torch from her coat pocket and flicked it on. Satisfied that it worked she headed towards the house which bore the sign 'Avalon'.

'It looks quiet enough,' said Tyler as he opened the gate.

'That's how it looked earlier,' Jo told him.

She moved impatiently forward but the farmer blocked her way. He shook his head.

'Let me go first,' he said, softly.

She agreed, allowing him to lead the way, furtively, up the garden path. They decided to break in via the back way in order to make themselves less conspicuous. Jo looked to her left, watching for any lights in the house of the woman she'd spoken to that morning. There were no lights to be seen anywhere.

The moon had been well and truly smothered by dark cloud so they hadn't even the advantage of natural light.

As they reached the back door Jo flicked on the torch.

'Shine it on the lock,' whispered Tyler, fumbling in his pocket. 'Shit,' he grunted. Then, turning to Jo, he asked, 'Have you got a hair clip or something like that?'

She hadn't.

Tyler pulled off his jacket, wrapped the garment around his elbow and, looking around one last time, drove it into the glass panelled door.

The pane spider-webbed but didn't break.

He hit it again, wincing as some glass smashed loudly on the kitchen floor inside. Then the farmer hurriedly slipped his hand through and unlocked the door. They both scuttled inside.

'Burglar I'm not,' he muttered, pulling his jacket back on. 'Now tell me what the hell we're looking for?'

Jo shone the torch around the kitchen, playing the beam over the beige walls. She picked out a calendar, a rack of knives, a couple of shelves and cupboards.

'I'm not even sure myself,' she told him, walking cautiously towards the door which led into the sitting room. Her high heels clicked loudly on the lino.

Tyler followed, noticing that one of the knives was missing from the rack. It was nothing extraordinary in itself but, with the rest of the room being so well ordered, this particular abberrance seemed all the more prominent.

The shape moved quietly from one bedroom to the next, listening to the muffled sounds of movement below. Finally it emerged on the landing and peered over the banister into the seething pit of Stygian blackness beneath.

The long-bladed kitchen knife, held in one black hand, seemed almost to be floating on air.

95

'Does this place look lived in to you?' said Jo, shining the torch around the sitting room.

'Well, someone's been here recently,' Tyler proclaimed, motioning towards an open drawer in the bureau. He hunted through it but found nothing. Jo moved to join him, picking up some pieces of paper which she discovered elsewhere on the cabinet.

'There might be notes of some kind,' she said.

'About what?' he enquired.

'I don't know. Anything, just to tell us where the hell Anderson is.'

Tyler moved into the hallway where he discovered the phone and the answering machine.

'Jo,' he called.

She joined him, shining the torch over the machine.

The cassette had been removed, the tape torn out. It hung like long streamers from the shattered cassette case. Even the plug on the machine itself had been removed.

'I told you there was something going on,' she said almost triumphantly.

'Let's not jump the gun,' said Tyler. 'There could be a logical explanation for this.'

'Like hell,' she rasped.

The American shone the torch around, bringing the beam to bear on the doormat.

There were two letters lying there, both addressed to Anderson and both bearing postmarks two days old. She looked at Tyler and an unspoken acknowledgement passed between them.

'Let's check upstairs,' said the farmer, taking the torch from her and mounting the first step.

The dark shape heard the sound of footfalls on the steps and it melted back into the darkness. It stepped into the bath and drew the shower curtain slowly around to

96

conceal itself still further. It gripped the knife tightly and listened intently as the stairs creaked.

'We can get it done quicker if we check the rooms separately,' said Jo. 'If you find anything, shout.'

He nodded and pushed open the door of the nearest room. She, for her own part, took the one to the left.

Tyler found himself in what appeared to be a spare bedroom. A single bed was made up neatly and the room smelt of fresh linen. There was a wardrobe too and he tried the key, wincing at the squeak as he turned it. The door came open and Tyler shone the torch inside.

Apart from a set of blankets, it was empty. No clothes, no shoes. Even the coat hangers were gone.

He pushed the door to and crossed to a bedside cabinet, sliding open a top drawer.

It too was empty.

Tyler frowned, repeating the procedure with the solid oak dressing table which stood beneath the window. The entire thing had been cleared, all the drawers were empty.

He exhaled deeply.

Jo, meanwhile, found herself in what looked like an office of some kind. There was a desk, a couple of filing cabinets and piles of paper and envelopes of varying sizes. The desk itself had just two pencils and a small writing pad on it. She checked the drawers which, to her surprise, were empty. Puzzled, she ran a hand through her hair and decided to flip through the pad. Several pages had been torn out, the tops of the perforated paper still in place.

She crossed to the filing cabinets and pulled the top one open. There were about three dozen manila files inside. All unmarked. All empty.

'Christ,' muttered Jo, her voice a mixture of anger and frustration. She pushed the cabinet shut a little too hard, the sound of metal on metal ringing around the silent house.

Tyler heard it and called to her.

She answered that she was OK.

The farmer moved into a second, larger bedroom.

Once more he was confronted with a wardrobe, a bigger one, and this one was locked. He tugged at the recalcitrant fastening. Finally putting down the torch and using both hands. It wouldn't budge. He looked around for something with which to break the handle and retrieved a brass paper weight from a nearby sideboard. He struck the handle twice and, on the second impact, it dropped away.

Jo heard the clatter but paid it no heed as she moved into the bathroom. She blinked hard, her eyes having become accustomed to the gloom, but in this particular room it seemed darker still. It was small, with just a toilet, a wash basin and a bath. The shower curtain, she noticed, was drawn.

Her heels sounded loud in the stillness as she crossed to the nylon curtain and prepared to pull it back.

Behind it, the shape raised the knife.

Jo took a firm hold on the curtain.

'Come here.'

The shout startled her. She spun round, letting go of the curtain, and headed in the direction of Tyler's voice.

She found him in the larger bedroom, two suitcases lying on the floor before him. They were both open. Both filled with clothes.

'If he'd gone away,' said the farmer. 'I think he might have taken his things with him.'

Jo nodded, looking down at the cases. Someone had gone through the wardrobe, removed every item of clothing and meticulously packed them into the tan suitcases.

'The wardrobe in the other room is empty too,' Tyler told her.

'I told you there was something wrong here,' she said.

'That still doesn't explain where Anderson is.'

'No,' murmured the American.

'I think we should call the police but not from here. This is out of our hands now. We'll report him as a missing person, tell them what's happened.'

'When?'

He looked at his watch beneath the torch light.

It was approaching 11.42.

'If he's already been missing for two days another few hours won't hurt. We'll wait until morning.'

Jo agreed.

They left everything as it was and made their way back down the stairs then outside once more. Tyler flicked off the torch as they reached the back door and they scuttled across the front lawn back to the waiting Chevette.

From the window of the larger bedroom the shape watched the car pull away, the kitchen knife still cradled in its hand.

Nineteen

As the sound of the Chevette's engine receded into the night, the curtain was slowly pushed back into position and the inside of Geoffrey Anderson's house once more became as black as pitch. Nevertheless, the lone intruder moved, as he always did at night, with an assurance few others possessed. His footsteps were as noiseless as before and he crossed to the larger bedroom, retracing his own steps and also those of Tyler and Jo.

He stood, a dark shape amongst so much gloom, gazing down at the open suitcases, the long bladed kitchen knife still gripped firmly in his hand. He hefted the lethal blade before him a second then dropped it onto the bed. His breathing was shallow but more guttural now and he suppressed a cough as he reached into his jacket pocket for a pack of Rothmans. There was one in the box, crumpled. What the hell, he'd make do. He'd started smoking when he was five and now, at fifty-three, he was on over eighty a day. His fingers, long and slender, were stained almost black with nicotine. He lit the cigarette and sucked hard on it. A spasm of coughing racked his body and he banged his chest angrily.

Carlo Fanducci was dying.

He knew it, he didn't need any doctor to tell him. He was fucking dying. The mornings when he coughed until he spat blood, the pains in his chest, the bouts of wheezing. They had told him that, he didn't need any goddam medical genius to confirm it. But what the hell, everybody had to die sometime. Fanducci smiled thinly, running a hand through his lank grey hair. Despite the fact that his hairline was receding, the lustrous grey strands still grew in abundance over his ears and the back of his head. Deep creases scarred almost every inch of his face, particularly his forehead which looked as though someone had pulled a fork across it. Someone had once told him he had a face like an unkept grave and he smiled once more at the recollection.

He sat down on the edge of the bed to finish his cigarette, the glowing tip the only light in the room.

Fanducci inhaled painfully.

He'd thought he was going to have to kill the man

and the girl when they'd entered the house. He didn't recognise the man but he'd seen the girl before. He'd listened in on the phone tap the night Anderson had called her then he'd watched her from the trees as she'd used the call box. He'd ripped the car light from inside the Chevette with his bare hands. He smiled and flexed his fingers. There was enormous strength in those hands. He might be dying but he sure as hell didn't intend going down weak and enfeebled.

The vision of the girl floated into his mind once more. He thought he'd seen her before that night in the lay-by. She was American, like himself. He had detected her accent – East Side, New York. Different from his own which was a curious amalgam of Italian and Lower Manhattan. He'd been born in Mott Street, at the very centre of 'Little Italy'. His father had been a bartender, running one of the joints owned by the Molinaro family, one of New York's largest and most powerful families. Fanducci himself had graduated, over the years, from collector to soldier and, finally, to trigger man.

Cosa Nostra. He almost said the words aloud. *Our thing. Our fucking thing*. Only he was no longer a part of it. Don Vito Molinaro had seen to that. The old bastard had given him a job to do. There had been a Union boss called Bishop. He wouldn't toe the line, wouldn't pay his dues to the collectors. Had even pulled a .45 on them, told them to fuck off and stop bothering him. Fanducci had been told to warn the Union leader off, frighten him a bit. So he had paid a visit to the man's factory, spoken to him. Ended up sticking the barrel of his .357 between the motherfucker's legs.

It hadn't been warning enough.

Old man Molinaro had finally given Fanducci the go ahead to push the button on Bishop. The Union Leader had to go and Fanducci was only too happy to do the job. He'd trailed the man home one night, then sat in his car until late finally emerging around midnight.

101

He'd cut through one of the windows with a glass cutter and entered the building.

Bishop had woken up as the Italian had entered the room and Fanducci could still remember the look of horrified realization on the Union leader's face as he saw the .357 being drawn. The big gun had not had the benefit of a silencer and the bang when it came had been thunderous. The hollow-tipped bullet had caught Bishop in the chest, exploding as it shattered bone, ripping an exit hole the size of a fist as it punched its way out of his back spraying Mrs Bishop with gobbets of lung and smashed scapula.

She'd started screaming when Fanducci had fired the second bullet into the nape of her husband's neck.

In the darkness her screams had seemed to be coming from some disembodied ghost but, in the pale light from outside, he could see her, drenched in her husband's blood. She continued to shriek. Then the two kids appeared from another room and *they* were screaming.

All of them were fucking screaming.

The only way to shut them up was by blowing their heads off and that was precisely what he'd done.

It had been plastered all over the papers the next day. Fanducci had been summoned before the Don and told that he was outcast. The family didn't want him any longer. Fuck them, he thought, and he went.

There was no shortage of buyers for his services. During his years as a family member he had met many top industrialists. These powerful men always needed bodyguards and Fanducci had found himself another employer with ease. He'd enjoyed that way of life. There had been more women in those years than he'd ever had before. One of them had become his wife.

By that time in his fiftieth year, Fanducci had married a girl half his age. She had the face and body of a movie star and a mind like a child. However, in bed she was something else. And, she was too much for him to handle. She had, he'd later discovered, a string of lovers but it wasn't until he walked in one night and found her being well and truly shafted by some goddam nigger that he'd found out. He'd beaten them both with a chair leg. Then he'd broken the nigger's fingers for good measure and thrown the girl out. Little bitch.

At roughly the same time, he'd been approached by John Stark. A mysterious man about six years younger than Fanducci himself. He'd asked the Italian what he was earning, then offered to double it. The condition was, he would have to up roots and move to England. Stark was opening a chemical research plant of some kind and he needed someone like Fanducci working for him. The Italian had agreed and, for the past three years he'd lived in England, working for what was to become Vanderburg Chemicals. He saw little of Stark, taking most of his orders from a guy called Thorndike, an Englishman who he could not learn to trust but then, Fanducci reasoned, trust was a hard thing to come by.

It had been Thorndike who had told him to kill Anderson. He hadn't reckoned on any interference though. Now, as he sat on the edge of the bed he tried to remember where he'd seen that dark-haired girl who'd not long ago left the house. Quite a looker, not the sort you'd easily forget – nice tits. No. The memory eluded him. He took one last suck on the cigarette, nipped it out and dropped the butt into his jacket pocket.

Then he set about his task.

Twenty

It was just after midnight as Jo and Tyler stood facing each other in the car park of 'The King George'. She had locked her own vehicle and now they stood beside the farmer's landrover.

'I'll meet you in the morning,' he said. 'We'll go to the police, tell them everything. They'll find Anderson.'

Jo nodded.

'Thanks for your help,' she said. 'I appreciate it.'

He leant forward and kissed her softly on the lips, feeling that familiar tingle run the length of his spine as he did so.

Jo felt the same sensation and she pulled Tyler closer, her lips parting, brushing the hard edges of his teeth before probing deeper into his mouth. He responded fiercely and they remained locked together for long moments, each enjoying the touch of the other. He felt her soft hair brush against his hand and he shuddered. As she slipped one hand inside his jacket it was all he could do to contain the erection he felt beginning. They finally broke apart, gazing into each other's eyes.

'I'd better go,' he said, opening the door of the landrover.

She watched as he climbed in and started the engine. He smiled at her, then spun the wheel and drove off. Jo stood in the car park for a moment longer, then she headed for the side entrance to the hotel.

There wasn't a soul in the reception as she entered. The American wandered into the darkened bar and found that too was deserted. She felt a sudden pang of hunger and knew she would have to eat something before she turned in for the night. Just a sandwich would do. Jo crossed to the reception and rang the bell.

No one appeared.

There were some papers on the desk top and a half

finished glass of beer but there didn't appear to be anyone around to claim them.

'Hello,' she called, her voice sounding strangely muffled in the silent confines of the reception.

The night porter or some member of staff had to be around she reasoned. Maybe they'd gone for a leak. She waited a moment longer, walking across to the open fire place, looking up at the two large pikes crossed above it. The weapons had been polished recently and glinted in the half light. Jo wandered back to the desk and rang the bell once more.

When the second attempt failed to secure any response, Jo lifted the flap which led behind the counter and walked through. There were two doors before her, both closed, both marked 'Private'. She knocked on the first one, peering inside when she got no answer. It was a small room, one wall being lined with leather chairs. There were a couple of coffee tables in there too, some magazines lying around. Jo guessed that it must be the staff room, a suspicion confirmed when she saw a rota pinned to a notice board on her right. There was another door before her which led through into the kitchen. This door was slightly ajar and she could see light spilling through the crack. There were vague sounds of movement from inside so she headed towards the door.

Of four banks of fluorescent lights set into the ceiling of the kitchen, only one was lit and, from where she stood, Jo could see a dark figure standing near to one of the fridges at the far end of the room.

As he turned, she saw that it was Mark Bates. She watched in silence as he opened the fridge door and took out a large piece of raw steak, the blood dripping from it as he removed it from the metal tray.

Jo was hidden from him by the darkness and by a rack of cooking utensils which hung before her. She watched, mesmerized, as he lifted the steak in one

105

hairy-palmed hand, looked at it for a moment, then tore off a chunk with his teeth. He chewed with difficulty, blood from the meat dripping from his chin. Bates grunted in satisfaction as he indulged his gluttony. Dark, rusty stains smeared his cheeks and some of the red liquid dripped from his long nails. When he opened his mouth, a gobbet fell to the floor and, quick as a flash, he scooped it up and rammed it back into his mouth.

Jo turned away, revolted, and fled from the kitchen. She felt sick and, when she finally reached her room, she drank several glasses of water before she felt the nausea pass off.

Downstairs, Bates stuffed the last of the steak into his mouth, then he fastidiously licked every last drop of blood from his fingers.

Twenty-one

The following morning, Jo ate a light breakfast of toast and jam washed down with a cup of coffee. She couldn't face the bacon and eggs which she saw one of the other guests tucking into, not after what she'd seen the previous night. She hadn't slept too well and there were dark rings beneath her eyes. Dressed in a pair of jeans and a red T-shirt she was already beginning to feel warm as, outside, the sun rose in a cloudless sky and began its merciless grilling of the land beneath.

She had looked for Bates but not seen him. There were just two waitresses and a porter, all three of whom looked lethargic and pale. Perhaps Tyler had been right? There might be a virus going around. She sipped at her coffee. A virus which caused hair to grow on the palm of a man's hand and made him eat raw meat? Jo almost chuckled aloud.

Her thoughts turned to other things. The incident at Anderson's house last night had unsettled her. Although at least now she felt secure in the knowledge that her hunch had been correct. There *was* something going on which he had known about and which someone at Vanderburg didn't want him to talk about. At least it looked that way. Obviously they wouldn't know for sure until they found him. She paused. *If* they found him. Jo hastily dismissed the idea. After all, this was England, not New York. Things like that didn't happen here. She finished her coffee, seeds of doubt already sown and growing in her mind. The American lit up a cigarette, took a few drags on it and left the dining room.

Tyler was waiting for her in reception.

'I wondered if you'd be up yet,' he said, smiling.

'With the lark,' she told him as they headed out to his waiting landrover.

As they drove to the police station she told him about Bates and the raw meat.

'Christ, what would make him do that?' Tyler wondered aloud.

She mentioned what he himself had said about a virus.

'It's possible I suppose but if it is a virus which is affecting so many people how the hell is it transmitted?'

'I'm a journalist not a doctor, Vic,' she said.

'Curiously enough, neither of my farm hands have turned up this morning but no one's rung in to say if they're sick or not. One of Stuart Nichols' blokes is taking care of things for me.'

They drove slowly through the quiet streets, noticing

just how few people there were about. Granted it was only ten o'clock but Wakely town centre was usually bustling by now. Those few people who were on the streets seemed to be moving in slow motion, heads bowed as if searching for something on the ground beneath them.

Tyler turned a corner, braking hard as a man stepped out in front of him.

'You silly sod,' Tyler shouted angrily. 'I could have killed you.'

The man merely looked round and both Jo and Tyler saw how bloodless his features were, the cheeks sunken, the eyes dark rimmed and yellowed. The man narrowed them against the glare of the sun. He gazed at the occupants of the landrover in bewilderment and, as he did so, Jo noticed that the flesh was flaking from his hands and curling back in almost transparent wisps. His nails were hooked, those that weren't broken. He stood motionless for a moment, then walked on as if nothing had happened.

Tyler looked anxiously at Jo and started the engine again.

'Maybe we should stop off at the doctor's surgery,' Jo said. 'See if he's had many cases like we've been seeing.'

'First things first, eh?' said the farmer. 'Let's find out where Geoffrey Anderson is. Besides, we don't know there *is* anything wrong with the people in Wakely yet.'

Jo opened her mouth to speak but Tyler cut her short.

'And even if there is, I don't see that there's much we can do about it.'

'But if it's affecting so many of them it must be communicable. What the hell is to stop us catching it?'

The farmer seemed not to have considered that possibility. As if troubled by the realization, he drove the rest of the way in silence.

There were two Panda cars parked outside Wakely police station, both with their windows wound down in an effort to let some air into the stifling confines of the vehicles. The police station itself was a large, white-washed building; just one storey, it was about the size of a supermarket and quite disproportionately large for the number of men on the force. Tyler knew four of them well, the other three just well enough to nod too.

He swung the landrover around and parked in front of the main doors, then he and Jo climbed out and strode down the six wide stone steps which led to the forecourt.

Inside the building it was cool, two powerful fans droning in opposite corners of the entry-way giving some respite from the blistering heat outside. Tyler crossed to a meshed glass partition and rapped sharply on it.

There were sounds of movement from behind, of a bolt being slipped and then the partition opened to reveal a red-faced man with a thick growth of beard. He had his white shirt rolled up to the elbows but there was still perspiration glistening on the thick hairs of his forearms. Rotund and quick to smile, he reminded Jo of a dark-haired, sweaty Santa Claus.

'Hello, Vic,' said Sergeant Don Mason. 'How are you?'

'Not so bad,' said Tyler, then he introduced Jo.

Mason smiled even more broadly and shook hands with the American who did her best to retain her smile as she felt her hand engulfed by the sticky puffiness of Mason's appendage.

'What's wrong? One of your pigs got lost has it?' Mason said, chuckling.

'I want to file a missing persons report,' the farmer told him.

Mason raised his eyebrows quizzically. He reached for the appropriate form and stood there, pen poised.

'What's the name?' he asked.

'Geoffrey Anderson,' Jo told him. 'He's been missing since Sunday.'

'Three days,' said Mason to himself, scribbling on the form. 'Description?'

There was an awkward silence.

Mason looked up.

Tyler exhaled deeply.

'We don't know what he looks like. Neither of us have ever seen him.'

'So how do you know he's missing?' Mason wanted to know.

'We broke into his house last night,' Jo said. 'All his clothes were packed as if he was going away but there was no sign of him. I think someone had been through the house.'

The policeman tapped on the desk top with the end of his pen.

'*You* broke into someone's house?' he said.

They both nodded.

'Perhaps I should be filling out a bloody charge sheet, not a missing persons form. What the hell were you doing breaking into somebody's house?'

'Don, for Heaven's sake listen to me,' said Tyler. 'I'm telling you, Anderson has disappeared.'

Mason wiped a bead of perspiration from his forehead.

'We'll soon sort this out,' he muttered. 'Peck.'

A constable appeared from one of the back rooms. He was tall, perhaps six five and he moved slowly as if each step were an effort. Both Jo and Tyler noticed the pallor of his skin, the way his teeth protruded from his swollen lips.

'Peck, drive out to this address,' said Mason handing the P.C. a page from his notebook. 'See what you can find.'

Peck nodded, blinked hard and rubbed his eyes.

110

'Come on, move yourself, lad, we haven't got all day. Radio in as soon as you've found out what's happening there.'

The constable nodded and made his way slowly out to one of the Pandas. They heard the engine being revved up, then the car pulled away.

'He needs a bloody bomb behind him that lad,' said Mason. 'He's been moping around looking like a wet weekend for the last week or so.'

'He looks ill,' said Jo.

'Well, if he is, he's not the only one on the force who is. Two of my constables called in sick five days ago and I haven't heard anything from them since and the others here, apart from myself and P.C. Dagless, look like death warmed up.'

'So do most of the people we've seen,' said Jo.

'I reckon there must be a virus or something going round,' Tyler added.

'Probably bloody flu,' Mason said, scornfully. He considered the missing persons report again. 'What makes this Anderson so important anyway?'

'He works for Vanderburg Chemicals,' Jo said. She paused. 'Or *worked*. He was a research scientist. He wanted to speak to me about something but he never got the chance.'

'So you two thought you'd break into his house and see if you could find him?' Mason said, sarcastically.

'Goddamit, we had no choice,' Jo snapped.

'Perhaps he's gone on holiday,' Mason insisted.

Tyler shook his head.

'No,' he said, emphatically.

The sergeant offered them some tea and they sat in the entry-way and drank it, waiting for Peck to radio in.

'When he gets inside he'll find the suitcases,' Jo said to Tyler. 'They'll know we're telling the truth then.'

There was a hiss of static from the microphone on

111

the desk close to Mason. He picked it up and flicked the transmitter switch. Tyler and Jo got up and crossed to the partition in an effort to hear the conversation.

'Tango One come in,' said Mason.

More static.

'Peck, for Christ's sake come in you idiot.'

'Sorry, sarge, I was having trouble with the handset.' The constable's voice sounded tinny.

'Have you checked the house out?' Mason asked.

'I didn't have to.'

'Why not?'

'Anderson's here.'

'What?' snapped Tyler.

Mason waved a hand for him to be quiet.

'You're sure it's him. Geoffrey Anderson. You have got the right address haven't you?'

'Sarge, it's him, I'm telling you. He said he was leaving for a few weeks' holiday. I saw his cases in the hall.'

Mason exhaled through clenched teeth, his eyes fixed on Jo and Tyler.

'OK, Peck, come back to the station. Over and out.' He flicked off the set.

Mason held up the missing persons report and very carefully tore it up.

'Next time, Vic, get your facts right before you come bothering me. Now clear out before I charge you both with breaking and entering.'

The two men glared at each other for long moments, then Tyler spun round and, followed by Jo, left.

As they clambered into the landrover Tyler banged the steering wheel angrily.

'What the bloody hell is going on?' he snarled.

'Vic, it couldn't have been Anderson,' Jo insisted.

'Well, as far as the police are concerned, it *was* and the case is closed.' He started the engine and turned the vehicle around, heading in the direction of his farm.

'I'm not letting it drop, Vic.'

'We were taken for mugs,' he snapped. 'Someone fooled both of us.'

They drove the rest of the way in silence.

Carlo Fanducci stood in the doorway and watched the Panda pull away. He couldn't resist a smile. Jesus, what a dumb bastard that cop had been. He hadn't even asked him for any I.D. A real lame fuck. Fanducci had said he was Geoffrey Anderson and the cop had believed him, even fallen for the line he'd shot him about going away for a few weeks. Dumb motherfucker. The ex-Mafia man chuckled to himself and closed the door.

He wondered if he'd get any more trouble from the two bastards he'd seen in the house last night.

If they wanted trouble, fine.

As he moved, the .357 Magnum felt heavy in its shoulder holster.

Twenty-two

The cow walked by slowly, followed by its calf. The larger of the two animals paused momentarily and looked at the two onlookers, then it found some grass and began eating. All over the field animals were doing likewise. In some places, the young were almost as big as the parents. It was difficult to distinguish them.

'See what I mean,' said Tyler, indicating one of the over-developed calves. 'Twice as big as they should be for their age.'

Jo nodded.

'But you said it wasn't just the cows.'

'It isn't,' said Tyler, heading back across the yard towards a barn. Jo followed him, trying to avoid the mud patches, muttering to herself when her heels sank into the sticky ooze. Tyler looked down at her feet and grinned.

'Not the most practical footwear for a farm,' he japed.

The American was about to say something when her left shoe was actually pulled off by the clinging mud. She hopped about on one leg, hurriedly tugged the shoe free and slipped it back on.

The farmer led her into a barn which contained a number of pigs. In small pens were about two dozen sows, most with litters. The noise in the building was almost deafening. Jo looked into the first pen and saw three large weaners feeding from their mother's teats. She shuddered involuntarily, remembering what had happened at the livestock market. In the next pen were more piglets, only here some of them were normal size. One lay motionless in the straw whilst another, larger one, sniffed at it.

'Some are affected, some are normal,' said Tyler, wearily.

'I don't know what to make of it.'

He turned and headed for the exit but Jo lingered for a moment, her attention caught by the small pig before her. It was still lying in the straw but whether or not it was dead she didn't know. Its larger companion continued to nuzzle against it until finally it gripped one of the creatures floppy ears in its mouth and tore it away.

Jo winced.

'Oh God,' she murmured, then she found the breath to call Tyler. He scuttled back to the pen and glanced in at the tableau before him. The larger piglet had taken another chunk out of the dead one and was chewing

114

hungrily. The smell of blood had created squeals of excitement amongst the remainder of the litter and, in seconds, they were crowding around the body of the dead weaner. Tyler reached for a nearby broom and, stepping over the rail, drove the litter away. He picked up the dead pig by one of its hind legs and lifted it out of the pen. The others returned to the sow as if nothing had happened.

Jo had turned pale and she headed for the door ahead of Tyler who carried the torn carcass of the dead weaner with him. He tossed it onto the ground outside and sighed.

'Are you OK?' he asked the journalist.

She nodded.

'When is this going to stop?' she wanted to know.

'I wish I knew.'

There was a large compost heap nearby, the stench even more unbearable due to the fact that the sun had been baking it for the past few weeks. Tyler tossed the weaner onto it and pitched a few forkfuls of the muck over the carcass. Beside the heap Jo noticed some large bags, like the bags supermarkets sold potatoes in. They were of a strong plastic, silver in colour and she could also see some red letters on them. The American squatted down and pulled one of the bags free.

'What was in here, Vic?' she asked.

'A new multi-purpose feed,' he told her.

They looked at one another as Jo uncovered the label:

VANDERBURG CHEMICALS.

The same thought struck them simultaneously.

'Then it is something to do with the feed,' she said. 'I mean, what's been happening to the animals? The accelerated growth, them turning crazy?'

Tyler nodded.

'I'm pretty sure none of this started happening until the Vanderburg feed was introduced to the stock. Hawley said that other farmers around here have been

115

having the same sort of problems as I have.' He scratched his chin thoughtfully.

'Christ,' he muttered. 'Stuart Nichols was using it, so was old Ben Thurston. They *did* both mention peculiarities in their stock.'

'Increased growth,' Jo added. 'I heard one of them say that when I was in the bar before the livestock market.'

'Still-born litters and Ben said his lambs were as big as dogs. It has to be the feed.'

'Maybe Anderson ties in to this somehow,' she said. Tyler frowned.

'Come on, Jo, you're obsessed with this bloody bloke. How could he have anything to do with what's been happening at the farms in Wakely?'

'Look, Anderson worked for Vanderburg Chemicals. These sacks belong to Vanderburg Chemicals. The feed they produce has caused abnormalities in livestock. There . . .'

He cut her short.

'We won't know that for *sure*, not until Dan Hawley completes the autopsies.'

'Goddamit, Vic, there has to be a link,' she shouted at him. She threw the bag down angrily.

'You want there to be a link,' he countered. 'Anderson probably doesn't even know anything about this multi-purpose feed, let alone its effects.'

'He was a research scientist for Christ's sake, he was one of the guys working on the project.'

'Where's your proof?'

She was silent for a moment. Her breath was coming in short gasps, her eyes aglow with anger.

'Let's see what Hawley says first,' Tyler said. 'But I think you're wrong about the link between Anderson and what's going on here.'

'Maybe you're right,' she conceded. 'Maybe I am

116

paranoid about Anderson but it's one hell of a coincidence.'

Tyler nodded. They stood for a moment longer, then he walked back to the house with her. He asked if she wanted a coffee. She said yes.

'I'll make you a cup when I've tried to reach my two farmhands.' He crossed to the phone.

'I can do it. Just tell me where everything is,' said Jo.

'In the kitchen, you can't miss it, it's still out from breakfast time.'

She wandered through into the kitchen. Tyler picked up the phone and dialled Harrison's number.

No answer.

He let it ring half a dozen times.

Still there was nothing.

Tyler put the phone down. If Harrison was that ill, then surely his wife would have called in for him. Unless she too was sick. But too sick to reach the telephone? He tried Jenkins's number. The result was the same. No answer.

He replaced the receiver and wandered into the kitchen where he found Jo standing over two steaming mugs of coffee. She handed one to him.

'No luck?' she asked.

He shook his head.

'Maybe they've got that virus,' she offered.

Tyler smiled thinly.

'Now you *are* clutching at straws. You'll be telling me next that Anderson's mixed up with that as well.'

Jo smiled wryly.

'I don't discount the possibility.'

'Don't journalists ever stop speculating?'

'No.'

They carried their coffee into the sitting room and Tyler seated himself on the sofa. Jo sat next to him, lighting up a cigarette. She looked around the room, taking in every detail.

'It's a nice house,' she said. 'Not what you'd expect a farmhouse to look like.'

'You mean where are the horse brasses and carved wood furniture?'

She chuckled.

'A bit of a cliché that,' he said, smiling. 'Farmers are businessmen these days. We're more concerned with stock figures and V.A.T. than we are with weaving our own sweaters and making oak tables.'

'I *never* had you figured as a cliché, Vic,' she told him. She noticed two photos on the mantelpiece over the fire.

'Your parents?' she asked, motioning towards them.

'Yes.'

Jo got to her feet and crossed to the fireplace, looking at the photograph of the man and then at Tyler.

'There's a resemblance.'

'Same face, same temperament my mother used to say.'

'Don't you ever get lonely out here by yourself?' she asked, returning to the seat beside him.

'No. I could ask you the same question, you're thousands of miles away from home. Don't you ever miss it?'

'I don't miss New York. Though maybe one day I'll go back, just to see if things have changed.'

She looked down into her coffee as if trying to discover her next few words there.

'Who am I kidding?' she confessed. 'I wouldn't dare go back.'

'You mean because of the Mafia?'

She nodded.

'They're like the goddam Mounties, they always get their man.'

Vic squeezed her hand and she turned to look at him. As on the previous night, Tyler sensed that curious duality within her. The raw, smouldering sexuality

118

mingling with the softness. It was a combination which aroused him deeply and he found himself gazing deep into those jade eyes. He leant forward and kissed her softly on the lips. Jo touched his stubbled cheek with one long nail, listening to it rasp across the bristles. Then she pulled him closer, her mouth eager to find his, her tongue probing deeply.

Tyler slid his right hand up her back until he felt her soft lustrous hair. Without breaking the kiss, Jo moved closer to him, her hands sliding inside his shirt to explore his muscular chest. He felt her long nails rake his flesh and the sensation sent waves of pleasure through him.

He slipped his free hand up her T-shirt, his eager fingers brushing her left nipple. It stiffened to a hard bud and he transferred his attention to the other one. Jo let out a low gasp of pleasure and lay back, allowing the farmer to reach her more easily. She pulled the T-shirt over her head and dropped it behind her, treating Tyler to the sight of her firm breasts. He bent forward and kissed each nipple in turn, drawing it between his teeth, leaving a trail of saliva as he licked his way down to her navel.

She loosened the button of her jeans, closing her eyes as he eased her zip down. She lifted her bottom so he could pull the denim free. He removed her jeans and panties in one movement. He nuzzled the area between her legs, his hands parting her thighs a little more. He kissed her mound, allowing his tongue to snake lower until he was flicking her clitoris.

Jo arched her back, pushing her pelvis hard against his questing, darting tongue, wanting him to push it into that most sensitive area. Her entire body felt as if it was on fire and, as he probed her moist cleft, she jerked spasmodically beneath the attentions of his tongue.

She opened her eyes and looked at him as he knelt

before her, freeing his own bulging erection. Jo reached for it eagerly, moving her hand gently up and down the shaft until Tyler himself began to shudder.

He entered her with ease, both of them gasping at the sensation and he began to move rhythmically inside her. Jo raised her hips to meet each of his thrusts, her hands resting on his buttocks as she drew him in deeper.

Tyler bent his head and lapped at her swollen nipples and he felt her body begin to tense.

She murmured something in his ear, her hair brushing against his shoulder as she leant forward. She licked some perspiration from his face, gritting her teeth as she felt the first sensations of impending orgasm. Tyler quickened his pace and, seconds later, Jo was moaning loudly, raking his back with her nails as the fury of her climax racked her body. Tyler tensed and, a moment later, he too joined her in ecstasy and she writhed with renewed pleasure as she felt his hot seed spurting into her.

For long moments they lay breathless, Jo running her fingers through his hair. Her body seemed to be glowing and both of them were covered by a thin film of perspiration. He withdrew gently from her, allowing his eyes to trace a pattern once more over her shapely body. Jo lay back, naked, on the sofa, her eyes closed.

Tyler ran his hand up her leg, pausing just short of her slippery cleft.

'It's more comfortable upstairs,' he said.

They both laughed.

Twenty-three

Wakely's only General Practitioner's surgery was crowded as usual. The waiting-room, which seated twenty people, was full and there were even patients standing in the corridors waiting their turn. A chorus of coughs and mutterings drifted from the room, mingling with the strident ringing of the phones on the front desk. One harrassed receptionist tried to deal with patients wanting appointments and manage those who already had them.

In a room to the right sat half-a-dozen more people, some clutching green cards, others pink ones. The pink cards signified blood tests and nurse Jan Williams peered through her appointment book to see how many more she had to do before she finished at one o'clock. She had a splitting headache, not helped by the glaring fluorescent lights above. As she swabbed the arm of a patient and steadied the syringe over the bulging vein, she blinked hard. The needle seemed to swim into separate images for a second before clarifying.

She'd had the headache for the past two days but the tablets which usually relieved it had not worked this time. She'd thought about phoning in to say she was going to have a day off but had decided against it. Besides, if she was at home she would only sit around feeling sorry for herself and the kids would drive her potty. They always did during the school holidays. They got so bored and ended up fighting. Jan had two children, both boys, both ten years old, identical twins in fact. They were the image of their father. Joe Williams had been made redundant two months ago from his job in Arkham and now spent his days sitting around the house worrying where the rent was going to come from. Jan didn't fancy a day at home in *that* atmosphere.

The patient got up and left and Jan transferred the

blood to a phial, placing it alongside the other eight which she had already collected that morning. As she gazed at the crimson liquid she felt her stomach churning and, for a moment, she thought she was going to be sick. She bowed her head and massaged her temples, a little disturbed to find flakes of skin coming away beneath her finger tips. Her hands and arms looked milk white and, when she caught sight of her face in an upturned kidney bowl, she thought she was looking at a skull. The distorted vision leered back at her, eyes sunken, the orbs bulging from the sockets. The blood vessels seemed swollen in places as if threatening to burst but the whites were sepia coloured.

Jan Williams closed her eyes, hoping that the pain in her head would go, but it showed no signs of abating.

She called her next patient.

A urine test this time. She gave the man a small bottle and directed him towards the lavatory, reminding him that the sample must be 'mid-stream'. He looked vague and she started to explain but then he smiled as if something had clicked and he marched off to the toilet.

Jan consulted her book once more, readying a fresh syringe as she saw that she had yet another blood test to do. She ushered the woman behind the curtain and sat her down, fastening the velcro pad around her bicep. Jan blinked hard under the light and stuck the needle in.

It missed the vein and the woman yelped in pain and surprise.

The nurse apologized and tried again. This time the needle punctured the pulsing vein. She let the tourniquet go and drew the required amount of blood. As before, she deposited it in a tube and reached for the seal but, as she held the bottle in her hand, she began to salivate wildly until streamers of sputum dribbled from her mouth. The pain in her head seemed to grow in intensity until it felt as if her eyes were going to burst from her skull.

The woman who had just had her blood taken sat mesmerized, watching the nurse who had clamped her hand around the bottle and was squeezing. With her free hand she reached for two more of the phials, crushing the glass inside her fist.

There was a loud crack as it broke.

Blood cascaded from her hands, pieces of glass falling also, other shards slicing open Jan's palms. She opened her hands to see that the glass had lacerated her hands badly. Broken pieces of crystal protruded from the torn flesh as thick crimson liquid pumped out.

Jan raised both hands to her mouth and lapped at the swiftly flowing blood.

The woman in the chair fainted.

The man returned from the lavatory, apologising for only having half filled the bottle but, when he saw what the nurse was doing, his bladder seemed to find hidden reserves and a dark stain appeared at the front of his trousers.

Jan Williams sank to her knees amidst the blood and glass, both hands held up, the crimson liquid running down her arms to stain her white overall. Ignoring the pieces of glass which cut her tongue, she sucked and licked frenziedly at the life fluid.

When a doctor tore back the curtain and looked down at her she merely turned and smiled, her teeth and lips dripping red, her hands in bloody tatters.

Her wild laughter began to fill the room.

Twenty-four

Dan Hawley wiped some perspiration from his forehead with the back of his hand and steadied the scalpel above the calf. The animal was lying spread-eagled on one of the dissection tables, the vet's trolley full of implements beside it. He cut carefully into it, just above the anus and opened the alimentary canal. A vile-smelling dark fluid spilled from the rent and, even though he was wearing a mask, Hawley winced slightly. He cut a piece of the slippery internal tube and placed it carefully on a microscope slide, then he turned his attention to the calf s stomach.

The accumulation of gas had caused it to swell up so that when the vet cut into it, it deflated rapidly. Bile spurted onto his gloved hand. He sliced off a section of the stomach wall and placed that on a slide too.

He coughed and supported himself against the work bench for a moment, wincing beneath the powerful overhead lights which blazed like minute suns. Then he pressed his eye to the microscope, slid the specimen beneath the powerful lens and peered at it. He adjusted the focus until things swam into crystal clarity, carefully scrutinizing what he saw before him.

Hawley exhaled deeply and reached for the second slide.

What he saw was the same.

Ordinarily, bacteria will survive in a dead body for anything up to three days before dying. The microscopic organisms which he saw before him had come from an animal that had been dead for two days and yet they were still moving amongst the other debris. But what surprised Hawley was the fact that they were multiplying.

Instead of dying, the bacteria were increasing.

He stepped back from the microscope and crossed to

a small incubator nearby. From it he took a third slide, one which held a section of the piglet's brain which Tyler had brought in the day before.

Hawley looked once more at the third slide.

The bacteria had begun to form spores.

He swallowed hard, his mouth feeling as if it were full of chalk. His tongue seemed swollen, his lips dry. He crossed to the sink and filled a plastic cup with water but, instead of slaking his thirst, it made him feel sick. The vet held his stomach for a moment, then returned to the spread-eagled calf. He took a saw from his trolley and set to work opening the skull. The tumescent growth on the side of the head had begun to shrivel like an old grape but, Hawley noticed, the eye which was attached to it still gazed glassily at him.

He prized away the portion of skull he'd cut, exposing the brain, then he retrieved his scalpel and carefully cut a sliver of the grey-red matter, dropping it onto a slide as he had done the other specimens.

There were spores in there too.

Whatever kind of bacteria it was, Hawley had never seen its like before. It was multiplying at a greatly accelerated speed, forming spores in order to hibernate. But why? He coughed again and pulled off his rubber gloves, then he walked across to a small bookshelf on the far wall. From it he took down a heavy tome and flicked agitatedly through it. There were diagrams of every known bacteria but nothing remotely like what he'd seen on his slides. He slammed the book shut and stood there for what seemed like an eternity then, pulling the gloves back on, he returned to the calf.

He'd already examined the cow which had given birth to it and found traces of exactly the same bacteria in both her bloodstream and placenta. It had also been present in the remains of the stomach.

The cow, the calf and the weaner. All three had

become breeding grounds for the new strain of bacteria, their carcasses infested with the microscopic life form.

Hawley took one last look at the writhing shapes on the slide, then he hurried to the phone and dialled Tyler's number.

Mandy Potter opened the door when Tyler and Jo arrived. She ushered them through into the surgery, then disappeared.

The hands of the wall clock had just crawled past noon.

As the farmer and the journalist entered the surgery they were immediately struck by the foul smell. The body of the calf had been covered by a rubber sheet but, nevertheless, the strong odour hung heavily in the air making Jo cough.

Hawley was sitting on a stool beside the microscope. The room was stuffy, the blinds down, the overhead lights having been turned off.

The vet looked up wearily as his two visitors entered.

'What have you found, Dan?' asked Tyler.

Hawley exhaled deeply.

'I wish I could tell you,' said the vet, enigmatically. He motioned for the farmer to look into the microscope which he did, squinting down the eye piece. He saw the bacteria moving rapidly amongst the tissue, then he stepped back to let Jo have a look.

'It's bacteria,' said Hawley, answering an unasked question. 'There are four separate specimens taken from the weaner, the calf's brain and stomach and from the cow. They're all identical.'

'What does that mean?' asked Jo.

'A virus?' asked Tyler.

'I don't think so,' the vet told him. 'The bacteria which cause viral infections in livestock aren't as. . . .' He struggled to find the word. 'They're not as powerful.

This bacteria is not only multiplying, it's creating spores.'

'Meaning what?' said Tyler.

'Meaning that it intends or intended to go into a period of dormancy, of hibernation. Now, very few bacteria are able to do that and those that do are normally confined to plants. This is a completely new strain. Not different. New. *I've* never seen anything like it before.'

'How does that explain what's been happening to the animals lately?' the farmer enquired. 'The cannibalism, the still-born litters, the increased growth?'

Hawley exhaled deeply.

'As I said, I took samples from the stomachs of all three animals. There was a greater abundance of the bacteria in the stomach of the cow. She ate something which induced the growth of this bacteria. It was passed on through her bloodstream to the calf. That was what happened with the sow and her piglets. That's what's been happening with *all* the livestock around here. The parent animal has been passing on the bacteria through the bloodstream to the unborn young which have been developing more rapidly. The bacteria have, somehow, caused a change in the DNA of the young animals.'

'What could they have eaten that would do this?' asked Jo.

'It's a toxic agent of some kind. It's impossible to say without a sample of it,' Hawley told her. 'All I do know is, whatever it is, it's inorganic.'

'You mean it's man-made?' said Tyler.

Hawley nodded.

'The feed,' said the farmer, wearily. 'The Vanderburg feed. It's the only inorganic compound that any of my animals have had lately.'

'What about the other farmers?' asked Jo.

'We'll have to find out.'

'I need to run some tests on this feed,' said Hawley. 'Break it down, find out what exactly it's comprised of.'

Tyler nodded.

'And then what?' Jo asked.

'I'm going to see how long the bacteria survive for,' Hawley told her. 'I need to know as much as possible about it if I'm going to help. Get me a sample of it.'

Tyler turned and headed for the door. Jo followed.

'I'll be in touch, Dan,' he said.

'Where are we going now?' she asked.

'Visiting,' Tyler said, enigmatically.

They sprinted across to the waiting landrover and climbed in and, in seconds, were heading out towards Stuart Nichols's farm.

Hawley stood before the bathroom mirror, reluctant to turn on the light above it. As if the sight of his own face were too abhorrent to him. But finally he did so, wincing painfully as the fluorescent sputtered into life. The vet inspected his skin, both surprised and anxious by its pale, dry appearance. He put a tentative finger to his cheek and rubbed, watching as a thin coil of skin came away. It left a red patch beneath and Hawley swallowed hard.

Perhaps Tyler was right. Perhaps there *was* some kind of virus going around.

The vet moaned and pressed both hands to his temples. The light seemed to sear his eyeballs until he could stand it no longer. He shot out a hand and switched if off.

In the silence of the bathroom he listened to his own low, guttural breathing. His body felt tight, his skin itched. With clumsy fingers he began unfastening his shirt finally pulling it free to expose the wasted flesh beneath.

Skin was coming off in great long tendrils, hanging from him like leprous rolls.

Hawley sucked in a frightened breath. He pulled at one of the coils and it came free, much like sunburnt flesh, but it felt moist. He dropped it into the sink and tried to wash it away. His throat was dry and sore and he scooped a handful of water from the swiftly flowing tap. It made him feel sick and he steadied himself against the basin, gazing through bloodshot eyes at his own ghastly visage.

He pulled another of the flesh coils from his chest, held it in his hand for a second, then pushed it into his mouth and chewed hungrily.

Twenty-five

The windows of the landrover were open but the slight breeze which they allowed in offered no respite from the scorching heat. Tyler wiped a hand across his forehead and brushed away the film of perspiration. Above them, the sun blazed with unrelenting fury.

Jo tossed the butt of her cigarette out of the window and gazed at the surrounding countryside. The road which led out of Wakely towards Stuart Nichols's farm was flanked on both sides by thick forest and gently sloping hills but, as they left the town further behind, the land flattened into rolling fields.

Ahead of them on the right, Jo spotted something.

'What's that?' she asked, pointing.

Tyler smiled and slowed down as they reached it.

'It's Wakely football club,' he told her.

'It used to be one of the best equipped non-League

clubs in the country. The old chairman was a builder. Now he's dead the whole place has gone to ruin.'

The ground was compact, surrounded on all sides by a high wooden fence which was now broken in many places. The six floodlight staunchions still rose into the air although somewhat less majestically than in the past. The steel girders were rusted, weeds and overgrown grass lapping at their bases like some kind of floral sea. The smaller stands were roofed with corrugated iron looking more like enlarged sheds and they too carried a patina of rust, so bad in some places that there were holes in them. The pitch was like a jungle, infested with weeds. Grass grew wildly in places but, in others, it had been trampled flat. The kids from the town cycled out to the old stadium in the summer and played in the disused goals but there were none to be seen on this particular day. Wakely Town F.C. had gone broke in the end after many years of struggling with low attendances – the same fate which was befalling many other league and non-league clubs. However, Tyler could still remember the days when people had come from all around to watch, filling the ground to capacity.

'I used to go there with my father when I was a kid,' said the farmer as they left the place behind. Soon, it was nothing more than a vague outline in the rear view mirror.

'How far to the farm?' asked Jo.

'It's just up ahead,' Tyler told her, pointing through some trees.

He swung the landrover off the main road onto a sun-baked track. The vehicle bounced over the hardened ruts and Jo gripped the door handle to prevent herself being shaken too badly. There was a clatter in the back as the farmer's shotgun fell from its hooks and skittered across the rear of the landrover. Tyler stuck it into a low gear and slowed down, lessening the effect

130

of the bumps. As he drove, he scanned the fields around them. His forehead puckered into a frown.

Jo glanced to one side and caught his worried expression.

'Something wrong?' she asked.

'I don't know yet,' he murmured.

The gate which led into the farm yard itself was open. Tyler swung the landrover around and brought it to a halt beside a large shed which he knew Nichols used for milking. They both got out.

Immediately, the silence seemed to wrap itself around them like a glove.

Tyler looked around and exhaled deeply.

'Where the hell are all the animals?' he mused.

There was a sty to the left but it was empty, the gate open. Even in the fields there was nothing to be seen and yet Nichols owned a herd of over 200 cattle. Tyler wandered into the milking shed, alert for any sign or sound of movement. Jo followed him, wrinkling her nose at the cloying stench inside the shed. It seemed even hotter inside the metal construction, like walking into an oven.

Tyler was the first one to spot the dead cow.

It was lying near the far exit of the shed and he walked cautiously across to it. The buzzing of flies could clearly be heard and there were dozens of the things crawling on the carcass. Tyler got as close as he needed to and peered at the cow. Its eyes were open, its tongue lolling from one side of its open mouth. Flies crawled eagerly over the glassy orbs. There were no external signs of damage to the animal. No wounds. No blood. He and Jo stood there for long moments gazing down at the body, then they turned and headed outside once more.

The yard was rectangular, sheds and barns forming the enclosure which led up to the farm house itself.

131

Lying in the open doorway of another barn were two dead pigs – big boars, saddlebacks by the look of them.

Tyler held up a hand for Jo to stay back, then he crossed to the door of the barn and looked in, careful to avoid the carcasses. The stench from them was appalling, exposed, as they were, to the sun. And, this time, as well as flies, the carcasses had drawn the attention of some ants. The insects crawled frenziedly over the bodies, some of the flies feasting on a gaping sore near one boar's ear.

Inside the barn were a number of pens, designed to hold pigs, very similar to the ones Tyler had on his own farm.

The gates to every single one were open, the animals gone.

'What is it?' asked Jo, appearing at his shoulder.

'See for yourself,' he said.

She peered into the barn, then stepped outside again, almost tripping over one of the dead boars. She looked down and noted with disgust that a large blow-fly was just disappearing into the animal's nostril.

'What could have killed them, Vic?' she asked.

'There's no sign of injury on any of them,' said the farmer. He shrugged helplessly.

'A disease?' she said, cryptically.

'Could be. But where the bloody hell are the rest of the stock?'

He turned and headed towards the farm house itself. It was a two-storey, pebble-dashed building with a grey slate roof and a genuine nineteenth-century chimney stack. In fact, the whole building looked somewhat anachronistic amongst the modern machinery which lay around in the yard.

As they approached the house, Jo noticed that the curtains, both upstairs and down, were drawn.

Tyler reached the front door and knocked hard.

It swung open.

132

'Stuart. Bet,' he called. 'It's Vic Tyler.'

Silence.

'We'd better take a look inside,' said Jo.

They walked into the hall, squinting in the gloom.

'Stuart,' Tyler shouted once more, passing into the sitting room. He bumped his leg on a table and cursed. It was so dark in the room. The place smelt fusty, the humidity wrapping itself around them like a sweaty glove. Jo felt her T-shirt sticking to her back and she ran both hands through her thick hair.

Tyler pushed open the door to the kitchen.

There was some food on the table. A piece of cheese and a couple of slices of bread, the edges curled up. The silence in the room was broken, yet again, by the loud buzzing of flies.

'Let's try upstairs,' said Tyler, leading the way.

As he opened the door from the hallway to the staircase he had to stop for a moment. The steps were immersed in a blackness so total it was virtually impossible to see a hand in front of him. He moved cautiously, slipping on a step half way up.

'Shit,' he grunted and continued his ascent, finally reaching the landing. There, he was grateful to find that the powerful rays of the sun had managed to find a chink in the curtains and a single powerful ray of light lit up the area. Jo joined him and they approached the first of three doors which confronted them. Tyler knocked loudly on the closest before turning the handle.

'Stuart,' he shouted.

They walked into the room.

It was empty. The bed was unmade, the sheets rumpled, one pillow lying on the floor close by. The room smelt of copper, a strange metallic smell which reminded the farmer of rotting meat.

'Let's try the next one,' he said.

133

He repeated the same procedure, banging loudly on the door, calling Nichols' name and then entering.

It seemed darker in the second room, a blanket having been pinned across the window as well as the drawn curtains.

Lying prone on the bed, arms by his sides, was Stuart Nichols.

Tyler and Jo moved quietly into the room, the only sound being the low, guttural breathing of the other man. His chest rose and fell almost imperceptibly, his mouth open to reveal protruding teeth. Even in the gloom, Tyler could see how pale Nichols's skin was. His hands, palms turned upward, bore the long hooked nails which both Jo and Tyler had come to recognise by now.

Tyler took a step closer, recoiling slightly from the stench which seemed to be emanating from Nichols's body. A combination of rancid sweat and an overpoweringly fetid odour which made the farmer cough.

'Stuart,' he said, reaching out a hand but not touching the motionless form of his friend.

Nichols didn't stir.

The pillow beneath his head was dirty and, as Tyler looked more closely, he saw that there were several sizeable growths of hair lying there. Not mere strands of it but thick hanks. Nichols's scalp was bared in places where the hair had come out, raw and angry as if it had been torn away.

'He looks as if he's in a coma,' said Jo. 'Maybe we ought to ring a doctor.'

There was a low rasping sound from nearby and both of them spun round, their eyes searching the gloom.

It came from behind them, from the other bed in the room.

So mesmerized had they been by the sight of Nichols, neither had noticed the hunched form of his wife lying on the other bed.

Bet Nichols was, Tyler remembered, a large woman but now, she looked as though she was suffering from anorexia. Her body, covered only by a thin nightdress, was emaciated, as if she hadn't eaten for days. For weeks. The pallor of her skin was even more alarming than that of her husband and her hair, usually done up in a bun, was hanging loose.

Tyler reached forward and shook Nichols, trying to rouse him from his deathly slumber.

'There's a phone downstairs,' said Jo, 'maybe we ought to ring a doctor.'

Tyler didn't speak, he was still gazing down at his friend. He touched Nichols's cheek, withdrawing his hand quickly as he felt how clammy the skin was but, after a moment's hesitation, he cautiously opened the other man's crusted eyelids. His eyes were dark ringed, the whites flecked with yellow, the normally steely eyes now dull and lifeless. Tyler shuddered. It was like looking at a corpse.

'Stuart,' Tyler called, shaking Nichols hard until he saw his eyelids flicker open.

He turned his head to look at Tyler, his cracked lips sliding back in a bestial sneer.

Tyler took a step backwards.

'What do you want?' Nichols croaked, trying to swing himself upright. He finally managed it and sat on the edge of the bed, head bowed.

'How long have you been like this?' Tyler asked him.

'I don't remember,' said the other farmer, sounding as if he had gravel in his throat. He put both hands to his temples and winced. Tyler crossed to the window and pulled down the blanket, then he dragged the curtains open, flooding the room with sunlight.

Nichols let out a howl. A deafening shriek torn raw from his throat, from the depths of his soul. A sound which was a mixture of rage and pain. He staggered to his feet, shielding his face from the powerful rays of the sun and Tyler looked on in horror as the flesh on his friend's arms rose swiftly into half a dozen reddening welts. The flesh was actually blistering as surely as if a red hot iron had been pressed to it.

'Shut them,' screamed Nichols.

He crashed into the bed and overbalanced, trying to slide down beside it to hide from the sunlight. He had one hand across his face, the other outstretched before him. Jo, too, saw the skin rise into a series of liquescent blisters which, all at once, burst. They left dark crimson gouges in the flesh and Nichols's fingers curled round, his nails tearing the palm of his hand.

'Shut the fucking curtains, for God's sake shut the fucking curtains,' he roared, dragging himself to his feet.

Tyler was in the process of doing what Nichols wanted when he heard the click of a shotgun hammer. The other farmer, his face now a malevolent mask of pain and anger, had snatched a twelve bore from beneath his bed and was aiming the barrels at Tyler.

'Shut them,' he bellowed once again.

Tyler complied hurriedly.

'Now get out of here,' snarled Nichols. 'Leave us. One side of his face looked as if someone had thrust a blow torch at it. Huge suppurating sores dribbled their sticky contents down his torn cheek, one of them having formed over his left eye, nearly closing it.

Bet Nichols writhed silently on her own bed, her flesh similarly scorched. But Nichols had taken the full brunt of the intruding sunlight and he swayed uncertainly, the shotgun levelled at Tyler's stomach. He edged cautiously towards the door, ushering Jo before him.

'Get out now,' rasped Nichols, licking his swollen lips. He raised the shotgun and, for one interminable second, Tyler thought he was going to fire but, as the farmer and the American stepped out of the room, he lowered it once again.

Tyler closed the door behind him.

There were sounds of movement from inside and, a second later, Nichols burst out of the room, staggering drunkenly.

'Don't come back here,' he said. 'If you do I'll kill you.'

'Stuart, you need help,' Tyler said, his eyes never leaving the gaping mouths of the twin barrels.

'I told you, just get away from me,' Nichols growled and he stood sentinel at the top of the darkened stairs as Jo and Tyler retreated. 'And don't try sending anyone else or I'll kill them too.'

Jo was the first to reach the hallway and she pulled open the door, hurrying out into the blazing sunlight. Tyler followed a second later.

'My God,' muttered Jo. 'What the hell happened to him?'

Tyler could only shake his head vacantly.

'It must be a disease of some sort,' he said, almost incredulously.

'Rabies?'

'No. He isn't exhibiting the symptoms.'

'Hawley said that the bacteria was a new strain. Maybe he's got a new kind of rabies.'

Tyler was unconvinced.

'Did you see what the sunlight did to his skin?' said Jo. 'I mean, it burned him for Christ's sake.' There was a note of desperation in her voice. 'Vic, what are we going to do?'

'Calling the police won't help, especially after that fiasco about Anderson. They'll probably lock us both up.'

'We should get a doctor out here,' she insisted.

'You heard what he said and I believed him. If anyone sticks their head around that door he'll kill them.' They stood facing one another for a moment, then Tyler

137

turned and headed back towards the landrover. 'Come on,' he said.

Jo hesitated, her eye caught by something close by, something which she hadn't noticed when they'd first approached the house.

To the right of the building was a small wooden shed, its door open. The sunlight was glinting on something silvery.

'Vic, come here,' she called and the farmer spun round.

Jo was standing in the doorway of the shed.

'Look at that,' she said.

Inside the shed, piled three or four high in places, were sacks of the Vanderburg multi-purpose feed.

Without a moment's hesitation, Tyler lifted one of the heavy sacks onto his shoulder and, together, they headed back to the landrover. He opened the rear door and threw the sack in alongside his own shotgun then he clambered into the driver's seat, waited until Jo was settled beside him, then turned on the engine. Tyler swung the vehicle around and floored the accelerator. The quicker they left this place the happier he'd be.

They were back in Wakely in less then ten minutes and only when they were safely back in the confines of the town did Tyler ease the pressure on his accelerator. The needle on the speedometer bounced from sixty to thirty and hovered there.

He drove slowly through the tree-lined streets, both he and Jo noticing how quiet things were. There weren't above six people moving about in the blossom-shrouded streets. Garden tools and toys lay discarded in some places, most houses had their curtains drawn and the few people who *were* moving around looked pale and lethargic.

And there was something else, something which

Tyler found even more disturbing than the absence of people, because it was even more inexplicable.

There were no dogs or cats to be seen.

Wakely was becoming a ghost town.

Carlo Fanducci lit up another cigarette, coughing as the acrid fumes burnt his chest, searing his lungs. He spat out of his open window, noticing that the sputum was flecked with blood. What the hell? It was nothing new.

Parked across the road from Dan Hawley's surgery, he had a clear view when Tyler pulled up.

The Italian watched as first the farmer then Jo clambered out, Tyler retrieving the sack of Vanderburg feed from the rear of the vehicle.

Fanducci ran an appreciative eye over Jo and sucked hard on his cigarette. The red T-shirt clung tightly to her body, highlighting the smooth swell of her breasts. Great tits, thought the Italian. He wondered what she was like in bed. A regular little ball-breaker no doubt about it.

And, he was sure now, he'd seen her somewhere before.

He watched as she followed Tyler up the path to Hawley's front door, then he lit up another cigarette, using the butt of the other one to do it. This time he didn't cough.

Fanducci loosened his tie slightly and relaxed back in his seat.

In time it would come to him. Eventually he would remember exactly who that girl was. His memory was one of the things he prided himself on. Names, places, dates. All filed away, waiting to be recalled.

A thin smile spread across his face.

The reporter from the *New York Times*. He'd seen her with that scum-bag Tony Hagen a couple of times. She'd blown the whistle on old man Scalise's rackets and he'd put out a contract on her.

Well, well. What a small world it was turning out to be. Fanducci chuckled to himself and eased the .357 from its holster. He released the cylinder, spun it once, then snapped it back into position. The Italian patted the butt gently.

Twenty-six

Helen Piper sat back on her haunches, laying the trowel before her. She was perspiring despite the fact that she only wore a bikini top and a pair of cut-off denim shorts. The sun had moved full circle in the sky and now, with the advent of afternoon, its rays weren't so powerful. Helen ran a hand through her long black hair and got stiffly to her feet. She'd been out in the garden for most of the day, digging, weeding, planting. Now she decided that it was time to go inside, she was parched. Besides, she'd have to start getting something to eat for herself and the children.

Phil wouldn't be home for another few hours. He'd gone to London on business and she didn't expect him until after seven. He'd been putting in extra hours for the last six months but still Helen was not satisfied. As she passed the pram which stood beneath the porch the sight of their five-month-old daughter, Lorraine, seemed to remind Helen just how badly they needed the money now. Of course everyone had been delighted when she'd announced that she was going to have another child, but she and Phil had already been saddled with a mortgage which they could just about

140

pay and now, with the arrival of the baby, it looked as though they were going to struggle again.

He told her not to worry but she took no notice. It was in her nature. She worried about the bills, she worried about the children. She worried about World War Three. Helen looked in at Lorraine as she passed and smiled down at the sleeping baby. Then she padded inside and put the kettle on.

The house was unusually quiet considering her five-year-old son, Kevin, was upstairs. He'd been up there for hours and she'd not heard a peep out of him. There must be a reason why. Helen decided to find out what he was up to.

As she passed the mirror in the hall she patted her stomach approvingly. She'd worked hard to regain her figure after Lorraine's birth and now, at thirty, she was in as good shape as she'd ever been. Helen moved quietly up the stairs, hoping to surprise her son in the act if he was doing anything he shouldn't be. She tip-toed across the landing and opened the door with the 'Star Wars' poster on it.

The room was in semi-darkness, the curtains drawn.

'Kevin,' she called, unable to see him at first, angry that he'd shut out the light. Then, in the gloom, she saw him crouched by the bed. There were toy soldiers spread across the carpet, the boxes emptied wantonly.

'What are you doing up here?' she asked him, crossing to the window and pulling open the curtains. 'You've been stuck in your room all day. Go out and get some fresh air while I get your tea ready.'

'Oh Mum,' he muttered, his brown hair plastered to his forehead by perspiration. 'I'd rather play in here.'

'Outside, Kevin, please,' she insisted.

'No,' he snapped.

'I told you to go outside, it's not good for you being cooped up in here and with your curtains drawn too.'

'I don't want to go outside. Leave me alone.'

141

Helen slapped him across the backside.

'Don't talk to me like that, Kevin,' she said. 'Now go on.'

She ushered him out, watching as he shuffled irritably down the stairs. Helen walked into her own bedroom and peered out of the window in time to see the boy emerge in the garden below. He kicked at a stone and, hands dug in the pockets of his jeans, began wandering up and down. She pulled the window closed, leaving just enough room to let some of the late afternoon breeze in.

In the garden, Kevin Piper shielded his eyes from the glare of the sun, glancing alternately up at the window where his mother had been and then at the pram where his baby sister lay. He had a headache and his stomach felt as though he'd eaten too much but he knew that wasn't true. He hadn't been able to eat all day. He hadn't felt like it. His head hurt. He didn't like the sun. Kevin kicked a stone and it banged against the side of the pram. He looked up at the window. No sign of his mother. He picked up a stone and threw it at the pram. The impact rocked it and, from inside, Lorraine began to whimper. He smiled and picked up another stone. A larger one.

This one he hurled with all his strength.

It struck the pram near the hood and Lorraine began to cry.

The shrill sound made his head hurt more.

He threw another stone, this time lobbing it into the pram.

Lorraine screamed and began sobbing loudly.

'Shut up,' grunted Kevin. 'Shut up.'

The crying went on. Louder.

'Shut up,' he shouted, advancing towards the pram.

The window above him opened and Helen looked out. She could hear Lorraine crying, but the porch obscured her view of the pram and also of Kevin.

He gripped the pram by the handle and began to pull on it, using all his weight.

Lorraine was screaming now, her sobs punctuated with racking gasps.

'Lorraine,' Helen called. 'Kevin, what are you doing?' She left the window open and hurried out of the room.

With one final surge of strength, Kevin managed to tip the pram up. It tottered on its back wheels for a second, then pitched forward, catapulting Lorraine out onto the grass. The baby continued screaming, lying helpless on her back before Kevin who was glaring down at her.

He reached for the trowel.

Helen ran down the stairs, tripping at the bottom, nearly losing her footing. She scrambled on, tugging open doors in her haste to reach the garden.

Kevin lifted the trowel in both hands and raised it above the screaming baby.

Helen burst from the back door in time to see him bury the pointed blade in the baby's stomach.

Now it was her turn to scream.

She tried to move towards him but her legs buckled and she could only crawl. Helen saw him bring the weapon down again, this time piercing the little girl's throat. A fountain of blood erupted from the wound, most of it splattering Kevin who bent his head to the jetting flow of crimson, allowing it to flood into his mouth, swallowing hungrily.

Helen Piper passed out.

143

Twenty-seven

'The one on the right is the broken-down Vanderburg feed, the one on the left is from the bloodstream of the calf.'

Hawley stepped back from the twin microscopes and invited Tyler to look. The farmer pressed his eye to the first of the magnifying instruments and peered at the rapidly moving organisms on the slide beneath. Then he passed to the next one. He looked at Hawley but said nothing. Jo was the next to inspect the findings. It was she who broke the brooding silence.

'They're identical,' she said.

Hawley nodded.

'The same strain of bacteria is present in both the calf's blood and the Vanderburg feed.'

'So the inorganic compound which caused the trouble with the animals *is* the one in the feed? said Tyler.

Hawley nodded.

'But what it is I don't know. It's bacteria, that's true, but what I'm getting at is the fact that the compound itself is made up of proteins. From a breakdown of the Vanderburg feed the other constituents are what you'd expect to find in any animal feed. Maize, barley, wheat, that kind of thing. It's just this protein that shouldn't be there.'

Tyler exhaled deeply.

'What do you mean, it shouldn't be there?' He looked agitated.

'It's been specially introduced into the feed. Manufactured and then added. But it's a synthetic protein. It has no peptide links.'

Tyler held up a hand.

'Look, Dan, can you keep it in a language we can all under stand?' he asked.

Hawley apologized, then continued.

144

'A protein molecule is made up of hundreds of thousands of amino-acid molecules. They're joined together by peptide links. By combining with oxygen, the amino-acid forms bonds which help keep the protein molecule together. The proteins in the Vanderburg feed have not been synthesized from amino-acid. They've been created artificially. That's another reason why the bacteria are still flourishing when they should have been dead ages ago, the proteins have been created from some kind of autotrophic organism. From something inorganic.'

'Man-made, like you said before,' Jo added.

Hawley nodded.

'That's right. This bacteria is virtually indestructible.'

A heavy silence fell over the trio in the room. The vet looked at his two companions, wondering if what he had said had made any sense to them. From the worried looks on their faces he assumed that it had. Tyler peered into the microscopes once more.

'Who could create protein like this?' he asked.

'Someone with very specialized knowledge in this particular field.'

'Like a research scientist?' said Tyler, looking at Jo.

'Anderson,' she said, quietly.

The farmer nodded.

'But why should the protein be consumed by bacteria?' asked Tyler.

'Because with normal protein molecules if you immerse them in water or salt solutions they form colloids. It's like a protective mechanism. These proteins are artificial, they have no protection so, after a while, they simply become engulfed by bacteria which feed off them.'

Tyler wiped a thumb across his eyebrow and swallowed hard.

'There's something else,' said Hawley, crossing to one of the dissection tables where the body of the

145

weaner lay covered by a sheet. He pulled it back, pointing to a small patch of grey coloured skin on the animal's side. 'Spores,' he said. 'The same ones that have been showing up in the bloodstreams and stomachs of the other animals.'

'Have they moved to the outer skin?' asked Tyler.

Hawley nodded.

'On a living animal they'd be invisible.'

'My God,' said Jo. 'What does it mean?'

The vet swallowed hard.

'It means that the idea about a virus spreading through Wakely, amongst its *human* population, is more than likely right,' he announced, wearily.

'But how?' Jo wanted to know. 'You said you didn't know how it was communicated.'

'I didn't before today,' the vet told her.

'So,' demanded Tyler. 'What's the answer?'

'All animals fed on the Vanderburg multi-purpose feed are likely to be carrying this bacteria in them, some more advanced than others. The bacteria, once it has formed spores, then transfers itself to the skin of the animal, sometimes on the hide itself, sometimes in the first layer of muscle.' He paused. 'Anyone who's eaten meat is liable to be infected.'

'Oh God,' muttered Tyler.

'Beef, pork, lamb, mutton, sausages, pies. *Anything* that contains meat is more than certainly contaminated and anyone consuming that meat will be infected.'

'What about poultry and fish?' asked Tyler.

'It hasn't affected them. The feed, as far as I can gather was only designed for use on larger stock.'

'That's something at least,' said Jo.

'At Stuart Nichols's farm we found some dead animals,' Tyler told the vet. 'Could the bacteria have killed them?'

'Some bacteria, once they've finished with the host animal or plant, form spores in order to disperse. To

146

move around. Most are air carried, others water carried.'

'What are you getting at?' asked the farmer.

'We don't know what form the dispersal of these spores takes,' Hawley said. 'The spores from the dead animals you found may already be in the air.'

'Then other people could be infected with this virus?' said Jo. 'People outside Wakely?'

Hawley was silent for long moments.

'Look, at the moment, the only thing I know for sure is that it's confined to animals fed on the Vanderburg compound. They're the ones carrying and transmitting the virus.'

There was another troubled silence.

'Anyone eating meat is at risk,' Hawley reiterated.

Tyler sucked in a weary breath.

'Have you any idea what this disease or virus might be, Dan?' he wanted to know.

'None at all,' the vet said. 'I'm not a doctor.'

The farmer looked at Hawley, noticing the paleness of his skin, the deep black rings around his eyes, the yellowed whites so heavily veined.

Hawley looked at him, aware that he was being stared at. He squinted as the bright lights overhead seemed to sear his eyes.

'Are you feeling all right?' Tyler asked.

'Yes,' he said, defensively. 'Shouldn't I be?'

'Just wondered.'

Hawley tried to swallow but his mouth tasted dry. He said nothing.

'I need to use your phone,' said Tyler.

Hawley motioned him through into reception, keeping his head bowed.

The farmer passed through into the other room and picked up the receiver. He thought for a moment, then dialled. At the other end the phone began to ring.

He let it ring a dozen times, then tried again.

There was still no answer from Wakely's doctor's surgery.

Tyler pressed the cradle down, listening to the persistent buzz for long seconds. There was no point in driving over to the surgery. He felt instinctively that it would prove fruitless. There was obviously no one there.

He dialled Ben Thurston's number.

Nothing.

He tried Reg Gentry's farm.

It was the same story.

Tyler hesitated for a moment, then dialled Thurston's farm once more. God, he hoped nothing had happened to the old boy. As he stood listening to the ringing at the other end, Tyler frowned, thoughts of his own father suddenly coming, unbidden, into his mind. Perhaps, he reasoned, it was because he identified old Ben so closely with his own late father. It would be like losing a parent all over again if Ben was dead.

The phone was still ringing.

'Come on, come on,' muttered Tyler, gripping the receiver more tightly.

He actually had it poised over the cradle when he heard the click which signalled that it had been picked up. He lifted it swiftly to his ear.

'Hello,' he said. 'Ben?'

Tyler heard low, guttural breathing.

'Ben. Is that you?'

A cough.

'It's Vic Tyler.'

'What do you want?'

He recognized the voice. It belonged to Frank Thurston, the eldest of Ben's boys. But the voice had a harsher, deeper quality to it which it didn't usually possess.

'Are you all right?' asked Tyler.

'I'm all right.' The voice was becoming weaker.

148

There was a long silence.

'Frank, let me talk to Ben will you?'

Another long silence.

'Frank, are you still there?'

'Still here.'

'I want to talk to Ben, is he there?'

There was a bang and Tyler heard footsteps shuffling away from the phone.

'Frank,' he called.

Jo, meantime, had appeared at his elbow.

'Did you reach anyone?' she asked.

Tyler held up a hand for her to be quiet.

More silence. A hiss of static.

'Hello, Vic, what can I do for you?'

Tyler smiled as he recognized Thurston's voice, as bright and cheery as usual.

'Ben, are you feeling OK?' asked Tyler.

'*I* am, but I can't say the same for my boys,' Thurston told him. 'They both look like death warmed up, they've been like it for a few days now. I've tried getting the doctor but there's no bloody answer from the surgery.'

Tyler exhaled deeply.

'What's on your mind, Vic?' Thurston asked.

Tyler looked at Jo. Should he tell Thurston about the virus?

'Nothing Ben, I called Reg Gentry's place but I couldn't reach him. I thought I'd try you. There's nothing wrong.'

'Well then, if you'll excuse me I'll get back outside, I'm doing everything here at the moment.' He chuckled.

Tyler nodded.

Thurston hung up.

'So,' Jo said. 'Not everyone's infected.'

'Not everyone.'

She reached for the phone.

'What are you doing?' he asked.

149

'Calling my paper, someone's got to know what's happening here,' she announced.

'Don't mention the virus,' Tyler said.

'Why, Vic? The people in Wakely need help.'

'Well, they're not going to get it by having reporters swarming all over them.'

She stepped back and looked deeply at him.

'What's that supposed to mean?' she demanded.

'If you tell your paper what's going on, word will spread. There'll be newsmen from all over the country converging on Wakely.'

'The public have a right to know what's happening. Especially if Vanderburg Chemicals are in back of all this. People's lives might be at risk, we don't know if this virus or disease or whatever it is can kill.'

'Exactly. That's why we don't want more people in the bloody town. They might pick it up, carry it to other places.'

'Goddamit, Vic, this is one hell of a story. Don't try to get in my way. The rest of the country has a right to know.'

'All right,' he said, softly, his voice muted but full of anger. 'Ring your office.' He lifted the receiver and pushed it towards her. 'Do it.'

She took it from him and dialled.

He saw her forehead wrinkle into a frown.

'What's wrong?' he asked.

She flicked the cradle.

'The line's dead.'

She tried again but still there was nothing.

She dialled her own home number.

No sound. Not even a hiss of static.

'The internal lines were all right,' he said.

Jo looked at the receiver for a moment then replaced it.

'Wait,' said Tyler, taking it from her. He dialled 100

150

and waited for the operator to answer. 'What's your home number?' he asked Jo.

She told him.

Tyler asked the operator to connect him with the number.

There was a moment's silence then a metallic voice told him: 'I'm afraid the number you have requested is no longer in use.'

Jo snatched the receiver from him.

'I want Arkham 62671,' she said.

'The number you have requested is no longer in use.'

Tyler left her with the recalcitrant phone and scuttled back into the surgery. He found Mandy Potter standing beside Hawley. She smiled at the farmer.

Jo re-entered the room a moment later, a worried expression on her face.

'They won't connect me with anywhere outside Wakely,' she said.

Mandy looked surprised.

Tyler glanced down at his watch and saw that it was nearly 7.00 p.m.

'There might be something on the local news,' he said, hopefully.

Mandy led them into the sitting room and turned on the television.

A blue screen greeted them, words spelt out in red letters gleaming like fresh blood against the glowing background:

THERE HAS BEEN A TRANSMITTER FAILURE
NORMAL SERVICE WILL CONTINUE SHORTLY.

Mandy tried the other channels but it was the same on each one. She excused herself and hurried upstairs to try the portable.

'Where's the nearest transmitter?' asked Jo.

'It's in Ducton, about thirty miles from here,' Tyler told her.

Mandy returned a few moments later.

'It's the same message,' she announced.

Tyler switched off the set, gazing at the blank screen for a second.

Through the open door into the surgery he could see Hawley slumped forward across one of the work-tops.

'Is he all right?' the farmer asked.

'He's been a bit under the weather lately,' Mandy explained. 'But he won't go to the doctor.' She shrugged.

'We'd better go,' said Tyler. Both he and Jo left via the surgery. 'Dan,' he called and Hawley turned. 'If you find anything else, anything at all, call me.'

Hawley nodded.

Tyler closed the door behind them as they left. They hurried from the surgery to the waiting landrover and climbed in.

The sky was stained darkly with the colour of the dying sun. Dusk settled over the countryside, the evening clouds gathering in the distance to form a purple shroud which would soon blacken to form the cloak of night.

Twenty-eight

The cassette whirred to a stop and ejected with a loud click.

'Oh sod it,' grunted Gordon Thompson.

Beneath him, her blonde hair plastered across her face, Tina Phillips moaned softly. As he went to pull away she held him close, the touch of their naked bodies causing sensations in her which she did not want to curtail.

'Leave it,' she whispered, running her fingers through his long brown hair.

She leant forward and kissed him, their tongues probing urgently against one another. Tina drew Thompson's bottom lip between her teeth and sucked gently, chuckling as she did. They broke and he rolled to one side, allowing her searching hand to find his erection. She began to move it rhythmically up and down the shaft, bringing her right leg over so that the sensitive area between her legs was rubbing against Thompson's thigh. He felt her wetness on his skin, mingling with the perspiration which was already there.

They had been living together for three months and, to Gordon Thompson, it seemed as if they'd spent all their time in bed. Not that he was complaining. Tina, twenty years old and a year younger than himself, was always eager. Her sexuality knew no bounds. They had never had much time together before, their love-making confined to hurried lunch hours at her home or snatched evenings at friends' dwellings. But now, in the security of their own place, they were taking full advantage.

She leant forward and kissed him again before sliding down and nibbling the flesh of his shoulder, drawing it between her white teeth, nipping him. He groaned, the pain of the small pinch tempered by the building pleasure he was feeling from her hand.

Still stroking his erection, she raised herself onto her knees and turned slightly. Thompson slipped a hand between her legs, his fingers tracing a pattern inside her thigh, probing at her liquescent cleft. He felt her stiffen as he gently stroked the hard bud of her clitoris.

Tina sucked at his chest, leaving a red mark, then

153

she lapped her way down to his stomach, repeating the procedure.

This time she bit a little too hard and Thompson let out a small yelp of pain but he said nothing, tensing as he felt her hand speeding up on his penis. Allowing him to move his eager fingers inside her, she sat back and looked into his face and, in the darkness of the room, he noticed how her eyes seemed to be ablaze. He had known her passion was intense but he'd never seen her quite so restless as tonight. She kissed him again, fiercely. This time she took his lip between her teeth and sucked harder.

'Jesus,' he gasped, pulling his head away and raising a hand to his mouth.

She had drawn blood.

'Be careful, love,' he said, dabbing a tentative finger at the small gash in his bottom lip.

She didn't speak but merely bent forward again and, this time, Thompson felt her warm breath on his swollen penis head. She manoeuvred herself above him, lowering her slippery sex towards his mouth. His tongue darted forward and he himself felt waves of pleasure run through him as she began to nibble at his stiff organ, finally slipping it into her mouth.

Tina's saliva mingled with the clear liquid which was seeping from the head of his shaft. He thrust forward into her hot mouth.

He felt her stiffen as, for his own part, he lapped at her vagina. She rubbed herself harder against him as she felt her orgasm approaching. Her eyes glowed and Thompson felt her chin nuzzling his pubic hairs as she continued to suck at him, her teeth raking his erection.

For fleeting seconds he realized what was happening.

She bit his penis in half, severing muscle and veins as she clamped her teeth together.

He let out a shriek of agony but it was muffled as she thrust herself at him. Thompson blacked out at once.

154

Tina sucked hard at the torn root of his manhood, eagerly swallowing the blood which pumped from it, staining the sheets beneath and gushing over his thighs. Her sharp nails tore his scrotum to bloody streamers, shredding the tender flesh.

She lay on top of him, her lips and chin dark with his life fluid.

Finally satiated, she rolled onto her back, ignoring the stench which emanated from Thompson's body.

The breeze which wafted in from the window stirred the strands of her hair. Those that weren't matted with blood.

She closed her eyes, a thin smile on her crimson lips.

PART TWO

'Turn up the lights, I don't want
to go home in the dark . . .'
   – O. Henry

'And the day burns through their blood,
like a white candle through a shuttered
hand . . .'
   – Roy Campbell

Twenty-nine

The meshed glass partition swung open as Tyler banged on it. The sound of squealing hinges was deafening in the unearthly silence of the police station. Even the two big fans which normally stood over the entry way were silent, the blades immobile.

'There's got to be someone here,' said the farmer, glancing out of the window to where the two Panda cars were parked.

During the short drive to the station that morning, they had seen perhaps two dozen people on the streets. No more.

Tyler reached round and slipped the bolt on the half-door. Jo followed him through. They stood behind the desk, the ticking of the clock above them the only noise in the stillness. The radio stood nearby and Tyler flicked at the 'On' switch. There was a loud crackle and a scream of feedback. He adjusted the volume.

'Ever used one of those things before?' Jo asked him.

Tyler shook his head, fiddling with the frequency regulator in an attempt to pick up a signal of some kind. All he got was a fluctuating buzz and occasional bouts of silence.

'Shit,' he muttered, glaring angrily at the radio. 'We'd better have a look around, the place can't be deserted.'

Jo moved towards a closed door on the left but Tyler stepped in front of her, his hand closing on the knob.

They found themselves in what he took to be the rest

room. There was a large notice board with rotas pinned to it and a couple of photos of cars. On the far wall was a dart board, the arrows jammed into the bull's-eye. The blinds were drawn in the room, plunging it into deep gloom but, in the corner, Tyler saw someone sitting down.

'Who's there?' a voice asked and Tyler recognized it as belonging to Don Mason.

He moved towards the sergeant who tried to rise from his seat. It seemed an effort and he gave up finally, sinking back into the plastic covered chair.

'Don, are you all right?' asked Tyler, drawing closer to the policeman. As he did, he saw that the sergeant's normally lustrous beard was greying, patches of raw skin showing through in places where the bristles had come out in thick hunks. As he raised his hands to his temples, Jo noticed how long his nails had become, the cuticles cracked and riven.

'I feel so bloody tired,' croaked Mason, accepting the hand which Tyler offered.

The farmer shuddered involuntarily as he felt the cold clamminess of the policeman's flesh against his own.

Mason swayed drunkenly for a second, then seemed to regain his footing.

'Where are the other men?' asked Tyler.

'Not here,' Mason told him, heading towards the door. He recoiled slightly as he reached the light and stood in the frame, momentarily frozen. He narrowed his eyes and groaned, one hand pressed to his temple, the other supporting him.

'I don't know what the hell is wrong with me,' he said.

'How long have you felt like this?' Jo asked him.

He shrugged.

'Started to feel bad yesterday afternoon. The wife, she's . . .' he hesitated, as if he'd forgotten what he was going to say next.

160

Jo and Tyler helped him into the other room where he groaned aloud at the lights and the sun pouring through the unshaded window.

'Is your wife ill too?' Jo wanted to know.

'I couldn't wake her up this morning. So tired.'

Tyler and Jo exchanged anxious glances.

'Look, Don, we've got to contact someone outside Wakely,' explained the farmer.

'Phone them.'

Jo picked up the nearby phone but the line was, as she'd expected, dead. She shook her head and replaced the receiver.

'The lines are down. You'll have to use the radio, Tyler insisted. 'Get in touch with the Arkham police.'

'Why?'

'Because people here in Wakely could be in danger. We need help.'

'A virus of some kind,' Jo added.

'What the hell are you going on about?' rasped Mason.

'Call the Arkham police,' Tyler said, firmly.

'No good. We're out of range. Arkham's too far from here, besides, they use a different frequency.'

'So find the frequency,' the farmer demanded.

Mason rounded on him.

'They're out of range,' he growled, his yellowed eyes glowing, the veins in them bulging.

'Try,' roared Tyler.

The two men faced each other for a moment, then Mason nodded painfully and reached for the modulator. He turned the dial, the high pitched screams of interference making him wince. Voices drifted, phantom-like, over the air-waves until, finally, Mason grunted and raised the microphone to his mouth.

'This is Wakely Police Station,' he croaked. 'Sergeant Don Mason speaking. Come in Arkham. Over.'

The hum of static was punctuated by sharp crackles, then a distant voice answered:

'This is Arkham. Go ahead. Over.'

Tyler took the microphone from Mason who offered no resistance.

'Arkham Police Station?' said the farmer.

'Affirmative. Please identify yourself.'

'Vic Tyler, I live in Wakely. Listen, send some men over here now I . . .'

'Are you a policeman?'

'No, I told you, I live in Wakely. Will you – '

Again he was cut short.

'You have no right to be using police property, it's an offence.'

'There's no one else here you silly bastard,' snarled the farmer. 'The people in Wakely are in danger, send some men. It's urgent.'

'We've received no reports from Wakely to that effect.'

'That's because the policemen here are gone. For God's sake listen to me . . .'

A hiss of static.

'Did you hear what I said?' Tyler rasped.

'We have received no reports concerning Wakely.'

'Well I'm giving you a fucking report now,' the farmer shouted. 'People are dying. We need help.'

'There have been no formal reports made.'

Tyler gripped the microphone until it threatened to break.

'Let me speak to someone in charge,' he demanded.

'We have received no formal reports. Over and out.'

There was a loud click and then silence.

Tyler hurled the microphone to one side in a paroxysm of rage.

'Bastards,' he fumed. 'Stupid bloody bastards.' He looked down at Mason who was shielding his face from the encroaching sunlight. He pushed past them, heading back into the darkened rest room.

Tyler exhaled deeply.

'There's nothing we can do here,' he said. 'Let's go.'

Tyler was surprised to see one or two members of staff present in 'The King George' hotel. The bar was open and there was even a man sitting on one of the stools sipping at a pint of beer. A rotund chambermaid was hoovering the carpet in reception. She looked up briefly as Jo and the farmer entered.

The American crossed to the desk and rang the bell, wondering if Mark Bates was going to appear. She thought back to the incident the other night when she'd discovered him devouring the raw meat. Was he going to emerge from the staff room with blood dripping from his hands? She hurriedly dismissed the thought.

'I'll have to get your key, miss,' said the chambermaid, appearing beside her. 'There's only a few of us here today.'

'Why is that?' asked the journalist.

'Some of the staff are off sick,' the maid explained. 'My husband, he's not been too good lately.'

'What's wrong with him?' asked Tyler.

'He looks so pale, sir, and during the day all he wants to do is sleep. He's not so bad at night though.' She shrugged.

'But *you* feel OK?' said Jo.

'I'm fine thank you.' The maid looked puzzled and she coloured slightly beneath the combined gaze of Jo and Tyler.

'Is there something wrong?' she asked, handing Jo her key.

The American smiled.

'No.'

The maid crossed to her hoover.

'It seems pointless doing this,' she mused.

'Why,' Tyler wanted to know.

She looked up.

'Well, what with there being hardly any guests here. And I can't see us getting many more in the near future the way things are.' She leant on the cleaner like a navvy on a shovel. 'I'll tell you something else, a lot of people have left the town. Don't ask me why but only two days ago the family who live next door to us moved out. And I've noticed how many people seem to be feeling off colour. You know, ill. I can't understand it.' She paused, shaking her head. 'It's a good job Mr Bates isn't here.'

'Who *is* Bates?' asked Jo.

'The Manager,' explained the maid. 'Why?'

Jo shook her head.

'I was just curious.'

The three of them stood in silence for another moment, then the maid started up her cleaner.

'I suppose I'd better get this done all the same,' she said and bustled off across reception.

Jo and Tyler headed for the lifts, both of which stood empty before them. For some unaccountable reason, the sight of people in the reception and lounge made them feel easier but, as the lift bumped to a halt and the doors slid back, the corridor which stretched away ahead of them seemed curiously forbidding.

They reached Jo's room and went inside.

It was large, containing a double bed, a sideboard and even a desk. The wardrobe had mirrors on its doors and through a white door was the bathroom. A latticed window looked out onto the car park at the back of the building. There were tea-making facilities so Jo filled the kettle from the tap in the bathroom and plugged it into the socket nearby.

Tyler sat down on the edge of the bed.

'If there are people leaving the town, like the maid

said, then that would be one explanation why there aren't so many about.'

'And the ones who haven't left?' said Jo, cryptically.

'We've got to assume they're infected with this virus, whatever it is.'

'You know I've noticed with a lot of them, sunlight or artificial light frightens them. It hurts them. Like that guy Nichols.' She sucked in an anxious breath. 'What kind of virus makes people afraid of the light?'

There was a long silence broken finally by Jo.

'I was thinking about what Hawley said. About the synthetic, man-made proteins in the Vanderburg feed. Geoffrey Anderson *would* have known about it. He would have known the effects it was going to have too. Tests must have been done.'

'What are you getting at, Jo?'

'That night he tried to talk to me, maybe that was what it was about. Anderson must have known what was in the feed. Someone didn't want him shooting his mouth off.'

'He may have known the effect it would have on animals but how could he have known what it would do to human beings?'

'I think he was told to keep quiet. When he wouldn't someone shut him up. Killed him.'

'Come on, Jo, this isn't New York,' said the farmer, wearily.

'Then where is he?' she barked. 'He was scared that night he rang me. He knew someone was on to him.'

'Like who?'

'That's what we've got to find out.'

Tyler exhaled deeply.

'We don't know he's dead. We don't know anything.'

'We know that this town is infected with some kind of virus. We know it's spread by eating contaminated meat. And we know that the victims can't come out in sunlight.'

165

'That adds up to nothing,' said Tyler. 'Why hasn't everyone in Wakely got this virus? Why haven't you and I caught it?'

'You don't eat meat. I haven't touched any since I arrived in Wakely.'

Tyler stroked his chin thoughtfully.

'If Vanderburg Chemicals are responsible for the virus,' he said, slowly. 'They wouldn't want any publicity. No outside interference.'

'You think they're behind the phone and TV blackouts?' Jo said, incredulously.

'It's a thought, although I doubt if they'd be able to do anything on that scale without help.'

'Help from whom?'

'That's what we've got to find out. We've got to get inside Vanderburg Chemicals.'

Jo looked at him, dumbstruck.

'Are you kidding? That place is like Fort Knox.'

'There has to be a way. We've got no choice.'

'When do we do it?'

'Tonight,' he announced, flatly.

'And in the meantime?'

'I think it would be best if I moved in here with you. I'm not leaving you alone. Not now.'

She kissed him softly on the cheek and he brushed a strand of hair from her forehead.

'What about your farm?' she asked.

'What farm?' he said, sardonically. 'Diseased animals are no good to a farmer. They'll have to be destroyed.' He got to his feet. 'I'll be back in an hour or two,' he said. Then he was gone.

The kettle had begun to boil but Jo didn't notice it. She was gazing out of the window, watching the scudding clouds.

It was just after 1.00 p.m.

Thirty

The oak table sparkled like ice beneath the fluorescent lights. The room smelt of polish and nicotine, the air filled with a bluish haze. It was a large room, twenty feet wide and thirty long, the table being its centre point. The white painted walls bore framed pictures, including an original Turner over the fire place. The painting looked somewhat anachronistic set over an electric fire. Indeed, the entire room seemed to be caught in a kind of chronological limbo. A clash of cultures and times mirrored in what it contained. Antique furniture sat side by side with such modern encumbrances as a computer terminal which, at present, showed a blank screen. The windows, large and airy, were double-glazed, offering added sound proofing.

Five men sat around the table, each with a note pad and pencil before him.

The wall clock ticked noisily in the stillness, the hands having crawled round to 3.00 p.m.

Sir Oliver Thorndike looked at his own watch and coughed exaggeratedly as if to still a babble of conversation, but all eyes were on him anyway.

Thorndike was fifty-three, a tall but heavy set man with thick white hair and sad eyes. He had been knighted in 1978 for his work in the field of genetics. He had worked for Vanderburg Chemicals since 1980. He coughed once more, brushing an imaginary speck of dust from the sleeve of his navy blue suit.

'Gentlemen,' he said. 'If we could begin.'

There were nods of approval.

Thorndike looked at the man closest to him on the right. Charles Muir finished lighting his pipe and sucked contentedly on it.

'The new synthetic compound is almost completed,'

said the older man, his voice a harsh Scots drawl. 'It should be ready for introduction within a week.'

'It will be treated with ultra-violet rays this time,' added Richard Neville.

At forty-five, Neville was the youngest man at the table. He pushed his glasses back on his nose and shuffled in his seat.

'It should have been treated before,' said Muir.

'We had no way of knowing what the effects of the synthetic protein would be,' Neville protested.

'You're a bacteriologist,' the Scot said, challengingly. 'You should have had some idea.'

Thorndike raised a hand.

'Gentlemen, please,' he said. 'We all appreciate that the first batch of the additive was, how shall we say, unproven. The results were merely unfortunate.'

'Why was it not thoroughly checked?' Muir persisted.

'For God's sake,' snapped Martin Glendenning. 'The damage is done now. We made a mistake. That mistake can be rectified this time.'

'Whatever we do now can't be of any help to the people of Wakely,' Muir said, chewing on the stem of his pipe.

'We all knew we were taking a chance,' said Thorndike, sweeping back his white hair. 'We were unfortunate.'

'A masterful understatement,' Muir chided.

'Do we know exactly how the viral infection is affecting the residents of Wakely?' asked Neville, toying with his wedding ring as he spoke.

Thorndike picked up a manilla file and flipped it open.

'First reports indicate that it's manifesting itself as something like pernicious anaemia. We haven't been able to discover the exact effects yet.'

'Does it really matter?' said Glendenning.

'Well, it only matters in as far as knowing its communicability,' Thorndike said. 'It seems confined to the town at the moment so it's reasonably safe to assume that the virus is passed on through ingestion of the affected meat.'

'Is there any possibility of outside interference?' asked Glendenning, plucking at the back of his hand.

'In what form?' Thorndike wanted to know.

'Police. Other authorities.'

Thorndike shook his head.

'If the need arises, we can seal Wakely off,' he said. 'From what I can gather, many of the residents have already left.'

'Infected or virus free?' Muir wanted to know.

Thorndike held up his hands.

'Charles, there's no possible way we could know who was or wasn't infected. Wakely has a population of just under 4,000. From that amount of people it would be impossible to guess how many had the virus.'

'*Try* guessing,' the Scot insisted.

Thorndike looked at the fifth man seated at the table, who was yet to speak, and then at Neville.

'From a population of 4,000,' the younger man began. 'One could expect perhaps a quarter of that number to have contracted the virus in some form.'

'What about those who aren't infected?' asked Glendenning.

'What about them?' Thorndike said.

'What's the likelihood of them contracting the virus?'

'Unless they eat the contaminated meat, they should be safe from the primary infection,' Thorndike told him.

'What about secondary infection?' asked Muir.

Thorndike exhaled deeply.

'As I said before, we have no way of knowing how or even if the virus is communicable except by ingestion.'

'There is the problem of cure,' said Neville. 'Can we find one?'

'It's not our business to find one,' snapped

Glendenning. 'This project is designed to maximize the growth of livestock by the infusion of synthetic proteins. Any adverse effects caused by that work are regrettable but, nonetheless, not our concern.'

'Not our concern,' said Muir, angrily, the pipe bouncing about in his mouth. 'We virtually wipe out an entire town and you say it's not our concern.' He paused. 'I say we should call off the project for the time being.'

A chorus of mutterings greeted his remark.

Thorndike stilled the babble and looked at the Scot.

'That is impractical and unnecessary, Charles, and you know it,' he said.

'Geoffrey Anderson agreed with me,' Muir said.

'To hell with Geoffrey Anderson.'

The voice came from the fifth man who got to his feet and walked to one of the windows which looked out into the grounds of Vanderburg Chemicals. He was tall, nearly six five and his black hair glinted beneath the lights. When he spoke it was with a strong American accent, Mid-West. He was wearing an expensive suit and, when he smiled, which was something of a rarity, a single gold tooth sparkled amidst the expanse of white enamel.

He reached into his pocket and pulled out an engraved silver hip-flask. Unscrewing the cap he took a hefty swig, then turned back to face the men around the table.

'Anderson was a pain in the ass,' said the dark haired man, vehemently. 'This project demands top secrecy at all times, that's why we're working with the co-operation of your Government.' His voice took on a hint of sarcasm. 'To further Anglo-American relations. Now if anybody else wants out that's fine with me but hear this, if one of you bastards breathes a word of what's been said in this room, you'll be wearing your asses for hats.'

170

John Stark took another swig from his flask, then returned to his seat. As chief financial backer to Vanderburg Chemicals he relished his own importance and was never slow to remind those around him of it too. He had founded the company three years earlier, shortly after the death of his wife, using her maiden name for the concern. She had been killed in a traffic accident, the brakes on her Trans-Am failing as she pulled in front of a Mack truck carrying a tank load of amyl nitrate. There hadn't been much left to bury.

'I don't think any of us want to leave, Mr Stark,' said Thorndike.

'Then what the hell is he bitching about?' snapped the American, pointing at Muir.

'Look, I'll work for you,' said the Scot. 'But that doesn't mean I have to stop caring about the people my work affects. Especially when it's something on this scale.'

'You win some, you lose some,' snapped Stark.

'And in this case we lost an entire town,' said Muir.

'You were the goddam scientists, you should have got it right first time. If anyone's to blame it's you.'

'Well,' said Thorndike, 'I'm sure matters have been put to rights this time.' He smiled at Stark but the gesture was not returned.

'Yeah, well there's something else.'

The men looked, vaguely, at the American.

'I'm talking about that girl and the guy in town, whoever the hell he is. They're too goddam curious.' A rare smile crept across Stark's face. 'Still, curiosity can kill more than cats.' He chuckled.

'What do you propose to do?' asked Glendenning.

'*You* spoke to the girl didn't you?' said Stark.

The older man nodded.

'She did seem rather . . . inquisitive. Especially about Anderson,' the scientist said.

'Too inquisitive.' He turned to Thorndike. 'I want

171

Wakely sealed off. Cops, telephones, TV, I know that's already been taken care of but, from now on, I don't want anyone leaving. I want this town sewn up tighter than a fish's ass and I mean water-tight. Make that phone call.'

Thorndike reached unhesitatingly for the phone close to him and dialled a London number. It rang for a moment, then the others sat watching as he spoke.

'I'd like to speak to the Minister,' said Thorndike.

The secretary asked for his name, then what he wanted.

'Tell him it's Erebus.'

There was a moment's silence at the other end of the line. A confusion of clicks and crackles as Thorndike was re-connected on another line.

Muir chewed on his pipe.

Stark took another swig from his hip-flask.

The other two men watched Thorndike as he moved the receiver agitatedly from one hand to the other.

Glendenning plucked at the flesh on the back of his hand.

Neville continued twisting his ring.

Thorndike suddenly became animated as he heard a voice at the other end of the phone.

'Yes, sir,' he said. 'This is Erebus.'

He swallowed hard.

'There have been difficulties. We need the town sealed off. No passage for residents or visitors.'

The voice asked what kind of difficulties.

'Project Erebus has precipitated some unforeseen confusion here. We need time to rectify the situation.'

How long, the voice wanted to know.

'Until further notice,' said Thorndike looking across at Stark.

The American nodded.

Thorndike listened for a moment.

'Yes, sir, I understand. No, there is no danger to the project itself.'

There were more hasty enquiries, then Thorndike spoke again.

'Yes, sir. Everything will be taken care of.'

He put the phone down and turned to the waiting American.

'It's done.'

'What, may I ask has been done?' Muir enquired.

'Within forty-eight hours,' Thorndike told him. 'Wakely will be completely sealed off from all outside contact.'

'How?' the Scot wanted to know.

'That's not your worry,' Stark told him.

'What's your solution, *Mr* Stark?' Muir began. 'Complete the annihilation of Wakely that was begun by Project Erebus?'

The American rounded on him.

'Listen to me,' he growled. 'This project is worth millions and we're not the only ones who are going to benefit. Why the hell do you think your Government is behind me too?' There was a long silence. 'Now, there's nothing else to be said. I don't think I have to keep you *gentlemen* from your work any longer.'

The assembled scientists rose and filed from the room. Stark took a swig from his hip-flask, then crossed to a desk in the far corner of the room. He flicked a switch on the console before him and muttered something into the intercom. A moment or two later there was a knock on the door.

'Come in,' he called.

Carlo Fanducci walked in, a cigarette hanging from his mouth. He closed the door behind him.

'The guy and the girl who've been doing the digging in town, who are they?' asked Stark.

Fanducci coughed, fighting to keep down the bitter phlegm.

'The girl's a reporter. She's from the East Side,' he said, his voice raw and gravelly. 'I knew I'd seen her someplace before. She was the one who fingered old man Scalise back in New York. She's been fucking around with this guy, Tyler, for a few days now.'

'Do you know where they are?' Stark asked.

'Tyler runs a farm about a mile outside town. The broad's staying at a hotel in Wakely. But, from what I've seen, he spends most of his time there.'

'What do they know?'

Fanducci shrugged.

'Waste them,' said Stark, flatly. 'And anyone who's with them.'

'When do you want it done?' asked Fanducci.

Stark took another swig from his flask.

'As soon as you can.'

The Italian nodded.

Thirty-one

The attic smelt fusty, the dust of neglect having settled thickly on everything. Particles of it swirled in the beam of Tyler's torch as he clambered up onto the thick rafters. It was a part of the farm house which he used to visit regularly as a youngster, sitting for hours with his father, listening as the older man spoke. Young Tyler would sit cross-legged before the man he held in awe, watching him clean his beloved guns. He had learnt all he knew about guns from his father and now, as he shone the torch around the attic, those memories

174

came flooding back. The beam glinted on some of the trophies which hung on the walls of this most hallowed retreat. Plaques, statuettes, certificates. Everything covered by a film of dust. On the far wall, however, was a canvas sheet. Pinned at either side, it protected the valuable collection beneath.

Tyler reached forward slowly and pulled it down.

There were four shotguns on the rack. Two nickel plated Purdeys, a Franchi automatic and a single barrelled Baikal. Beneath them, in a large cupboard, were countless boxes of ammunition. Tyler still held his own Purdey by his side. It had been given to him on his sixteenth birthday by his father, the stock still bore his faded initials. They had been carved by his father.

Tyler's mother had never been keen on guns, her own brother having been wounded in a hunting acci-dent, but Jack Tyler had taught his son how to use them carefully and skilfully. Many hours of practice and aching shoulders had turned Tyler into a proficient marksman and, at seventeen, he had won the county championships for clay pigeon shooting. Still the youn-gest person ever to do so.

Now he looked at his own gun and at those of his father.

Already he could feel the tears welling up inside him, not so much for the fact that the memories of his father were so strong but for the purpose to which he intended to put these beloved weapons.

He took down the top gun from the duo of Purdeys and hefted it before him. Then he selected the Franchi. That done, he unlocked the ammunition cupboard and took out as many shells as he could stuff into the pockets of his jacket. He could, he reasoned, come back for more if he needed them. Then, carrying all three weapons, he made his way back down the rickety step ladder which led up to the attic. He paused at the bottom and loaded his own gun and the other two, thumbing five cartridges into the automatic.

When he emerged into the late afternoon sunlight, Tyler felt sick and he had to steady himself against a fence for a moment.

He sucked in huge lungfuls of air, realizing what he had to do but feeling something akin to disgust with himself.

Many of the animals were already gone. Pens and fields were empty. Elsewhere, animals lay dead, some partially decomposed in the heat. But there were still three or four dozen in and around the farm.

Tyler knew they were diseased. He knew they must be destroyed but it made his task no easier. He looked up at the attic window as if expecting to see his father standing there watching him, shaking his head reproachfully as he saw what use his guns were being put to.

Tyler picked up the Franchi and worked the pump action, chambering a round. He crossed to the pig sty and looked in at the oversized weaners, raising the weapon to his shoulder.

He aimed and fired in one movement.

The first animal dropped into the mud as the roar of the shotgun was joined by another. And another. The weaners made no attempt to move as the shot tore into them and, finally, when the hammer slammed down on an empty chamber, the sty was full of carcasses. A bluish haze of smoke wafted gently into the air and the stink of cordite was strong in Tyler's nostrils.

He re-loaded and walked purposefully across to the nearest shed which housed half a dozen cows due for milking.

Tyler gritted his teeth and opened fire, tears now flowing swiftly from his stinging eyes as his ears were filled with the deafening retort of the gun and the loud bellowings of the cattle. And there was another sound.

His own moans of distress.

The smoke cleared slowly and, before it had dispersed, he was firing again. Choking back sobs, trying to keep his aim straight. His shoulder ached from the constant thudding against it of the stock as each fresh impact slammed against him.

He was muttering soundlessly to himself as he fired, passing from one shed to the other. From cattle to pigs, to sheep. The Franchi began to glow red in his hands so he dropped it and, with bloodstained hands, broke the nickel-plated Purdey and checked that it was loaded.

It was.

He gave both barrels to a large bull, watching as the animal went down as if pole-axed.

He felt hot salty tears running freely down his cheeks now because he realized that, in the thundering discharge of those shotgun blasts he was destroying not just diseased animals. He was destroying everything his father had built up. He was slaughtering his own memories. The Purdey roared in his hand.

Each blazing explosion was like an accusatory shout.

Tyler shouted aloud at each discharge, his sorrow gradually giving way to anger as he continued with his grisly task.

The ground was littered with empty shell cases, but there were always plenty more at hand.

'Vanderburg,' he muttered, his jaw set firm.

The rage seemed to grow.

'Bastards,' he growled. He would find out why this had happened. Someone would pay. Tyler was determined that somebody would suffer for what had been done.

The slaughter continued.

It took Tyler over an hour to despatch what livestock he could find on the farm. By the time he'd finished, his arms felt like lead weights. His eyes stung and his nostrils were full of the stench of gun oil and cordite. He dropped to his knees and gulped down the air, trying to ignore the pungent odour of blood which was so strong.

Finally, he got up and trudged wearily back to the house. He collected as much ammunition as he could carry and put it into the landrover with the three shotguns, then he climbed into the vehicle and sat behind the wheel for what seemed like an eternity.

'I'm sorry,' he whispered, wondering whether the words were spoken to the memory of his parents or to appease his own tortured conscience.

He started the engine and swung the vehicle out of the yard. He didn't once look back.

Jo sat on the edge of the bed listening. But for the odd sound of movement from downstairs, the hotel was in silence. The American got to her feet and crossed to her door. She paused for a moment, then opened it, peering to her right and left.

The corridor was empty, the doors to the other rooms were closed.

Jo dropped her own key into the back pocket of her jeans and quietly closed her door behind her. She moved noiselessly towards the first and nearest door and turned the knob. It wouldn't budge. She dropped to one knee and squinted through the keyhole.

The room was well lit inside, the curtains drawn back.

Jo got to her feet and moved down the corridor. It turned at right angles as it approached the lifts, both of which were stationary. The American moved to another door, glancing behind her at the lifts, as if expecting someone to emerge at any second.

She wondered how many of the guests were infected with the mysterious virus, if any. Some of the staff of the hotel certainly were – she knew that only too well after the incident with Bates – and of the other guests she knew nothing.

The second door she tried was also locked.

Jo was about to move away from it when she heard a noise from inside.

She pressed her ear to the white wood and listened.

It came again. A low, guttural rasping. Like asthmatic breathing.

She knelt once more to try and look through the key hole, but all that greeted her prying eye was darkness.

The breathing seemed to grow louder for a moment, then ceased.

The American knocked gently.

The breathing began once more, slow and strained.

Jo paused a moment longer, then moved along to a door which, she noticed, was ajar.

It was dark inside the room and she opened the door inch by inch, allowing the light to dispel the gloom.

It was as quiet as a grave in that room and Jo shuddered involuntarily as she passed across the portal and into the blackness.

The room was like her own except for the fact that it showed no signs of being inhabited. The bed was made, the smell of carpet cleaner strong in the air.

She moved towards the bathroom and pushed open the door, slapping on the light as she did so.

There was hair in the sink. Thick dark hunks of it. Not strands but tufts which had clogged the plug hole. Jo prodded at it with her key, noticing something else too. A thin, almost transparent substance which reminded her of mucous. She turned away, stifling a scream as she looked into the bath.

The white enamel was splashed with blood.

Jo swallowed hard and leant over the bath, dipping one finger tentatively into the crimson liquid.

It was fresh.

She got up and hastily left the room, intent on

returning to her own. The corridor turned at right angles again and Jo realized that she had come almost full circle in her search. Out of curiosity, she tried each door as she went. Finding every one locked.

However, the room next to hers was not locked.

The handle turned smoothly in her grip, the door opening a fraction.

The American hesitated. This was no bedroom. From the smell of freshly laundered sheets she realized that it was the linen cupboard. She wondered whether or not it was worth looking into, then something caught her eye. Something crumpled lying on the floor about two feet inside the room.

She stepped inside.

Had Jo been in the corridor, she may well have seen the lights on the lift flash brightly but, hidden inside the laundry room, she was oblivious to what was going on.

One of the lifts was rising.

Jo took a closer look at the crumpled mass on the floor, prodding it with her key.

It looked like the transparent stuff she'd seen in the sink of the other room. But what the hell was it? She looked around and found a pile of towels nearby. She pulled the top one down and wrapped it around her hand.

The lift bumped to a halt and the doors slid quietly open.

Jo picked up the sticky substance, noticing how tendrils of it hung like rotting streamers. It had a revolting familiarity about it. As she held it before her, it seemed to take on a shape.

Unfolding, the slimy mass fell away like unravelling paper.

Jo saw hair attached to it and she finally realized what she was holding.

It was a large coil of human skin, shed as a snake would shed its old hide.

She dropped it in disgust and got to her feet, backing out of the room, eyes fixed on the lump of skin as if it were a living thing.

The hand closed on her shoulder.

Jo screamed and spun round.

'Sorry,' said Tyler, apologetically.

She could only stand and stare at him, her heart hammering madly against her ribs.

'Didn't you hear the lift coming up?' he asked.

Jo shook her head.

'What's wrong?' Tyler wanted to know.

'Well,' she panted. 'Aside from the fact that I nearly had a goddam heart attack, I've found a couple of things.'

'Like what?'

'Like that.' She pointed to the sloughed skin.

Tyler knelt and glanced at it.

'Skin?' he asked.

She nodded.

'That's not all.'

Jo showed him the blood and hair in the other room, then led him to the locked bedroom where she had heard the breathing.

'There's someone asleep in there,' he said.

'It's four thirty in the afternoon,' she snapped. 'Who sleeps at this time of the day?'

'And what do you propose we do? Kick the door down?' he said. 'There's probably a perfectly logical explanation for . . .'

She cut him short.

'Don't give me that crap,' she rasped.

The door was suddenly pulled open.

Both of them stepped back, surprised to see Mark Bates standing there.

'What are you doing here?' he rasped.

'I heard you breathing,' said Jo. 'I thought maybe you were sick.'

Bates regarded them warily and, in the light, they both saw how the skin had peeled from his face and neck, leaving red and angry patches beneath. He shielded his face from the light, the thick growths of hair on the palms of his hands clearly visible.

'What do you want?' he demanded.

'Nothing,' said Tyler, pulling Jo aside. 'Sorry if we disturbed you.'

Bates glared at them, then slammed the door once more and locked it.

Jo and Tyler were left in the corridor, gazing at the closed door. It was the farmer who made the first movement, urging Jo to join him as he walked back to their own room. Once inside he locked the door behind them.

'Do you think it's safe here?' the American asked him.

Tyler nodded. He crossed to the window and looked out. Jo studied his broad outline as he stood there, unusually silent.

'Vic.' She spoke his name softly. 'What's on your mind?'

He told her what had happened at the farm prior to his return.

'My father built that place up from nothing,' he said. 'Every time I pulled that trigger it was as if I was destroying a piece of his dream.'

Jo crossed to the window and slid her arm around his waist. He pulled her closer.

'You had no choice,' she said.

The words brought him little comfort, but the sadness which had lain so heavy inside him had now turned into a knotted ball of fury. He wanted revenge.

The sun vanished momentarily behind a bank of dark cloud and, in the distance, they could both see the

182

shadow which it cast over the land. Jo shuddered and Tyler held her tighter.

'It'll be dark in a few hours,' he said.

At 7.30 p.m. they returned to the room where they'd found Bates and, surprisingly enough, found the door open.

Tyler checked out the entire room.

Bates was gone.

Thirty-two

Night lay heavy over Wakely. An impenetrable blanket of darkness denied even the welcoming glow of the moon. A few stars glinted against the velvet back-drop but even they were mostly obscured by banks of thick cloud which spread across the gloomy heavens like ink stains on a blotter. There was a storm in the air. The heat of the day had become a cloying humidity and, even as Jo and Tyler sat in the dining room of 'The King George' prodding at the remnants of their dinners, the first low rumblings of thunder could be heard away to the north.

'The fences around Vanderburg Chemicals are electrified,' Jo began. 'If we get past those there's Security guards and patrol dogs. Vic, I'm telling you, it'd take a team of Green Berets to break in there.'

'We'll see,' said Tyler, defiantly.

'So, once we're in, assuming we can *get* in, we're not even sure what we're looking for.'

'Somebody's been doing everything they can to stop us finding out the facts about what's going on in Wakely. The only people who would need to do that are the people at Vanderburg Chemicals.' He paused. 'No phones, no television, not even any police or newsmen. The whole set up is too . . . organized to be a coincidence.'

'You said you thought that Vanderburg couldn't do anything like that without help,' she said.

'I don't. I think someone else is involved. Don't ask me who.'

'Who's powerful enough to seal off an entire town?' Jo said, the question hanging lazily in the air.

Tyler had no answer for her.

A troubled silence descended over them.

Carlo Fanducci brought the car to a halt across the street from the hotel. He lit up another cigarette and inhaled the smoke, gritting his teeth as he felt the pain begin to gnaw at his chest and throat. He coughed, wincing at the effort. Son of a bitch, he thought. It was getting worse. Fucking cancer must have eaten away most of his lung by now. What the hell, there was no good crying about it. He hawked and spat onto the pavement, the bloodied sputum looking black beneath the dull glow of the street lamp.

The lights on the front of the hotel glowed with a rare brilliance and Fanducci noticed how none of the people on the streets went near to the building.

He could see them in the gloom, moving furtively. Like tangible shadows they scuttled about in side streets and doorways, always careful to keep clear of the puddles of yellow light given off by the sodium lamps. Fanducci himself felt at home in the darkness and, as he drew the .357 from its shoulder holster, he did not need to see the heavy cylinder. He knew, from the sound it made as he spun it that every chamber was full. Each one carrying a lethal hollow tipped bullet.

Satisfied, he slid the revolver back into position and reached onto the back seat where he found the Ingram The machine gun, no bigger than a shoe box, was also loaded, the thirty-two round magazine rammed tight into it. Fanducci pulled back the bolt, priming it.

His little baby. It fired over 1,500 rounds a minute and, from close range, would cut a man in half. He wrapped the leather carrying strap around his wrist and hefted the weapon before him. When he got out of the car, the Ingram dangled at his side.

Fanducci stood for long moments watching the front of the building. Nothing stirred, only the long strands of ivy which clawed at the stone work moved in the shallow breeze.

There was a back entrance which he'd found the other day. Shit, he'd go in that way. Give them a little surprise.

The Italian smiled to himself and set off towards the hotel.

Overhead, the first soundless flash of lightning tore its way across the heavens.

Jo and Tyler walked through the darkened reception towards the lifts and the American jabbed a button. The lights on either side glowed brilliantly for a second, then dimmed. There was a loud rumble of thunder. The lights blazed with their usual power once more.

'Bloody storm,' muttered Tyler.

They were now the only ones in the reception. Off to the left the door to the staff room stood closed. To the right, the bar was empty as well.

The lift purred to a halt and the doors slid open. Outside there was a whiplash crack of lightning followed by a growl of thunder which seemed to shake the building to its foundations. They both stepped into the lift and Jo pressed the button marked 'l'. The car began to rise.

Even inside the lift, insulated to a certain degree against the noise from outside, the storm raged with nerve-shredding fury, the celestial explosions continuing at an ever increasing rate as the storm reached its full magnitude.

The lights went out.

The lift was plunged into a blackness so total that Tyler could not see his companion even though she stood just two feet from him. At the same instant, the lift stopped dead.

'Oh Christ.' murmured the farmer.

They stood for interminable seconds, waiting for power to be restored but nothing happened.

'Perhaps the storm's brought down a power line,' said Jo.

'We must be between floors,' Tyler said. 'Perhaps I can get these doors open, then we can see.' He fumbled his way across the small compartment to the sliding doors and worked his fingers into the tiny gap between them, then, with a grunt, he began to pull in both directions. His muscles bulged as he fought to open the doors, the veins throbbing at his temples.

They began to open a fraction.

Jo held up her lighter, the meagre light which it gave off being sufficient to show them that they were, indeed, between floors. But the top of the car showed about two feet above the floor of what would be the first storey.

Tyler suddenly let the doors go as the pressure became too much to bear.

Jo flicked off her lighter and the two of them stood in the gloom. Disembodied voices floated on a sea of darkness.

'Can we climb up through the gap?' asked Jo.

'*You* can,' Tyler said. 'I'll hold the doors open as far as I can, you'll have to try and squeeze through.'

'What about you?'

'There should be an emergency exit in the top of the lift. A maintenance opening or something. If I can get through that, perhaps I can make it to the second floor.'

'No, it s too dangerous. Maybe we should wait until the power comes back on.'

'And if it doesn't?'

The question hung ominously in the air.

'I'll try the doors again,' said Tyler, bracing himself. Jo slipped her shoes off, realizing that she was going to have to clamber over the farmer to reach the small gap. The floor of the compartment felt cold beneath her bare feet and a chill ran through her though she was convinced that not all of it was induced by the cold. She shuddered involuntarily.

Tyler, by now, had managed to force the doors open far enough for her to attempt to slip through. Jo was grateful that she was slim, a few more pounds around the backside and she'd be stuck.

'Ready?' grunted Tyler.

'Ready,' she assured him.

The entire lift was rocked by a powerful impact from above.

Tyler fell back, the doors sliding swiftly shut, nearly trapping his hands.

The car was shaking slightly and they could both hear loud scratching sounds coming from above.

'What the hell is that?' Tyler said, looking up.

Jo was silent, straining her eyes to see.

There was someone on the top of the lift.

The shaking continued for a moment, only to be replaced by what sounded like heavy footsteps

'How could they have got up there?' asked Jo, a note of fear in her voice.

'From the second floor,' Tyler offered. 'They must have climbed down the cable.'

There was a loud scraping sound filling the lift now and, as Jo flicked on her lighter, they both saw that the maintenance hatch was being opened.

Whoever was up there would be through in a minute or two.

The lighter grew hot in Jo's hand and she dropped it, plunging them back into darkness once more. She dropped to her knees, fumbling to find it. Groping like a blind person, her ears ever alert for the sounds from above as the hatch was pulled away.

Tyler felt helpless. Unable to see a hand in front of him, he could only stand there impotently and wait for the intruder to drop from above.

The lights suddenly came back on, the lift simultaneously bucking into action. It rose the required few feet and bumped to a halt on the first floor.

'Get out, quick,' Tyler shouted, pushing her through the half-open doors.

Jo stumbled and fell into the corridor, looking behind her to see Tyler following.

The maintenance hatch was torn free.

Tyler backed off slightly, looking around for something to defend himself with. There was a small fire extinguisher nearby and he snatched it up, hefting it before him like a club. But no one came from the lift and, as the doors slid quietly shut, the farmer lowered his make-shift weapon.

Jo had struggled to her feet and was standing behind him.

'Who was it?' she said, breathlessly.

Tyler merely shook his head.

'You go back to the room, lock yourself in,' he told her. 'Don't open the door for any reason.'

'Where are *you* going?' she demanded.

He dropped the fire extinguisher and headed for the stairs.

'To get us some protection.'

Jo stood for long seconds, listening to his footsteps receding, then she turned and headed up the corridor towards their room, fumbling in her pocket for the key.

She glanced anxiously to her left and right as she walked, watching for the slightest signs of movement from any of the other rooms.

She was in the process of inserting the key in the lock when the lights went out again.

Jo suppressed a scream, relaxing as, a moment later, the power came back on. The thunder rolled ominously around the building and, through the window at the far end of the corridor, she glimpsed jagged barbs of lightning ripping through the thick clouds.

She stepped inside the room and hurriedly locked it.

Across the corridor, the door directly opposite hers opened a fraction.

Carlo Fanducci gripped the Ingram sub-machine gun firmly by its butt and leant against the door. It opened effortlessly and the ex-Mafia man moved silently through the kitchen of the hotel. He strode through the darkness with assurance, his own black shape causing him to melt into it, only his low breathing signalled his presence at all.

He stopped as he heard footsteps in the reception beyond but then he scuttled to the door in time to see Tyler disappear out of the front entrance.

Fanducci smiled. The girl was obviously upstairs alone. Both together or one at a time – it didn't bother him how he had to take them out. He pushed against the door and found himself in reception, behind the desk. The Italian cursed as the light above it flickered again but he flipped open the registration book and ran one nicotine-stained finger down the list of names.

189

He found Jo's name and checked it against the number of her room.

Behind him, the door to the staff room opened slightly.

Fanducci released the safety catch on the Ingram and steadied the weapon in his hand, eyes fixed on the front entrance. On the glass doors which he knew Tyler must use to re-enter the building.

Away to his left, just out of his field of vision, there was movement. Two shadowy figures, hidden by the gloom, moved closer.

Fanducci ducked down behind the desk, just enough to keep himself hidden but to provide a good view of the main doors. Finger resting on the trigger, he waited.

Tyler unlocked the rear door of the landrover and pulled out the nickel plated Purdey. He broke it and thumbed two cartridges into the hungry chambers. As he looked up the sky seemed to grow darker, clouds gathering like predatory birds above him as the thunder and lightning continued their deafening symphony. The farmer stuffed a box of shells into his jacket pocket then, taking care to lock the vehicle once more, he turned and headed back to the hotel. The rain would not hold off for much longer, Tyler reasoned, although a possible downpour was the last thing on his mind as he trekked back towards the hotel. His mind was in a turmoil.

What *had* happened while they were in the lift? Tyler tried to think of a logical explanation but, lately, things in Wakely had begun to defy rationality.

As he approached the front of the hotel, the farmer glanced behind him.

Across the street, hidden by the deep shadows in a shop doorway, he could see two people. Further down the pavement there were others. Even though he couldn't see their faces he knew they were watching him. Tyler paused for a moment, trying to count the dark shapes, but it was useless. They seemed to move and writhe as one, a large undulating mass which defied close scrutiny.

He walked into the hotel, slowing his pace as he entered the darkened reception. For some reason, it seemed even more forbidding than the storm-blasted street.

Tyler saw the staff room door open and he took a step back.

Fanducci, who was already straightening up, saw the farmer move and thought he'd been spotted. The Italian rose from behind the desk like a malevolent Jack-in-the-box, the Ingram pointed towards Tyler. The farmer barely had time to hurl himself behind one of the oak beams near the door when Fanducci opened up. The hit-man squeezed the trigger and the reception was filled with the staccato rattle of automatic fire. Bullets, sprayed in a wide arc, ploughed through wood, plastic and ricocheted off metal. The sound of breaking glass added to the racket as the shells shattered the doors. Shards of crystal sprayed in all directions and Fanducci kept his finger on the trigger until the hammer struck an empty chamber. He swiftly pulled a fresh magazine from his belt and rammed it in, opening up immediately. Spent cartridge cases rained down like brass confetti as he raked the area where Tyler had been standing.

Tyler hugged the beam, the Purdey gripped in one hand, wondering what was happening. The room smelt of gun oil and cordite and a thick haze of smoke was drifting in the air.

The firing suddenly ceased and Tyler took his chance. He leapt out from behind the beam, throwing the shotgun before him, rolling over until he was sheltered behind a couple of chairs. From his vantage point he could see Fanducci reloading.

He could also see two figures who had emerged from the blackness and were almost upon the Italian.

Despite himself, Tyler shouted a warning.

Fanducci spun round and, for a second, he froze.

Both the figures facing him were dressed in the uniform of the hotel. One of them a maid, the other a chef. The latter of the two carried a kitchen knife.

He struck with lightning speed, slicing open Fanducci's left arm from shoulder to elbow. Blood spurted from the rent and the ex-Mafia man yelped in rage and pain, his finger tightening on the trigger of the Ingram. It spat out its stream of hot lead, the impact blasting both figures against the wall. Bullet holes the size of fists gaped in their chests and stomachs and the wall behind them was splattered crimson.

Immediately, Fanducci turned his attention back to Tyler, the machine gun stuttering loudly.

The farmer ducked low but it was useless.

One of the high powered slugs caught him in the shoulder. It slammed him backward, erupting from his back just above the right scapula. He rolled over, trying to fire the Purdey, pressing the butt to his injured shoulder. He screamed in agony as he fired, the stock slamming into the wound as the recoil shook him. The twin barrels erupted, the discharge missing Fanducci. The power of the explosion blew a hole in the reception desk itself and Tyler fumbled in his pocket for fresh cartridges. He could see his assailant emerging from behind the desk, drawing a revolver.

The first of another two figures in the bar reached up and tore the long pike from the wall, levelling it at Fanducci.

The Italian heard the noise and turned, not sure, for the first time in his life, what to do. He knew Tyler was re-loading but he now found he had two more enemies to deal with.

Tyler saw the figures, a man dressed in a dark suit

who held the pike and a girl in her late thirties, her hair hanging loosely to her shoulders. Patches of her scalp were exposed, raw and angry. Both of them were as white as milk. The man's face was dotted with streaming blisters, his cracked lips drawn back to reveal long teeth now brown in colour.

Fanducci heard the loud metallic snap as Tyler successfully closed the Purdey.

Pike or shotgun?

It all seemed to happen at once.

The diseased man thrust forward with the pike, the vicious point burying itself in Fanducci's side just below the armpit, knocking him over. He went down in a bleeding heap, one hand clapped to the gaping wound which the girl leapt for with a speed that amazed Tyler. She was upon the Italian in seconds, her mouth hungrily seeking the bloody gash. He writhed in agony as she tried to tear his shirt free in an attempt to reach the wound now spilling crimson fluid so freely.

Tyler, his shoulder burning with pain, pulled both triggers, watching as the concentrated shot struck the woman in the back. It lifted her off Fanducci, tearing open her back, snapping her spine as it ripped through her torso to burst forth from her chest, destroying one breast and spattering the pike-carrying man with gobbets of viscera.

The man seemed intent on reaching Fanducci however and he drove the pike forward again, putting all his weight behind it. The wicked point punctured the dying man's stomach, pinning him to the floor like a butterfly to a board. He let out a keening wail of agony which was smothered as blood bubbled up his windpipe and filled his mouth.

Tyler managed to get to his feet, holding the shotgun in one hand, the pain in his shoulder gnawing away at him. He ran for the stairs, by-passing the scene of slaughter before him and ignoring the man who had his face buried in the torn hollow of Fanducci's stomach. The farmer could hear liquid slurping from behind him as the man feasted on the Italian's blood.

He stumbled half way up the stairs, the shotgun falling from his grasp. Tyler turned to retrieve it and saw that the man was now following him. And he was moving with surprising speed.

Tyler snatched up the shotgun and stumbled on, not daring to look round.

As he reached the landing he saw Jo standing in the corridor. She'd heard the noise from downstairs and come to investigate.

'Get back,' screamed Tyler.

The diseased man caught up with him as he stopped to load the shotgun.

Tyler's attacker launched himself at the farmer, crashing into him with the force of a steam train. Both of them slammed into the nearby wall, Tyler already weakened from loss of blood. He rolled onto his back, trying to keep the man's hands away from his throat. He felt long nails gouging his flesh as his attacker fastened both hands around his windpipe in a vice-like grip. Tyler could smell the fetid stench from his opponent, he could feel the strength in those hands, see the fire in the eyes.

The farmer struck out with his good hand, driving two fingers into the man's left eye.

He shrieked but merely tightened his grip.

Jo stood mesmerized for a second, then snatched up the shotgun.

'Do it,' croaked Tyler, his face turning the colour of dark grapes.

The American levelled the shotgun until it was pointing at the man's head. He was straddling Tyler now, using all his power to throttle his victim, but he turned his head and opened his mouth in a defiant roar.

Jo saw blood and pieces of intestine sticking to his

long teeth, more of the red fluid and ragged pieces of flesh hanging from the gaping maw which was his mouth.

'Kill him,' Tyler urged, now a second away from unconsciousness.

Jo gritted her teeth and pulled the trigger.

The roar was deafening, the barrels flaming white for devastating seconds.

From such close range the effect of the blast was incredible. The man's head was literally torn from his shoulders. A sticky mess of crimson and grey porridge was splattered against the far wall and the body, the arteries still jetting blood, remained upright for a second before toppling over.

Tyler was on the point of blacking out. He managed to roll away, gazing up through pain-blurred eyes as Jo dropped the gun and fought to keep down the hot vomit which was clawing its way up her throat.

Further up the corridor, unseen by either of them, Mark Bates moved silently from the room opposite Jo's. He paused, then slipped inside her room, closing the door behind him.

He waited

Tyler propped himself up on one elbow, his free hand reaching for the handkerchief in his trouser pocket. He pressed it to the wound in his shoulder, alarmed at how quickly the linen was soaked with blood. He coughed, finding it difficult to swallow. There were several deep indentations in the flesh of his neck from his attacker's powerful hands and the farmer spat as, once again, he felt his throat stinging from the pressure which had been put upon it.

Jo stood against the other wall, trying to look away from the headless remains of Tyler's assailant. The Purdey lay at her feet, the open chambers smoking.

'Jo,' Tyler rasped.

She was milk white, her breath coming in short gasps.

'Jo.' He said it more forcefully and she seemed to regain her senses somewhat. She looked at him, her green eyes a little glazed.

'Help me,' he said, trying to get up.

She finally tore her gaze from the dead man and aided Tyler as he struggled upright. He took his hand from the wounded shoulder and slipped one arm around Jo for support. His right arm and hand felt numb and he kept flexing his fingers to ensure that he still had control over the appendage. He wondered, for one terrifying moment, whether the bullet had severed some vital nerve, but as he continued flexing his fingers he realized that it hadn't.

Outside, the storm continued to rage across the sky and, as the two of them moved slowly towards their room, the lights in the corridor flickered once more.

'What happened?' Jo asked, finally. Her voice low. 'I heard shooting.'

He nodded.

'There was someone down there with a machine gun,' Tyler said.

'One of the townspeople?'

'No.'

'Is he still down there?'

'He's dead. Two of them killed him.' He paused. 'Tore him apart.'

'Oh God,' she murmured. 'That man who attacked you . . .' The sentence trailed off.

'Diseased. And there was a woman with him. I shot her.'

They reached the door of the room and Jo pushed it open. She frowned, flicking at the light switch.

'Dammit, I thought I left this on,' she said. She tried the switch again but there was still no light.

'The power's on,' said Tyler. 'The corridor lights are working.'

'The bulb must have blown,' she surmised.

Tyler walked across to the bed and sat down, pulling off his jacket carefully, wincing as he did so. The blood had congealed thickly in and around the wound, the material of his shirt and jacket stiff with the red substance.

'You'd better come into the bathroom,' said Jo. 'I'll clean that up for you.' She indicated the wound.

Tyler got up again and crossed to the door, grimacing as he turned the handle.

'Let me,' said Jo.

She twisted the knob.

From inside the bathroom, a clawed hand snaked out and gripped her by the wrist.

She screamed uncontrollably as she felt the hairy palm pressing against her flesh, the long nails tearing into her skin. The door was opening, the attacker emerging.

They both saw that it was Mark Bates.

Jo tried to pull away from him but the strength of his grip was too great. Eyes bulging madly, saliva dripping in reeking ribbons from his swollen lips he advanced from the darkness of the bathroom, pulling Jo towards him.

Her screams drummed in Tyler's ears and he looked around for some way to fight this new horror.

Forgetting the pain in his shoulder, he leapt at Bates and all three of them went down in a heap, Bates releasing his grip on Jo. He seemed more interested in the blood which was now flowing once again from Tyler's bullet-torn shoulder. The farmer may have been injured but he fought with a new-found strength born of desperation. He grabbed Bates by the hair, stepping back in horror as a huge tuft of it came away in his hand to reveal bloodied scalp beneath. But his reactions

197

were fast and he drove his knee up hard into Bates' face. The impact sent the man reeling. He crashed against the open bathroom door, slipping on the floor inside. Tyler was upon him in an instant, driving kicks into his torso, almost shouting in triumph as he heard ribs cracking.

Tyler dragged Bates to his feet and forced him over the bath, bending his back at an impossible angle.

Despite his wound, the farmer was still too heavy for Bates who clawed impotently at his opponent.

Tyler, his face a mask of rage and fear, brought one forearm crashing down on Bates' throat.

There was a sound like splintering wood and the man's spine broke.

Tyler remained lying across the body, pressing down ever harder as if he feared Bates would get up if he released his hold but, finally, he slid off. The corpse dropped to the floor with a forlorn thump.

Jo stood frozen in the doorway, unable to speak.

The farmer hauled himself upright, looking down at the body of his attacker. Bates' eyes were open and staring, the pupils now dilated and glazed. His face, like that of the man further down the corridor, was covered in numerous large blisters, some of which had burst and were weeping watery pus. Others, just forming, appeared like bulges beneath the pale skin.

'Let's get out of here,' said Tyler.

'But where are we going to go?' Jo asked, exasperatedly. 'There could be more of them outside. We can't leave the hotel.' There were tears in her eyes and the farmer could see that she was having trouble holding them back. He pulled her close to him, the burning pain in his shoulder having lessened somewhat.

'Vic, what are we going to do?' she whimpered.

'It's OK,' he said. 'We'll be OK.'

He wasn't sure if he was reassuring Jo or himself.

She looked up at him, wiping the tears away angrily. 'I'm sorry,' she said, 'coming apart on you, like this.'

198

He said nothing.

Jo laughed sardonically.

'I wasn't this scared when the Mafia were after me.'

Tyler brushed a tear from her cheek.

'We'll move to another room for tonight. Barricade the door if we have to.'

'What about the bodies?' she asked.

'We can't do anything about them until morning.'

He led her across to the room where Bates had been hiding and was relieved to find the key in the lock.

'I've got to get the gun,' he said.

'We ought to check on the guy downstairs. The one who shot you.'

'Right. You stay here. Lock this door and . . .'

She cut him short.

'No way. You're not leaving me alone again. I'm going with you.'

Tyler didn't argue. They walked down the corridor to where Jo had dropped the shotgun. Tyler stooped and retrieved it, breaking it with difficulty, the pain in his shoulder intensifying. The American took it from him and thumbed in two cartridges. Both of them were careful to avoid looking at the body of the headless attacker. They made their way cautiously down the stairs, pausing momentarily as the lights flickered again and a deafening clap of thunder shook the building. Tyler had the Purdey cradled over the crook of his good arm, his finger resting gently on the fore-trigger.

As they emerged into the reception, Jo saw the bodies.

The diseased woman, nearly cut in half by the shotgun blast.

The two staff members, riddled with bullets from the sub-machine gun which lay nearby.

And Fanducci.

He was lying spread-eagled, arms outstretched in the pattern of a crucifixion. His stomach and chest had been ripped open and what remained of his intestines and other internal organs were scattered over the blood-soaked carpet around him. The .357 lay close by, the hammer still pulled back.

'Oh my God,' muttered Jo.

Tyler crossed to the eviscerated corpse and, reining back his revulsion, began fumbling inside the dead man's jacket. The stench which rose from the body was overpowering and Tyler was forced to pause for a second to suck in a reasonably unpolluted breath. Resuming with his task he finally discovered a wallet in the Italian's inside pocket. Tyler wiped the blood from it and flipped the slim leather folder open.

It contained about fifty pounds, mostly in fives, some dollar bills stuffed at the back, a receipt for something and a few other inconsequential pieces of paper.

The I.D. card fell out almost by accident.

Tyler picked it up, looking first at the slim plastic strip.

'Jo,' he said. 'Look at this.'

She appeared at his side, trying to keep her eyes off the riven corpse. Jo read aloud the details on the card.

'Carlo Fanducci, Number 23958. Born 1930.'

And below that was the all too familiar logo with the red and silver initials joined at the curve of the C.

'Vanderburg Chemicals.'

Jo looked at the body then at Tyler.

'Jesus H. Christ,' she murmured.

'Someone at Vanderburg wants us dead,' Tyler observed. 'Why I wonder?'

'Whoever it is thinks we're important enough to go to the trouble of hiring a hit man,' she murmured, looking across at the discarded .357 and the Ingram.

'And we don't know if he's the only one,' the farmer said, nodding towards Fanducci's body. 'When they find out this one's dead they might send others after us.' He slipped the I.D. card into his jacket pocket and turned to pick up the nearby Magnum. The pistol felt heavy in his fist and he passed it to Jo.

'Have you ever used one of these things?' he asked.

'I'll learn,' she told him.

The farmer put one hand to his throbbing shoulder.

'We've wasted enough time,' he said. 'We must get inside Vanderburg Chemicals.'

'Not with your shoulder in that state,' she protested.

'We've got to,' he snapped.

There was a long silence, their eyes locked, neither flinching.

'We've still got five or six hours before daybreak,' said Tyler.

Jo nodded slowly.

'Let's get you patched up first,' she said, wearily.

Outside, there was a whiplash crack of lightning and, in the momentary brilliance, they both glimpsed figures moving in the blackness beyond – writhing and moving like monstrous automatons.

And then there was only darkness again.

Thirty-three

Tyler lay on the bed, watching as Jo cut away his bloodied shirt with a pair of scissors. As she pulled at the gore-stiffened material it stuck to the ragged edges of the wound and pulled some tiny slivers of skin away with it. The farmer winced.

'Sorry,' said Jo, picking up the wet towel which lay beside her. She cleaned the rust-coloured area around the bullet hole, asking Tyler to lean forward while she attended to the exit hole which was slightly larger than her thumb. 'You were lucky,' she told him. 'The bullet couldn't have hit you direct, it must have ricocheted. The deflection took most of the power out of it otherwise it would have taken your arm off.' She wiped away the blood from the exit wound, apologizing once again as she accidentally pulled away a piece of ragged flesh. 'I don't think there's anything broken, it went clean through.'

He worked it around tentatively, making a fist of his right hand as he did so.

'How does it feel?' she asked.

'Sore,' he told her.

They looked into each other's eyes for long moments, then Jo wadded up a clean handkerchief and pressed it to the wound. She did the same at the back, securing the makeshift dressing with lengths of sheet which she had taken from the bed in their room. It lay, torn up, in the corner.

'Tie it tight,' the farmer told her.

When she'd finished he lay back again, one large hand reaching for hers. She looked tired, her mascara had run in places, her hair, normally so lustrous, was matted with blood and her jeans were spattered with dried gore.

She looked down at herself and sighed.

'I feel like shit,' she said. 'I'm going to take a shower.'

He nodded, watching as she walked wearily to the bathroom. Tyler could hear the sputter as the water began to flow from the shower spray. He picked up the .357 which lay beside him and inspected the weapon before finally laying it on the bedside table. The shotgun, together with a dozen or so cartridges, lay beside the bed.

The farmer looked at the I.D. card which bore Fanducci's name and photo and also that red and silver

VC. Their suspicions about Vanderburg Chemicals had obviously been right and also, doubtless, their fears about Geoffrey Anderson. If someone at the chemical plant was willing to kill *them* then Anderson had most probably suffered the ultimate fate. Was the secret of the feed *that* important? Important enough to kill for? Obviously it was, he reasoned. And how many of the townspeople had died or were dying? How many of the people he had known all his life had been transformed into savages by the effects of the contaminated feed? In the past few weeks Tyler had seen his entire world crumble.

He dropped the card and swung himself off the bed, padding across to the door of the bathroom.

Jo had not bothered to pull the shower curtain and the farmer ran appreciative eyes over her tanned body as she stood naked beneath the spurting shower. He watched as she soaped her hands, running them over her breasts and neck, shaking her head to allow the water to run through her hair.

'You're a very beautiful woman,' he said.

Jo turned quickly.

'You scared me,' she said, not attempting to hide herself. 'I didn't know you were standing there.'

'Sorry,' he said, smiling.

She turned off the shower spray and stepped out onto the mat, water dripping from her hair. Tyler noticed how it glistened invitingly on the tightly curled mound beneath her navel. He walked across to her and pulled her close to him, feeling the water on his skin.

Jo shuddered in his arms, her hands fumbling with his trousers which she hurriedly unfastened. Tyler stepped out of them and they stood naked, facing each other, her left hand gently squeezing his penis. It began to stiffen. They kissed and she felt his hands stroking the wet skin of her back, pausing there a second before gliding to her breasts. He kneaded the firm globes, bending his head towards her nipples which had risen to red peaks. She gasped as she felt his tongue licking around them, flicking water away in the process.

She knelt slowly, her hand still on his hard shaft and Tyler ran his hands through the silky slickness of her wet hair. She took one testicle in her mouth and sucked gently before transferring her attention to the other one, then she moved back slightly, fastening her lips around the bulging purple head of his organ.

Her own fluid was flowing now, mingling with the water from the shower and she slid one hand between her own legs as she sucked Tyler's penis, teasing the nub of her clitoris until it too stiffened and grew erect.

Jo stood up slowly, a strand of saliva dripping from the end of Tyler's organ. He felt her hard nipples brush his belly and then his chest as she straightened up and his hand replaced hers in that most delicate area between her legs. She felt only liquid pleasure there, her excitement growing stronger as he pushed two fingers inside her.

Jo pressed her pelvis hard against him, bucking hard on those fingers which probed so deeply. She slipped one leg around his, resting herself on the hard muscle of his thigh, grinding herself against it.

He realized what she was doing and bent his knee slightly, gripping her buttocks in order to add to her movements. The water from the shower dripped onto his thigh but it was her warm moistness which lathered his flesh. Her breathing became more rapid, her movements more frenetic and Tyler held her as tight as he could.

He slid one more finger into her slippery cleft, running the index finger of his other hand over the smooth skin of her back.

She pressed her head against his chest and speeded up her movements, her entire body shaking as the orgasm swept through her. Tyler gripped her tight, still moving his fingers inside her, pressing his thumb to her clitoris, prolonging the moment of pleasure for her until she cried out huskily. She muttered something under her breath and kissed him, now moving slowly against his hard thigh. Finally she pulled free, her face flushed, the upper part of her body glowing pink.

Immediately she began stroking his throbbing penis, tracing the outline of the bulging veins with her long nail. She raised herself onto her toes, allowing him to seek and then find the entrance to her burning sex with the head of his organ. He slid into her and she stepped back, taking the weight against one wall as he moved inside her and, from deep within, she felt that wonderful glow blazing in every fibre of her body.

Their mouths locked, tongues entwining, stirring the warm wetness within.

Tyler gripped her waist and began to thrust urgently. As he reached his climax, Jo felt renewed contractions between her legs and, for the second time, she was enveloped by the most powerful of physical explosions.

They clung to each other for a long moment, then Tyler gently withdrew.

Jo picked up a towel which was lying nearby and began to dry herself.

They both changed into fresh clothes, Tyler slipping on a black shirt, grunting in pain as he pulled it over the makeshift bandage. He clenched his fist, relieved that the numbness and burning sensation had diminished considerably. Then, he checked that the guns were loaded.

Jo glanced at her watch.

'Ready?' he asked.

She nodded.

They had four hours of darkness to hide them. The drive to Vanderburg Chemicals would take them about fifteen minutes.

Thirty-four

The grass was wet beneath his feet and, more than once, Tyler almost slipped over. Hs shot out a hand to steady himself, grasping a nearby tree branch. The wire cutters fell from his belt and he cursed under his breath.

'It's OK,' Jo whispered, stooping before him. 'I've got them.'

She handed the implement back to the farmer who stuck it in his jacket pocket along with the handful of large crocodile clips he'd taken from an electrical store near the centre of Wakely. Jo held a long coil of insulated wire which came from the same source.

They paused, hidden by the enveloping darkness, gazing at the tall wire fence which confronted them. Every fifty yards there were large spotlamps but between these radiant oases the desert of night was impenetrable. Tyler looked to his right and left then, satisfied that nothing was moving, he scuttled towards the fence. Forced to lie on his belly, he could feel the wetness soaking through his clothes. Jo crouched beside him and hastily wound lengths of wire around the ends of the crocodile clips, attaching the mouths to the fence. Then she watched as he slid the wire cutters from his pocket and fastened the sharp jaws on the fence between the crocodile clips.

The wire was thick and it took all of Tyler's considerable strength to cut through it. Fresh pain began to gnaw at his shoulder but he continued with his task, cutting a hole big enough for them to crawl through. If there had been an alarm attached, it had not been activated. Perhaps, Tyler thought, the knowledge that over 60,000 volts coursed through the protective barrier was deterrent enough for most intruders. Not so for Jo and himself.

He finished cutting and wriggled through, turning

on his stomach to help Jo. They both straightened up, Jo brushing the moisture from her clothes as best she could. Tyler stuck the wire cutters back in his belt, his hand brushing against the .357 as he did. The weapon was fully loaded although he doubted his ability to use it if the need arose. Shotguns were one thing, high-powered pistols another.

They both squinted through the gloom, their eyes picking out the massive bulk of the Vanderburg buildings about two hundred yards ahead of them. The ground between them and the buildings was open and Tyler was aware of the spotlights. He ducked low, pulling Jo down with him and, hunched over, they ran as fast as they were able.

They were half-way towards the nearest building when they heard the dog bark.

As if at a given signal, both of them froze.

The barking was close, perhaps fifty or sixty yards to their right. It was coming from the direction of the fence.

Beneath the light from one of the lamps, a Security guard, clad in the familiar Vanderburg dark blue, stood and lit a cigarette. With his other hand he kept a firm hold on the leash of a large black Alsatian. The animal was turned towards Jo and Tyler, its loud barks splitting the stillness.

The guard seemed to pay it no heed. He jerked on the lead and wandered on, casting just a cursory glance in their direction.

The noise the dog was making gradually receded.

'Come on,' Tyler whispered and they continued their sprint, finally coming to a halt against a cold stone wall.

Both stood panting for long seconds, surveying the scene before them.

The gigantic bulk of the main building faced them across a tarmac area about eighty feet wide. There were lights on in one or two of the rooms but most merely reflected the dull glint of the stars above. The main entrance beckoned but Tyler hesitated, sucking in a troubled breath as he saw two Security men walk across the tarmac, one of them holding a Dobermann pinscher by a thick chain. The men were chatting happily, oblivious of the two onlookers.

Jo swallowed hard, frowning when she saw them come to a halt outside the main doors.

'Shit,' she murmured. 'What now?'

Tyler didn't answer, his gaze was fixed on the men and the dog which, he noticed, had pricked up its ears and was looking back and forth. He motioned for Jo to move back further into the shadows.

The dog looked in their direction, froze for a moment, then barked loudly three times.

The farmer slid the sheath knife from its leather scabbard and gripped the handle tightly.

'Have they seen us?' Jo whispered, unable to see the Security men from where she was.

'I don't know,' Tyler answered but he had his suspicions.

The dog continued to bark, straining hard on its chain now. The guard who held it, a tall thin individual, bent and released it and, immediately, the dog bounded towards Tyler and Jo.

'Don't make a sound,' said Tyler, crouching down as the dog drew nearer. He held the knife steady and waited.

The Dobermann came hurtling around the corner of the building, its nose full of scent, but it skidded to a temporary halt in the darkness. The few seconds' respite was all Tyler needed. He threw himself at the animal, raking the knife down its side until it struck bone. He grabbed for its muzzle, trying to avoid the sharp teeth and also to shut the creature up. He succeeded in neither task.

Strong jaws clamped around his forearm for fleeting

moments and, as he struck upwards with the knife a second time, the Dobermann let out a high-pitched wail.

Tyler pushed the lifeless carcass aside, his ears detecting the sound of running feet as the Security men approached.

They, like the dog, came around the corner and paused as they were met by a solid wall of blackness.

The farmer caught the first one across the forehead with the wire cutters, the blow felling him immediately. The second man turned to run but Tyler ran after him, kicking his legs away. The man went down heavily on the tarmac, cracking his head on the wet surface. Yet still he tried to rise and the farmer was forced to drive a boot into the man's face to immobilize him completely. The guard flopped onto his back like a beached fish, blood running from his shattered nose.

'Search them,' said Jo, moving across to the prone bodies, rummaging through their pockets. She found a bunch of keys in the breast pocket of the taller man.

'C-5 report.'

The metallic voice cut through the stillness like a razor blade.

'C-5.'

There was a two-way radio lying nearby.

'Bill, if you're having a piss just say so will you?'

Tyler looked first at Jo and then at the two-way.

'C-5 come in,' the voice demanded. 'Bill, for fuck's sake, what are you playing at?'

Tyler picked up the hand-set.

'C-5' he said, praying that the static on the set would be sufficient to disguise his voice.

'What the bloody hell are you doing down there? Why didn't you answer?' the voice demanded.

'Sorry,' Tyler said, cautiously.

'Is your sector clear?' the voice asked.

'Yes.'

There was a long silence. Jo and Tyler exchanged worried glances.

'Sector is clear,' Tyler repeated, trying to hide the tension in his voice.

There was a harsh chuckle.

'You've been humping that fucking dog again haven't you?' the voice said, merrily.

Tyler gripped the set tightly.

'Sector is clear,' he repeated.

'Yeah, right, I heard you first time. Check back in an hour.' The two-way went dead.

The farmer breathed an audible sigh of relief and wiped his forehead with the back of his hand. Taking another look at the motionless guards, he and Jo crept through the shadows towards the main building.

The massive edifice towered above them, a mass of concrete and glass which looked as impregnable as a fortress. Tyler wondered how they were going to get inside. The entrances, he reasoned, would be alarmed. They couldn't break in without alerting every guard on the site. He glanced behind him. The two unconscious men weren't going to stay out forever. He and Jo didn't have much time.

The farmer reached for the small two-way which he'd slipped into his pocket. He held it before him for a second, his finger poised over the 'ON' button.

'What the hell are you doing, Vic?' Jo gaped, watching as he switched it on.

He waved a hand for her to be quiet.

'C-5,' he said.

Jo shook her head, glancing around anxiously.

The radio crackled.

'C-5' Tyler repeated. 'I have a request.'

'Come in, C-5,' said the metallic voice.

Tyler swallowed hard.

'Intruder sighted,' he said.

'Where?' the voice demanded.

'Main building. Request permission to search.'

'Do you need any help?'

'No,' said the farmer, perhaps a little too quickly.

The radio went silent again.

'Come in,' he said.

Silence.

A bead of perspiration popped onto his forehead.

'Come in,' he said again.

'The alarms are off, the voice told him. 'Report back immediately if you find anyone.'

He flicked the set off and proceeded towards the main door, followed by Jo. They found that the doors opened easily. Both of them walked into the reception area of Vanderburg Chemicals. The shadows swallowed them up. Jo could feel her heart beating faster as they moved quickly but quietly towards one of the many corridors which grew, spoke-like, from the central hub of the main reception.

'Where do we start?' whispered Tyler, exasperatedly.

'What about the laboratories?' Jo offered.

He nodded.

'If we can find them.'

They walked the length of the corridor, each door which faced them was firmly locked. Tyler suggested searching the first floor. They found the stairs and began ascending, stepping as lightly as possible on the cold stone.

'C-5 report.'

The metallic voice sounded thunderous in the silence of the stair-well.

Tyler grabbed for the hand-set and switched it on.

'C-5, any sign of intruder?'

'No,' said the farmer.

'Check the second floor, if any one *is* inside make sure you stop them before they get to E-1.'

'E-1?' Tyler sounded vague.

Jo shot him an anxious glance, then started up the

stairs to the second floor. He tried to hold her back but she was already disappearing through a set of fire doors at the top of the steps. He followed and found himself in a corridor, at the far end there was a large oak door. Jo was in the process of turning the handle.

'Stop them reaching E-1,' the voice repeated.

'Check,' Tyler snapped.

'I'm going to send more units to help you.'

'No,' the farmer blurted.

There was an ominous silence.

'C-5 identify. Number and code name.'

Jo pushed open the door of the room.

The radio rasped in Tyler's hand again.

'Identify. Number and code name.'

He held the hand-set for long seconds, then hurled it to one side. It smashed against the wall.

'Jo, come on, we've got to get out,' he yelled but she was gazing around the room in amazement.

Computer terminals, filing cabinets and all manner of blue-prints vied for space in the large room which was completely windowless. Thick ring binders were stacked as high as a man in places where they wouldn't fit on the wooden shelves. There were half a dozen large oak desks in the room too. Jo crossed to one of the manilla files laid out on the nearest desk and flipped it open:

BIO-SYNTHETIC MUTATION

She read the top sheet to herself, reaching for another file.

'Jo, for God's sake, this place is going to be swarming with Security men in a minute,' Tyler told her.

'But Vic, it's here,' she said, grabbing up another file headed:

PROTEIN CONSTRUCTION

'Everything we need is here.'

'Come on,' he snarled, gripping her arm, pulling her forcibly from the room.

They ran back down the stairs, the far off sounds of dogs drawing nearer.

'Not the front way,' said Tyler as they reached the reception. He pushed her towards another corridor which ran off to the right. They hurtled along it, the farmer throwing his weight against a flimsy wooden door which barred their way. The impact nearly tore it from the hinges and, as he dashed through, Tyler was thankful that he had hit it with his good shoulder. The wound in his other one was throbbing anyway.

They reached a window and he flung it open. Moist air rushed in and Tyler helped Jo through, then scrambled after her.

The Security men were in the reception by now and two of them let their dogs loose. Confused by the mixture of scents, one ran up the stairs, the other scampered towards the room where the intruders had been.

Outside, Tyler and Jo jumped to the ground, Jo falling on the slick surface but the farmer hauled her upright and they were running again. He prayed that they would make it to the fence.

Lights were beginning to flash on inside the main Vanderburg building now and, from somewhere in the darkness, they heard a siren, its strident wailing filling their ears.

Jo was gasping for breath but she found new strength as she saw the fence drawing closer. Tyler urged her on, glancing around to see dark uniformed men following them. He made sure that she scrambled through the hole in the fence then crawled after her. They got to their feet and rushed into the trees, welcomed by the enveloping darkness. Not until they reached the landrover did they stop running. Tyler wrenched open the door and leapt behind the wheel, starting the engine. Jo slumped into the passenger seat, thrown back as Tyler stepped hard on the accelerator and the vehicle shot forward like some kind of projectile. He spun the wheel, guiding it onto the road back into Wakely, glancing in the rear-view mirror to see if anyone was following.

They weren't.

'Vic, it was there in those files,' Jo gasped, trying to catch her breath. 'I'm sure that was the proof we needed.'

He nodded.

'The Vanderburg scientists *must* have conducted tests. They *knew* the feed was harmful but they went ahead with the project anyway,' she said.

Tyler didn't ease his foot off the pedal, not even when the needle on the speedometer touched sixty.

'Vic, are you listening to me?' she demanded. 'What are we going to do?'

'What we should have done in the first place,' he said. 'Tomorrow morning we'll search the town, see if there's anyone else unaffected by the virus. Then, we'll get out. Leave Wakely.'

Jo nodded.

'Then we'll call every fucking newspaper and TV station we can get hold of and see what they make of Vanderburg's little game.' There was a hard edge to his voice.

Jo sat back in her seat and closed her eyes. She knew she should sleep, she needed to but her mind was too full of ideas, overflowing with thoughts. And fears?

She opened her eyes again and gazed out into the night.

In two hours it would be daylight.

Thirty-five

'Shouldn't we bury them?'

Jo ran a distasteful eye over the pile of corpses which faced her. She had helped Tyler drag them out into the car park of the hotel earlier, now she stood gazing at the untidy heap of bodies. Fanducci's gutted corpse lay face down on top of the others. There were six, counting his.

'We can't take any chances,' said Tyler, reaching for the can of petrol which he'd found amongst many in a shed to the rear of the hotel. There was a cellar beneath, approachable also by a service entrance inside the hotel itself. While he'd been down there he'd discovered a great deal of canned and dried food, hundreds of bottles of wine and a small generator which, he guessed, acted as a source of auxiliary power should anything happen to the mains supply. He began to splash the amber liquid over the corpses.

'We've got to destroy any traces of the bacteria,' he told her, the smell of petrol mingling with that of putrescent flesh. 'If Hawley said it lived on in the dead animals there's every reason to believe it'll live on in the victims.'

Jo shivered, despite the fact that she wore a thick sweatshirt. The watery sun provided little warmth and the early morning dew still lay like a glistening cowl over the ground.

It was 9.17 a.m.

Tyler emptied the last of the petrol over the bodies, then tossed the can onto the make-shift pyre with them. He stepped back, striking a match. For long seconds he hesitated, the sightless eyes of Mark Bates pinning him in a reproachful stare, then the farmer tossed the match onto the pile of corpses.

There was a loud whump as the petrol went up, the

215

flames eagerly devouring the still forms. Like a collection of obscene effigies on Guy Fawkes night they blazed, the acrid stench of scorched flesh now filling the air, rising with the thick black plume of smoke which billowed from the mound.

Tyler touched his right shoulder, rotating it slightly to remove some of the stiffness. He felt Jo's hand grasp his and he looked at her.

'Are you all right?' he asked.

She nodded, her eyes still fixed on the burning pile of cadavers.

They watched the greedy flames for a moment longer, then turned and headed back to the landrover. They both climbed in, Tyler checking the three shotguns which lay in the back of the vehicle. He had the .357 jammed into his belt.

They looked at one another and there was steel in that gaze. Tyler started the engine.

The streets of Wakely were deserted, the sound of the landrover's engine seeming louder than usual in the stillness. Tyler drove slowly, looking to both sides as well as ahead, not even sure what he was looking for.

'Vic, over there.'

Jo's shout startled him and he stepped hard on the brake. She was pointing at something to the left of them. They both got out of the landrover, Tyler picking up the Franchi as he did so. He left the engine idling and walked slowly across to the shapeless thing which was hunched in the nearby shop doorway.

It was a man. He was squatting, knees drawn up to hide his bowed head, arms dangling limply on either side of him.

Jo looked first at the man and then at Tyler who had not taken his eyes from the motionless figure. He approached within five feet, ensuring that Jo stayed behind him.

The man did not move.

The farmer worked the pump action of the shotgun, chambering a round. He took a step closer and prodded the man with the end of the barrel, one finger hooked around it. Just in case.

The body toppled sideways, face to the sky.

His throat had been cut.

There were three or four ragged tears in the skin, each about the size of a child's fist. Lying close by was a broken bottle, its razor sharp edges stained with dark fluid. And yet, around the body itself, despite the savagery of the cuts, there was little or no blood. Only the front of the man's shirt was stained crimson.

Tyler remarked on it to Jo.

'Maybe the rain washed it away,' she suggested.

Tyler didn't speak. He looked closely at the gaping wounds, noticing a darker, purplish discoloration around them. Like bruising. He stood up.

'Why is there no blood?' he pondered aloud.

Tyler and Jo walked back to the landrover and he drove off, keeping to a steady fifteen as they cruised the deserted streets.

'Maybe all the unaffected people have already left,' Jo suggested.

Tyler shook his head.

'The bloke back there with his throat cut, he wasn't infected. There must be others. Not everyone eats red meat.'

'So where are they?' Jo wanted to know.

'They're probably frightened.'

'I know the feeling,' she muttered.

There were more bodies.

Two of them lay prone in the middle of the road. A man and a small child. The man had been stabbed, his ripped shirt revealing numerous wounds in his chest and stomach.

The child, a boy about five, had been bludgeoned to

death. His head was a shattered ruin. There were pieces of skin and fragments of bone close by, indicating that he'd been killed by having his head slammed repeatedly into the tarmac of the road.

Once again, there was a noticeable lack of blood around the bodies and also, Tyler noticed, the discoloration which tinged the extremities of each wound.

Neither victim was diseased.

Flies swarmed frenziedly over both corpses, entering each orifice eagerly and the farmer watched in disgust as two of them crawled over the child's blackened tongue.

As before he remarked on the lack of blood.

'What are you thinking, Vic?' asked the American.

'I don't know what I'm thinking,' he said. 'If I told you you'd probably laugh.'

'Try me.'

'From what I saw of those infected people last night and what we've found today, I think this disease forces its victims to drink blood.'

He waited for her to say something but she didn't.

'With wounds like these,' he indicated the stabbed man, 'there'd be blood all over the place, the same as that other bloke we found. He'd bleed for ages with a cut throat. There wasn't enough rain last night to wash *that* much blood away.'

'The piglets at the cattle market,' said Jo, 'they attacked the sow. They could have been trying to drink her blood. What we thought was cannibalism was blood-lust.'

There was a long silence.

'Vampires,' Jo murmured, softly.

Tyler didn't hear her. His eyes were fixed on the wounds on the dead man's torso but, more particularly, on the dark areas around the gashes. The flesh looked as if it had been sucked; the wound milked of its

218

crimson fluid by hungry mouths. The very thought disgusted him.

They both stood there looking at the bodies for a moment longer, then Tyler turned and headed back to the landrover.

Jo hesitated, looking first at the corpses and then at the windows of the shops which surrounded them. She wondered what was waiting inside.

The thought made her shudder and she hurried back to the waiting vehicle.

'Let's try Dan Hawley,' said Tyler.

Jo counted half a dozen more bodies on the drive to the vet's surgery. Tyler merely slowed the landrover down as they passed. Neither of them bothered to get out and inspect the corpses.

The farmer finally brought the vehicle to a halt in Hawley's driveway. He clambered down, taking care to bring the shotgun with him, looking up at the drawn curtains of the building as he approached it. Jo was close beside him, her heels clicking noisily on the concrete approach.

Tyler knocked on the door, a little surprised when it swung open at the first impact. He held the shotgun across his chest and stepped into the reception. The curtains downstairs were open, the weak sun lighting their way as they moved cautiously into the surgery itself.

'Dan,' Tyler called, his voice echoing off the white walls.

There was no answer.

Jo paused in the reception and picked up the phone.

It was dead. Not even the hiss of static on the line.

Tyler nudged open the surgery door and found that the blinds were down, the room having been plunged into stifling gloom.

219

He muttered under his breath as he surveyed the mess before him.

The surgery had been wrecked. Instrument trolleys were turned over, specimen jars smashed, filing cabinets upended. Glass crunched beneath his boots as he walked further into the dusky room. The pungent odour of formaldehyde was strong in the air. Scalpels, probes, saws and all manner of other instruments lay on the floor, combining with ripped and discarded pieces of paper to form a chaotic jigsaw of destruction.

Jo joined him in the room, her eyes widening in shocked surprise. While Tyler moved around the surgery, the American opened the door which led through from the main room into the living quarters beyond.

She found herself in a hallway which, in turn, led through into a spacious living room.

The scene in there was the same. The sofa was upended, a large bookcase had been pulled over, spilling its load on the carpet. Even a fish tank, once a proud possession, had been torn from its base and hurled across the room. There were pieces of broken glass everywhere and, amidst the shattered crystal and tiny stones, lay the stiffened bodies of tropical fish. The room smelt damp. Jo passed through it into a kitchen and from there to the stairs.

She climbed them cautiously, ears alert for the slightest sound of movement. She reached the dim landing and headed for the door closest to her.

She paused in the doorway.

The room had been devastated. As with those downstairs, it looked as if someone had systematically gone through the house and destroyed everything they could lay their hands on. Jo moved cautiously into the room, noticing that several china figures lay smashed at her feet. She bent to inspect one.

Behind her, the door of the wardrobe opened slightly.

220

Jo held the tiny figure in her hand, shaking her head gently. It seemed as if nothing had escaped the fury.

The hinges on the wardrobe door creaked loudly and Jo spun round.

She saw the knife as it was lifted high above her.

When he heard the scream, Tyler burst from the surgery, not even pausing in the wrecked sitting room. He blundered up the stairs, shotgun held at the ready.

The sight which met him caused him to freeze.

Jo was sitting on the edge of the bed and, beside her, sobbing uncontrollably, was Mandy Potter. She still held the long knife in her shaking hand.

'What happened?' Tyler asked, softly, lowering the gun.

Mandy looked up to see him. She dropped the knife, using both hands to wipe away the tears which were streaming down her cheeks.

'Mandy,' he said. 'The surgery. Did Dan do that? Did he wreck the place?'

Mandy nodded.

'He tried to kill me,' she blubbered, revealing several deep indentations near the top of her arm. They looked like claw marks. Her blouse was ripped and there were flecks of blood on it. Her throat too bore scratches and there was a nasty gash on her left cheek.

'I stabbed him,' she said, her voice a harsh whisper. 'I don't know if I killed him. He ran away. She began to cry once more and Jo slipped a comforting arm around her shoulder. 'He was like an animal. Mad.'

They stood over her for long moments, Tyler watching as she removed her glasses and wiped them on the sheet.

'I'm sorry,' she said, holding up the knife. 'I could have killed you.'

'I'd have done the same thing,' said Jo, smiling.

221

'We've got to leave here, Mandy,' said Tyler. 'Will you be all right?'

'You're not leaving me alone,' she gasped.

He shook his head.

'I mean all of us, we've got to leave Wakely. Now.'

Mandy nodded.

While they waited downstairs, she cleaned herself up and changed into some fresh clothes. When she joined them in the hall way she looked more assured. Stronger.

'I'm OK,' she said, sniffing slightly.

The three of them walked out, back into the welcoming glow of the sunlight.

'What's happening?' asked Mandy as they climbed into the landrover. 'First the animals, now the people?'

Jo explained briefly what was going on. Mandy sat in silence, not even speaking when she'd finished. She just nodded.

'Are we the only ones left?' she asked, finally.

'That's what we've been trying to find out,' said Tyler. 'So far you're the only uncontaminated person we've found alive. The others have been killed.'

He swung the landrover around a corner, narrowly avoiding the body of a young woman which lay by the kerb.

Mandy looked briefly at it, then closed her eyes.

'Where are we going?' she asked.

'To the nearest big city,' Tyler informed her. 'We've got to let people outside Wakely know what's going on. Someone's got to stop it before it spreads.'

The streets seemed to crowd in on them as they drove, the houses glowering down like watching gargoyles, the sun reflecting off windows which glinted like hundreds of blind eyes.

'There,' shouted Jo, pointing towards a small group of shops nearby.

Tyler slammed on the brakes, the vehicle skidding slightly.

'What is it?' he asked.

'I saw something move in one of those buildings,' said Jo.

Tyler reached for one of the shotguns, his hand closing around the Franchi.

Four buildings confronted them: a small supermarket, a newsagent's, a confectioner's and a butcher's shop.

'Stay here,' Tyler said to Mandy. He and Jo climbed out of the landrover and approached the supermarket. The doors were closed but when Tyler struck at them with the butt of the shotgun they swung open. No alarms went off. Total silence prevailed.

It was relatively light inside the supermarket, the sun cast bright rays through the large windows at the front of the building.

Jo wrinkled her nose. The place smelt of bad food. The fridges were off and some of the frozen produce had begun to rot, as had the fresh vegetables. She passed a pile of apples which were now brown and putrescent. Flies swarmed hungrily over them.

There was a large storeroom at the back of the building but they found it empty. Tyler stood in the middle of the stacked boxes and cans of food and shook his head.

'I know I saw something,' said Jo before he could speak. 'Maybe whoever it was is afraid to come out.'

'Let's try the other buildings,' he said.

The newsagent's was empty. So was the confectioner's.

They moved on to the butcher's.

'There has to be someone here, I know I saw them,' Jo insisted. He nodded and pushed the door.

It was locked.

Without hesitation, the farmer put his weight against the glass and wood partition and drove his shoulder into it. The door flew open, the glass rattling in the frame as it crashed back on its hinges. The blinds were down so Tyler reached for the nearby light switch, waiting until the fluorescents overhead had sputtered into life before walking inside the shop. Both of them moved cautiously, having learnt to fear darkened rooms over the last few days. Now the only sound was the intermittent clicking of Jo's heels on the wooden floor and the steady hum of a fan. It must, Tyler assumed, be on the same circuit as the lights.

The shop itself was large, the two long glass counters forming an 'L' shape. The counters were full of display trays bearing different types of meat. Jo shuddered involuntarily as she looked at the array of beef, lamb and offal, thinking how much damage food like that had done to the residents of Wakely. Once more, there was a smell of decay, a sickly sweet odour which made her wince. Maggots writhed frenziedly on a piece of rotten steak.

Tyler walked behind the counter, touching a couple of discarded knives as he passed a large wooden chopping board. It was stained darkly with blood.

At the back of the shop was the freezer, a large room almost as big as the shop itself, where the carcasses of countless animals hung from meat hooks. There were also several large white fridges at the far end of the room and another work bench where the joints were actually prepared.

There was a man lying on the wooden surface.

His arms were dangling limply from either side of the bench and there was a meat cleaver embedded in his chest. His throat had been sliced open – probably, Tyler thought, with the large knife which lay on the floor beneath him. Apart from a small puddle of frozen blood around the man's head, there was little of the crimson fluid to be found.

'Vic, look,' Jo whispered, pointing to one of the fridges.

Several long slicks of blood had dribbled from the top of one fridge, freezing half-way down.

Tyler crossed to it and hooked two fingers under the lid, the shotgun lowered.

He flipped it open.

The fridge was empty.

Jo shrugged and opened the next one.

The man inside seemed to sit up and grab her as if he possessed some uncanny form of radar. He snatched handfuls of her hair in his clawed hands and pulled her towards him.

Jo shrieked, trying to pull away from the madman's grasp, but felt him rising.

Tyler dare not use the shotgun for fear of hitting Jo. He could only watch for agonizing seconds as the butcher rose from the fridge and grabbed Jo around the throat. She struck out at him with one hand, her nails raking his dry flesh. Tyler ran at the man and reached for his face, clawing at his eyes. He punched hard and felt brittle bone splinter under the impact but the man merely hurled Jo to one side and turned his full attention to Tyler. It was then that the farmer noticed his adversary held a meat hook.

Jo, thrown by the butcher, had crashed into the nearby bacon slicer which promptly burst into life, its circular blade spinning at over 500 revolutions a minute. She looked up, the droning sound loud in her ears. The diseased man was out of the fridge now, between Tyler and the discarded shotgun. He swung the meat hook in a vicious arc, missing the farmer by inches. Tyler leapt to one side, trying to keep the butcher away from Jo who was still dazed after her fall.

The drone of the moving bacon slicer filled the room, covering the low raspings which the diseased man made as he came at Tyler once more.

The farmer avoided another swipe of the hook, this time managing to grab the meat cleaver. He tore it free of the corpse and brandished it before him. The butcher was grinning, thick streamers of saliva dripping from his mouth as he advanced on the farmer. The hook lashed forward again, this time burying itself in a nearby carcass of meat. Tyler took his chance and brought the cleaver down with bone crushing force.

His aim was good. The vicious blade thudded into the butcher's shoulder, shattering the scapula, scything through an inch or two of muscle. Blood burst from the wound and the injured man backed off.

It was his groping hands that found the shotgun.

Tyler realized that he must act fast. He hurled himself headlong at the madman, knocking him backwards. The gun clattered to the floor and the two of them toppled over. The butcher roared in pain and anger and grabbed Tyler's head between his huge hands, pressing inward. The farmer struck out wildly in an attempt to free himself but the butcher, despite the wound in his arm, was an enormously powerful man and, inch by inch, Tyler felt himself being pushed back.

The man was grinning insanely and, in a moment of panic, the farmer realized that the butcher was forcing his head towards the spinning blade of the bacon slicer.

Jo dragged herself upright moaning aloud as she saw what was about to happen to Tyler.

She looked around desperately for something to attack the butcher with and, she too, found the cleaver. Hefting it in both hands, she went at him.

Tyler gripped the big man's wrists, trying to prise them apart, attempting to relieve the pressure on his skull. It seemed merely a matter of whether his skull was crushed like an egg or his head sliced in two by the swiftly rotating blade. In a few seconds it would all be over. He could actually see the blade out of the corner of his eye.

226

Screaming in desperation, Jo struck out with the cleaver. It sank into the big man's back just below the nape of the neck. She dragged it free and struck again, this time lower. The swipe laid open his lumbar region and, through a haze of pain, Tyler saw blood begin to dribble from the butcher's mouth. His eyes rolled upward in their sockets and he released his pressure on the farmer's head.

Tyler scrambled clear, grabbing the big man by the hair, forcing his head downwards onto the spinning blade.

There was a sound like sharp nails on a blackboard as the bacon slicer shaved off a sizeable portion of the butcher's skull, exposing the sticky grey matter beneath. The large body bucked violently, blood gushing from the numerous wounds, then he rolled over, the blade of the bacon slicer taking off a chunk of his bottom jaw. He fell to the ground and lay still.

Tyler turned to see Jo standing motionless, the dripping cleaver still held firmly in her hands. She swallowed hard and looked at him, dropping the weapon as she saw the blood spilling out around the corpse at her feet.

He reached out and switched the machine off. Silence descended once more.

'Jo,' he said, softly.

'Yeah, I'm OK,' she told him.

She gazed at the body of the butcher for a moment longer then dropped the cleaver.

Tyler took her in his arms and held her tightly.

After a moment, they walked back out of the shop, leaving the two corpses.

'What happened in there?' asked Mandy.

Tyler told her, keeping details to a minimum.

It was Mandy who heard the far off roar of a car engine. The sound travelled easily in the silence and it didn't take any of them long to realise that it was coming from the centre of town. Without hesitation, Tyler leapt behind the wheel and brought the landrover full circle.

He stepped on the accelerator and drove back into the town centre.

Thirty-six

Tyler brought the landrover skidding to a halt opposite the hotel.

There was a silver-grey Capri outside, its engine idling. The driver's side door opened and a short, tubby man with brown hair and a thick moustache got out to confront Vic who held a shotgun firmly in his grip.

'Do you intend using that?' said the man, his voice as crisp as November frost.

'Who are you?' said Tyler.

'My name is Clayton. Doctor Alec Clayton,' he motioned to the woman who sat in the passenger seat. 'That's my wife, Maria. Might I ask who you are and what you're doing with a shotgun?'

'I'm Vic Tyler, I used to run a farm on the outskirts of Wakely.'

He introduced Jo and Mandy.

'You're not from Wakely,' Tyler said, looking the newcomer up and down.

'No, we've come from Sussex, we've been driving most of the night.'

'What do you want?' asked the farmer.

'I think that's my business, Mr Tyler,' Clayton told him.

'That's true, but we don't get too many strangers around here.'

The doctor's wife got out of the car.

'The town seems deserted,' she said. 'We didn't see a soul on our way through the streets.'

'Where is everyone?' Clayton echoed.

Tyler sighed.

'It's a long story,' he said.

'We've got time,' Clayton told him.

It took Jo and Tyler over an hour to explain what had been happening in Wakely, or at least as much as they knew. Mandy was lying down in the lounge of 'The King George', but the remaining quartet sat in the bar, with the destruction of the previous night still visible, speaking in subdued tones as if in reverence for a town which was no more.

When the whole story had been told Clayton merely sat gazing into the bottom of his wine glass, as if seeking inspiration.

'It's incredible,' he said, softly.

'That's one word for it,' said Tyler. The farmer studied the features of the newcomer. He guessed that Clayton was in his middle forties, his wife about the same age. She was a tall, willowy woman, elegantly dressed in a black two-piece.

'So,' Jo asked. 'Why are you in Wakely?'

'My brother, Edward, and his wife,' said Clayton. 'They live here. We hadn't heard anything from them for a couple of weeks. When I tried to phone two days ago there was a recorded message on the line saying that the number was unavailable.'

Jo looked at Tyler, anxiously.

'I tried two other numbers, friends of Edward, but every time it was the same. A recorded message saying

229

those numbers were no longer in use.' He took a sip from his wine glass. 'I wondered what was wrong. I was worried about Edward anyway. He usually phones or writes regularly. Eventually, we decided to come and see for ourselves.'

'Have you been to his house?' asked Tyler.

Clayton nodded.

'There was no one there but all their belongings were in place. It was as if they'd just walked out. Or vanished.'

'Most people have left the town,' said Tyler. 'Those who haven't are either infected or . . .' He let the sentence trail off.

'Dead,' said Clayton.

There was a long silence. Clayton plucked at his moustache.

'A disease passed on by eating red meat,' he mused, 'it may be some form of food poisoning. You said the strain of bacteria which produced the virus was new, so it stands to reason the symptoms are going to manifest themselves in new ways as well.'

'Food poisoning my ass,' snapped Jo. 'What kind of virus do you know that turns people into vampires?'

Even Tyler looked at her in surprise.

'Vampires?' said Clayton, frowning.

'The contaminated people only come out at night, they have claws, they have large teeth. They drink blood.'

Clayton smiled humourlessly.

'So do haematophiliacs, Miss Ward,' he said.

Jo looked puzzled.

'Have you ever heard of Haigh? John George Haigh?' asked the doctor.

'I've heard the name,' Jo said.

'He was a murderer wasn't he?' added Tyler.

The doctor nodded.

'He was executed in 1949. His defence council tried

230

to claim he was insane because he confessed to drinking a wine glass full of his victim's blood before he dissolved them in acid. Haigh was haematophiliac. He was aroused by blood. There was a case similar to his in Germany in the 1920s. A man named Peter Kurten killed at least a dozen people and drank their blood. They nicknamed him "The Vampire of Düsseldorf".'

'Could the people in Wakely be suffering from the same disease as Haigh and Kurten?' asked Tyler.

'No. They were not physically ill. An obsession with blood whether it involves drinking it or not, is a psychological problem, not a pathological one,' Clayton explained. He looked at Jo. 'As for your theory about vampires, Miss Ward, they're creatures of folklore. What's happening in Wakely has nothing supernatural about it.'

'Well, whatever the answer is, we've all got to get out of here. Now.'

'I can't leave until I've found my brother,' Clayton protested.

'Doctor,' said Tyler, quietly, 'if your brother is still in Wakely then the chances are he's infected with this virus. I wouldn't advise you to hang around.'

'If my brother *is* infected then he needs help, all the people suffering need help. I can't just turn my back on them,' Clayton said.

'If you're staying you'll need this,' said Tyler, handing him the nickel-plated Purdey.

The doctor regarded the shotgun with horror, drawing back from it as if it were about to strike out at him.

'Take it,' urged Tyler.

'And what am I supposed to do with it?'

'Kill any of them that find you.'

'Tyler, for God's sake, they're human beings. They're ill.'

231

'They're animals,' snapped the farmer. 'Homicidal maniacs.'

'And your solution is to murder them?' said Clayton, sardonically. 'How many have you already killed?'

'You haven't seen what they're capable of,' growled the farmer.

'What in God's name gives you the right to act as judge, jury and executioner on these people?'

'If you want to find your brother, fine. But if he's infected then he's better off dead and he'll try and kill *you* if he can.'

'Is mindless violence your only answer?' asked the doctor.

Tyler turned to Jo.

'Get Mandy, we're leaving,' he said.

'Tyler,' Clayton shouted. 'We're talking about people, not cattle to be slaughtered. Is that what you'd do with every rabies victim? Shoot them?'

Jo returned a moment later with Mandy who looked on as the two men faced each other.

'You should come with us too,' said Tyler, looking at Maria Clayton.

'My wife's staying with me,' Clayton said, defiantly.

'Suit yourself,' Tyler said and tossed the shotgun onto a nearby chair. Then he turned his back on the doctor and, followed by Jo and Mandy, left the hotel.

They all climbed into the waiting landrover and the farmer started his engine.

The hotel gradually disappeared from view.

Thirty-seven

Tyler looked down at his watch and noticed that it was almost 5.00 p.m. The trees which flanked either side of the road from Wakely to Arkham crowded in like dark battalions, their leaves stirred by the strong breeze which had sprung up. Grey clouds scudded across the late afternoon sky and birds looked like black arrowheads against the dull background.

Dusk was approaching fast and, as if sensing this, Tyler put more pressure on the accelerator, coaxing extra speed from the landrover.

'What do you think will happen to the doctor and his wife?' said Mandy.

Tyler shrugged.

'If they stay inside they should be all right,' he said. 'But, they were warned.'

The road sloped upward sharply, simultaneously curving to the right.

'Jesus Christ,' gasped Tyler, slamming on the brakes.

The road block was about fifty yards from them and he could see uniformed men moving about near to a large truck which was parked on the verge. The men were wearing army uniforms.

As quickly and unobtrusively as possible, the farmer stuck the landrover into reverse and swung it off the road into an outcrop of trees. He let the engine idle and squinted towards the barrier.

'Troops?' said Jo, uncomprehendingly. 'To keep people out?'

Tyler shook his head.

'If they wanted to keep people out they'd have the road block facing the other way,' he said, cryptically.

'You mean it's to keep us *in*?' Jo whispered.

Tyler pointed to a dark-coated man who was talking

to a couple of the soldiers. The man wore the unmistakeable uniform of a Vanderburg Security guard.

'It looks like they're even more thorough than we thought,' said the farmer.

He turned his wheel and drove back the way they'd come, branching off at a junction, taking the road which led to Ducton.

'How the bloody hell did they manage to drag the army into this?' he pondered aloud.

Jo had no answer for him.

Mandy gazed out of the windows in bewilderment, watching as the trees sped past and, beyond them, rolling fields.

Clouds were gathering in greater abundance now.

It took them nearly thirty minutes to reach the Wakely–Ducton road.

The second road block consisted of two large trucks parked bumper to bumper. The troops who manned the obstruction could not have failed to see the approaching landrover but they merely stood, immobile, watching it. Tyler and the two women stared back. They sat there for what seemed like an eternity, then he swung the vehicle around once more, banging the wheel angrily as he drove away.

'We'll have to go across country,' he said and, with that, drove through a gorse hedge which fringed the road. The wheels of the landrover spun on the wet ground for a moment, then gained a grip and the heavy vehicle sped on, bumping over mounds and divots in the earth as it went.

About half a mile ahead of them was a range of low hills, the clouds already gathering ominously above them. Like dusky fingers, they crept over the hills, darkening the sky.

'They can't have covered everywhere,' Tyler said as the landrover reached the top of the hill. He peered through the windscreen and was relieved to see that there were no troops, no trucks. Nothing. A slight smile creased his face. It was clear.

'Next stop Arkham,' he said, triumphantly, and put his foot down. 'We can get back on the road in a while. There's a track about two miles further on, we'll by-pass the block.'

The vehicle moved easily through the mud and grass but after a minute or two Jo gripped his arm.

Ahead of them, clearly visible in the earth, were five or six freshly dug places each about a foot in diameter. Mandy, looking out of the back, noticed more behind them.

'Vic,' said Jo, pointing to the mounds. 'What are they?'

Tyler stepped on the brake and stiffened as if an electric current were being pumped through him. He gripped the wheel until his knuckles turned white.

'We're in a mine-field,' he said, softly.

Thirty-eight

'Sector One report.'

John Stark held the walkie-talkie in one hand and stood poised over the map of Wakely and its surrounding districts which was spread out on the desk before him.

The radio crackled loudly, then a voice came floating into the room.

'Sector One secure,' said the voice.

Stark nodded to himself and drew a large cross on

the black line which represented the Wakely-Arkham road.

'Sector Two report.'

He got a similar answer from the remaining four men he contacted and, at each affirmation, the American drew another cross at the appointed location on the map. The main roads which linked Wakely with the towns around it were blocked, the remainder of the town was ringed by troops.

They had arrived less than three hours ago. Stark didn't know what the troops had been told by their superiors. He didn't really give a shit anyway. The only thing that mattered was that they were there. Wakely was sealed off.

With each unit of troops was a Vanderburg Security man, just to keep an eye on things and, if the need arose, to quell any speculation as to why the troops were where they were. For all they knew, it was some kind of exercise. The only thing which might have puzzled them was the fact that they had been ordered to load up with live ammunition.

Stark wondered how many people *were* still alive in Wakely. He drew a large ring right around the town then dropped his pen. However many there were, they sure as hell weren't going anywhere.

He smiled and took out his hip-flask.

'How long do you propose to keep the troops there?' asked Sir Oliver Thorndike, who was also looking down at the map.

'Until this little mess is cleaned up,' Stark told him.

'And when is that likely to be?'

'What am I, a fortune teller? How the hell do I know?'

'You can't keep troops around the town indefinitely.'

Stark rounded on him.

'Don't tell me what I can or can't do, Thorndike,' rasped the American. 'I wasn't the one who put them there, remember. It was *your* Government. I asked for assistance, they sent troops.'

'It seems rather like using a sledgehammer to swat a fly,' Thorndike said.

'Stop talking in riddles, dammit,' Stark snapped.

'You're after Tyler and the girl. Don't you think using a battalion of troops is being too . . .'

Stark cut him short.

'Look, there could be other people alive in that town. I don't want any of them leaving.'

There was a long silence.

'I'd like to know why the hell Fanducci isn't back yet,' Stark said, finally, unscrewing the cap on his hip-flask. He took a hefty swig.

There was a knock on the office door.

'Come in,' Stark called and looked up as Charles Muir entered.

The Scot had his pipe in his mouth but it wasn't lit. He was carrying a large clip-file.

'The reports on the new additive,' he said, passing the file to Thorndike. 'It should be ready for introduction into the feed in a day or two.'

Thorndike nodded and passed the file on to Stark.

'Any problems?' asked the American.

Muir shrugged.

'It's early days,' he said. 'There didn't seem to be any problems, at first, with the initial batch did there?'

Stark looked at him through eyes narrowed to steely slits.

'You were hired to work here, Muir, not to pass moral judgement on what you're doing.'

'Well,' said the Scot, 'let's see how much damage we can do with the second batch shall we?' His voice was heavy with sarcasm.

Stark slammed the file down.

'I've had it with your complaining,' he snapped. 'If you don't like the work then clear out.'

'Just walk away?' said Muir. 'You'd let me do that, knowing everything I know?' He smiled humourlessly and shook his head. 'I'm not that green *Mr* Stark.'

'Charles, the tests done this time were far more exhaustive,' said Thorndike, trying to put a wedge between the two men.

'I know,' snarled the Scot. 'I've just come from the laboratory. My God, have you seen what it's done to some of the specimens?' His own anger was now rising. 'This . . . "miracle feed" is lethal. How many more towns do you have to wipe out before you realize that, Stark?'

'Why don't you just get the fuck out of here,' Stark rasped. 'You came to work here in the beginning because you were offered a lot of money. What's wrong? Is your conscience starting to get at you? *You* helped wipe out that town, Muir.' Stark pointed an accusatory finger at him. 'You and the rest of you fucking geniuses.' He looked at Thorndike too. 'Well now *I'm* clearing up the mess you made. And I'm doing it my own way.'

A heavy silence filled the room, then the Scot turned and headed for the door.

Thorndike tried to call him back but Muir was already gone.

'He's your friend, right?' said Stark.

Thorndike nodded.

'Then keep him quiet or I swear to Christ he'll wind up like Geoffrey Anderson.'

'Does that apply to any dissenting voice?' asked Thorndike, warily.

Stark looked him in the eye.

'Yes,' he said flatly.

Charles Muir rode alone in the lift. He chewed agitatedly on the stem of his pipe and exhaled deeply.

238

Conflicting thoughts and emotions raged through him.

Anger. Frustration.

Guilt?

He knew Stark was right about his involvement in the Wakely catastrophe and that made it worse.

Guilt.

Hatred.

Charles Muir had taken all he was going to take from John Stark and Vanderburg Chemicals.

He chewed his pipe and wondered how best to approach the idea he had.

Thirty-nine

Mines.

The word blazed like a beacon in Tyler's mind. No wonder there had been no troops in this area. There had been no need for any. He sat behind the wheel of the landrover staring at the small mounds of earth all around them. They were spread quite well apart and the farmer shuddered as he thought how they had driven so easily and unsuspectingly into the trap. The thing was, how far into the mine-field were they?

'Get out,' he said, pushing open the passenger side door.

Jo hesitated.

'Get out, both of you,' Tyler said more forcefully. 'You'll have to guide me through it.'

Mandy sat immobile in the rear of the vehicle.

239

'Come on, Mandy. Now.' Tyler felt a bead of perspiration pop onto his forehead.

She shook her head.

'Move,' he bellowed, his voice a mixture of rage and desperation.

The shout seemed to galvanise her into action and, carefully, helped by Jo, she climbed out of the vehicle. The two women stood beside the landrover, looking at the ground around them, moving cautiously towards the back of the vehicle when Tyler instructed them. He pushed open his own door and peered over his shoulder.

Mandy was clinging to Jo's arm and, as they reached the back of the landrover, she slipped.

For interminable seconds, Jo thought she was going to be pulled off balance, only to topple onto one of the waiting booby traps, but she managed to steady herself and, gripping Mandy's hand, she picked her way backward. They both stepped over the mounds carefully.

'All right,' called Jo. 'Come back, slowly.'

Tyler stuck the landrover into reverse and pressed down as lightly as he could on the accelerator. The vehicle began to move.

He could see the first of the mines and tugged on the steering wheel to manoeuvre past it.

'Keep coming,' Jo called, herself backing off, careful to avoid the lethal traps. Mandy was shivering uncontrollably.

Above them, the sky was darkening. Clouds rolling across the heavens like fearful portents.

'There's one to your left,' Jo called, watching as Tyler adjusted the vehicle's path slightly.

He was breathing heavily now, his throat dry.

Mandy screamed as she slipped and fell.

Tyler slammed on his brakes and looked round.

Mandy was lying prone, her head less than a foot from the nearest mine. From where she lay she could see the two prongs which nudged up from beneath the earth. If anything should brush against those. . . .

Jo helped her up.

Tyler cursed under his breath and stuck the vehicle into reverse again, having put it in neutral when he heard the commotion from behind. Now, it edged back tortuously, guided by a combination of Jo's directions and his own careful driving.

'There's another to the left,' Jo called.

To avoid it, Tyler was forced to swing the landrover to his right, up a sharp incline.

His foot slipped from the accelerator and the engine stalled.

The landrover began sliding towards the mine.

'Vic,' screamed Jo.

The farmer grabbed his ignition key and twisted it madly.

The vehicle wouldn't start, it continued sliding inexorably towards the mine.

'Come on,' he shouted, turning it once more.

This time the engine fired and Tyler swung the land-rover back, praying that the ground was clear behind him.

Jo leapt to one side, pulling Mandy with her, both of them watching as the rear offside wheel missed a mine by a matter of inches. Tyler brought the vehicle to a halt and sat stiffly behind the wheel. He tried to swallow but couldn't.

Jo too found that her breath was coming in gasps.

Mandy could only stare, wide-eyed as the landrover continued its snail-like progress backwards.

'Another few yards and it's clear,' Jo told him.

At least she hoped it was. The ground behind her was free from any bumps or mounds. Unless, she thought, with a shudder, some other, more insidious form of booby-trap lay hidden beneath the dirt. One invisible until it was too late. It was at that point the thought struck her. The mines had been left conspicuous. As if they were waiting to be found. Silent warnings.

'Keep coming,' she called and Tyler finally reversed to safety.

He allowed his head to sag forward onto the wheel. His palms were sweaty on the plastic which he still gripped as if threatening to break it. Mandy, aided by Jo, clambered back inside the landrover and then the journalist herself got in. They all sat in silence for long moments.

'There's no way out of the town,' said Tyler, quietly. 'We're trapped.'

'What are we going to do?' Jo wanted to know.

'We'll have to go back into Wakely, to the hotel. We've got no choice.'

He spun the wheel, completing a 'U' turn, then he drove back towards the road.

'But it'll be dark soon,' Mandy protested. 'What about the infected people in the town? They'll be on the streets.' She was becoming more and more distraught. 'They'll kill us.'

'We'll make it,' said Tyler, forcefully.

He glanced up at the sky and shuddered. Rain clouds were forming in vast black banks, hastening the onset of evening. He found he was forced to flick his side-lights on as he drove back towards the centre of Wakely. The trees, bustling in the strong wind, seemed even more menacing in the dull light. They bent and snatched at the speeding vehicle as it roared past, skeletal branches tapping on the roof every now and then.

The outskirts of the town loomed nearer and Tyler allowed one hand to drop to his side where the Franchi lay.

Jo gripped his arm momentarily and he could feel her shaking.

242

A dark shape moved ahead of them, disappearing into the deep shadows.

'I told you they'd be around,' Mandy babbled.

No one answered her.

Tyler swung the landrover around a corner and saw more of the townspeople emerging from shop doorways. They looked at the vehicle as it hurtled past, hunger in their eyes.

'How far to go?' Jo asked.

'About three-quarters of a mile,' he told her. They had been forced to enter Wakely from a different direction. One which, Tyler knew, would add to the journey time.

The man ran out into the street as if appearing from nowhere. He raised both hands towards the speeding landrover, illuminated briefly in the dim light it cast.

The landrover struck him doing about sixty. The impact hurling the body to one side. Tyler flicked on his headlamps, able to see more of the dark shapes now.

They recoiled from the twin beams, skulking back into the shadows, only able to watch as the machine roared past.

The hotel was close now, Tyler could see its lights.

He swung the vehicle around the next corner, almost tipping it over.

Jo screamed.

There was an overturned car blocking the road.

Tyler had no time to stop, he merely twisted the steering wheel and tried to guide the vehicle around the car. The landrover bumped as it mounted the pavement, skidding on the concrete as its rear end spun round. There was a loud crash as it ploughed through the window of a shop. Glass cascaded down from the smashed sheet and Tyler cursed as the impact slammed him against the steering column.

A dozen of the dark shapes converged on the vehicle.

Tyler wrestled with the ignition key as the towns-people drew nearer. Jo snatched up the Franchi, stuck the barrel out of the window and fired. The noise inside the landrover was deafening and Jo shouted aloud as the recoil made her ears ring.

Mandy screamed repeatedly, grabbing the handle of the vehicle's rear doors, anxious to be out of it.

'Mandy, no,' shouted Tyler as the landrover bucked into life again. But it was too late, she had pushed open the rear doors and jumped out onto the pavement, running as fast as she could away from the attacking shapes. In the rear-view mirror, the farmer saw her disappear from view around a corner.

'We can't leave her out there,' said Jo.

Tyler stepped on the accelerator and brought the landrover full circle, speeding away from the frenzied shapes and after Mandy.

When he turned the corner there was no sign of her.

'Shit,' he snarled, scanning the darkened street ahead.

The vehicle was moving slowly now as both he and Jo squinted into the gloom in an effort to catch sight of the terrified girl.

The streets were empty.

He reversed.

'What are you doing?' Jo gasped. 'We've got to find her.'

'We're not risking our lives too,' he snapped.

'Vic, for God's sake.'

The scream came like a knife in soft flesh, ringing through the darkness. A piercing ululation which set their nerves jangling.

Tyler grabbed a shotgun and pushed open his door.

'Keep the lights trained on me,' he said and ran towards the place where the scream had come from. Jo shuffled across into the driver's seat, glancing around her anxiously. She was quivering.

244

Tyler had pinpointed the sound of the scream, realizing that it came from a house just ahead of him. He kicked open the front door and moved inside, the shotgun held at the ready.

The house smelt fusty from disuse and he wondered how long it had been uninhabited.

In the glow from the landrover's headlamps he saw something glistening on the floor ahead of him.

It was blood.

There was more of it on the stairs.

Tyler moved cautiously upward, working the pump action of the shotgun. He swallowed with difficulty, his throat dry and chalky.

He reached the landing and advanced towards one of the doors which faced him. The farmer braced himself and kicked it open.

Mandy Potter lay on the bed naked. Her clothes lay in bloodied tatters beside her like gory confetti. In her nudity, she looked even more pathetic and Tyler lowered his eyes briefly but it was the nature of her injuries which caused him to look away for a moment. She was still wearing her glasses which, Tyler noticed, had been smashed. Thick lumps of glass had punctured her eyes and blood ran down her cheeks like crimson tears. One breast had been practically ripped off, the other was covered by claw marks – deep, red furrows which made it look as if someone had pulled a rake across her torso. Her mouth was open in a soundless scream, her swollen tongue lolling from one side of it. An inch or so below her left breast there was a large hole. Clogged with black clots of congealed blood it yawned like a monstrous mouth.

On the bed beside her was her heart.

The organ looked grey in colour, parts of it having been gouged open.

Tyler crossed to the body and pulled a blanket over

it, covering both the horrific mutilation and Mandy's nakedness.

Only as he stepped back did Tyler suddenly realize that whoever had done this must still be in the house. He spun round, the shotgun lowered.

Nothing moved.

He made his way back onto the landing, then down the stairs, pausing every now and then to listen for sounds of movement.

There were none.

Above him he heard deep guttural breathing, but he kept on edging down the stairs, the light from the landrover's headlamps beckoning him.

He reached the front door, then turned and ran back to the waiting vehicle.

'Mandy?' Jo said.

He shook his head.

Jo understood.

Tyler stepped on the accelerator and drove as fast as he could in the direction of the hotel.

'I thought you were leaving.'

There was no surprise on Alec Clayton's face as he saw Jo and Tyler enter the hotel. Only Maria showed any signs of bewilderment.

'What happened?' she asked.

They told her about the road blocks. About the troops. About the mine-fields.

About Mandy.

'There's no way out of Wakely,' said Tyler, flatly.

Clayton looked a little shocked.

Tyler crossed to the bar and poured himself a large vodka.

'So what are we going to do?' asked Clayton.

The farmer shrugged.

'I wish I knew.'

Forty

Apart from the red and white collision lights which glowed on the skids and sides of the helicopter, the craft flew in darkness. The steady sweep of its powerful rotor blades cut rapidly through the air until it sounded like a loud sewing machine.

The pilot, a man in his early thirties, was bundled up in a heavy leather flying jacket, his black clothing making him almost invisible in the gloom. The lights from the complex instrument panel before him cast a weak glow across his face, highlighting the parts of his skin which were visible above his scarf. His flesh looked pale in the false light, his cheek bones standing out prominently. It seemed as though the chopper was being flown by a disembodied skull.

In the seat alongside him, John Stark pulled the engraved silver hip-flask from his coat pocket and took a hefty swig. He smacked his lips appreciatively, feeling the brandy burn its way to his stomach. Jesus, it was cold. He wore a thick, fur-lined parka but he was still shivering. He rubbed his hands together, slapping the gloved appendages against his thighs. Beneath him, a blanket of cloud had settled over Wakely, virtually blotting the town from view. There were few lights to be seen. Technicians from Vanderburg Chemicals had shut off the main power supply to the town that very afternoon.

Stark jabbed a finger earthward and nudged the pilot.

'Take her lower,' he shouted, forced to raise his voice to make himself heard above the whoosh of the rotors.

The helicopter dipped violently for a moment, caught for precious seconds in a thermo-draught, but it soon straightened out as the young pilot manipulated the controls and lowered the machine to less than 500 feet.

It skimmed through the air effortlessly, dropping ever lower as Stark demanded a better view of the town.

'I thought you said he was your best man,' said Oliver Thorndike who was sitting behind Stark.

'He was,' snapped the American.

'Then why hasn't he reported back?'

The American didn't answer, he merely took another sip from his flask and peered out into the darkness.

'Could Fanducci have caught the disease?' he asked.

Thorndike cupped a hand to his ear, finding it difficult to hear above the noise of the helicopter. He was cold too, his fingers numb.

'What did you say?' he asked.

Stark repeated his question, raising his voice as he did so.

Thorndike shook his head.

'No. He knew about the meat. Perhaps the girl and her friend were too clever for him.'

'Bullshit,' snapped Stark. 'He's never made a mistake yet.'

The helicopter danced in the air, dipping and swerving until it was just a hundred feet or so above the rooftops.

'We're on the outskirts of Wakely, Mr Stark,' said the pilot. 'Do you want me to land?'

'Are you kidding?' shouted the American. 'Just fly over the place, I want to take a look but only from up here.'

The pilot smiled.

'Just what do you expect to see?' Thorndike asked him.

Stark didn't answer. He reached beneath his seat and pulled out a pair of binoculars, squinting through them at the streets below. He adjusted the focus until everything swam into crystal clarity. In the darkness of the streets he could see moving shapes, dozens of them.

'Take a look,' he said, handing the binoculars to Thorndike. 'There are people down there.'

The scientist leant forward in his seat and looked out. 'They're the infected ones,' he said, studying the black shapes beneath them. 'There's still quite a few left.' He swept the binoculars back and forth as the chopper swung in low over the town. '*They* could have killed Fanducci.'

Once more Stark didn't answer.

He suddenly spotted something about 500 yards ahead and nudged the pilot to get closer.

'Give me the glasses back,' he said to Thorndike who willingly obliged.

As the helicopter drew nearer, Stark trained the twin lenses on the light which he had seen. He found that there were over a dozen large lights glowing in a large building a spot near the centre of Wakely. It took him just a moment or two to realize that it was the hotel.

'Son of a bitch,' he murmured under his breath.

He could actually see some of the diseased townspeople moving about beyond the glare of the hotel lights, skulking in shop doorways and standing in black-shrouded streets nearby looking at the one cursed centre of luminosity in the entire town. The hotel stood out like a beacon amidst the stifling Stygian gloom.

'If the girl and the guy are still in town, I'll lay good money they're in there,' Stark said, pointing towards the hotel. He turned to the pilot. 'Circle it a couple of times.'

The man nodded, taking the chopper up slightly before beginning the first of his sweeps.

Forty-one

The auxiliary power provided by the hotel generator had cut in as soon as the mains supply had gone off and Tyler thought again how fortunate they were to have this reserve. What would have occurred had the hotel been plunged into complete darkness he dared not think. As it was, the street lights were out. Wakely was under a blanket of impenetrable gloom – a premonitory blackness which made all four occupants of the hotel feel somewhat uneasy.

Clayton sat at the bar drinking. Maria paced nervously up and down the lounge. Jo stood close to Tyler, gazing out of the window towards the hordes of people barely visible beyond the range of the hotel's powerful lights.

'What do they want?' said Jo, quietly.

'Us,' Tyler said, flatly.

There was a long pause broken by Tyler himself.

'Fresh blood,' he muttered.

Jo frowned.

'What did you say?'

'I think they need fresh blood. Uncontaminated blood,' he explained. 'Up until now, all the victims we've found had been unaffected by the virus. I think that's why they want us.' He gripped the shotgun tighter. 'I wonder how many are out there?'

No one answered.

'I've been thinking,' Tyler continued. 'Apart from the odd victim of the virus we've found, the majority seem to disappear during the day and yet, at night, they all emerge at roughly the same time.'

'What are you getting at, Vic?' Jo asked.

'I think they're all together. In one communal . . . nest, if you like.'

'It would need to be a big building,' said Jo.

Tyler nodded.

'Are you sure this place is secure, Mr Tyler?' asked Maria, anxiously.

'As long as the lights are on they won't come near us,' Tyler reassured her. He looked down as he felt Jo squeezing his arm. He leant over and kissed her softly on the forehead.

It was Clayton who heard it first.

'Listen,' he said, raising a hand for silence.

'What is it?' asked Tyler.

The doctor cocked an ear towards the imagined sound.

'Listen,' he repeated.

The noise grew louder and they all heard it.

'It's a goddam chopper,' said Jo, peering through the window. She pointed towards the red and white lights which glowed brightly on the craft, appearing suddenly, then soaring out of sight.

'It might be someone from another town, the police perhaps,' said Maria, hopefully.

The sound of the rotor blades receded for a moment, then grew louder as the helicopter swept over the building once more.

'Isn't there some way we can signal to him?' said Clayton. 'He might be looking for somewhere to land.'

The chopper completed another circle and Tyler shook his head almost imperceptibly.

'If he wanted to land he could drop it in the street, the road's wide enough,' said the farmer.

'So why doesn't he?' Maria wondered aloud.

The helicopter passed overhead once more, swinging off to the left and hovering like some gigantic insect preparing to alight on a plant, the thrumming of the rotors sounding like a swarm of bees. In the glare of the hotel lights Jo thought she spotted something. A symbol which she had seen before – a red and silver VC. But in the gloom, could she be sure? She watched the chopper as it hovered, trying to make out the markings on its sides. Was it the Vanderburg logo? She couldn't be sure. The sound of its engine gradually receded.

'Why didn't they land?' said Maria, dejectedly.

No one else spoke.

Clayton returned to the bar and began sipping at his drink once more.

'Why don't you try and get some sleep,' said Tyler to Jo.

'I'm fine,' she said, smiling.

The hands of the wall clock had crawled around to 11.26 p.m.

There was an explosion of glass as the first stone shattered the window.

Tyler jumped back, pulling Jo to one side in an attempt to shield her from the shards of crystal which sprayed inwards. He cursed as he felt a jagged splinter nick his cheek.

Another rock came flying at the glass and smashed through. And, suddenly, they were coming with increasing rapidity.

'What the hell are they doing?' said Clayton, knocking his drink over as he moved towards the window.

'Stay back,' Tyler yelled at him as another stone came hurtling at them.

There was another volley of rocks, then a lull.

Tyler peered out through the broken partition, trying to get a look at the hordes beyond the reach of the hotel lights. He could see them, moving like ghosts, almost invisible in the gloom. He could see enough to realize that a number of them were pointing at the building. Many still held lumps of stone and brick, but it was as if they were awaiting some kind of signal.

The farmer swung the shotgun up to his shoulder and aimed.

'What are you doing?' shouted Clayton, rushing towards him.

Tyler actually had his finger hooked around the trigger when the doctor pulled the barrel down.

The farmer turned on him.

'You stupid bastard, Clayton,' he rasped. 'I should use this on you.'

'I shouldn't imagine you'd find it too difficult,' said the doctor sardonically.

'I've told you before, stay out of my way,' Tyler snarled, turning back towards the window.

'Vic, look,' Jo said, pointing at the townspeople. They had unleashed their salvo of stones but they were aiming higher, many of the projectiles falling on the concrete in front of the main doors. Elsewhere, the occupants of the hotel heard more glass smashing.

'My God, they're trying to smash the lights,' said Tyler and, this time, he raised the Franchi and fired all in one movement. There was a deafening roar as the barrel flamed and he saw one of the diseased horde fall. Swiftly working the pump action of the gun, he fired again.

Maria screamed as another stone came crashing through the glass near to her whilst others were hurled at the lights which covered the front of the building.

Tyler squeezed the trigger a third time, watching as two women dragged the bleeding bodies away into the darkness. He could guess what their motives were and the thought sickened him.

He fired again, killing the first of the women.

'You mad bastard,' roared Clayton, trying to pull the gun away from Tyler. The farmer pushed him hard, knocking him over, then he hurriedly thumbed fresh cartridges into the smoking weapon.

The lights flickered once.

'What's that?' Maria gasped.

Tyler saw the shapes moving back into the shadows,

watching as the hotel illuminations began to perform like strobes, flickering on and off more rapidly now.

'Christ, it must be the generator,' said Tyler, anxiously. 'The fuel must be down.'

The lights glowed brightly for brief seconds then died.

The entire hotel was plunged into darkness.

Forty-two

'Get upstairs now,' Tyler said.

'Where are you going?' Jo wanted to know.

'To see about that bloody generator.' He snatched up the Purdey which was lying close by. 'Clayton, take this,' he said, thrusting the weapon towards the doctor.

Clayton merely shook his head.

Jo took it instead.

'Go quickly,' Tyler shouted, heading for the cellar door which lay to his right through the bar. He heard the sound of their footsteps as they clattered up the stairs. For his own part, he fumbled for his torch, wrenched open the door and hurried, as best he could, down the stone steps into the abyss which was the cellar. He stumbled at the bottom, sprawling on the cold stone, the shotgun falling from his grasp, the torch rolling away from him.

The impact had caused it to go out.

Like a blind man, Tyler groped around.

He heard the sounds of hammering on the outside

cellar door and realized that they were trying to break in.

At last his hand closed over the shotgun but, still in darkness, he continued groping for the torch.

The pounding on the door grew louder.

Outside, the diseased horde ran towards the darkened hotel, some climbing the rope-like ivy which clung to the walls of the building, others pounding at the doors or smashing windows to gain access.

Tyler found the torch and flicked it on, swinging the beam around until it fastened on the outside door. He could see the handle being turned, see the wood bowing inward as more pressure was exerted on it from the outside. He dashed across the cellar and up the other flight of steps, dropping the metal locking bar in place, securing the door. Then, he scurried towards the generator, running the torch beam over the various gauges on it. The needles of all three were lying limply on the red side of the dial indicating that it had indeed run out of fuel. He snatched up a can of petrol and began pouring.

There was enough natural light for Jo and the others to see where they were going once they reached the top of the stairs. Jo ushered them towards the nearest room and they locked the door behind them. The American checked that the shotgun was loaded, praying that Tyler could get the lights back on before she had need to use it.

There was a deafening crash as the window was broken and a large man came hurtling into the room.

He rolled over once, then hauled himself upright. He was followed by two others. A shorter man and a willowy woman. The taller man was carrying a hammer.

Jo aimed for him, but the massive recoil of the shotgun pulled the barrels to one side and the blast hit the shorter man. It lifted him off his feet and slammed him against the far wall where he left a large blot of crimson as he slid down.

The tallest man turned to the three terrified onlookers, the hammer gripped tight in his fist.

Alec Clayton found himself staring into the mad, bulging eyes of his brother.

'Edward,' he said, taking a step towards the man who had once been blood kin but was now little more than a raving maniac.

'Stay away from him,' shouted Jo, trying to aim the gun again.

Maria too was staring dumbfoundedly at Edward and it was towards her that he moved.

The blow from the hammer was both well-aimed and powerful. It caught Maria just below the left temple and stove in most of the side of her face, her cheek bone splintering beneath the impact. She fell sideways and Edward Clayton dropped to his knees, bringing the weapon down again. The head punched a hole in Maria's skull, exposing part of her brain. She was dead by the time he struck again, this time using the claw end of the hammer to tear open the soft flesh of her neck. Great gouts of blood rose from the rent and spattered Edward. The woman with him also moved towards the corpse but Jo squeezed the trigger of the Purdey, shouting aloud as the massive recoil slammed her backwards.

Once more her aim was off. It caused the gun to veer to one side and the blast caught the woman in the arm, almost severing it at the shoulder as it ripped away most of her chest in the pulverizing discharge.

Jo fumbled in her pocket for more cartridges, her eyes fixed on Edward Clayton who, by now, had bent his head to the jetting fountain of blood spurting from Maria's throat. He drank voraciously.

The sight finally seemed to galvanize the doctor into

action and he ran at his diseased brother, knocking him away from Maria.

Edward snarled, his mouth open to reveal dripping teeth.

Jo looked up and saw that more of the killers were attempting to clamber through the smashed window.

She unlocked the bedroom door and tugged at Clayton's arm.

'Come on,' she screamed.

He stood transfixed, gazing at his dead wife and then at his diseased brother, the awful realisation finally sweeping through him.

More of the killers were crashing into the room.

'For God's sake, move,' Jo shouted, almost pulling the doctor over and, as he looked up and found himself pinned in the stare of so many mad eyes, he finally found the strength to move. He and Jo ran from the room, charging headlong down the corridor.

Behind them, three of the townspeople followed.

'Up the stairs,' Jo said, taking them two at a time and nearly falling. She could hear the intruders drawing nearer, their feet pounding as they chased their prey.

Clayton banged into a table as he turned a corner, jarring his hip but he kept going, not daring to look behind him.

They turned into another corner, the killers less than twenty yards behind them.

It was a dead end.

Jo raced towards the door, praying that it would be unlocked.

She twisted the knob frantically but it wouldn't budge.

Clayton kicked at it while Jo held the shotgun ready, waiting for the pursuers to round the corner.

The first to appear was a woman carrying a chisel.

Jo gripped the shotgun tight and pulled the fore-trigger. The weapon bucked violently in her hand, almost knocking her off balance. The blast hit the woman in the thighs and she went down as if pole-axed.

Clayton drove his foot against the door once more and it flew open, crashing back against the wall. He dashed in, followed by Jo, then both of them struggled to pull a chest of drawers across the gap as the people outside tried to force their way in.

Jo was shaking, Clayton was finding it hard to get his breath.

'He killed her,' the doctor gasped. 'Edward killed my wife.'

Jo could hear his voice cracking but she had more important things to think about.

The door was already beginning to open a fraction and there was nothing else in the room to block it with. Another minute or so and the killers would be in and, this time, there was nowhere else to run.

Tyler threw another empty can of petrol to one side and unscrewed the cap of another. He couldn't remember how many gallons he'd poured into the hungry generator yet still the machine seemed to swallow every drop. The sound of the shotgun blasts from above had caused him to quicken his efforts and now, as he tossed yet another container aside, he reached for the switch that would activate the generator.

The needles on the dials rose a fraction, then dropped again.

The hotel remained in darkness.

Jo levelled the shotgun at the door, Clayton picked up a chair leg and prepared to defend himself as the door began to crack from the monumental blows it was receiving. The wood had already split in two places, great long vein-like seams running its full length. The

258

hinges groaned as the furious onslaught seemed to grow in intensity and both Jo and Clayton jumped as a fist burst through the door, clawing at the splintered wood, ripping away the panels. Through the gap they could see the crazed faces, the yellowed eyes gleaming with mad desire as the intruders realized they had almost reached their prey. The chest of drawers, the final obstacle between them, began to topple.

Tyler was sweating as he poured yet another can of petrol into the generator. He hurled it aside and threw the switch. The machine spluttered for a second then hummed into life. He breathed a sigh of relief as the lights came back on, brighter than ever. He switched off the torch, stuck it in his pocket and ran towards the cellar steps.

Jo almost laughed aloud as the lights burst into life. The entire hotel seemed to glow brilliantly and from outside the splintered door both she and Clayton heard screams of pain and rage. As helpless in the brightness as their victims had been in the gloom, the infected group ran for the windows in an effort to escape the searing power of the lights. They stumbled awkwardly, falling over each other in their haste to escape back into the night.

Clayton wrenched the chest of drawers away from the door and ran out into the corridor, watching as one of the intruders writhed contortedly in front of him. Jo too watched mesmerized as the man's skin rose in large welts which burst to emit a thick mucoid fluid. His face began to turn red and the clear pus took on a crimson tinge. He opened his mouth to scream, a furred tongue lolling from his mouth, his swollen lips cracking under the lights until they were shredded by numerous small clefts, each one weeping blood. They saw his eyes bulging in pain as he continued to squirm like an eel on a hot skillet, his fingers opening and closing as he shook violently. Finally, with a last racking spasm, he coughed loudly and a foul-smelling mixture of bile and pus spilled over his lips.

Jo prodded the body with the barrel of the shotgun, looking up as Clayton hurried past in the direction of the room they had first come from.

He paused in the doorway, looking down at the body of his wife.

'Oh God,' he whimpered. 'No, no.'

He knelt beside the body, clasping her hand, tears coursing down his cheeks as he saw the extent of her mutilations.

Her clothes had been torn off, her torso punctured in a dozen different places by various weapons.

'Maria,' he whispered, sobbing uncontrollably but, as he saw another of the killers lying close by, that grief slowly became blind anger. He began kicking at the body, driving great powerful kicks into the neck and head until the bone shattered under the impact.

'No. No,' he sobbed. 'Maria.' He snarled down at the diseased body. 'You filthy bastard. Animal. Murderer.' He continued driving kicks into the body.

By this time Tyler had entered the room. He looked at Jo with relief on seeing that she was uninjured.

'Clayton?' he asked.

'In there,' Jo said, pointing towards the room. 'Maria was killed.'

'Oh Christ,' said Tyler, wearily. He looked down at the body in the corridor and then walked to where Clayton was still raining blows on the dead body of the killer. Almost exhausted now, he was on his knees, digging his thumbs and fingers into the ruined face of his adversary. Punching the still form, his body still lurched violently as the tears stained his cheeks.

Tyler shook his head as he looked down at Maria's body, then he crossed to Clayton and tried to lift him off the pulverized corpse at which he was still clawing.

260

'They killed her,' he rasped. 'Look what they did to her.'

Tyler nodded.

'If I'd listened to you, this wouldn't have happened,' croaked Clayton.

'It wasn't your fault,' Jo said.

He seemed to quieten down somewhat, his gaze returning to the mutilated body of his wife.

'My brother did this,' he said.

Tyler looked shocked.

'You saw your brother?' he asked.

The doctor nodded.

'He killed my wife.'

There was another heavy silence.

'I should have listened to you, Tyler,' said the older man. 'I should have listened.' He walked out of the room.

Jo put her arm around Tyler's waist and squeezed him tightly.

'Are you all right?' he asked.

She nodded, her eyes drawn to the two bodies lying before them. How easily one of them could have been herself she thought, and the realization made her shudder. Tyler crossed to the window and looked out. There was nothing to be seen out there in the oozing darkness, only the bodies of those he'd killed earlier. The breeze which blew in brought with it the smell of death. It mingled with the stench which already filled the room.

When they walked back out into the corridor, Clayton was nowhere to be seen. Tyler paused for a moment, looking down at the scorched corpse of the killer in the corridor, then he took hold of the ankles, dragged it into the room with the other one and locked the door.

'What about Maria's body?' asked Jo, apparently concerned that it was sharing a room with two other corpses.

261

'We can't do anything before morning,' Tyler said and, together, they walked downstairs.

They found Clayton in the bar pouring himself a large measure of Scotch which he downed in one, hastily refilling his glass.

He slammed the bottle down on top of the bar and ran his index finger around the rim.

'I want to bury my wife, Tyler,' he said, quietly. 'I want . . .' The sentence trailed off. He exhaled deeply and took another hefty swig from his glass. 'We'd been married for fifteen years. She was all I cared about, we had no children.' He drained what was left in his glass and poured himself another. 'I'm sorry for that little outburst earlier on,' he smiled, sardonically. 'I've had to tell about twenty patients that they were terminally ill during my time as a doctor. Twenty people in over eighteen years is quite a lot. But it was always from a distance, if you know what I mean. Death never had a tangible face until tonight.' He swallowed more of the fiery liquid. 'Death has my brother's face.' Clayton laughed humourlessly. There was a long silence finally broken by the doctor once more. 'I want to kill him. I want to kill my brother. I will destroy death.' He smiled thinly and raised his glass in salute.

The doctor pulled two more glasses from beneath the bar and filled them with the amber fluid.

'Join me?' he said.

Tyler nodded.

'Why not?' Jo echoed.

They sat on the high stools facing the doctor.

'Whatever you want to do,' said Clayton. 'I'll help you. I owe it to my wife.' He gritted his teeth, the knot of muscles at the side of his jaw pulsing.

'I don't think this is the time to talk about it,' said the farmer.

Clayton shook his head.

'I insist,' he said, his voice taking on a hard edge. 'I want someone to pay for what happened tonight.'

Tyler exhaled deeply.

'We can't get out of here, out of Wakely,' he said. 'As I see it, there's only one thing left for us to do. Something that will bring the whole country down on us.'

Jo frowned.

'What?' she asked.

'Destroy Vanderburg Chemicals,' he said.

Jo was speechless.

'And the infected people in the town?' asked Clayton.

'We've got to destroy them too.'

Jo sipped at her drink.

'You find the townspeople,' she said to Tyler. 'I'll see to Vanderburg.'

'You're not going alone,' he told her.

'She won't be alone,' Clayton interjected. 'I'll go with you, Miss Ward.'

He finished his drink and walked out from behind the bar.

'If you'll excuse me,' he said, quietly. 'I'd like to be alone for a while.'

They watched him as he walked wearily away, turning as he reached the exit.

'Tyler,' he said. 'What about that shotgun?'

The farmer tossed him the nickel-plated Purdey and a box of cartridges, watching as he hefted the weapon before him.

Outside, the dark shapes had returned but, this time, they merely stood motionless, staring at the hotel.

It would be daylight in two hours.

Forty-three

Doctor Alec Clayton placed one solitary flower on the small mound of earth in the hotel garden. Tyler and Jo stood to his right, eyes lowered. The sun had risen bright and shining, casting its warm rays over the sombre proceedings.

It had taken them less than half an hour to bury Maria Clayton. They had dug a makeshift grave using tools from the hardware shop across the street, then they had wrapped the body in a sheet and lowered it gently into the hole. No more than two feet deep, it lay beneath a small willow and, as they stood there, pieces of blossom fell like pink tears to join the flowers atop the grave.

Clayton said a short prayer, his voice cracking halfway through, then he brushed the earth from his hands and walked away.

Tyler felt an uncomfortable familiarity about the ritual, remembering the funeral of his own father not so long ago; the act which had brought him back to his birth-place, now a place of death and disease.

Before they had buried Maria, Tyler had driven alone to Dan Hawley's surgery where he had collected a couple of microscopes, some slides and other paraphernalia which Clayton had asked for. On the journey there and back he had found bodies in the streets, some savaged as Clayton's wife had been, others disfigured almost beyond recognition. And amongst those bodies he had recognized people he knew.

Reg Gentry was one of the men who had farmed around Wakely all his life. Tyler had found him with his eyes torn out and his throat cut.

He had found Ronald Faber, a man he remembered as owning a clothes shop. Faber, normally a fat individual, had wasted away to practically nothing, his skin covered everywhere by hideous growths and sores.

It had seemed to Tyler, as if he were driving through a gigantic graveyard where no one had bothered to bury the dead.

Nevertheless, he had returned with the required instruments and then set about helping Clayton bury his wife. As he had helped lift the body onto the sheet, Tyler had not failed to notice the severity of the mutilations which she had suffered. It seemed as if the ferocity of the attacks was growing worse. And, beside her, had lain the body of one of the diseased killers, the body even more broken and disfigured by the pounding which Clayton himself had given it, venting his frustration and pain on the immobile cadaver. Tyler had looked at it, at the monstrous deformity and obscene appearance and it had reminded him, somehow, of the deformed calf which he had killed. How long ago was it now? A week? Two weeks? Three? It seemed like an eternity. Memories and thoughts flooded through his mind and he was sure the others felt the same way. Each carried their own secret to be stored in the darkest recesses of their minds.

Tyler wondered how much more they would see before it was all over.

The body lay on one of the large stainless steel benches in the kitchen of the hotel. Completely naked, the skin had a yellowish tinge to it, that at least, which wasn't covered by unhealed sores and festering blisters. The stench which rose from the corpse was a pungent mixture of putrefying flesh and blood. Tyler and Clayton had carried it from the room upstairs and stripped it, wearing some rubber gloves which Jo had found in a store cupboard. Now, together with the instruments from his own black bag, Clayton had before him two large butcher's knives, a smaller freezer knife

265

(capable of cutting through bone) and a meat saw. They were not the best implements with which to conduct an autopsy but he had little choice.

The doctor prodded the body with the end of his finger, noticing how tightly the skin was pulled across the bones. In places, it looked as if it were going to break or tear. Small pieces flaked off as he rubbed, exposing grey muscle beneath.

'Very little surface lividity,' he said, reaching for the largest of the butcher's knives. 'The skin looks jaundiced.'

Tyler and Jo watched as he inspected the body, peering closely at the face, probing at one of the gaping blisters with the point of the knife. A small trickle of clear fluid oozed from it and Clayton transferred it onto a microscope slide. 'These lesions look as if they've been caused by a reaction *within* the skin cells,' he said, peering through the microscope. He stroked his chin thoughtfully and returned to the body. Jo gritted her teeth as he pushed the knife into the abdomen of the corpse just below the sternum. With an expert movement, the doctor opened the torso as far as the pelvis.

A cloying stench erupted from the hollow and he waved a hand in front of him for a moment before reaching for a syringe. He located the bladder and ran the syringe deep into the swollen organ, withdrawing about 25ml of fluid which he also deposited on a slide. One drop of it glistened beneath the lights.

'Interesting,' he said, abstractedly. 'The bladder is undamaged yet it's full of blood and, from what I can see, there's no damage to either the liver or kidneys. Filtration of waste has been happening as it would in any normal person.' He pointed to the liver with the end of the knife. 'If the skin coloration was caused by jaundice, or hepatitis, then at least half of the liver cells would be damaged.'

266

He opened the mouth and inspected the teeth and gums.

'Gum shrinkage,' he said, moving down to the hands with their long fingernails. The doctor also looked at the hair which grew in a thick clump in the palms of both appendages. 'This is very unusual,' he said, pulling at the hairs.

'Have you ever seen anything like it before?' asked Tyler.

Clayton was silent for long moments then he nodded almost imperceptibly.

'Yes, I have,' he said. 'But, it was impossible to make the diagnosis without a full examination of a sufferer.'

'So what is it for God's sake?' asked Tyler.

Clayton looked at Jo.

'It's probably the answer to most of Eastern European myth and folklore,' he said.

'What's that supposed to mean?' Tyler said, agitatedly.

'It was Miss Ward who first mentioned vampires wasn't it?' said the doctor.

Tyler shook his head.

'Oh no, come on Clayton, you're not going to tell me that the people of Wakely have been turned into vampires? What do you think this is, some kind of joke? You'll be telling me next there are werewolves running around here.'

'Vic, let him finish,' said Jo, trying to calm the farmer down.

'This man,' he indicated the body before him, 'in fact, all the infected residents of the town, are suffering from a highly advanced form of a disease known as porphyria.'

'What's that got to do with vampires?' asked Jo.

'You've seen the symptoms yourself,' Clayton said. 'Fear of sunlight, sensitivity to light, growth of nails and teeth, swelling of the lips, yellowing of the skin.

267

Even the hair on the palms of the hands. The blood-lust, the psychosis. They're all symptoms of porphyria. What, in a less enlightened age, might well have been labelled vampirism.'

'My God,' said Jo, softly.

'Why the need to drink blood?' asked Tyler.

'Porphyria is basically a deficiency of iron in the blood stream,' Clayton told him. 'What is known as a disorder of haem synthesis. The blood cannot absorb iron. At first the symptoms look like anaemia and, much of the time, that's as far as it goes. We still know very little about the diseases.'

'You mean there's more than one strain of it?' Jo enquired.

Clayton nodded.

'There are at least six, each manifesting a different severity of symptoms. The people of Wakely seem to be suffering from an advanced form of *porphyria cutanea tarda*. It can be precipitated by alcohol, oestrogen as is found in some birth control pills, or by any toxic agent. In this case, it would seem to be the bacteria in the Vanderburg feed which was passed on to the humans by way of the diseased animals.'

'I still don't understand the significance of the blood,' said Tyler.

'Blood itself is rich in iron,' Clayton began, 'probably the richest source of iron in nature. As I said, anyone with porphyria would find it impossible to absorb iron but, nevertheless, they would need to replace the lost iron. The quickest way of doing that would be to drink blood. That's why the victims of those infected have been mutilated.' His voice dropped slightly and he lowered his gaze. 'The killers wanted blood.'

'Jesus,' murmured Jo. 'It's not hard to see why or how the vampire myth started.'

'There's another thing which links porphyria to myths,' Clayton told her. 'Vampires, according to folklore, are afraid of garlic. There's an enzyme in garlic which breaks down iron in the blood. It stands to reason that anyone suffering the disease would want to keep well away from garlic. The sufferer also only comes out during the night because once the disease has reached a certain stage the iron-free porphyrins build up under the skin. Any exposure to light or sun causes a chemical reaction leading to these lesions.' He pointed to the disfiguring scars and welts on the face of the corpse.

There was a long silence, broken once more by Clayton.

'At the moment, only one person in every 25,000 suffers from porphyria but that number could increase, with or without the influence of the Vanderburg feed. That has just acted as a catalyst in this case but, as I said before, *any* toxic agent could induce it, even something as simple as alcohol or the birth control pill.'

'How is it cured?' asked Jo.

'It isn't,' Clayton said, flatly. 'So little is known about it that no one knows how to perfect a cure. I only recognize the disease because I've seen it in a much milder form many years ago, but never as virulent as this. The problem with the most common form of the disease, *Erythrohepatic porphyria*, is that people can have it and not even realize they're infected.'

A troubled silence settled over the trio, Tyler looked almost accusingly at the gutted body on the slab before him.

'Is it fatal?' Tyler asked.

Clayton stroked his chin, thoughtfully.

'Normally, no,' he said.

Tyler shook his head.

'In the early stages, the people who were infected must have realized there was something wrong with them, so why didn't they go to the doctor?'

'The disease attacks the central nervous system,' Clayton told him. 'It causes disorders of thought and reason. Eventually, it leads to erosion of brain cells. That's what causes the psychosis.'

'So, theoretically, the people who are already infected may die in a few days anyway?' Jo offered.

'It's impossible to say,' said Clayton. 'Days. Weeks. Months. There's no way of knowing.'

'Which doesn't help us in the meantime,' Tyler added, cryptically.

'Thank God the infected people are inactive during the day,' said Jo.

'Inactive perhaps but, unlike the vampires of myth, they don't go into a coma during the daylight hours. Once awoken, providing they are clear of any kind of light, they're just as dangerous.'

'So, are they vampires or not?' asked Jo.

'They're as close to the concept of the mythical vampire as we'll ever see,' said Clayton. 'Or want to see,' he added as an afterthought.

'Then all those legends were created because people didn't understand about diseases like this?' said Tyler.

'Man has a habit of attaching labels to things,' Clayton said. 'It makes us all feel more secure if we can pigeon-hole people or even beliefs. Ignorance spawned legend in many cases, certainly where porphyria is concerned. If you couple the symptoms of it with the fact that there were also a great many more cases of catatonic coma and premature burial in the middle ages, it's not difficult to see how the legends of vampires, were-wolves and even the living dead came about. If we can't rationalize something, we tend to push it into the area of the sub-normal, the supernatural. We're afraid of what we don't understand. And, what we're afraid of, we tend to destroy.'

There was another long silence.

Tyler looked at his watch and saw that it was almost 12.05 p.m.

'We haven't got much time,' he said. 'Less than seven

hours of daylight and there's a lot of ground to cover. We'd better get moving.'

Forty-four

Sir Oliver Thorndike paced agitatedly back and forth in front of his desk, pausing every few seconds to look at his watch. He brushed first one sleeve then the other, as if the gesture would somehow ensure that the time passed more rapidly. He glanced over at the manilla file on his desk and swallowed hard.

There was a knock on the door.

'Come in,' said Thorndike but Stark was already half-way through the door as he said it.

The American looked at the scientist indifferently.

'OK, what's so goddam important?' he said, seating himself in one of the high-backed leather chairs which faced the older man's desk.

Thorndike walked behind the mahogany cabinet and picked up the file, brandishing it almost accusingly before him.

'This is the report on the latest batch of feed,' he said.

'I read it,' Stark told him, reaching into his pocket for the ever-present hip-flask.

'Then you'll have noticed that it too did not reach the specifications required for an adequate safety level.'

'Cut the crap, Thorndike. If there's something on your mind say it.'

'The protein additive which we are, at this very moment, adding to the new batch of feed, is no safer than the first lot. And look what happened because of that. The Government won't tolerate any more incidents on the scale of the one in Wakely.'

'This Government will tolerate anything once they realize the overall financial gain. Why the hell do you think they agreed to co-operate with this project in the beginning?'

'In a covert capacity, yes, but they won't stand for much more. This incident can't be kept quiet forever.' Thorndike swallowed hard. 'Call a temporary halt to Project Erebus.'

'No,' said the American, flatly. 'The new batch of feed is treated and ready for shipment.'

'How many more people are going to die before your conscience begins to prick you?' Thorndike demanded.

'It seems to me I've heard this shit somewhere before. Have you been talking to Muir?' snarled Stark, vehemently. 'You knew the risks involved when this project was launched, you and all the other men working on it – so don't start lecturing me about conscience, you hypocritical son of a bitch.'

'Deciding to call it Erebus has become somewhat prophetic don't you think?'

'What's that supposed to mean?'

Thorndike threw down the file.

'Erebus. The God of Darkness, ruler of the region beyond Hades. Well, it seems we've created our own little hell just a mile or so away.'

Stark got to his feet.

'Don't try to hand me any of your intellectual crap. You're not indispensable, Thorndike.'

The scientist grinned but there was no humour there.

'It seems to me I've heard *that* somewhere before,' he said. 'First Anderson, then Charles Muir, then myself, is that it?'

'Forget your conscience,' the American said, his voice full of menace. 'There's no room for it anymore.'

He walked out, leaving Thorndike to stare impotently at the discarded file. He sat down, head cradled in his hands.

The file lay there like an accusation.

Forty-five

The map of Wakely which was pinned to the notice-board in the hotel was criss-crossed with red and black pen marks, entire streets had been coloured over. Tyler inked over another part of the map and stepped back in resignation.

'There's nowhere left they could be hiding,' he said.

'Have you searched everywhere?' asked Clayton.

'I think I've been to some places twice, I seem to be going around in circles.'

'What's that?' asked Jo, pointing to an untouched black square towards the north of the town.

'The old cinema,' said Tyler, quietly. He gazed at the map for long moments, thoughts tumbling through his mind.

Clayton looked at him.

'Is it big enough?' he asked.

Tyler nodded.

'How the bloody hell did I miss it?' he muttered to himself.

'You try there then, Vic,' Jo said.

'Are we decided on what to do now?' the doctor added, running over the plans which they had formulated earlier.

273

'I'll search the rest of the buildings, any that I haven't tried,' said Tyler. 'You and Jo drive out to Vanderburg Chemicals, see what you can find.' He reached into his pocket and pulled out the I.D. card which he'd taken from the body of Carlo Fanducci days earlier. 'Use this to get past the guards,' Tyler said, handing it to the doctor.

'And what if they know who Fanducci is?' asked Clayton.

'Then you'll have to find some other way of getting in.'

'It seems like madness doing it in broad daylight,' said the doctor. 'We'd have a much better chance at night.'

'You know as well as I do that we daren't risk being outside in the dark, not until these . . . creatures have been destroyed.'

Tyler fumbled in his coat pocket, checking that he had enough cartridges for the Franchi. His landrover was already loaded up with a dozen cans of petrol. He felt as secure as he was likely to.

'And we meet back here at eight?' said Jo.

Tyler nodded.

The trio stood in silence for long moments, then Clayton excused himself, walking out of the front door of the hotel. Jo and Tyler gazed into each other's eyes, questions hovering there. Unspoken fears.

He finally reached out and pulled her towards him. She responded fiercely.

'Vic, I'm scared,' she said.

'Join the club,' he mused.

'I don't want to lose you. Not now.'

'You won't,' he reassured her, wishing he could add more conviction to his voice.

'Please be careful,' she said.

'You too,' he told her, smiling. Then they kissed, mouths joined firmly, tongues probing urgently.

274

When she pulled away, there was a single tear trickling down her cheek which Tyler wiped away with his index finger.

'What happened to the tough lady reporter?' he asked, smiling.

'I think she stayed in New York,' said Jo, angry at herself. When she looked up at him, her eyes were glistening. 'I love you, Vic,' she whispered.

He looked momentarily surprised by the exclamation but then he pulled her close once more.

They remained like that for what seemed like an eternity then, without speaking, they walked outside and around to the rear of the hotel where they found Clayton. The doctor was on his knees, head bowed, beside the small mound of earth which marked the resting place of his dead wife. Tyler could see the man's mouth moving as he spoke silent prayers, muttering inaudible phrases.

Feeling like intruders at the private ritual, Jo and Tyler slipped away to wait for him.

He returned minutes later looking somewhat drawn.

'I'm sorry,' he said, smiling, thinly. 'There was something I had to do.'

Tyler nodded but didn't speak.

The three of them walked out to the car park together, Tyler watching as Clayton unlocked the boot of his Capri, ensuring that there was enough room inside for Jo to lie comfortably. It was an unfortunate necessity. The security men at Vanderburg had seen her. They may not recognise her again but it was a chance no one was willing to take.

Tyler climbed into his landrover and laid the shotgun on the passenger seat. In the rear of the vehicle were several cans of petrol which he'd taken from the hotel cellar.

He watched as Jo slid into the boot of the Capri.

275

Clayton shut it and walked around to the driver's side door.

He looked at his watch and then up at the sky.

Rain clouds were gathering to the west, a vast grey expanse which stretched across the sky like a shroud, drawing nearer by the minute.

The two men exchanged brief glances then, without speaking, Tyler drove off.

Clayton watched the landrover disappear around a corner, then he too started his engine, guiding the Capri out into the road.

The drive to Vanderburg Chemicals would take less than fifteen minutes.

Forty-six

Tyler glanced anxiously at the sky as he pulled the landrover to a halt. More and more of the blue canopy above him was being obscured by smoky grey cloud which moved in rolling banks towards the town. A light breeze had sprung up and he shivered a little as he stepped out of the vehicle, gripping the Franchi tightly.

The cinema stood before him, a towering red brick building built over forty years earlier. It had been allowed to fall into disrepair, its stonework chipped in places, windows broken here and there. There were still posters up outside, advertising forthcoming attractions and, as Tyler approached the building, he glanced at them. There would be no audience for them this time, he thought. Tyler rattled the glass doors, seeing that they still bore chains and padlocks. If he was going to get in he would have to find a different entrance. He wandered slowly around to one side of the large edifice and tugged on the bar of the twin wooden safety doors.

They wouldn't budge.

He decided to check the rear.

Skirting the building meant passing along a narrow alley way which ran between the cinema and the yard of a furniture store next to it. Tyler had already checked out the store, but it had not struck him to search the cinema until now. He moved slowly down the alley, glancing up at the overcast sky every so often.

Old cans and newspapers lay around his feet as he walked and the breeze whipped one up at him. Tyler pulled it away from him irritably and turned a corner.

The woman's body was lying amidst a pile of rubbish, almost hidden from view. Just her feet and the lower part of her torso were visible.

Tyler crossed to the untidy heap and prodded the corpse with the end of the shotgun, knocking some boxes away in order to get a better look at her. She was lying face down but her head was turned to one side. A woman in her thirties, her hair had come out in thick wads, even her eyebrows were mere tufts. Her eyes, dark rimmed and bloodshot, were open, as was her mouth and Tyler saw that there were several flies crawling eagerly over the corpse, their attention focused on the festering wound just below her right ear. It was already beginning to turn gangrenous, mottled blue and green in places. The knife which had been used to inflict the wound lay a foot or so away, its blade rusty with dried blood. Tyler could see that her throat had been slashed in several other places too.

He exhaled deeply and walked on, past the large incinerator where rubbish from the cinema was burned, finally reaching the other side exit.

It was slightly ajar.

Tyler approached it cautiously, noticing how clammy his hands felt against the wood and metal of the gun. He prodded the door with the end of the barrel and it shrieked alarmingly as it swung open. The farmer paused for long seconds, reaching for his torch, then he moved cautiously inside.

He found himself confronted by a set of stone steps which, he knew, led up to the balcony. As he began to climb them his boots echoed loudly within the cold passageway and Tyler cursed under his breath. It was dark on the staircase but there was enough natural light coming through the frosted glass window ahead to prevent him using the torch. He trod carefully, the shotgun lowered.

The steps finally flattened out into a landing. He needed to turn a corner to climb the other flight, which would take him into the balcony itself. Tyler could hear water dripping from the pipes in the toilets behind him. The steady 'plink, plink' jarred his nerves as he slowly ascended the second flight of steps. The darkness grew more pronounced, closing around him like a glove as he finally reached the doors which were his final obstacle.

He flicked on the torch and leant against the door.

It wouldn't move. Something, Tyler decided, was stopping its passage.

He stepped back a pace then drove a boot into the partition and, this time, it swung open to reveal the gaping black maw within. It was like walking into a coal mine. Even the beam of the torch had difficulty cutting through the all-enveloping darkness. He shone the beam down, bringing it to bear on the object which had been blocking the door.

It was another body, a man this time. His shirt and jacket lay open to reveal a pulped rib-cage and the tattered remnants of intestines. A fetid odour of decay filled the farmer's nostrils and he stepped over the corpse, moving slowly across the balcony, sweeping the torch beam back and forth. The place smelt damp and fusty but there was the ever-present odour of death and decay which he'd come to know only too well in the past week or so.

Something brushed against his ankle.

Tyler almost shouted aloud in surprise, swinging the torch around in an effort to discover what had touched him.

He held the shotgun in one hand, not daring to put the torch down but aware that, if someone did come at him, he would more than likely break his wrist firing the weapon with one hand. He felt a bead of perspiration pop onto his forehead as his eyes scanned the unyielding gloom.

He shone the torch around his feet.

'Oh Christ,' he murmured, softly.

A dismembered hand lay close by, the fingers outstretched. The hand had been torn, not cut, off. Long tendrils of flesh hung from it and Tyler swallowed hard. From the hair on the back of it, the hand looked as if it had belonged to a man.

He heard a slow, rhythmic thudding and it was drawing closer.

The farmer stood bolt upright, the torch moving wildly in his grip as the beam sought out the source of the movement.

The soft thudding grew louder.

It was close now. Very close.

His finger tightened a fraction on the trigger.

Something heavy struck his leg and he almost fired. He swung the torch down immediately, his breath stuck in his throat.

Lying at his feet was the severed head of Ben Thurston. The old man's eyes were open, gazing past Tyler as if looking for his killer. His own movements, he guessed, had dislodged the head.

Tyler gritted his teeth and shone the torch ahead of

him. The rest of Thurston's body lay a few feet away. The head had been severed by a small axe which was still embedded in the back of the corpse. The hand was missing too.

'You bastards,' Tyler shouted and his voice echoed around the cavernous interior, bouncing off the walls until it seemed to rise to a high-pitched scream of anguish.

Only silence greeted his outburst.

He was shaking slightly, as much from rage as from shock. The discovery of Thurston, the man he had loved like his own father, had shaken him more than he'd expected, and what made things worse was the fact that the old man had not been infected. He had been another helpless victim of the diseased killers. Vampires. The word drifted into Tyler's mind. Standing here in this deserted cinema with the severed head of a friend at his feet, surrounded by impenetrable darkness, the word seemed to have a terrifying reality about it.

'Vampires,' he said, quietly.

He stood for long seconds, now sure that the creatures were not hiding in the cinema. But where were they? He'd searched everywhere in town.

The thought struck him like a thunderbolt.

What a fool he'd been. It was so obvious it was ridiculous. He felt, simultaneously, elated and angry. Angry with himself for not having thought of it earlier. He turned and ran for the door.

There was only one place where they could possibly be.

Forty-seven

Clayton wound down his window as the first of the security guards approached, the familiar red and silver Vanderburg logo on his breast pocket.

'Afternoon, sir,' said the guard, running appraising eyes over both Clayton and the car.

The doctor nodded a greeting. He didn't want to speak but even if he'd needed to, he doubted if he could. It was as if someone had clamped a steel vice around his throat and were turning it one notch at a time. He tried to swallow but couldn't.

'There's no unauthorized personnel allowed in,' the guard said. 'If you want to see someone you'll . . .'

Clayton reached into his pocket and produced the I.D. card which had been taken from Fanducci. The guard took it from him, not noticing that the doctor's hands were shaking slightly. He looked at the card and then at Clayton. After a moment he handed the card back, his eyes still fixed on the doctor.

'OK,' said the security man and signalled to his partner. The barrier which blocked the drive was lifted and Clayton drove on. As he guided the vehicle up the long driveway, he peered into his rear-view mirror and saw one of the two guards pointing at the car. Clayton swallowed hard, still watching as the man disappeared inside the yellow porta-cabin. His companion followed closely.

Clayton wiped his sweating palms on his trousers and drove on, finally bringing the car to a halt next to one of the large manufacturing sheds. There was a narrow gap between the shed and the main building and he reversed towards that.

Inside the boot, Jo heard him switch off the engine.

She waited a few moments then slipped the catch, climbing out.

She felt appallingly conspicuous for a moment as she stood behind the car but she rapidly ducked down and sprinted along the narrow passage towards a window in the main building. Clayton watched her in his rear-view mirror, then he scanned the area before him.

A large container lorry had just pulled up in front of the main building. The driver got out.

He looked across, saw Clayton and headed towards the car.

The doctor was frantic as the man drew nearer, glancing at his piece of paper and then at the parked Capri.

Clayton shuffled nervously in his seat. What the hell did this man want?

Jo had disappeared from view behind him. He was alone.

And the man was getting closer.

Clayton heard a loud whistle and looked to his right where another man, dressed in a white overall, was signalling to the driver of the lorry. The man in the overall beckoned the driver to him and Clayton saw them chatting animatedly. The driver returned to his lorry and started it up, guiding the massive juggernaut into its appointed position near the loading bay of the closest manufacturing shed.

The rear end of the lorry now blocked Clayton's exit.

Jo knew the lab coat was too big and she felt conscious of it. She tried tucking the sleeves up but they kept coming down, covering her hands. She pulled it tightly across her and waited for the lift to descend.

She was standing in the main foyer of Vanderburg Chemicals, muzak filling her ears as she waited impatiently, for the metal doors to slide open.

The window by which she had gained entry into the building had led her into a deserted office. She had found the lab coat hanging on a hook on the back of the door. It bore the red and silver VC on the pocket but, from the weight and size of it, Jo was convinced that it belonged to a man. She hoped he didn't come looking for it. However, as she stood watching the numbers light up above her, signalling the approach of the lift, she found that her heart had stopped pounding so hard. Few people had looked at her and, those who had, had cast only cursory glances at her. Hold onto yourself, she thought. Don't get paranoid now.

'Where are you going?'

The voice startled her and she turned to see another young woman standing beside her. The woman, in her late twenties, was carrying several thick files. She too wore the monogrammed lab coat.

'I was looking for the research labs,' said Jo, the lie ready on her tongue. 'I'm new here, I can't find my way around too well yet.'

The other girl smiled.

'I know what you mean, I was like that for the first few *weeks* after I started. This place is like a maze.'

'How long have you worked here?' asked Jo.

'Two years,' said the girl. 'My name's Ruth Wicks by the way.'

'Hi, I'm Janet Grant,' Jo lied.

The lift bumped to a halt and they stepped inside.

'Which floor?' asked Ruth, finger hovering over the buttons.

Jo swallowed hard.

The other girl continued to smile.

The American glanced at the array of buttons.

'Three,' she said, praying she'd said the right thing.

Ruth jabbed the button marked '3' and the doors slid shut.

'You're working with Glendenning then?' she said.

Jo nodded.

'He's away all day, there's no one in the labs,' Ruth said.

283

'I just thought I'd have a look around, familiarize myself with the place,' the journalist said.

Ruth eyed her, the smile fading slightly.

'I don't think they like people just walking in and out of the labs, not with the work they're doing.'

'Well, like I said, I wanted to get the feel of the place. What kind of work *are* they doing exactly?'

'Didn't they tell you that when you were interviewed?' asked Ruth, the smile now completely gone.

'Not everything,' said Jo, sensing that she was losing her grip here. 'Do *you* know?'

'Yes.'

There was an awkward silence. The lift came to a halt at the second floor and Ruth stepped out.

'Perhaps I'll see you later,' she said.

Jo nodded vigorously, anxious for the girl to leave.

As the doors slid shut, the American breathed an audible sigh of relief. A sound which caught in her throat as, a second later, they opened again.

'By the way,' said Ruth, the smile having returned. 'I'd get them to find you a lab coat that's the right size.'

Jo laughed exaggeratedly, watching as the girl walked away. She jabbed the '3' button again and the lift rose one more floor.

When she stepped out she found that she was in a windowless corridor, fluorescents blazing brightly above her. The passageway ran arrow-straight ahead of her for about twenty yards, then it angled sharply to the right. Jo began walking, her eyes scanning the doors on either side of her, expecting one to open at any moment. There were names on some of them, numbers on others. She sought out the door with Glendenning's name on it. She knew that name from somewhere, she knew him, had spoken to him. Of that she was sure and, as she turned the corner, the realization gradually spread through her. He had been the man she'd spoken to when she'd first visited Vanderburg Chemicals in search of Geoffrey Anderson.

One of the doors she passed was thick, sheet steel and on it was the yellow and black sign which warned of radiation. Jo paused beside the door, looking in front and behind her, listening for the slightest sound of movement. Then, she moved on.

Still the doors showed no signs of Glendenning's name. She tried the handle of one but it was locked.

Jo spun round as she heard a low whimpering sound.

In the stillness of the corridor, with just the steady hum of the fluorescents, the sound seemed louder.

She listened and it came again. It sounded like a dog in pain but a big dog and even then the whining was curiously resonant. She put it down to the acoustics in the corridor.

Jo crossed to the door from behind which the sound was coming. She twisted the knob, surprised to find it unlocked. The blinds in the room were drawn, it was difficult to see. The overcast weather outside offered her very little natural light either. But she was able to see that the room was about twenty feet square. One wall was completely covered by filing cabinets, the centre of it was divided into aisles formed by three workbenches and dozens of cages.

In each of the cages there was a different animal. They were surprisingly quiet as Jo approached them, only the dog continued to whine.

She peered into the first cage where a rhesus monkey lay motionless on the floor, its tail twitching slightly.

It had no eyes.

Where the glistening orbs should have been there were just red-rimmed holes. And yet, when Jo moved, the monkey sat up, following her with those bloodied pits as if tracking her with radar. She shuddered, almost shouting aloud as the bats in the next cage flapped their wings excitedly at her approach. There were two of them, fruit bats or flying foxes she guessed from the size.

Both were completely white, their eyes glinting with a vile pink lustre.

And then she saw the dog.

It was a labrador, at least she thought it was. Its coat had no brilliant sheen to it, rather a dull appearance which made it look dirty. Its muzzle was virtually non-existent, its mouth consisting of a huge gaping maw from which long fangs protruded. One ear was missing and, as Jo looked closely, the dog moved.

There was a long growth sprouting from one of its rear legs and the American was sure she could see claws growing at the end of it. The dog had five legs. It shuffled helplessly in the cage, that cavernous mouth dripping saliva as it watched her with eyes that glowed red.

Jo passed the last of the cages and found two or three files laid out on the nearest work-bench. One of them was open. She scanned the title page:

GENETIC RE-CONSTRUCTION

She looked at the cages behind her, then back at the file. Another lay beside it marked:

PROTEIN SYNTHESIS

Something at the back of her mind clicked. It had been Dan Hawley who had first mentioned proteins. An artificially created protein. The plague carrier. The thing which had transformed the residents of Wakely into the vulpine denizens of legend.

These files were what she sought.

There was another marked simply:

DISTRIBUTION

She picked that one up too, stuffing all three under her arm. As she turned to leave she noticed the steaming mug of coffee on the work-bench nearby. Someone had obviously been working in here and might well return.

Jo swallowed hard and made for the door.

She had taken less than two paces when it opened and Richard Neville stepped inside.

'What are you doing in here?' he snapped. 'This is a restricted area.' He noticed that her lab coat did not fit and, something which Ruth Wicks had not noticed, the absence of an identity tag on her lapel. 'Who are you?' he demanded.

Jo took a step back, her hand brushing against the mug of coffee.

As Neville advanced towards her, she hurled it at him.

The boiling liquid hit the scientist full in the face and he shrieked, clawing madly at his eyes.

Jo side-stepped him and ran for the door.

'Stop,' screamed Neville, his skin blistered by the red hot coffee, his arms flailing about uselessly.

Jo wrenched open the door and ran for the lifts.

The scientist dragged himself upright and staggered blindly across the room towards the alarm on the far wall, crashing into some of the cages as he did so.

There was an explosive cacophony of squawks, shrieks and buckling metal as the cages went flying, some of them bursting open to release their occupants.

A cat with a large tumorous growth on its back scampered free and hid beneath the work-bench. The monkey began to howl, baring long fangs, gripping the bars with the stubby nubs of fingers.

Neville reached the alarm and broke the glass with the heel of his hand. Immediately, the strident wail of a klaxon filled the air, reverberating throughout the entire building.

Alec Clayton heard the siren and he gripped the wheel of the Capri tighter, feeling the plastic slip beneath his sweating palms. The sound could have been started by anyone he reasoned. It may even be a fault in the mechanism, a drill which the employees were obliged to endure every so often. He sought desperately for explanations but his mind could accept nothing but what he knew must be the real reason for the sirens. He wondered if they had caught Jo. Should he start his engine and get away? What if he was wrong? Questions piled up in his tortured mind. Perhaps if he created a diversion of some kind . . . The thought trailed off. He looked anxiously around him. What could he do?

He twisted the key in the ignition and started his engine.

'Security alarm,' said John Stark getting to his feet. He crossed to the window of his office and looked out. Nothing moved. He returned to his desk and flicked one of the switches on the console before him.

'What the hell is going on?' he demanded. 'Who set that alarm off?'

The voice which answered him sounded metallic over the intercom. It belonged to Thorndike.

'There's been a disturbance in one of the laboratories,' he said. 'Neville said that a woman stole some files.'

'A woman?' Stark exclaimed, angrily. 'What does she look like?'

'Neville didn't get a good look at her,' Thorndike said. 'He seemed more concerned about the files. She took the files on the Erebus project.'

The American gritted his teeth and flipped another switch.

'Security, this is a general alert, there is an unauthorized person in the building. No one is to leave. Repeat, no one is to leave.' He flicked the switch off and supped deeply from his flask, grunting angrily. 'Fucking bitch,' he rasped to himself.

Jo gripped the files tightly under her arm as the lift descended. The sound of the siren was loud in her ears, even inside the enclosure. There was a loudspeaker in there too and she heard Stark's angry words. She wondered how she was going to get past the security men downstairs.

Indeed, as the lift doors slid open she stepped out into the cavernous reception area to find blue-uniformed men standing at the exit doors. One was speaking into a two-way radio. Jo hesitated for long seconds, wondering what to do. She dared not try and slip out through the window she had gained entry by, and yet she couldn't stand helplessly staring at the guards. The files suddenly seemed enormous and she felt painfully conspicuous, dressed in her ridiculously ill-fitting lab coat.

She was still trying to decide what to do when one of the security men began walking towards her.

Alec Clayton stuck the Capri into gear and guided it slowly towards the front of the main building. The siren continued to wail and he could see the blue-coated security men blocking the exits.

His shirt was sticking to his back, the perspiration beaded heavily on his face. He gripped the wheel tightly and peered through the double sets of glass doors, his roving eyes finally spotting Jo.

He could see that one of the security men was approaching her. Clayton swallowed hard, realizing what he must do. He put the car into reverse and stepped on the accelerator, pulling back about thirty yards.

Already he could see other security men approaching in his rear view mirror.

He ignored them, gripping the wheel even tighter, ducking as low as he could behind it. Then he pushed his foot down hard on the accelerator, glancing down to see the needle touch forty. There was a scream of burning rubber as the back wheels spun for long seconds, then the Capri shot forward as if fired from a gigantic cannon. It sped towards the glass doors and Clayton opened his mouth in a silent scream as he saw them rushing towards him.

The Capri hurtled into the double doors with the force of a steam train. There was an ear-piercing explosion of glass as the car obliterated the entry way. Huge shards of crystal flew through the air, pieces of wood and metal buckling under the impact. The Capri skidded inside the reception, the rear end swinging round to thud into a security guard. The impact catapulted him several feet and he rolled over in the cascade of glass splinters. The windscreen of the car was cracked but not broken, the front bumper bent badly. Clayton himself sat for long seconds gasping to regain his breath, groaning as he touched his chest. The steering column had slammed into him as he hit the doors but he was sure he hadn't broken any bones.

Jo took advantage of the shattering entrance and lashed out at the security man nearest her, driving her foot hard into his groin. He went down in a heap at her feet. She vaulted him and ran for the car, wrenching open the passenger side door and leaping in.

'Go,' she shouted and Clayton reversed, back over the jagged splinters of crystal, through the pulverized doors.

There was a loud bang and the side window exploded into a thousand pieces as a bullet struck it.

Clayton floored the accelerator, anxious to get away from the two security men who had appeared from another building and were pointing guns in the direction of the Capri. He saw one actually sight the pistol and fire. The bullet ripped off a wing mirror and ricocheted off the bonnet, gouging a deep furrow in the paintwork.

Another security guard emerged from one of the

manufacturing sheds, levelling a .38 at the speeding car.

Clayton spun the wheel, slamming the car into the man before he had a chance to fire. The impact catapulted the guard into the air. His body seemed to hang there for interminable seconds, as if suspended on invisible wires, then it crashed down on the roof of the vehicle before bouncing off.

Clayton drove for the main gate, trying to urge more speed from the Capri.

Both he and Jo saw that the barrier had been dropped. The two guards were both kneeling down, aiming their pistols. A salvo of shots hit the car, one shattering the windscreen. The glass spider-webbed, leaving Clayton momentarily unsighted. The Capri skidded violently and Jo clutched the door handle as the car lurched across the driveway. The doctor punched his fist through the shattered glass, enabling him to see out. He twisted the wheel, ducking low once more as they approached the barrier.

There was another salvo of shots and one of them caught Clayton in the shoulder.

The impact slammed him back in his seat and he yelped in pain as the bullet punched its way through his back leaving an exit hole the size of a fist. His right arm went momentarily numb and the Capri skidded but the doctor gripped the wheel as tightly as he could with his good hand and, seconds later, the car hit the barrier.

What was left of the windscreen was smashed in by the impact and Jo screamed as she was showered with glass. A sliver cut her arm as she shielded her face and she heard the groan of metal as the roof of the vehicle was almost torn free by the collision.

More bullets ploughed into the back of the vehicle as it burst miraculously through the barrier. Behind them,

Jo could see the two security men clambering into a rangerover.

'They're coming after us,' she yelled, watching as the large vehicle roared away in pursuit.

Clayton didn't answer. His face was the colour of rancid butter, blood running freely from the wound in his shoulder. But it was the pain which kept him conscious and, as he too saw the rangerover speeding after them, he seemed able to coax yet more speed from the Capri until the needle on the dashboard nudged eighty.

The Range Rover kept on coming.

Forty-eight

Tyler stood before the main gates of Wakely football ground, the Franchi cradled in his arms.

Above him, the grey clouds were gathering ever more rapidly and, as he pushed open one of the gates, he felt the first light spots of rain begin to fall.

The farmer realized that he would have to move fast. He was no longer safe in weather like this. The floodlights loomed menacingly over him as he walked slowly towards the broken rail which separated the stone embankment steps from the pitch itself. The ground was enclosed by a high wooden fence but, as a child, Tyler could remember sneaking through the gaps to watch the Wakely side play. Now he moved across the steps cautiously, eyes alert for any sign of movement.

292

There were stands on either side of the pitch and one behind each goal, only the part of the ground which he now patrolled was not under cover. As the rain began to fall more heavily, Tyler hurried to the canopy which overhung the nearest stand.

He pushed open the rusty iron gate and walked through, past the turnstile and the tiny box-like structure which had once been the ticket office. A mouldy yellow sign still proclaimed:

MAIN STAND: ADULTS £1.00 CHILDREN 25p

Tyler looked up at the stand, its roof battered and holed by the ravages of years gone by. However, at the very top, up a flight of covered stairs, was what looked like a press box. It was a room about fifteen feet long and twelve wide, its windows now crusted with dirt and broken in many places.

He had been allowed up there once when he was ten. His father had known most of the ground staff at the club and, as a special treat, young Tyler had been taken up to that special room to see how the floodlights were activated. He could still remember even after all these years.

He stood by the stairs which led up to the first row of stand seats and inhaled. The air smelt of wet grass and decay. He gripped the shotgun tighter and decided to check out the other stands first.

The farmer chose to walk across the pitch itself, coming to the smaller stand directly opposite. It had about 200 seats in it, most of them now rotten, some torn from their brackets and tossed into the aisles. Tyler scanned the delapidated structure hastily then clambered over the rail back onto the pitch.

The goal posts were still standing, the paint peeling and chipped from them like scabrous flesh.

He checked the area behind the right hand goal, it was little more than a covered embankment, then he walked the full length of the pitch and did the same at the other end. Weeds had fought their way up through gaps in the concrete and, here and there, rusted tin cans lay in piles or rolled gently, coaxed by the breeze. A piece of paper, the team sheet from a programme, fluttered mournfully in the air.

Tyler turned and headed back towards the main stand, pausing at the players' tunnel.

Twelve stone steps led down into the maze-like catacombs of changing rooms and showers below. It was as black as pitch down there and the farmer reached for his torch, flicking it on when he was half-way down. An overpoweringly fetid odour rose from the subterranean tunnels but it was not the familiar fusty smell of damp and neglect. It was the pungent, nauseating odour of dead flesh.

Tyler paused as he reached the bottom of the stairs, shining the torch ahead of him. It cut through the blackness, revealing a tunnel. It ran for about twenty yards, then branched off at a sharp angle to both right and left. Tyler advanced cautiously, reigning back his revulsion as the stench grew stronger.

The walls were coated with mildew and he could feel it slimy against his hand as he felt his way along the tunnel.

As he turned to the right he almost tripped over the first of the creatures.

It was a man in his early twenties, huddled up in a foetal position, his mouth open to reveal his long teeth. But for the almost imperceptible rise of his shoulders, Tyler could have mistaken the immobile form for a corpse.

He stepped over the young man, moving as slowly as he could, desperate not to make a sound. As the torch beam cut through the darkness it picked out six, seven. A dozen more sleeping forms. Two dozen.

The tunnel was widening, opening out into another

294

corridor and, sprawled on the floor were more of them. Many more.

To his left in what had once been the showers he saw three dozen of them huddled close by. To his right, more. The entire place was full of the infected townspeople. Tyler re-traced his steps, careful not to wake any of the sleeping creatures. He tried the other way.

It was the same story. Dozens and dozens of contaminated killers all sleeping in the reeking blackness.

At his feet lay Stuart Nichols. Tyler fought to control himself, a combination of fear and loathing welling up inside him until he felt he would have to scream. The silence was broken only by the occasional rasping ululation, a liquid gurgling. Thick, mucoid snortings.

The farmer tried to control his breathing, to still his hammering heart for fear that they would hear it.

The smell was unbelievable.

All around him they lay, some dead, killed by their own. There were the remnants of corpses lying with those who still breathed and the sight made Tyler feel even sicker. It was like standing in hell itself, in the dank, reeking subterranean gloom surrounded by these monstrosities.

He moved backwards slowly, trying to avoid the numerous sleeping forms, the shotgun hovering in his grip. If he woke them now . . .

Tyler forced himself to think of something else.

He sensed that he was near to the tunnel bend, just a few more yards and he would be back in the players' entrance, able to flee upward from this pit of horror. He could feel the perspiration on his forehead. His throat felt dry and he couldn't swallow.

He would burn them, he decided. There was enough petrol in the landrover, all he had to do was seal the exits from beneath the stand and then set light to the place. Burn every one of them.

Ten yards and he would be able to run.

His torch went out.

Tyler could not restrain himself. A cry of panic escaped him as he shook the useless light, blind in the Stygian darkness.

He turned to run.

A hand caught his ankle and tripped him.

He went sprawling but managed to retain his grip on the shotgun. As he felt the deformed figure clawing at him, he tightened his finger on the trigger.

The blast not only gutted his attacker, it also gave him a second of precious light. In that second, Tyler saw that they were rising. But, there was no slow deliberation to their movements, almost as one they were awake, alert and on their feet. Dozens of them spilled from their hiding places to fill the corridor, hungry eyes fixing him with baleful stares.

Tyler turned and ran, the monstrous horde after him. He hurtled up from beneath the ground, slipping on the wet grass, rolling over in time to see the first of them emerge from the tunnel. The farmer swung the shotgun up and fired, the blast ripping away most of the man's face. The body was catapulted backwards, momentarily blocking the entrance, giving Tyler time to get to his feet.

He was moving without thinking, sheer instinct kept him going and he vaulted the rail, heading for the steps which led up to the main stand.

He could hear the fastest of them clattering up the steps behind him and he turned to see Don Mason approaching him.

Tyler didn't hesitate. He squeezed the trigger, watching as the wad of shot cut through the policeman's chest, splattering those behind with gobbets of lung and fragments of bone. But they kept coming, clambering over Mason's body in their frantic effort to reach Tyler. To reach fresh blood.

He could see the others spilling onto the pitch, looking up at the grey sky as if in gratitude.

If only the sun had been out thought Tyler as he leapt up the next flight of stone steps, the ones which would take him to the little room on top of the stand itself. He took them two at a time, slipping once, looking back to see that there were three of the creatures following him. Led by Stuart Nichols. His face was almost unrecognizable, disfigured by the ravages of the disease but, through all that, his eyes gleamed madly as he sought to catch Tyler.

Tyler reached the door of the room and twisted the handle.

The door was locked.

Nichols was about ten yards from him now and Tyler tugged hard on the recalcitrant handle.

Finally, he realized he had no choice. He spun round and fired. The close range blast eviscerated Nichols, the impact catapulting him backward, blasting him off the steps. He fell screaming.

Tyler realized he had just one cartridge left in the gun. He blew the second attacker's head off, then using the butt of the shotgun as a club, went for his final opponent. The man was in his forties, overweight and a little sluggish. Tyler easily avoided his clumsy gropings and ducked under the first punch, bringing the stock up under the man's chin. The blow staggered him and Tyler struck again, feeling bone splinter as he crushed the man's nose. Blood burst from the ruptured appendage and the farmer pressed his advantage, kicking his opponent hard in the groin.

The man overbalanced and tumbled heavily down the steps. Tyler turned and kicked at the lock of the door, driving desperate blows into it until it finally surrendered to the pressure and flew inwards.

He dashed in, finding himself confronted by a bank of switches and dials. The accumulation of dust made him cough but he scanned the array before him, glancing periodically out of the window down to the pitch below.

Every square inch of grass seemed to be occupied. He could only guess at how many of them there were.

Two hundred? Three hundred? More?

They stood glaring up at the room where he remained. Not one of them attempted to move now. They knew he had to come down eventually. They need do nothing but wait.

Tyler's breath was coming in gasps, as much from frustration as exertion. He looked desperately for some sign on the large control panel which might help him. His fingers traced patterns in the thick dust, brushing it away from the controls.

There was a switch marked:

POWER

He flicked to 'ON' and, somewhere, far below him, there was a rumbling. Like thunder only it sounded as if it were going to erupt from the earth itself. The thrumming grew louder.

Now he saw other switches:

COLUMN ONE
COLUMN TWO

And through to six.

He swallowed hard, the floodlights. The switches had to control the floodlights.

He looked out of the grime-encrusted window once again. The diseased creatures were still standing, looking up at him.

'Just stay there you bastards,' he whispered, fingers poised over the first three switches.

He prayed that the lights would work.

The rumbling from below was now shaking the room. It was time.

All Tyler heard was a maniacal scream and then

298

something heavy crashed into him, driving him into the control panel, knocking the breath from him.

He looked up to see Dan Hawley standing over him.

At least what had once been Dan Hawley.

The vet's face was a patchwork of sores and blisters, some of which had burst and were weeping clear pus. Elsewhere, patches of skin had peeled off to reveal raw skin beneath. He had lost most of his hair, his scalp was now infested with suppurating boils. Nails stained darkly with dried blood curved from the ends of his fingers and he snarled at Tyler in a gesture that was more animal than human.

For what seemed like an eternity, they faced each other, then, Hawley launched himself at the farmer. Vic rolled to one side. He lashed out at his attacker as he did so, driving a powerful kick into his stomach.

The vet grunted and rolled over, his bony hand closing over the leg of a broken chair which lay nearby. He brought it down with bone crushing force, missing Tyler by inches, the nail which protruded from the end striking sparks on the control panel.

Tyler grabbed Hawley's arm and twisted it hard against the joint, trying to make him drop the weapon but the vet merely tore at Tyler's face with his long claws, drawing blood.

The farmer backed off, looking for his shotgun.

He snatched it up, hefting it before him like a club. Hawley struck again but Tyler deflected the blow, striking out himself, catching the vet on the temple. The impact sent him reeling and Tyler swung the gun once again, using it like a baseball bat. He drove the stock into Hawley's face, shattering his bottom jaw. But still the vet kept coming, ignoring the blood which oozed from the vicious rent in his flesh. He ducked beneath Tyler's next blow, striking for the farmer's thigh.

Tyler yelped in pain as the nail punctured his flesh.

Blood spurted from the hole and he felt his skin and muscle being torn as Hawley wrenched the spike free.

The farmer had cartridges in his pocket but he knew that he'd never re-load in time and, as he glanced out of the window down onto the pitch, he saw that the others were beginning to move. They could see what was happening in the room on top of the stand and they were becoming restless. Hungry.

Tyler hurled his gun at Hawley but the vet merely ducked and ran at him, bringing the chair leg down in a wide arc.

More by luck than judgement, Tyler managed to grab his assailant's wrist, gripping as hard as he could. Then, using all his strength, he swung Hawley around and hurled him towards the window.

Propelled by Tyler's throw and his own momentum, the vet could not stop himself.

He crashed through the glass with a scream of rage and horror. For what seemed like an eternity, he clutched at empty air, then, with a last caterwaul of despair, he plummeted down, smashing through the rusted roof of the stand and thudding to earth more than fifty feet below. He rolled over once, then lay still in a widening pool of blood.

Tyler threw all six switches.

The floodlights burst into life, bathing the pitch in powerful white light. Thirty bulbs, two hundred watts each, shone from every tower. In all 180 searing points of energy were trained on the vampires of Wakely, pinning them like moths in a candle flame.

Tyler saw them start to fall, hands raised to the offending brightness as their skin blistered and innumerable screams of agony began to rise like a swelling organ note from the contaminated hordes. They writhed helplessly as the light burned them, scorching their flesh as surely as if they'd been put to the torch. Some ran back and forth in an effort to escape their agony but there was no way out. They were trapped by the beams, paralysed into immobility by their pain. Like rabbits before a snake, they remained hypnotised by the blistering lights, unable to look away but dying in consequence. Their eyes were seared in the sockets, their skin stripped away as if by acid and, on all of them, the welts and sores rose like blossoming flowers. The brilliant light blazed down over the field like some purging fire – a white blanket which brought death to all beneath it. Like hundreds of artificial suns, the bulbs poured out their energy.

Tyler watched mesmerised as the last of the infected townspeople died, flopping around like beached fish until, finally, there was no movement at all.

He bowed his head, his breath coming in gasps.

The puncture in his thigh was throbbing madly and he pressed his handkerchief to it as he walked, hobbling from the little room to stand in the rain.

Tyler stood there for a full thirty minutes, eyes scanning the piles of corpses stretched out on the pitch. His whole body ached but he knew that there was one more thing he had to do.

After turning the lights off, Tyler hobbled down from the control room and wandered out to the landrover. From there he drove the vehicle inside the football ground and, working as thoroughly as possible, used up the cans of petrol, sprinkling the golden fluid over as many corpses as possible.

Now he stood watching as the bodies roasted, the acrid stench of burning flesh filling his nostrils, great black plumes of smoke rising above the scene of death.

It was another hour before he left.

Forty-nine

Charles Muir heard the sirens but he paid them no heed, nor did he stop to ask anyone what had happened. He continued walking purposefully towards the oak-panelled door at the end of the windowless corridor. A technician passed him, running, but the Scot didn't spare the man a second glance.

He entered the room and found two other Vanderburg workers there. One, a man in his late thirties, was looking through the maze of filing cabinets. The other, a woman, was seated at one of the computer consoles.

Muir smiled politely at the woman.

'Could you fetch Mr Stark for me,' he asked.

The woman looked puzzled for a moment, then got to her feet and left the room. Muir took her place at the console.

'If you wouldn't mind leaving?' he said to the man.

The technician put down the file he had and followed the woman outside. The Scot heard the sound of their footsteps receding down the corridor. Stark, he guessed, would arrive in five or six minutes.

Perfect timing. He smiled thinly.

The sirens continued to screech but Muir ignored them, turning his attention instead to the keyboard and V.D.U. before him. He pressed a button and the screen went blank, then, after pausing a second, he tapped in the first commands.

Luminous green letters appeared on the screen:

INTERFACE 3095. READY FOR ENQUIRY

Muir hastily relayed his next instruction.

REQUEST PROGRAM

The computer acknowledged.

ALL TERMINALS ERASE

He sat back, looking at what was displayed before him.

DOES NOT COMPUTE

The display unit glowed.

Muir chewed on the stem of his pipe.

ALL TERMINALS SELF-DESTRUCT

NEGATIVE

Muir hit the keyboard harder.

EMERGENCY COMMAND OVERRIDE. ALL
TERMINALS SELF-DESTRUCT

FULL POWER

He sat back, watching as the letters on the V.D.U. began first to flash and then to turn red. The room began to fill with a high-pitched whine, drowning out even the siren, but Muir just sat there, the unlit pipe clenched between his teeth.

KEY

He typed:

COMMAND IRREVERSIBLE

Now there was no turning back.

Consoles all over Vanderburg Chemicals began to display the same two words and more than one employee began making for the nearest door.

Muir knew what he had done. He was even quite proud of himself. Once the power began to overload, every electrical circuit in the building would go up. Not just short out but the huge amounts of power running through the circuits would cause fires and, eventually, explosions.

The Scot sat and stared at the screen.

He had known for a while now that it must come to this. The feedstuff programme had to be stopped somehow but, more importantly, John Stark had to be stopped. What he had said to Muir had struck a note deep inside him. As he sat staring at the flashing screen he realized that this was his atonement. It was the only way he could hope to find peace after what he had helped to create. The Vanderburg feed, as he had told Stark, was indeed lethal.

The door opened and John Stark blundered in.

Muir turned slowly in his chair to greet the American.

'What in God's name are you doing?' snarled Stark, peering at the console.

It was beginning to flash wildly:

OVERLOAD

Muir said nothing.

'Stop it, now,' shouted Stark, trying to raise his voice above the sirens and the high-pitched screech which was reaching ever greater intensity.

'There's no way of stopping it, *Mr* Stark, said the Scot. 'It's all over. Your plans. Everything.'

Stark leapt at Muir and fastened both hands around his throat.

'Turn it off,' he snarled as the first crackles of over-loading circuitry began to fill his ears.

Muir tried to force the American's hands away but there was a furious desperation in Stark's grip, something which gave him added strength. The two of them crashed onto the console, Stark slamming the Scot's head repeatedly against the desk top.

'Turn it off,' he roared.

As if a switch had been thrown the entire room suddenly exploded in a searing welter of blistering flame. The walls, as if pushed by gigantic fists, erupted outwards. Huge lumps of stone flew through the air like shrapnel.

Elsewhere on the second floor other terminals exploded, hungry tongues of flame licking through their circuitry. A chorus of deafening blasts rocked the main building as every electrical appliance overloaded. Screams began to punctuate the growing roar of fire. Those fortunate enough to be outside the building ran for their lives as glass from the upper storeys rained down in lethal crystal showers. Long, spear-like shards sped to earth like clear javelins.

A security guard, mesmerised by the sight before

304

him, was transfixed by a razor sharp length of window which buried itself in his chest.

On the third floor, a blast of seismic proportions sent bodies hurtling through windows as the chemicals in the labs also caught alight. The cries of animals now joined the cacophony of sounds as specimens were burned alive in their cages.

Men and women were picked up, as if by invisible hands, and flung through the air, slamming into walls or crashing through glass. A woman, her hair and clothes ablaze ran screaming down a corridor until another explosion brought the ceiling down on her. Metal began to melt under the intense heat and even the stone steps grew hot as the fires continued to sear everything they touched.

Here and there, people were attempting to fight the fires with extinguishers but it was like trying to put out a forest blaze with a thimbleful of water. Two security men, using extinguishers, tried to make a path for several women through the hungry flames but the fire seemed to rear up at them and they were forced back towards a room near the end of a corridor. It housed several hundred bottles of chemical and, a moment later, an ear-splitting blast simply brushed aside everyone within a hundred yards. Bodies were tossed like bloodied rag dolls, hurtling through the air as if fired from cannons.

In the forecourt below, a lorry exploded, the driver catapulted through the windscreen as the vehicle disappeared beneath a shrieking ball of red and white flame. Lumps of metal went spinning in all directions.

It seemed as if the entire complex which made up Vanderburg Chemicals was ablaze, a roaring beacon which could be seen for miles around.

Powerful explosions continued to rock the place, tearing it apart. Those who could, ran. Those trapped inside were either incinerated or blasted to atoms.

And, above it all, a gigantic mushroom cloud of black smoke rose fully two hundred feet into the air. Like some massive man-made cloud it hung, shroud-like, over the remnants of the complex.

Then, finally, as if the other blasts had been mere portents, there was an explosion which threatened to split the very earth itself: the final, cataclysmic death knell which brought the remnants of Vanderburg Chemicals down like a house of cards. A concussion wave flattened everything within a 500 yard radius and then, almost as an after-thought, there was a vehement detonation which levelled anything left standing. Flames screamed defiantly in the air, shrieking geysers of fire which rose like blazing fingers to point accusingly at the sky.

Even the clouds seemed to be on fire.

Fifty

Jo ducked low in her seat as Clayton swung the car around a tight bend in the road. Behind them, the driver of the rangerover slowed slightly to take the corner but then stepped on the accelerator as the road straightened out once more. His companion was leaning out of the side window trying to aim a gun at the tyre of the speeding Capri.

Jo heard the report but, thankfully, the bullet missed its appointed mark, scraping the side of the vehicle instead.

The doctor gripped the steering wheel as tightly as

he could, blood from the wound in his shoulder seeping down his arm. As she looked at him, Jo could see a shining nub of bone protruding from the ragged wound. The bullet had smashed his scapula.

She peered out of the back window to see that the rangerover was gaining.

'Oh no,' murmured Clayton.

'What is it?' she demanded.

'We're nearly out of petrol,' Clayton told her, indicating the gauge.

He swung the car around another corner and stepped on the brake.

'What the hell are you doing?' Jo asked, in amazement.

'Get out,' he said, watching the rear view mirror.

'Why?'

'Get out,' he bellowed at her. 'Take the files. One of us has got to get away.'

'I can't . . .'

He cut her short, pushing the door open and practically shoving her out. He passed her the files.

'Run,' he told her. 'Go on. There's nothing left for me now. You save yourself. Get to Tyler if you can.'

Before she could protest, he had reached across and slammed the door, spinning the wheel of the Capri, bringing it around in a 'U' turn until it was facing the opposite way.

A second later, the rangerover came hurtling round the corner.

The driver was a little puzzled at first to see the Capri heading back towards them, and that puzzlement turned to horror as he realized what Clayton was doing.

Jo, too, saw what was to happen.

'No,' she shouted but, a second later, her voice was drowned out by a thunderous explosion.

The two vehicles hit each other head on and blew up immediately. There was a blinding ball of fire followed by a billowing orange and black cloud of smoke. Lumps of red hot metal flew into the air and Jo blenched as she saw a severed arm rise on the funnel of flame which erupted from the roaring blast. A wave of pressure rocked her and she shielded her face as the heat rolled over her. The air was filled with the roar of raging flames.

She stood gazing at the pulverized vehicles for as long as she dared, then clutching the three files, she set off across the fields towards town.

It was nearly 6.39 p.m. when Tyler walked into the hotel. He found Jo sitting at the bar, the files before her. As he limped in, she ran to him, throwing her arms around his neck. He responded with equal warmth and relief.

'Thank God you're alive,' she said. Then, stepping back, she asked: 'Is it done?'

He nodded.

'I killed them all,' he told her. 'At least I think I did. There's no way of knowing for sure.' He swallowed hard. 'Jo, I knew so many of them.' He was silent for a moment.

'Clayton's dead,' she told him.

'How?'

Jo explained everything, finally showing him the files.

'But you destroyed Vanderburg Chemicals,' he said, wearily.

She shook her head.

'Not us.'

'I saw the fires,' he said.

'Vic, I don't know *what* happened. But, they're gone.'

Tyler picked up the file marked:

DISTRIBUTION

There was a column on the left hand side of the page which bore the names of cities.

'London. Manchester. Liverpool. Glasgow,' he read.

308

'Paris. Bonn. Brussels. Vienna.' Tyler swallowed hard. 'New York. Houston. Quebec.' He looked at Jo. 'Jesus, do you realize what this means?'

'They're all places where the new Vanderburg feed is supposed to be distributed, to be sold by their outlets in those cities,' she said. 'Now we have the files we can stop the shipments.'

Tyler shook his head, running his finger across the page.

'The despatch dates on most of these are weeks old,' he said, anxiously.

The smile faded from Jo's face.

'These shipments have already gone,' the farmer said, softly.

'My God,' murmured Jo. 'The virus will spread.' Her voice took on a note of desperation. 'Isn't there any way of stopping it?'

Tyler dropped the file onto the table before him.

'Vic, there has to be a way,' she gasped. 'There must be something.'

He sat down heavily.

'There's nothing,' he said, flatly.

Outside, it began to get dark.

Author's Note

All characters in this novel are figments of my imagination, as are the towns of Wakely and Arkham. There is also no company called Vanderburg Chemicals.

The disease porphyria, on the other hand, *does* exist and the facts given, in *Erebus*, by Dr Alec Clayton are correct. While it is true that one person in every 25,000 suffers from this rare affliction, it is not expected that figures will increase much beyond that particular statistic.

However . . .

Shaun Hutson

Victims

THIS BOOK IS DEDICATED TO
STEVE HARRIS, BRUCE DICKINSON, DAVE MURRAY,
ADRIAN SMITH AND NICKO McBRAIN –
QUITE SIMPLY THE BEST.
WITH THANKS AND ADMIRATION,
SOMEWHERE ON STAGE . . .

Acknowledgements

Writing this book was not easy but the following people, for various reasons, made the task less painful. For those who offered either advice, expertise, friendship, support, love or inspiration, I extend my warmest thanks.

To Mr Bill Waddell, Curator of New Scotland Yard's Black Museum, who put me right on a number of research points. To my agent, Sheelagh Thomas, and my editor, Bill Massey (thanks for the tea bags). To Bob Tanner, Ray Mudie and 'The Wild Bunch'. To everyone else at W. H. Allen.

Thanks also, for different reasons to Bill Young at Chiltern Radio ('The Attila of the Airwaves', frequenter of more beer tents than Watneys). To Mick Wall (I don't care what you say, I still owe you and by the way, it's your round). To Malcolm 'Miracle Man' Dome (who's going to win the league? And it's your turn to buy the lunch). To Krusher 'Jimmy Page' Joule. To Steve McTaggart, Geoff Barton, Karoline and all at 'Kerrang', thank you from your tea-boy . . .

Thanks to Cheap (from Fulham pubs mighty bands do grow). To Scrapheap (today 'The Comedy Store' tomorrow the world).

Extra special thanks to Rod Smallwood and all those at Smallwood-Taylor who made three days 'on the road' so special for me. To all the road crew as well, thank you.

Thak you to Liverpool F.C. for one of the greatest days of my life. To Queensrÿche, to Joan Ingram (I promise not to pay for any more tickets, honest) and to Ray Pocock (a great 'Harpist').

And finally, as ever, to my Mum and Dad, for everything. And to Belinda, who suffered this one with me. Just being there was enough . . .

Shaun Hutson

'It takes two to make a murder. There are born victims, born to have their throats cut, as the cut-throats are born to be hanged. You can see it in their faces.'

Aldous Huxley

Prologue

A thin mist of cigarette smoke hung like a dirty curtain between the watchers and the lone figure at the blackboard.

The man eventually turned, rubbing his hands together in an effort to remove the chalk dust. Then he pointed to what he had just written.

'I don't know if those names mean anything to you?' he said.

From the subsequent silence he guessed that they were unfamiliar to the assembled throng. Edward Malone jabbed at the first name with his stubby index finger.

'Franz Werfel. A German, as you may have gathered. In 1920 he wrote a novel called *Not the Murderer but the Victim is Guilty*. But it is this man,' he pointed to the second name, 'this psychologist, who concerns us. Dr Hans Von Hentig. In 1949 he was responsible for what has become a classic study, *The Criminal and the Victim*. He maintained that in many murder cases the victim is as responsible as the murderer for the act of violence, albeit by provocation. This is particularly true in domestic killings and in many cases concerning women and sex crimes. Provocative behaviour is often the cause of murder.' He gazed around at his audience. 'As policemen I don't need to tell you that. Individuals often behave in ways which invite violence. For instance, a woman who dresses alluringly and frequents, shall we say, "dubious" premises, one who habitually picks up a series of different men, must be classed as a potential victim. The same goes for a man, but to a lesser degree. It's a kind of Russian roulette. If a woman sleeps with ten different men in rapid succession then the odds are that one of those ten is likely to be either disturbed or perhaps violent. The same premise can be applied in some cases of child murder. If we use Von Hentig's theory then it's easy to see that it is sometimes the child who invites violence by its own behaviour. Many children like to play games with adults and perhaps, if those games get out of hand, the child may struggle . . .' He allowed the sentence to trail off. 'I realize that this is a generalization, the case of the Moors Murders being an exception, but the theory applies in many instances.

'Provocative behaviour was the subject of Von Hentig's studies but there was something which he didn't explore fully. The idea of the *born* victim. Someone actually destined from birth to become a murder victim. It could be anyone. Even one of us in this room now. There is some kind of psychological beacon given off by all murder victims which the killer homes in on, like a dog to a scent.

'No one knows what it is. No one can identify it. Von Hentig and, later, Jung, called it "Victimology". It might just be a case of being in the wrong place at the wrong time, especially in the case of people murdered by total strangers, such as the victim of Leopold and Loeb, but the fact remains that all of us give off certain unconscious signals, *vibes* if you like.

'The killer is triggered, we think, by some kind of subliminal means. As far as we are aware there are no external stimuli, something registers subliminally in the mind *and* eye of the killer. Something he himself may even be unaware of. But the psychological lure is there for a killer to see.

'Tests carried out on muggers showed that they picked out their victims by the way they walk. A mugger will steer clear of someone with a forceful stride but instantly consider a person of timid appearance or manner as fair game. The same theory applies to murderers; it's just that they home in on a different type of body language. The problem of course is that we have yet to discover what makes the victims so attractive to their killers.'

Malone wrote one single word on the blackboard in block capitals:

VICTIMS

Initiation

The coffin was covered by flowers. Bouquets, wreaths and as many other floral tributes as could be balanced on the lid of the box. The child watched as the four black-coated men lifted the casket gently from the back of the hearse and made their way towards the grave which yawned open like a waiting mouth, ready to swallow the offered article.

In the trees nearby birds sang, oblivious to the sound of sobbing, unaware of the moans of anguish which periodically rose from the assembled group close to the grave.

Bees buzzed around the coffin flowers, one of them settling on a wreath of red carnations.

The child looked up and around at the faces of those who stood by, some tear-stained and drained of colour.

As the coffin bearers approached the graveside one of the bouquets slipped and fell into the open grave. The child watched it disappear into the black maw, wanting to go over and look in, to see how deep the hole was, but the restraining hand on its shoulder prevented any such opportunity.

The priest spoke his words softly as the coffin was lowered slowly into the ground. The child watched the clergyman, studying his face — the heavy jowls, the thick lips dotted with spittle which he wiped away after every few sentences.

The sound of sobbing rose to a crescendo as the straps which held the coffin were pulled free and the box at last lay in the waiting earth. Again the child wanted to rush across and peer down into the hole, to look at the coffin. To look through the wooden lid at the body which lay within.

The priest finished speaking and beckoned the first group of

11

mourners forward and the child felt itself being pushed ahead. Towards the grave.

The hand never left the child's shoulder but now, as it looked down at the casket, nothing else seemed to register. There was the grave and the coffin. Nothing else.

The child stood mesmerized, eyes flicking back and forth over the object, from the brass name-plate to the six screws which held the lid down. The polished wood reflected the child's own image for a moment and it was as if positions had briefly been reversed. The child tried to imagine looking up at the faces which gazed down into the grave. Tried to imagine lying in the cold silk which lined the coffin, encased in a kind of cocoon, but one which was never likely to burst forth with life. This encasement was for the slow disintegration of a body, not the renewal.

The child wondered what it felt like to be dead. Never to hear those birds which still sang in the trees nearby or see the insects which hovered around the flowers at the graveside.

Then a handful of earth hit the coffin lid and the child looked at the priest who had thrown it. He was brushing the dirt from his palms as he backed away.

More dirt followed, thrown by others at the graveside, and now the child took a handful and stood over the box, noticing how the name-plate was all but covered by the scattered earth. The child finally released what it held in its hand, listening to the fragments bouncing off the polished wood.

Then hands tried to coax it away from the hole, but the child did not want to move. It wanted to stay and stare, wanted to climb down into the hole and look more closely. It wanted to lie on top of the coffin and look up at the twisted, anguished faces.

The hands tugged more urgently and the child moved away, the sound of muffled sobs now loud in its ears.

The wailing and the chorus of pain grew in volume but the child was unmoved. This was the music of death.

It was a tune which the child found pleasing.

It stared back at the open grave.

Wondering.

PART ONE

'Rather murder an infant in its cradle than
nurse unsatisfied desire.'

William Blake

'He's not a victim,
You can see it in his face.'

Kiss

One

He knew the child was somewhere inside the house.

Since her disappearance two days earlier he had known.

He had known that she had been taken to this decaying shell of a building. A testament to the insanity of some architect now long dead.

He had known but, until now, he had not been able to summon up the courage to enter the house to search for her.

He had been disgusted with himself. Disgusted with his own reluctance to retrieve his child.

But that disgust had been tempered by fear.

Fear of entering the building and searching its dusty rooms and cavernous corridors.

But now he had no choice and, as he moved slowly into the towering hallway, he felt the muscles of his stomach tighten into a hard knot until he found it difficult to get his breath. He trod the floorboards softly, his footfalls deadened by the odorous carpet of mildew which covered the wood. He paused at the foot of the staircase, one hand resting on the banister. Beneath his hand the slime felt like cold mucus and he withdrew it rapidly, wiping the noxious fluid on his trousers. He peered up into the gloom which made the upper landing almost invisible. Then, slowly, he began to ascend.

The steps creaked protestingly beneath his weight and he paused for a moment, ears and eyes alert for the slightest hint of sound or movement. There was none. He continued to climb.

The torch which was jammed in his belt was useless. He had smashed the bulb whilst breaking in. Now its only use was as a weapon should he need to defend himself. The idea brought beads of perspiration to his forehead.

He stood still at the top of the stairs, pulling the lighter from the pocket of his jeans, lifting its meagre flame above his head. The puddle of light which fanned out around him was woefully inadequate in the darkness, but he moved on, one hand gripping the rotten balustrade.

Ahead of him were three doors.

He crossed to the first of them, his hand shaking as he reached for the handle. He turned it and the mouldy brass knob twisted loosely in his grip.

He tried again, putting his weight against the thick wood this time. With gritted teeth he drove his shoulder into it.

The door swung back on hinges which had not tasted oil for years and the pitiful whine which they emitted reminded him of an injured dog.

He stood in the doorway for long seconds, flicking the lighter on once more, trying to discern some shapes in the cloying blackness inside the room.

But for some rotting pieces of furniture, the room appeared to be empty. He backed out onto the landing.

Somewhere ahead of him he heard a low, almost mucoid exhalation. Soft and sibilant.

He squinted through the darkness, trying to pick out the exact location of the sound. Easing the heavy torch from his belt he raised it before him like a truncheon and moved further along the corridor.

Outside the second door he saw something apallingly familiar.

The breath caught in his throat as he recognized his daughter's shoe.

Gasping, he dropped to one knee and picked it up. The tiny article was splashed with blood and he felt his own life-fluid freeze slightly as he held the shoe before him, listening for the sound once more.

Silence.

Only the pounding of his heart and the rushing of the blood in his ears greeted his vigilance.

He got to his feet and tried the handle of the second door,

pausing a moment before shoving it open. Immediately he flicked on the lighter.

The sickly yellow light spilled into the room, illuminating a torn cardigan. He crossed to it, sickness now replacing the knot of fear in his stomach. The cardigan was almost shredded and, like the shoe, it was spattered with blood. He whispered his daughter's name under his breath and turned back to the landing, approaching the third and final door. The lighter was growing hot in his hand and he was forced to flick it off, standing blindly in the darkness for what seemed like an eternity, his eyes darting to and fro in a vain attempt to pierce the stygian gloom. Finally, satisfied that the lighter had cooled down, he lit it again and prepared to enter the third room.

His hand was actually on the brass knob when it was turned from the inside.

The door swung open as if bidding him to enter and he stepped across the threshold, the lighter held above his head.

Had he been able to, he would have screamed.

As it was, all he could do was sag helplessly against the door frame, sickness sweeping over him, his stomach contracting and threatening to expel its contents. His eyes bulged madly in their sockets as he stared at the sight before him.

His daughter was hanging upside down from a hook and chain attached to the ceiling, dangling there like a joint in a butcher's shop. Both her arms had been severed at the shoulders, her throat slashed clumsily. The floor beneath her was awash with blood, some of which had begun to congeal, forming a sticky red porridge.

Of her severed arms there was no sign.

He staggered back, slamming the door behind him, anxious to block out the appalling sight, wishing that he could block it from his mind too. The lighter fell from his hand and the darkness closed around him once more. He felt as if his legs were going to buckle beneath him but, summoning some hidden reserves of strength, he managed to run for the stairs.

He was roughly level with the first door when it flew open.

The creature which came hurtling at him was straight out of a nightmare.

17

It was as tall as a man, its body slightly hunched due to the weight of its large head. A head which was covered by torn and shredded skin, revealing bulging veins and pustules beneath. Long wisps of white hair cascaded behind it as it ran at him, its eyes blazing. Twin orbs which seemed to have no pupils. Two burning red pools like boiling blood. As it opened its mouth a huge tongue flickered out, reaching past its chin, dripping yellow saliva.

In one clawed hand it held a machete.

He raised a hand to shield himself but the suddenness and ferocity of the attack were overwhelming.

The blade of the machete caught him just below the sternum, powering effortlessly through his belly until it reached his pelvis. His body split open like an overripe peach, entrails spilling out like a plague of bleeding ringworm. He screamed and fell, feeling the creature throw itself upon him, its claws burrowing into the cavity of his torso. Digging deeper until they closed around the object they sought.

The creature tore his heart free, squeezing the throbbing organ in its powerful hand, holding the blood-drenched trophy aloft while, all the time, its tumefied reptilian tongue writhed like a spittle-covered worm.

It squeezed the heart more tightly, watching the blood spew from the torn arteries. The creature raised it towards its mouth.

It was then that the lights came on.

Two

'Cut it.'

The voice was accompanied by a sudden explosion of brilliance from the banks of lights overhead and the darkened landing was bathed in a cold white glow.

Phillip Dickinson clambered off the camera crane which was poised beside the two actors and jumped down, careful to avoid the continuity girl who was busily snapping photos of the little tableau. She was taking no chances when shooting resumed. Only last week a character with a scar on his right cheek in one scene had appeared with the disfigurement miraculously transferred to the left cheek in the following scene. Only careful study of the rushes had revealed the mistake but now the actor had returned to America and it would cost too much to recall him. This time she didn't intend anything to go wrong. She measured positions while the two actors remained still, the one on the ground smiling up at her as she busied herself.

With the coming of light the film set once more became a scene of organized pandemonium as technicians consulted the shooting script to see what was next on the agenda. Actors were called onto the set, others stood around smoking and chatting.

Three grips were busily assembling the tracks onto which they intended lowering the heavy panavision camera and its trolley. The next scene called for a travelling shot of the deformed creature carrying the heart of its newest victim down to the cellar to its growing companions.

Dickinson looked down as he heard the voice of assistant director Colin Robson bellowing to some crew members to be careful as they moved a large spotlight into position. Robson was tall and lean, yet to reach his thirty-fifth birthday. He was four years younger than Dickinson who now stood looking at the scenes of activity around him, brushing a hand through his shoulder-length brown hair. He reached into the pocket of his jeans and pulled out a stick of chewing gum which he pushed into his mouth. He looked first at his watch, then at the continuity girl.

'Come on, Sarah,' he said, 'We haven't got all day.'

Despite having been born in Sussex, Dickinson had commuted back and forth between Britain and the States enough times for his accent to carry a slight American twang. He'd been directing for the past eight years, having graduated from scripting a couple of long-running American cop series which he then went on to direct. However, the constraints of television, he felt, had stifled his real creative leanings, so he'd decided to try films. He'd worked as a second-unit director on several films in the States but his big break had finally come when he'd travelled to Italy two weeks after his thirty-first birthday and met the head of DAC Films.

Dickinson had been hired to direct *The Mutilator*, which on release in the States made over ten million dollars and, more importantly, gave him a foothold in the American business. But in his eagerness to succeed he found himself directing a succession of horror movies and now, eight years later, the novelty hadn't so much worn off as been permanently eroded.

Now the director stood, hands planted firmly on his hips, looking down at the actor who was sprawled on the floor, his clothes saturated by stage blood. He shook his head and sighed wearily.

'Something wrong, Phil?'

The voice made him turn and he saw Frank Miller approaching from the top of the landing. Miller was dressed in a dark sweatshirt and jeans and he was carrying a small silver hip-flask in one hand. His brown hair was uncombed and, like his moustache, it carried traces of grey. His face was heavily stubbled, and as he scratched his cheek the bristles made a rasping sound. Miller, despite appearances to the contrary, was six years younger than Dickinson but the deeply cut lines in his forehead and around his eyes belied his youth. He took a swig from his hip flask then jammed it back into the back pocket of his jeans.

'You don't look very happy,' Miller said, patting the director on the shoulder as he passed.

As Dickinson watched, the younger man began pulling a network of thin tubes from around the back of the actor sprawled on the ground. They had carried the blood which had so realistically spurted from his torn stomach in the scene they'd just completed. Worked by three small and well-concealed pumps also attached to the actor's body, the device had been operated by remote control by Miller himself, who now looked on with some pride at his bloody handiwork.

'Can I go and wash this off now?' asked the bloodstained actor.

Dickinson nodded.

'Why not? I think we'll all take a break.' He looked at his watch then turned and, cupping both hands to his mouth bellowed across the set, 'We'll break it here. Everybody back on set in an hour.'

Murmurs of approval greeted his latest instruction and technicians and actors alike trooped off the set, heading for the canteen which had been set up in two large caravans outside the sound stage.

'What about this, Frank?' asked the rotting creature, still clutching the heart.

'Leave it here,' Miller said, watching as the heavily made-up actor deposited the organ on the ground beside him. Then, both monster and victim ambled off for lunch, leaving Dickinson and Miller alone. The silence suddenly seemed oppressive after the frenzied activity of between-scenes preparation.

'Got any of that to spare?' asked Dickinson, pointing at Miller's hip flask.

The younger man pulled the receptacle from his pocket and handed it to the director.

'I could be forgiven for thinking that you're not happy in your work,' Miller observed, winding the bloodied tubes into a ball.

'You'd be right,' Dickinson said, handing back the flask. He wiped his mouth with the back of his hand and watched as Miller stuffed the plastic tubing into a bag. He then picked up the heart and dropped that in as well. 'Christ, they give me a budget of four million bucks, a crew I've never seen before and a piece of shit for a script, send me over here and tell me to come back with a movie that's going to make them fifteen million. What the hell am I supposed to do?' He sighed wearily.

'They call it trying to make a silk purse out of a sow's ear,' Miller said sardonically.

'I'm lucky they let me pick my own special effects man. At least one part of this mess is going to look good.'

Miller smiled proudly. He knew that what Dickinson said was true; he hadn't earned a reputation as one of the film world's top special effects men for nothing. Twice nominated for his work in prosthetics, he'd finally won an award at the Trieste Fantasy Film Festival a year ago for his make-up and effects work on *Brainsucker Part 2*. Although his work throughout the film had been excellent, Miller had been particularly proud of the scene in which he'd been forced to contrive the illusion that the creature of the title was actually inserting its long proboscis into the ear of its victim and feeding on the brain. He'd achieved the effect through a mixture of false heads, stop-frame animation and live action.

Dickinson had directed on that occasion too.

'So why did you take this job?' Miller asked as the two men wandered down the staircase. 'You knew the script was crap.'

'It's a contract job,' the director answered. 'I signed for three movies. At least this one's an original,' he grunted. 'The last two were both sequels to somebody else's work. I sometimes wonder what would happen to the film business if no one had ever thought of sequels. So, what happens? I tell the chief executive that I don't want to direct any more sequels. He hands me this fucking script his son's written.'

Miller smiled thinly as the director continued.

'He rings me at home two days later and asks what I think of it. Fortunately, he told me how much they were going to pay me before I had to give an opinion.'

'It's all about money, Phil, you don't need me to tell you that,' the effects man reminded him. 'If you've got the money, who cares. Like they say, life's a shit sandwich. The more bread you've got, the less shit you have to eat.'

'Very philosophical,' Dickinson remarked. 'I'll just be glad when this damned picture's finished. I'm going to pick up my pay-cheque and run.'

'That's one of the things I love about you, your dedication,' Miller chuckled.

'You're the one who should know about dedication. I've been in this business for nearly fifteen years altogether and I've never seen effects as realistic as yours. Like that heart.' He motioned towards the bag which Miller was carrying. 'It looks so real and you only had twelve hours to model it. I don't know how the hell you do it.'

'Trade secret,' Miller told him, reaching for the hip flask again.

'You coming for lunch?' Dickinson asked.

'I want to take this stuff back first,' Miller said, holding up the bag and its contents. 'I'll leave it in my make-up room. I'll see you in the canteen in about ten minutes.'

Dickinson nodded and walked off.

Miller paused for a moment then wandered off in the opposite direction. Pushing open the exit door from the sound-stage he stepped out into the drizzle beyond. Above, the sky was grey and swollen with cloud. Puddles had begun to form on the tarmac round about. Miller's make-up room cum mobile workshop was a converted caravan as were the dressing rooms of the cast. He looked across towards his own temporary quarters then turned and headed for the toilets.

The special effects man paused as he entered, checking that he was alone. Satisfied that all the cubicles were empty, he entered the first one and slid the bolt behind him.

Locked inside, he opened the bag, recoiling slightly from the smell that rose from within. He picked up the heart then dropped it down the pan.

For long moments he stood looking down at it, bloated and bloodied, staining the water, lying there like the swollen remains of some hideous miscarriage. Then he flushed the toilet, watching as the entire pan turned red.

The heart stuck for a moment then, as he flushed again, it finally disappeared in a cascade of clear water.

Miller hurried from the toilet to his caravan, dumped the tangle of rubber tubing, then headed for the canteen.

On the way he checked in the toilet once more.

The heart had disappeared.

Three

Pieces of chicken stuck to the thick, cracked lips of the creature as it shovelled food into its mouth.

'Fuck this,' rasped Kevin Brady, his words somewhat slurred because he was unable to open his mouth more than half an inch. He pulled the greasy blobs of chicken from the lips of the mask and, instead, attempted to take a sip of his tea. The hot liquid dribbled down his chin but he felt nothing because the prosthetic skin protected his own flesh. Finally he retrieved a straw and sucked the tea through that.

'If this is what they call suffering in the cause of art then they can stuff it,' Brady grunted, his face feeling as though someone had coated it with concrete. He had been in make-up since six o'clock that morning and now, as the hands of his watch reached one-fifteen he was beginning to feel more like the man in the iron mask. Miller had told the actor when he applied the make-up that too much movement would cause it to crack and, as it took over two hours to transform him into one of the 'astro-cannibals' of the film's title, neither actor or make-up artist relished the prospect of a repeat performance that same day.

Frank Miller sat over his plate of egg and chips watching Brady, a slight smile on his face. The canteen was a hive of activity, a blur of sounds and conversation. A number of the cast were in make-up and Miller turned to see two hideously scarred burn victims queuing up for their lunch, chatting happily as the woman behind the counter did her best to look away from them. The effects man grinned more broadly.

'Are you eating that?' asked another man and, as Miller shook his head, a clawed hand with one finger torn off reached across

25

and claimed the jam doughnut which lay close by.

Two men, both with gaping bullet wounds in their foreheads, sat at the next table smoking.

'It took me an hour to get this stuff off last night,' Brady said, prodding his face. 'I know you removed most of it before I left the set but I had to use soap and water to get the rest off.'

'I told you,' Miller explained. 'Use surgical spirit, it's more effective.' He pushed his plate away and reached for his hip flask, glancing around him at his other creations.

A woman with one ear torn off and her throat cut was busily combing her hair. The front of her ripped top was stained with blood and Brady caught sight of a tantalizing flash of nipple through one of the strategically placed gashes in the material. As the actress got to her feet he tried to raise his eyebrows but the make-up prevented that simple gesture. He ran appraising red eyes up and down her long, slender legs as she strode from the canteen.

'There's times when having a tongue like this might come in handy,' he said, chuckling, prodding the long worm-like accessory which he wore over his own tongue once shooting began.

'Especially if you could breathe through your ears,' said Miller, swigging from his flask.

A chorus of guffaws greeted his remark.

'You get to put make-up on lots of actresses don't you?' Brady said. 'You know, body make-up.' He tried to smile but the effort was almost painful as he felt the rubberized skin tighten on his flesh.

'So?' Miller asked. 'It's only like an artist putting paint on a canvas. It's just that I use living canvas.'

'Yes, but artists don't paint on tits do they?' Brady replied lecherously.

Miller took another sip from his flask.

'Oh, I don't know,' he said. 'I mean, I put make-up on *you*. That must class as painting a tit if anything does.'

An outburst of laughter rang around the table. Brady, however, didn't see the joke. He regarded the effects man malevolently for a moment then returned to his lunch.

Miller massaged the bridge of his nose between his thumb and forefinger and tried to shut out the cacophony of sounds inside the canteen. He closed his eyes, as if that act would lessen the noise, shut it out of his mind. Needless to say it didn't work and he sighed almost painfully.

Miller didn't really feel comfortable in crowds, he never had. Probably a legacy of having been an only child, he told himself. He had grown used to his own company and, over the years, had seen the presence of others as, at best, a nuisance and, in the most extreme cases, an intrusion.

His jobs after leaving school had perpetuated his liking for solitude. He'd spent five years at a photographic college then decided, with the help of his father, to go freelance. At the age of twenty-three he had sold his first photographs to a national newspaper. There'd been an outbreak of foot-and-mouth disease on a farm close to where he lived and the pictures of the stricken animals had been used by the *Mail*. When a car crash had claimed the life of a local dignitary Miller had been on hand when the fire brigade were cutting the remains of him and his wife from the wreckage. He had managed to get some shots of the bodies before anyone could drape them with blankets.

The tabloids went crazy for those.

The pay was good but sporadic, so when he was finally offered a full-time position with the *Express* he moved to London and into digs. He made friends easily or, more to the point, he attracted people to him. Miller was hesitant to use the word *friend* about anyone. To him, people were never more than acquaintances; he wanted nothing more from them and he made sure that no one ever got too close to him. He had his work, that was all that mattered.

The assignments began to take on a depressingly familiar pattern. He was always first at any accident, camera at the ready. During the height of the IRA bomb blitz of London in the late seventies he found that his best friends were death and pain. Those friends paid his rent. Wherever there was suffering, Miller was never far away, ready to record the event for posterity and for a big cheque. When a woman had jumped from the seventh floor of the Ritz hotel he had been the one who had captured her image in mid-air as she plummeted to the ground. That photo had won him a prize. The one that he'd taken *after* she hit the ground hadn't been so popular but Miller was nothing if not thorough.

The police work seemed to be a natural progression. From taking photos of accidental deaths it seemed only logical that he should progress to snapping the aftermath of premeditated destruction.

The ten-year-old boy who'd been raped by a homosexual, so badly assaulted that his anus had been torn open. Then his killer had strangled him with barbed wire.

The young woman who had been found with her face pressed onto the ring of an electric cooker, a weighted suitcase holding her head there.

In time he even managed to look on the dead babies with an impassioned eye. Like the six-month-old girl who had been beaten so severely that part of her brain had burst through one of the holes in her skull. She had been killed by her mentally retarded mother who had been so fascinated by the fact that her daughter's fontanelle was still visible beneath the thin skin she had pushed three fingers into the child's head.

And then there had been the bigger jobs. Those that reminded him of his days on the newspaper. He had been one of the first on the scene at the Moorgate tube disaster, he'd watched as the remains of complete human beings were shovelled into plastic bags. Bodies had been mangled almost beyond belief. Certainly beyond any artistic acceptance. For in that blood-drenched tunnel Miller had finally learned that death and mutilation also had an aesthetic face. No one had seen him re-arrange one of the pulped corpses so that all of it was showing when he took the picture. After all, he was a photographer first and foremost and he'd never forgotten that the composition of a photo is important.

Even if, sometimes, it does mean having to wipe slicks of brain matter off your shoes afterwards.

He'd been twenty-six when that happened and it was around that time he had begun to drink heavily.

Miller's thoughts were interrupted by a hand on his shoulder.

He turned to see Dickinson standing there.

'Have you got a minute, Frank?' the director asked. 'I wanted to talk about the scene we're shooting next.'

'I'm all ears, Phil,' he said, swigging from his flask. The effects man got to his feet and followed the director out of the canteen. As he left a young woman smiled at him.

Miller smiled back.

She was a good looking girl.

Even if one of her eyes *was* missing and part of her nose *had* been hacked away.

Four

There was a loud metallic rattle as Dickinson worked the pump action of the shotgun. He raised the weapon to his shoulder, drew a bead on Kevin Brady and gently squeezed the trigger.

As the hammer slammed down on an empty magazine, the director squinted along the sight towards the actor who was standing with both arms upraised while Miller carefully attached a metal plate about the size of a man's fist to his chest. Holding a strip of surgical tape between his teeth, Miller secured the plate to the actor's bare flesh, grinning when he saw that the sticky band covered some of the hair on Brady's torso.

'That's going to be a bit painful when you pull it off,' said the effects man as he inspected his handiwork.

Brady nodded resignedly and prodded the small metal plate. It was backed by foam rubber to absorb what small recoil would come from the detonation.

'I hope these bloody things are safe,' said the actor, watching as Miller attached the tiny explosive charge to the metal.

'That's what we're going to find out,' Miller said, flatly, the solemnness in his voice making Brady feel suddenly nervous. 'OK, hold still,' the effects man said and retrieved a small handset from a nearby table. With one eye on the squib he selected the appropriate button on the remote and pressed.

There was a dull bang and a smokeless explosion as the squib went off.

Brady moved involuntarily as he felt the small impact on his chest.

'Do you want to try it with the blood bag, Phil?' Miller asked, taking a swift swig from his hip flask.

Dickinson nodded, handing the shotgun to another actor who was watching in fascination as Miller took hold of the small metal plate and, with one tug, pulled it free of Brady's chest. Several dark hairs came with it and the actor cursed, rubbing his sore skin.

He seated himself on the edge of the table, watching as Miller pulled a piece of rubber from his pocket and laid it out before him. Brady looked at the smooth latex, convinced that it looked familiar.

It took him only a second to realize that it was a contraceptive.

'I left some of my gear at home this morning,' Miller announced, carefully filling the contraceptive with a thick red fluid. 'It's a good job there's a chemist near the set.'

'How many did you buy?' Brady wanted to know.

'Six packets,' Miller told him, smiling. 'The woman behind the counter must have thought I was in for a heavy night.'

Brady and the others who were watching chuckled as Miller completed his task. The teat and the first quarter of the sheath were now full of the imitation blood. The effects man wiped some of it on his jeans and Brady noticed how realistic the stain appeared. As if he'd cut himself and wiped the wound on the material. Next he tied the contraceptive into a tight knot, pushing the blood into the end of its receptacle to form a bag. It looked as if someone had filled it with crimson ejaculate.

Colin Robson, the assistant director, wandered over to tell Dickinson that the cameras were in position, then, that task completed, he paused for a moment to watch as Miller attached another metal plate to Brady's chest. This one he also fastened on with surgical tape then, carefully, he positioned the blood bag on the plate, ensuring that it was directly over the fresh squib. That done, Miller retired a foot or so and picked up the remote control.

'Ready?' he said to Brady.

The actor nodded.

Miller took another swig from his hip flask, then nonchalantly pressed the small red button on the remote.

The squib went off, rupturing the rubber bag which burst

like a throbbing boil, spilling its sticky contents down Brady's chest.

'Terrific,' said Dickinson. 'We'll go for the shot now.'

As Miller set about securing another of the blood bags and squibs to Brady's body the director turned to Pat Sullivan, who was holding the shotgun. Sullivan was in his early twenties, a thin, gangling youth with long brown hair.

'Now, just run towards Kevin,' Dickinson said. 'Lift the shotgun up to your shoulder then stand there as if you're horrified. As if you can't bring yourself to believe what you're seeing. Kevin will run at you and it's then that you fire at him. Don't worry about the gun, it'll be loaded with blanks. There'll be lots of noise but it's safe enough. We'll dub on the sound later. Blanks always sound too hollow.'

'I was supposed to speak a line before I fired, according to the script,' Sullivan offered.

'Fuck the script,' snapped Dickinson. 'The line was crap anyway.'

'I just thought that it was necessary in the context of the character,' the young actor suggested.

'For Christ's sake, this is a horror film not a bloody social documentary. I'm not here to make great movies, I'm here to make money. Now forget the line, right. Just fire the shotgun at him. I'll be holding on a two-shot until you fire, then I'll move in for a close-up on you, then on Kevin when he's hit.'

Miller had all but completed his work. He had fixed four of the squibs and their accompanying blood bags to Brady's chest. With practised care he fastened one last one at the point of the actor's shoulder.

'With five of them on you, it's odds-on you're going to feel some impact,' Miller said.

'I'm more worried about pulling the bloody things off when we've finished,' Brady told him, his voice still slurred because of the thick make-up he wore.

High above them two powerful arc lights were lowered into position while the lighting cameraman checked the scene with a light meter, conferring with the cinematographer who was perched on top of a camera crane.

32

Miller glanced round as he saw the flash of a bulb and he recognized the photographer as one of the regulars from *Photoplay*. He nodded at the effects man then scuttled off to get some photos of the other technicians who were swarming over the set like flies over a dead dog.

'Are we ready to go?' Dickinson said wearily.

'Come on everybody,' the assistant director shouted. 'We *are* supposed to be professionals.'

A chorus of jeers and laughter greeted his remark.

Lights dimmed as Brady and Sullivan took up their positions.

'Right, no run-through. We go with it first time,' called Dickinson. 'Ready?'

'One ready,' a cameraman replied and his two companions signalled in affirmation.

'Turn over,' Dickinson shouted.

There was the harsh clack of a clapperboard and Miller heard the words 'Fifty-eight, take one.'

Dickinson took one last look around him then stepped back.

'Action,' he called and Sullivan stepped forward onto the set.

Miller moved closer to the director, the remote control panel held in his hand, the hip flask held in the other. He took a long swig from it as he waited for his cue.

The camera crane swung in low over Sullivan as he raised the shotgun.

'Right, Frank,' whispered Dickinson and Miller allowed his finger to hover over the red button on the remote. A few more seconds and he would, through his effects expertise, make it appear that most of Brady's chest had been destroyed by a shotgun blast. He watched the two actors confront each other, Brady now sporting the lolling plastic tongue which he'd worn in previous scenes.

Dickinson watched impassively as the actors played out the scene, his impatience growing as Sullivan paused a fraction too long before squeezing the trigger of the shotgun.

There was a dull boom as he did so, the blank cartridges going off with a deafening roar.

Miller jabbed the button on the remote.

Nothing happened.

33

'Oh, shit,' hissed the effects man, shaking the small box angrily.

'Cut it,' Dickinson shouted, wearily. 'Right, nobody move. This'll be fixed in a couple of minutes.' He looked at Miller who was already examining the squibs.

'What happened?' Brady wanted to know as the effects man fiddled with the small explosive charges.

'Something could have jammed the signal,' Miller said. 'If it doesn't work this time I'll have to wire them up to a control board.' He bent closer, squinting at the minute detonators, adjusting them slightly.

Brady could smell the whisky on the effects man's breath.

Miller muttered to himself as he re-adjusted the squibs, looking round to see where he'd put the remote.

It was lying on the table behind him.

He decided that he'd be better off trying the squibs first, before the cameras started rolling. He didn't want any more cock-ups.

He bent closer to the squibs, his face only an inch or two from them.

Pat Sullivan rubbed his shoulder, surprised that the recoil on the shotgun had been so violent, considering the weapon had fired only blanks.

Miller prodded the detonator of the fourth squib, bending closer to adjust it.

Sullivan put the shotgun down on top of the remote.

Miller heard the warning shout but there was nothing he could do.

All five squibs went off simultaneously.

He saw a brief blinding light then all he felt was searing pain as the charges exploded in his face, the bursts of fire scorching his eyes. He screamed in pain as he felt sticky liquid spurting onto him as the blood bags burst and splattered him with fake life-fluid. But the most powerful sensation was that of pain. Excruciating agony which seemed to fill his head as he clawed at his burning eyes. Fragments of rubber mingled with the shower of sparks which roasted the sensitive orbs. Miller fell to his knees roaring in pain, striking out blindly.

He heard screams and shouts around him but they came from an interminable darkness which would not lift while all the time he clawed at his eyes which felt as if someone had poured acid into them. Stage blood mingled with his own and ran down his face to stain his cheeks which were already blackened by the five miniature explosions.

He fell forward, the pain finally growing too great and, almost gratefully, he felt himself beginning to lose consciousness.

Before he blacked out completely he heard Dickinson's voice loud above the cacophony of shrieks and calls.

'Get an ambulance, quick.'

That was the last thing he heard.

Five

He heard the crash as the ambulance doors were flung open, then suddenly he felt cold air on his face as he was lifted onto a waiting gurney.

At least that was what he imagined to be happening. He could see nothing.

Miller had regained consciousness only minutes after being placed in the emergency vehicle and he had been forced to lie in agony as the ambulance sped through the streets towards the hospital. He'd been vaguely aware of the sensation of speed, he'd heard the strident wailing of the siren and, closer to him, the voice of a medic offering reassurance and, more to the point, morphine. In the darkness he had been grateful for the pain-killing drug.

The journey had taken less than ten minutes but it had seemed like an eternity. Now, in his blindness, he felt himself being trundled towards the main entrance of Casualty.

Voices swirled and eddied around him, disembodied sounds in the perpetual night which had descended upon him. He heard nurses speaking quickly, caught fleeting words here and there.

'. . . his eyes . . .'

'. . . straight to surgery . . .'

'. . . badly damaged . . . in pain . . .'

Miller felt like adding his own contribution to the patchwork of words and sounds, but when he tried to speak his lips merely moved soundlessly. It felt as if someone had filled his mouth with chalk. When he tried to swallow his throat merely constricted, preventing even that simple action.

The gurney bumped against something and, in his blindness,

he called out. A sound he'd felt incapable of making came out as a low croak. The smell of disinfectant was strong in his nostrils now, an odour which meant he was being pushed along one of the hospital corridors. He felt hands brushing his skin. Warm hands. There was reassurance in the touch.

Jesus, if only he could see something.

He blinked but the action only increased his pain and he groaned again, realizing that the effects of the morphine were wearing off.

'Get out the way . . .'

'. . . emergency . . .'

'. . . OR three, now . . .'

Miller could feel the bandages around his head and he prayed that was the reason he could not see. He gritted his teeth as he felt the gurney come to a halt.

'He's lost a lot of blood,' a voice above him said. Miller wanted to say something, wanted to tell them that most of the crimson fluid which covered his face was of the fake variety. Like some kind of joke. Funny fucking joke. You're blind, you stupid bastard, he told himself. Now let's hear you laugh.

'What happened?' the voice asked again and Miller heard brief details of the accident being relayed from somewhere to his right. He also felt hands gently removing the bandages, peeling back the layers of gauze until his eyes were exposed. He braced himself for the onslaught of the light, for the pain which would come when he opened his eyes. And he prayed for that pain.

He prayed for the light.

The cotton wool pads were removed.

Miller opened his eyes.

Darkness.

'Oh Christ,' he moaned, the noise sounding alien. As if someone else had spoken the words. 'I can't see.' His breath was coming in short gasps now. '*I can't fucking see!*' he roared, his voice a mixture of fear and frustration. He turned his head from side to side as if expecting his vision to return, as if everything was going to suddenly become clear, as if the disembodied voices were about to be given substance.

But there was only the blackness.

Miller tried to sit up but the pain tore though him and he slumped back as if he'd been struck by a heavy object, as if the outburst had sapped any strength he possessed. He lay helplessly on the gurney, restrained now by more firm but caring hands.

He heard other words, some he didn't understand, then he felt hands on his right arm, rolling the material of his sweatshirt up, exposing the crook of his arm and the vein which pulsed there. He turned instinctively towards the movements, angered now by his inability to see, wanting to know what these people were doing to him. Wanting to see them.

He hissed as he felt the needle being run into his arm and he tensed momentarily as the steel was pushed home, held there, then withdrawn.

'Lie still . . .'

'. . . get him ready . . .'

'. . . must hurry . . .'

More invisible words. He felt the gurney being moved again and he sank back onto the pillow which supported his head. It still felt as if his eyes were on fire but that pain was gradually beginning to subside. Everything was becoming distant. The voices were beginning to resonate inside his head like words spoken inside an echo chamber. He was floating but he fought against the feeling, blinking his blind eyes hard, squeezing his torn lids together. But even the renewed stab of pain could not prevent his steady slide into unconsciousness. It was a battle he knew he couldn't win, but he fought it nevertheless until, finally, he lay back and the darkness which filled his eyes filled his brain.

'The damage to the left eye looks more severe,' said Doctor George Cook as he gazed down at Miller's face.

Apart from the low breathing of the unconscious effects man and the odd murmurings of the surgical team the only sound to be heard in the operating room was the steady blip of the oscilloscope. Every now and then Greg Vincent would glance across at the machine but the anaesthetist did it out of habit rather than any concern for the patient. Miller was in good hands.

Cook picked up a scalpel from the nearby trolley and with minute skill slid it beneath the upper lid of Miller's left eye, exposing the ruined orb more fully. The surgeon carefully wiped away a dribble of vitreous jelly which spilled from the eye as he inspected it. Tiny clips held the lids open, allowing the doctor and his team a full view of their patient's injuries.

'There doesn't appear to be any damage to either retina or optic nerve,' muttered Cook. 'But the lens of this left eye is completely destroyed.' He sighed. 'I don't think we have any choice. We either remove the remains of the cornea and the lens or he'll lose the whole eye.'

'What about the right eye?' asked Doctor Simon Thompson.

Cook looked at it, using the point of the scalpel to remove a small piece of black matter from the lower lid. The skin round the eye was scorched in places but the orb itself seemed to have escaped damage. He shook his head and returned his attention to its neighbour.

'I'm going to remove the cornea and lens,' Cook repeated.

He steadied himself and, working with incredible delicacy for such a big man, pushed the point of the scalpel carefully into the pulped eye. Using a slight cutting action he sheared a small section of the cornea away, lifting it free with the razor sharp blade. A nurse moved forward and offered a metal dish, watching as the surgeon dropped the piece of almost transparent tissue into it before continuing with his task. He cut deeper this time, ignoring the watery trickle of blood and fluid which ran from the incision. His cut was circular, freeing what remained of the lens. It seemed to float on the vitreous liquid until Cook removed it and placed it in the dish.

The contents looked like slivers of bloodied cling-film.

'The suspensory ligaments and the ciliary muscles are badly burned,' he mused aloud, cutting away a small piece of flesh from beneath the inner lid of the eye.

It joined the cornea and the lens in the metal dish.

The steady blip of the oscilloscope accompanied his expert ministrations.

As if he were peeling away the layers of an onion, Cook separated pieces of translucent flesh and pulled them from the ravaged eye with the aid of a scalpel and tweezers. Then, when the last of the tissue had been lifted away he discarded the scalpel and set to work stitching together the small hole left by the removal of the lens.

'Will he be blind in that eye, sir?' asked a nurse who stood nearby.

Cook exhaled, the breath rasping against his mask.

'Possibly,' he said, thoughtfully. 'However, he does have a choice.'

Dr Thompson threw the surgeon a puzzled glance, his brow furrowing slightly.

Cook saw the other doctor's reaction but didn't acknowledge it. He merely regarded his colleague over the top of his mask.

The oscilloscope continued its tuneless refrain.

Six

At first he couldn't work out whether he was still asleep.

Miller tried to sit up but found the effort beyond him. He sighed and lay back against the pillows, breathing heavily. It was still dark. Everything around him was silent, none of the shouting and yelling in his ears which had greeted him on arrival at the hospital. Maybe it was just night time. Perhaps that explained the darkness. Perhaps.

He opened his eyes.

He saw nothing.

Miller reached up, aware that once more his eyes were covered by cotton wool pads. He touched the tape which held them in place, feeling the pads with the tips of his fingers as a blind person might trace their hands across a page of braille.

A blind person.

You are blind, he told himself. Get used to touching things, because you're never going to see them again. The thought made him sigh once more and he raised both hands to his temples, his breath coming in short gasps.

'Mr Miller.'

The voice startled him.

'Who's that?' he murmured, sitting up awkwardly, instinctively looking round even though he couldn't see who had spoken the words. Immediately he groaned as he felt the stiffness in his back and legs. He lay back once more.

'How are you feeling?' the voice asked. A soft, feminine voice with a slight Irish lilt to it.

He shrugged his shoulders.

'You've been unconscious for six hours,' the voice told him.

41

'Where am I?' Miller wanted to know.

'In your room in the hospital,' he was told.

'And who are you? You'll have to excuse me but being blind puts me at a slight disadvantage,' Miller said acidly.

'I'm Nurse Brennan,' she told him.

'I'd like to say it's nice to see you but, as you've probably gathered, that'd be rather inappropriate at the moment,' Miller said. He raised both hands to his bandaged eyes and exhaled deeply. 'Christ,' he murmured. 'I'm sorry . . .'

'No need to apologize,' she said and Miller heard her move closer to the bed. Next thing he felt her hand behind his back, pushing him forwards. She re-arranged the pillows behind him so that he was sitting upright then he heard the clink of cutlery on crockery and the smell of food reached his nostrils.

'I'd rather have a drink,' he said, listening as she cut up his food.

She took his hand and closed it around the fork, guiding it towards his mouth. He chewed, wrinkling his nose slightly.

'Perhaps it's just as well I *can't* see what I'm eating,' he said, allowing her to cut up more of his food.

He swallowed two or three more mouthfuls then waved a hand in front of him.

'You've got to eat, Mr Miller,' she told him.

'I haven't got much of an appetite at the moment, nurse,' he said, indifferently. 'You could say I've got more important things on my mind. Like whether I'm going to be blind for the rest of my life.'

'I'm not the one to tell you that, Mr Miller.'

'Well, is there any chance of me speaking to someone who can?' he snapped.

The momentary silence inside the room was broken by a knock on the door. Again, Miller turned instinctively towards the sound, aware that a newcomer had entered the room.

'That's all for now, nurse,' Miller heard, noting the authority in the voice. Nurse Brennan left the room, closing the door behind her.

There was a moment's silence finally broken by the new arrival.

'I'm not going to ask you how you feel, Mr Miller,' said George Cook, lifting the chart from the bottom of Miller's bed and scanning it. 'I can imagine.'

'Yeah, it's easy. Just close your eyes,' Miller said sarcastically.

Cook introduced himself, then crossed to the window, gazing out at the rain-sodden sky. High above, hidden from view by the low-lying cloud, a plane passed over, its low rumble sounding like thunder.

'It's not very often we get a celebrity in here,' the surgeon said. 'Someone from the film world. Special effects isn't it?'

Miller nodded.

'Only this time they weren't so special,' he said wearily.

Cook looked across at his patient who was lying with his arms by his sides.

'Am I going to be blind for the rest of my life?' Miller asked, a note of fear in his voice.

'That's difficult to say. The injuries, to the left eye in particular, were bad. It's difficult, as I said.'

'Well, try an educated guess.'

'It's likely, yes,' Cook said, quietly. 'However, it's not certain. In fact, there is a chance that your sight could be restored fully.'

Miller sat up, his head turning in the direction of the surgeon.

'How?' he demanded, the depression in his voice suddenly replaced by a hint of hope.

'I only said that there was a *chance*, Mr Miller. Your right eye may well return to normal in time without the aid of surgery but the left was beyond help by the time you were brought to us.'

'Just tell me what you meant by a possibility of restoring my sight fully,' Miller demanded.

'A transplant,' said the surgeon. 'We've done them before at this hospital, successfully too.' He turned as he heard the first drops of rain spattering the glass of the window pane.

'Is there a donor available now?' Miller asked, involuntarily touching his left eye.

Cook hesitated for a moment.

'Yes there is,' he said quietly.

43

'How soon could you do the operation?' Miller wanted to know.

'The earliest would be a week – '

Miller interrupted him. 'A week? Why so long? If there's a donor why can't you do it immediately?'

'It isn't like changing a light bulb, Mr Miller,' the surgeon said. 'There have to be all sorts of tests done, tissue-typing, blood-group compatability. It's a complicated process.'

There was a long silence, broken by the surgeon.

'And there is always the possibility that the operation may not be completely successful,' he said. 'There's no guarantee it will work. I'm merely offering you an option.'

Miller nodded.

'I understand. It's a risk I want to take.'

Cook announced that he was leaving and headed for the door.

'Dr Cook,' Miller called after him. 'Thanks.'

'Thank me when the operation's over,' the surgeon said, then he was gone.

Miller sank back further onto his pillows, aware that his hands were shaking as he rubbed them across his forehead. Cook had at least given him something to cling to. Some hope. If Miller had believed in God he might well have offered up a prayer. As it was he rubbed his stomach and wondered if there was some way he could get a drink.

'George, can I have a word?'

Cook turned to see Dr Simon Thompson striding towards him down the corridor.

'Is it important?' the surgeon asked.

Thompson nodded and the two of them continued down the corridor to Cook's room. Once inside the surgeon closed the door.

'You've been speaking to Miller,' Thompson said. 'Did you mention the possibility of a transplant?'

'He's all for it. He wants us to go ahead as soon as possible. I told him that the tests would have to be carried out first, but he's willing to go along with that.'

Thompson exhaled deeply.

44

'I can't see your objection, Simon,' said Cook. 'We have a suitable donor, we have the opportunity to give Miller his sight back.'

'You know my objections,' Thompson said. 'What did he say when you told him who the donor was?'

'I didn't tell him.'

'Why not?' Thompson demanded.

'What difference does it make? The specimens are in perfect order, why should it matter who they've come from? All Miller's interested in is getting back his sight and, as doctors, our only concern should be in completing the operation successfully.'

'He has a right to know,' Thompson persisted.

'Do you think it's going to make him change his mind? Do you think he's going to choose to remain blind when he could have his sight restored?' Cook said, irritably.

Thompson regarded his colleague angrily.

'He's not to be told about the donor,' Cook insisted. 'You know that's general policy in all transplant cases anyway.'

'I think this case is exceptional,' the other doctor argued. 'I think that Miller has the right to know he's being given the eye of a murderer.'

Seven

He didn't know how long he'd been asleep.

Miller raised his hands to his face with the intention of rubbing his eyes, but when he felt the gauze against his finger-tips he realized that instinctive action was impossible.

Miller cursed under his breath. He felt so bloody helpless, not even able to see what the time was. He could hear the steady ticking of a clock on his bedside table and he reached out towards it as if the mere touch of the timepiece would give him the information he sought.

His hand brushed against a water jug and the receptacle topped from its perch.

It hit the floor and shattered.

'Shit,' hissed Miller, slumping back onto his pillows.

A moment later the door of the room opened and he heard footsteps scuttling across to him.

'Are you all right, Mr Miller?' the nurse asked, looking first at the effects man then down at the glass and water beside the bed.

'I didn't know that bloody jug was there,' he said. 'I'm sorry. I didn't know what the time was. I was reaching for the clock . . .' He allowed the sentence to trail off.

'As long as you didn't hurt yourself,' the nurse said, busying herself beside the bed retrieving the pieces of glass. She informed him that she'd send an orderly in to mop up the mess then she retreated from the room to fetch him some more water.

'Put a drop of Scotch in it, will you?' Miller murmured as she left the room. He heard new footsteps and then a male voice close by him followed by the slopping of a mop.

The orderly looked down at the man on the bed, studying his

46

bandaged features.

'I heard that you were in films,' the orderly finally said sheepishly.

'Sort of,' Miller said.

'Are you an actor?'

'No, I do effects.'

The orderly squeezed some water into his bucket and continued with his task.

'What kind of effects?' the orderly persisted.

'Decapitations, disembowellings, shootings,' Miller said wearily. 'The usual sort of family entertainment.'

The other man didn't pick up the note of sarcasm in the effects man's voice.

'I was reading this book the other day and there was one bit where this bloke had his head pushed onto a bacon slicer. That'd look good in a film wouldn't it?' he chuckled.

'Great,' said Miller with a distinct lack of enthusiasm.

The orderly finished his task, said a cheerful goodbye and left.

Miller lay in the silence, listening again to the ticking of the clock. He smiled to himself. Head on a bacon slicer, he thought. Well, at least it was original. Nearly as original as blinding yourself with your own squibs. His smile faded as he sucked in an angry breath. Under any other circumstances, the irony of the accident might have struck him as amusing. But now all he felt was frustration and anger. And fear. The thought of blindness terrified him. If he'd been deafened by the accident, he told himself, he could have learned to live with that. But to face the prospect of living in never-ending night was one which made him shudder. If the operation worked, though, he would be fine. And if it failed . . .? He tried to push the negative thoughts out of his mind but they showed a marked reluctance to go. He almost smiled again. 'The best special effects man in the business' he'd been called on numerous occasions, and now he was in hospital, victim of one of his own devices. Miller thought back to the first time he'd worked on a film set. His introduction to the film world had been by way of still photography. He'd finally left New Scotland Yard, his mind numbed to suffering, his soul anaesthetized against pain after photographing the dead for so long. He'd found himself in a bar one evening drinking with a man who he later discovered was the second-unit director on a large American production shooting interiors at Elstree. The man – Miller couldn't even remember his name – had offered him a job and he'd taken it without hesitation.

The move into make-up and special effects had also been a piece of good fortune. Filming a scene in which a man had supposedly been shot in the head, Miller had remarked on how little blood the make-up man was using. After all, he'd seen enough gunshot victims to know that the head contains some of the largest blood vessels in the body. Head wounds bled profusely. He had the pictures to prove it. Miller had re-arranged the scene himself, adding the nauseating details of death which he knew so well.

After that episode he was often consulted on such matters and it was just a question of time before he moved into effects permanently. His time as a press and police photographer had been perfect training for the grisly effects he was called upon to create and Miller had read that top American make-up man Tom Savini drew on his own memories as a war photographer in Vietnam to create the gory effects which had made *him* famous.

Miller rubbed his cheeks, feeling the stubble against his finger-tips. There was a further irony to the situation, he thought. He created illusions with imitation flesh and blood, he'd been blinded by fake gunfire and now his only hope of regaining his sight was with someone else's eye. Once more he almost smiled. Almost.

The nurse returned with a fresh jug of water which she placed on the bedside table, away from the clock. Miller heard the sound of something being unscrewed and turned his head towards the noise.

'I've removed the front of the clock,' the nurse told him. 'That way you can feel the hands and you'll be able to tell the time yourself if you need to.'

'Well, it'll be good practice,' said Miller sarcastically. 'I'll start with the clock and work my way up to braille.'

48

'Why don't you try and sleep?' the nurse said, quietly.

'I've done nothing *but* sleep ever since I was brought in.'

'Try to rest, please.'

'Yeah, good idea. If I don't get eight hours I'll hardly be able to keep my eyes open will I?'

The nurse sighed softly, almost stung by the bitterness in his voice.

She squeezed his arm gently, then turned and left the room.

Outside it was still raining.

Eight

The green light on the switchboard flickered insistently, like some myopic eye in the gloom.

Nurse Brennan put down her book, folding the corner of the page, and reached for the phone. As she picked up the receiver she glanced across at the clock.

It was almost 12.08 a.m.

'Ward Nine B,' she said, stifling a yawn.

Silence.

'Nine B,' she repeated. 'Can I help you?'

The phone went dead and the nurse replaced it, reaching for her book once more, flipping the paperback open again. The words swam momentarily before her and she rubbed her eyes. Only another twenty minutes and she would finish her shift, able to return to the warmth of her bed. She'd been on the ward since eight that morning.

The switchboard light glowed green again and she picked up the phone.

'Hello, Ward Nine B.'

Again silence.

She sighed. Perhaps the receptionist hadn't connected the caller properly.

'Hello,' Nurse Brennan persisted.

'I want to speak to Frank Miller.'

The voice was low and rasping and the suddenness of the words startled her.

'Who is this, please?' she asked.

Silence.

'Who's calling, please?'

'I want to speak to Miller, now.'

'Are you a relative?' the nurse asked.

'Let me speak to him.'

'Mr Miller is asleep. I can give him a message when he wakes up if you'll tell me your name.'

Only silence greeted her enquiry, but on the other end of the line she could hear breathing.

'Who is this, please?' she persisted.

'Tell Miller we've got things to discuss,' the voice snapped, then Nurse Brennan jumped as the phone was slammed down. The sound rattled in her ear then all she heard was the dull drone of a dead line. She held the receiver before her for a moment then slowly replaced it.

As she did, she wondered why her hand was shaking.

Nine

'You must keep your eyes closed until I tell you otherwise.'

Miller heard Dr Cook's voice as he felt the bandages around his eyes being slowly and carefully removed.

Miller was trying to control his breathing but, like his heartbeat, it seemed to accelerate with every passing second. He swallowed hard as the last of the dressings were removed and only two patches of gauze covered his eyes.

The seconds ticked by.

Everything during the last two weeks had happened with what had seemed like agonizing slowness.

The tests.

The waiting.

The operation.

And now, finally, a week after the transplant had been completed, the moment of truth loomed. Miller knew that he was moments away from learning whether he would see again or if he was to be condemned to a life in darkness. The muscles in his stomach contracted like a fist.

Beside him he heard the clock ticking. Someone had told him it was just after two in the afternoon. He heard other voices in the room, low and almost conspiratorial, but above them all was the voice of the surgeon. It was he who now took a pair of tweezers and gripped the pad which covered Miller's right eye. He inspected the lid quickly, dropped the gauze into a dish and then repeated the action with the left eye.

'Close those blinds,' he snapped to a nurse who stood behind him and Miller felt the tension and fear building inside him as he heard them rattle. In a few seconds he would know.

'All right, Mr Miller, I want you to open your eyes. Slowly,' Cook told him.

Miller twitched his eyelids and felt a slight pain but he persevered, gradually forcing them open.

Light flooded into his eyes, despite the relative gloom inside the room, but he ignored the discomfort until his lids were fully open.

Hazy shapes swam before him and he blinked hard, trying to focus. The shapes remained mere blurs.

'Can you see anything?' asked Cook, looking down at him.

Miller glanced up at the surgeon, squinting in order to sharpen his vision, but it did no good. It was like looking at the man through frosted glass.

'Everything's blurred,' he said. 'I can see shapes but not their definition. It's not clear.'

'Close your right eye,' Cook instructed.

Miller did as he was told, gazing through the new eye.

Through someone else's eye. The thought made him shudder involuntarily.

'Now the left,' the surgeon said.

'There isn't much difference,' Miller said. 'I can't make out details. I can see your face but I'm not even sure what kind of expression is on it.' He raised his own hands and looked at them.

'What can you see?' Simon Thompson asked.

'I can see my hands but the fingers are blurred into one,' Miller said. He spread them but still the vision remained the same. He blinked again but found that it achieved nothing.

There was a heavy silence in the room as the nursing staff looked on.

'It'll take time for the eyes to settle down, especially the transplanted one. You've got to give it time,' Cook told him.

'But how much time?' Miller wanted to know.

'Rest your eyes now,' Thompson urged.

'It might be an idea if we kept them covered for another day or two,' said Cook, motioning the nurse forward.

'And after that?' Miller demanded.

'We've done as much as we can do,' the surgeon told him. 'You have to be patient now.'

53

Miller sighed and nodded resignedly, watching the hazy shape of the nurse as she drew closer to him. He closed his eyes as he felt the first of the fresh cotton pads being eased into place.

'Have you any pain?' Cook asked.

'None,' Miller told him as the nurse worked busily at her task.

There was another uncomfortable silence.

'I know it's difficult for you, Mr Miller,' the surgeon said. 'But all you can do now is wait.'

'The fact that you've even got some semblance of vision back is a good sign,' Thompson reassured him.

The nurse finished bandaging Miller's face and stepped back.

'We'll leave you now,' Cook said. 'I'll check on you later.'

Miller merely lay still, his fists clenched beside him. He heard footsteps as the medical entourage trooped out, leaving him alone. Alone in his room. Alone inside the darkness once again. He reached up and touched the bandages, trying to feel the outline of his eyes beneath the pads. He finally gave up and allowed his hands to drop to his sides once more.

'*All you can do is wait.*'

Cook's words echoed inside his head.

Beneath the cotton pads he blinked but he felt nothing. He rolled onto his side trying to blot out the ticking of the clock.

Each minute that passed seemed like a lifetime.

He waited.

Miller didn't know which floor of the hospital he was on but he guessed that he must be fairly high up as he could hear no sounds of traffic from the car park. Outside in the corridor he heard footsteps passing back and forth, sometimes at a leisurely pace, sometimes more frenetically. Apart from that, all he heard was the ever-present ticking of the clock, and it was a sound which was beginning to grate on his nerves. It was as if the rhythmic tick-tock was growing louder inside his head. Each movement of the second hand seemed to be more pronounced than the last.

Tick-tock. Tick-tock.

Like a splinter in his brain, driven deeper each time.

54

Tick-tock.

He rolled onto his back.

Tick-tock.

Something warm and wet rolled slowly down his cheek causing him to jump at the sudden, unexpected, sensation.

He wiped the tear away with the back of his hand.

A feeling of vague hope suddenly swept through him. Perhaps his eyes were beginning to function once more. Maybe the production of tears was a sign.

He felt another of the moist droplets dribble from beneath the bandages.

And another.

He blinked beneath the pads of gauze and the flow seemed to increase slightly. Miller winced as he felt a slight pain from his left eye.

He wiped the driblets away with his fingers, the digits brushing against his nose in the process.

Miller froze.

He felt the fluid flowing freely down both cheeks now and, as he struggled to brush it from his face he recognized the coppery stench which covered his hands.

It was blood.

His eyes were bleeding.

The thought struck him like a thunderbolt and he sat up, his hands shaking, trying to wipe away the fluid spilling from the ruined orbs. He put a hand to the bandages and felt that the gauze was soaked.

'Oh God,' he breathed in horror, trying to pull himself out of bed. In his blind terror he gasped aloud, almost falling as he felt his feet touch the cold floor.

He had to get help. Had to stop the bleeding.

Miller could feel the blood running down his face and neck, the smell strong in his nostrils. He tore at the bandages, trying to pull them off, not knowing quite what to do, wondering where the emergency button was, wondering how he could reach the door. He tried to call out but his throat seemed to have closed up. When he tried to scream blood ran into his mouth.

He coughed, gagging on the bitter-tasting fluid which ran

55

from his eyes.

Miller stumbled, crashed into a wall. He shot out one quivering hand and slapped at the wall leaving a bloodied handprint on the white paint.

'Jesus, Jesus,' he gasped as he banged into a chair. Fresh pain shot up his leg and he overbalanced, landing heavily on his shoulder, lying helplessly on the cold floor while the blood continued to run from his eyes.

Miller dragged himself upright, arms flailing uselessly. Then he slumped against a wall, his face a mask of blood. With shaking hands he tore the bandages free, tugging at the pieces of gauze which covered his weeping, throbbing orbs. The lumps of gauze were like sodden sponges, soaked in crimson. But Miller could see none of it. He could only smell the odour of life-fluid as it drained from him through the gaping wounds which had once been his eyes. And yet somehow, through that red torrent, he found that he could see.

He could see.

God in Heaven, he could see.

Despite the pain and the blood he almost smiled, the smile of a man who is losing his mind, for, close to him, with almost frightening clarity, he saw a mirror and using all his strength he dragged himself towards it.

Blood had soaked into his pyjamas and run down his legs. In his blind fear he had wet himself and the acidly pungent odour of urine mingled with that of the blood. But Miller didn't seem to care, all he wanted to do was reach the mirror. To look upon his ravaged face, possibly for the last time.

He stared into the reflecting glass.

His eyes were little more than swollen clots of dark fluid, oozing sores which bulged and throbbed like blood blisters which seemed on the point of bursting. Two grotesque pustules of crimson that opened and closed like slobbering, riven lips expelling their thick contents over his face.

As the blood-soaked image stared back at him he finally found the breath to scream.

Ten

His scream brought him hurtling from the nightmare.

Miller sat bolt upright, heart hammering madly against his ribs, the perspiration sheathing his body like a film of condensation.

He put a hand to his face and felt moisture there. He wiped it away, then sniffed it, satisfied that the wetness was nothing more than sweat.

He let out one huge, shuddering sigh and slumped back.

Immediately the door was flung open and he heard someone approaching him.

'Mr Miller,' Nurse Brennan said, her voice full of concern.

'A nightmare,' he said, softly, trying to catch his breath. 'I was dreaming. I'm sorry.' He tried to swallow but it felt as if his throat was encircled by an iron clamp.

Nurse Brennan poured him a glass of water and held it while he sipped.

'I'm all right,' he told her. 'Honest. It was just a dream.' His breathing was beginning to slow down now. He even managed a thin smile.

'Are you sure there's nothing you want?' she asked.

'Maybe something stronger than water?' he asked hopefully.

She smiled down at him, even though he couldn't see the gesture, then she took one of the tissues from beside the bed and wiped some perspiration from his face.

'I'll be back with your dinner at six o'clock,' she told him. 'Try and get some rest until then.'

Miller nodded, listening as she walked across the room and closed the door behind her.

Six o'clock.

He reached out carefully, feeling his way over the bedside cabinet with one hand until he found the clock. He touched the hands gently and worked out that it was almost 3.00 p.m. Miller replaced the timepiece and lay back, listening to the insistent ticking. He rolled onto his side, then his back, but found that he could not get comfortable. Finally, cursing, he sat up, touching the pads of gauze which covered his eyes. Sucking in a deep breath, he swung himself out of bed, steadying himself against the bedside cabinet. He gripped a handful of sheet and seemed to drag himself to the end of the bed, his feet slapping against the cold floor. His breathing was low but rapid as he gripped the metal bedstead. Another yard and he would be walking without support.

Miller knew that the sink was to his left, so he turned slowly in that direction and padded towards it, arms outstretched like some grotesque parody of the Frankenstein monster taking its first faltering steps. He reached out, hissing in pain when his fingers touched the radiator. He stood still, trying to re-orientate himself for a moment, then he continued onwards towards the sink. Every step seemed a monumental effort, as if someone had weighted his legs with lumps of lead, but he finally reached his goal, his hands closing over the cold porcelain.

Miller smiled thinly and exhaled deeply. Then, after a moment, he reached up and began undoing the bandages around his eyes.

He wobbled uncertainly for a moment but propped himself against the sink as he persisted with his task, his heart thudding faster.

The first layer of bandages came away and he dropped them into the sink.

He set to work on the next layer until finally, only the gauze pads remained.

His hands were shaking as he removed the one over his right eye, keeping his lids firmly closed.

He repeated the procedure with the left. Then, with agonizing slowness, he opened his eyes.

It felt as if someone had glued his lids together, but he perse-

58

vered, gripping the edge of the sink more tightly as he struggled to open them.

The right eye opened first and Miller was aware that he was now sweating profusely.

Miller opened his left eye, allowing the lids to roll back gradually until both glistening orbs were exposed. He gazed ahead of him towards the mirror above the sink.

Staring back at him was a clear image of his own face.

He tried to swallow but couldn't.

'Oh God,' he breathed, scarcely able to believe. Not daring to believe.

He could see.

Miller regarded his reflection as if he were looking at a stranger, but gradually the realization began to sweep over him. He turned to one side, wincing at the light which streamed through the window, but the brightness was glorious. He didn't care if he had to shield his eyes. He could see and that was all that mattered. He could see the bed, the door of the room, the four white-painted walls. Miller crossed to the window and looked out.

Below him, he guessed seven or eight floors, he could see the car park, vehicles and people coming and going. And he could see it with amazing clarity.

He closed both his eyes for as long as he dared, fearing that simple act might cost him his sight, but when he opened them again everything was as clear as before.

Miller turned towards the bed, towards the emergency button above it.

Shooting out a hand he hit the button, smiling as he did so.

He stood by the bed and watched the door.

By the time it was opened, he was laughing like an idiot.

Eleven

'Does that hurt?'

Dr George Cook aimed the pen-light at Miller's left eye.

'Nothing I can't get used to,' Miller said, sitting up in bed.

Cook inspected the right eye, watching the pupillary dilations and enlargements as he shone the light at the sensitive orb. Finally he flicked it off and dropped it into his top pocket.

'It would be wise to keep your eyes covered for the next few days,' the surgeon said. 'Just with sunglasses. We don't want to undo all our work now.'

'How long before you know that my sight is restored permanently?' Miller wanted to know.

'That's impossible to say,' Cook told him. 'We'll just have to hope there isn't any kind of reaction, particularly in the left eye. There's always a danger of rejection. That's a consideration in the transplantation of any organ.'

Miller nodded.

'When can I get out of here,' the effects man asked.

'Leave the hospital?' Cook said, almost incredulously. 'I couldn't allow you to leave until we were completely sure there were no adverse reactions to the new eye. It may take a fortnight, perhaps longer.'

'Sorry, Doc,' said Miller defiantly. 'But if you think I'm staying here for another two weeks you can forget it.'

'It doesn't matter whether you want to or not. You have no choice,' the surgeon insisted angrily.

'No, it's *you* who have no choice,' Miller reminded him. 'If I decide to discharge myself there's nothing you can do about it.'

'That would be ridiculous. Without adequate supervision

your condition could deteriorate again. If you leave I can't be responsible for what happens.'

'I'm not asking you to be responsible. When I walk out of here it'll be because I want to.'

Cook shook his head.

'If there was some kind of reaction then you could lose your sight for good and there'd be nothing we could do to help you.'

'Well, that's a chance I'll have to take,' Miller told the surgeon. 'I can see, that's all that matters. I've got you to thank for that and I'm grateful, but I can't stay cooped up in this bloody hospital for two weeks while you watch my progress. I'd go crazy. I realize the implications if I leave and I accept them.'

'As you say, it's your decision,' the surgeon sighed. 'But I wish I could make you change your mind.'

Miller smiled.

'You've done enough. You've restored my sight, that's the most important thing,' he said. 'You and the poor sod who donated his eyes to medicine,' Miller added as an afterthought. 'Who was he?'

Cook swallowed hard.

'I can't disclose details like that,' he said, quickly. Then he shook his head and raised his arms in a gesture which signalled defeat. 'If you choose to leave, that's your decision. My responsibility ends when you walk out of this hospital.'

Miller nodded.

Miller looked across at the clock.

5.35 p.m.

He swung himself out of bed and crossed to the small wardrobe which stood against the far wall. Inside he found his clothes. Rummaging in the pocket of his jacket he discovered what he was looking for.

The hip flask was all but empty. Nevertheless, he hastily unscrewed the cap and swallowed the contents. The whisky tasted slightly warm but it didn't put him off. He wiped his mouth with the back of his hand and replaced the flask in his pocket before closing the wardrobe and wandering across to the window once more.

He looked down at the car park then up at the rain-soaked sky, watching a low-flying plane cutting its way through the clouds.

At first he thought the plane had been swallowed up by the thick banks of grey, but then he realized that the window-frame itself was becoming hazy.

He blinked hard.

His vision was beginning to blur.

Miller closed his eyes for a moment, gripping the window-sill hard.

He opened them again.

Still the haze distorted his vision, like condensation on a car windscreen.

'Come on, come on,' he whispered, squeezing his lids together even more tightly. He stood there like that until his eyes began to ache, then, with almost painful slowness, he opened them.

Shapes and images in the room developed into crystal clarity and Miller breathed an audible sigh of relief.

He was still standing at the window when the door opened and Nurse Brennan entered, followed by an orderly.

Miller watched as the man set down the object he was carrying on the table at the end of the bed.

It was a small portable television.

'We thought you might be getting tired of your own company,' said Nurse Brennan, plugging the set in.

Miller smiled as she switched it on. He watched the shapes take form, delighting in the coloured images as if it was the first time he'd ever seen a TV.

'I'll be back with your dinner in about twenty minutes,' the nurse told him as he lay on the bed, eyes riveted to the set.

As she closed the door, Miller began to laugh.

He was watching an advertisment for spectacles.

Twelve

Miller blinked hard as his vision dissolved once more.

He kept his eyes screwed up, counting to five before he opened them again.

The clarity had returned and he exhaled slowly, resisting the temptation to rub the left eye. There was a maddening itch in the corner of it but he was reluctant to touch the tender orb. He closed his eyes once more, listening to the drone of the TV set at the bottom of his bed. Beside him he could hear the ticking of the clock.

In the corridor outside his room he heard the sound of footsteps coming and going. It was approaching seven-thirty in the evening and visiting hours had brought forth the usual torrent of well-wishers into the wards outside. Miller himself had received a call from Phillip Dickinson asking after his health, and a huge bouquet of flowers had arrived earlier that afternoon with a card signed by everyone on the set. Miller glanced across at the bouquet. Right now he would gladly have exchanged it for just one glass of whisky. His mouth felt dry, his throat parched, but by a thirst which mere water could not satisfy. It wasn't thirst he was experiencing, it was a craving.

He sat up, propping himself up on his pillows, his attention riveted to the screen in an effort to forget the gnawing desire within him. But what he saw did little to engage his mind. It was one of the many vacuous soap operas which proliferated on the networks now. No programme schedule seemed complete without one. Or two. Or three.

Miller reached for the remote control and changed channels. He flicked through stations as if he were skim-reading a book until finally he found a news programme. Pouring himself another tumbler of water he watched, blinking hard as his vision momentarily blurred again.

'. . . the sixth such murder in the last two months.'

Miller sipped his water, listening as the presenter talked with a photo of a woman projected behind him. The woman was in her early twenties, pretty despite the fact that her front teeth protruded slightly.

'For an up to date report we hand over to Terri Warner,' said the presenter, and the screen was suddenly filled with the face of a dark haired girl in her late twenties. She was dressed in a thick anorak and held her microphone in a gloved hand. The strong wind tossed her hair almost angrily, forcing her, periodically, to brush strands from her face. In the background, Miller could see other shapes moving about. Uniformed shapes. Policemen. Ambulancemen. The reporter was standing in the front garden of a well maintained house in what looked like a residential area. Every now and then Miller saw by-standers gathered close to the fence which overlooked the garden. A uniformed constable was doing his best to move them on but their interest in seeing a corpse was apparently greater than their fear of being arrested for causing an obstruction.

Terri Warner ran a hand through her hair and looked into the camera.

On the screen beneath her, beside the station logo, her name appeared.

'In the house behind me less than thirty minutes ago,' she began, 'the body of a woman was found, and police on the scene are reasonably certain that she was killed by the same person who has so far claimed the lives of five others in the last two months. The woman's body was found by a neighbour who is currently being treated for shock. The victim has been identified as Bernadette Evans, aged twenty-three.'

Miller re-filled his tumbler, then he turned up the sound slightly.

'With me I have the detective in charge of the investigation,' Terri continued. 'Detective Inspector Stuart Gibson.'

Miller smiled thinly as he recognized the policeman.

'Gibson,' he murmured, studying the DI's features.

The two of them had worked together many times when Miller was employed by New Scotland Yard and still met up for the occasional drink. The years, and the job, had woven their own pattern of lines and wrinkles into the face of the policeman. But his blue eyes still sparkled with their customary defiance. Miller smiled again as he saw his former colleague standing agitatedly before the camera. He never had liked the media.

'Is it safe to assume that the latest victim was killed by the same person responsible for the other murders?' Terri asked, pushing the microphone towards the DI.

'It's possible,' Gibson said curtly.

'Was the victim mutilated?'

'No comment.'

'Are you any closer to finding a clue to the killer's identity?'

'No comment,' said the policeman, moving back slightly as if anxious to be away from the probing questions and ever-watchful eye of the camera. 'That's all I've got to say.'

'Is this latest murder motiveless?' Terri persisted, following him a couple of steps.

'No comment,' he said with an air of finality. Then, with one last look at the camera, Gibson moved away.

'So, it would appear that the police are still baffled by this series of murders which has shocked the whole country,' she said. She paused for a moment. 'This is Terri Warner for Independent News.'

Her face disappeared and that of the presenter replaced it.

'There'll be a further report from Terri Warner in our next bulletin later tonight,' he said, moving onto the next story.

Miller turned the sound down once more.

Number six.

He'd read about the murders in the paper and seen Terri herself on the box. She seemed to be making quite a name for herself reporting on the killings. He shook his head wondering how many more would die before the murderer was caught.

His thoughts were interrupted as his sight began to deteriorate once again. This time he could not resist the urge to rub his eyes. Sharp pain shot through him as he did so, but despite the discomfort he was relieved to find that his vision was no longer impaired. He blinked hard a couple of times and wiped some moisture from his lower lid.

As he did so he heard the sound of heavy footsteps outside his room and the voice of Nurse Brennan speaking loudly, almost protestingly. Miller frowned as a second later the door opened.

Miller looked up to see the nurse standing there, her face flushed.

'There's someone to see you, Mr Miller,' she said curtly then stepped back out into the corridor.

Miller gazed at the door waiting for his visitor to enter.

The newcomer appeared and Miller felt the blood draining from his face.

He swallowed hard, his face now pale.

The visitor closed the door behind him and stood looking at Miller.

'What the hell are you doing here?' Miller said, his voice a combination of anger and fear. 'How did you find me?'

Thirteen

For once Detective Inspector Stuart Gibson was grateful for the smell of cigarette smoke.

It masked the stench of blood.

The policeman stood looking down at the body, sucking his teeth in an effort to remove a small fragment of the sandwich he'd eaten earlier.

Beside him Detective Sergeant Chandler took another long drag on the Marlboro and blew out a thin stream of smoke. He too was looking down at the corpse.

Bernadette Evans had been a pretty girl in life, that much they knew from her photo. But not any more.

She lay naked in the sitting room of the house she had shared with two other girls. They were both staying with friends while police investigations were carried out, both had been out when the murder happened. Otherwise, Gibson thought, he might have been looking at a trio of corpses. And at this stage one was bad enough.

The dead girl lay spreadeagled, one hand already beginning to close up as rigor mortis set in. The body was beginning to take on a bluish tinge, mainly due to the massive loss of blood which had occurred. The crimson fluid was splattered all over the carpet and furniture. It looked as if some irate artist had wandered into the sitting room and hurled several tins of thick red paint over everything.

Her head, at least what remained of it, had been pulped almost beyond recognition by several dozen pile-driver blows delivered by an antique brass poker which lay close by. The bone hadn't merely been broken, it had been battered into hundreds of tiny fragments by the deluge of blows. The skull had been completely destroyed, as had most of the other bones and tissue above the lower jaw. A sticky flux of blood, bone and brain-matter was spread out around the pulverized head. A fearful stench rose from the corpse and Gibson coughed slightly as he moved closer, inspecting the damage inflicted on the rest of the body, for, if anything, it was worse than what had been done to her head.

The chest and breasts were relatively untouched, except for three or four minor cuts around the right nipple, one of which had narrowly missed the shrunken bud, though the stomach was a patchwork of gashes and lacerations. In at least two places portions of intestine bulged from the rents, thick with congealed blood. But it was around the girl's vagina that the most horrendous damage had been inflicted. Her mound, hips and inner thighs had been punctured so many times that all the wounds seemed to flow into one massive, reeking crater, bloated with congealing gore. Her outer vaginal lips had been clumsily but effectively sliced away and lay beneath her like strips of bleeding steak, now shrivelled and discoloured. There was no doubt about the knife used to inflict the wounds. It was a broad, razor-sharp kitchen knife.

It was embedded, up to the hilt, in her vagina. Jammed there in a final act of obscene frenzy like a steel penis.

'If it's any consolation,' said Sam Loomis, pulling a sheet over the mangled genital area, 'I'm sure *that* was done after she was dead.' The pathologist looked at Gibson and raised his eyebrows.

'It isn't any consolation,' said the DI quietly. He turned and beckoned two waiting ambulancemen forward, watching as the men carefully lifted the ravaged body onto a stretcher. Through the front room window, Gibson could see the emergency vehicle parked outside, its red lights turning silently in the gloom.

'Six victims, six different MOs,' the DI mused aloud. 'You wouldn't think it was possible, would you?' The question was directed at no one in particular.

'Well, we've got the bodies to prove it,' said Chandler, grinding a piece of fallen ash into the carpet. He took a last suck on his cigarette then stubbed it out in a nearby ashtray, waited a moment and lit another. Gibson regarded him with irritation.

'Is that bloody TV crew still outside?' Gibson called to a uniformed man standing near the front door.

The man looked out and nodded.

'Why don't you speak to that girl?' Chandler said, smiling. 'You'll probably get on the ten o'clock news as well.' He blew a stream of smoke past his superior.

'She's been on this bloody case as long as we have,' Gibson said.

'I wonder if she knows anything we don't. It seems we could do with all the help we can get,' said Chandler bitterly.

'I don't see you coming up with too many clues, Sherlock,' the DI countered, glaring at his colleague.

'I'm as baffled as you,' Chandler admitted. 'But then I don't have as much responsibility as you, do I? I wasn't the one who was promoted.'

'No,' said Gibson, looking at the older man. 'You weren't.'

'I'll let you have my report as soon as I can, Stuart,' Loomis said, trying to interrupt the verbal sparring of the two detectives.

'Cheers, Sam,' Gibson said. 'Look, are you sure this one was done by the same murderer? Like I said, the different MOs . . .'

'I'm sure of it,' Loomis said, cutting him short. 'The wounds on the body were delivered with a strong right hand cut that matches up with the wounds on victim number four, remember?'

'How could I forget,' said Gibson.

The fourth victim, Nicholas Blake, had been found three weeks earlier on a bench in Hyde Park, his throat cut in six places, his head practically severed. No murder weapon had been found. No weapon. No fingerprints. No clues.

There were never any clues.

'Can you be sure there isn't more than one killer, Sam?' Gibson asked the pathologist.

'As I said,' Loomis began, 'the cutting action is the same in two cases. But the fact that all the victims were found in roughly the same prone position shows a certain consistency which also points to a single killer. The first victim was shot while lying on his side, then pushed over onto his back. Maybe the killer wants us to know he's working alone.'

'Why?' Chandler asked.

Loomis shrugged. 'Don't ask me. I'm a pathologist, not a psychiatrist.'

'Oh Christ,' sighed Gibson, seating himself on the arm of the nearby sofa, his eyes fixed on the crimson stain which covered the carpet. 'And I promised my kids I'd spend some time with them tomorrow.'

'Occupational hazard,' said Chandler, matter-of-factly. 'With position comes responsibility.'

Gibson wasn't slow to catch the sarcasm in his colleague's voice. He got to his feet angrily.

'That's right,' he snapped. 'And don't you forget *who's* in charge, Chandler. They promoted *me*. You and all your moaning and groaning won't change that, so why don't you just get on with your job?' The DI headed for the door but turned as he reached it. 'Before they decide to replace you with someone else. Someone younger.'

Chandler's face darkened and he murmured angrily under his breath as his superior left the room.

Someone younger. It was bad enough having to take orders from Gibson, the DS thought. At forty-five he was seven years older than his superior. Seven years more experienced, he thought bitterly. But, when the time had come, it had been the younger man who'd been promoted. He had pondered over and over again why he should have been passed by. Could it have been because he once took back-handers from a video dealer in Soho when he was with the vice squad? No, he reasoned, no one had ever found out about that or he'd have been out on his ear. It was departmental politics, he was sure of that. Gibson was married with a couple of kids while Chandler himself lived alone with only an Alsation for company. Gibson presented a better front to the powers-that-be higher up the ladder. He appeared more settled, more reliable. And, besides that, he'd been instrumental in tracking down the members of an armed gang who'd robbed a security truck of £750,000 six months earlier. They'd cut a hole in the truck with a chainsaw then promptly used the lethal implement on a guard who'd decided to play the hero. One of the other guards had been paralysed for life by a shotgun blast which had blown away part of his spine while the third member of the group had been relatively lucky to escape with only mild brain damage when a pick-axe had been driven through his helmet and into his skull.

Gibson had supervised the hunt for the gang who, it turned out, were a professional team from overseas. However, by sealing off air terminals and ferry routes and confining the search to central London, Gibson and his men had chanced upon some of the money and traced it back to one of the drivers used in the escape. Under interrogation he'd cracked and informed on his companions. Within four days they were all locked up and awaiting trial.

At the time of the raid and the track-down Chandler had been laid up at home with a slipped disc, so he'd missed the operation. Gibson had picked up the praise *and* the promotion.

Chandler took a last drag on his cigarette then dropped it into the ashtray on the table. He wandered outside to see Gibson talking to the TV reporter. She'd been present at every scene ever since the killings began. She ought to keep out of the way, he thought, running appraising eyes up and down her shapely form. The jeans which she wore tucked into a pair of ankle boots clung invitingly to her legs and buttocks. Tight, mused the DS as he passed.

'Look, what can you tell me off the record?' Terri asked the DI.

'Nothing's ever off the record with you lot,' said Gibson, scornfully. 'If I told you anything it'd be the main story in the next bulletin.'

'The public have a right to know what's going on,' the reporter told him. 'If there's a maniac running around butchering people then you shouldn't hide facts from them.'

'When it's time for the public to know all the facts they'll be told by New Scotland Yard not by a bloody TV reporter,' Gibson rasped. 'You must think I'm stupid. You've been on this bloody case from the beginning, I know it's making *you* a household name, no wonder you're interested.'

'I'm only doing my job,' Terri told him.

Gibson nodded. 'Yeah, and it makes great television doesn't it?' he snapped. 'Well I'm trying to do my job too but part of that job doesn't include giving press interviews at the scene of every murder.'

'Do you think there'll be more?' she asked.

Gibson eyed her suspiciously for a moment and thought about walking away but he hesitated, his voice losing some of its harshness.

He shrugged wearily.

'It seems possible considering the type of nutcase we're dealing with.' He fixed her with a cold stare. 'But don't quote me on that.'

Terri smiled and shook her head.

Gibson walked past her, heading for the blue Fiesta which was parked close by the ambulance. Chandler sat in the driving seat, a cigarette dangling from one corner of his mouth. As he clambered inside, Gibson waved a hand in front of him in an effort to disperse the smoke which was rapidly filling the vehicle.

Chandler started the engine as the DI belted himself in.

The car sped away.

Terri watched it go, feeling the first spots of rain on her face. High above her, dark clouds began to fill the sky.

The drive back into central London took less than thirty minutes, but in the uneasy silence which descended between Gibson and Chandler the journey seemed to take an eternity. The DI had his eyes closed, thoughts tumbled through his mind. Every now and then he would look up to see the rain which spattered the windscreen being swept away by the rapidly moving wiper blades. The lights of passing vehicles and neon glow of cinema and theatre hoardings seemed to merge into a liquid mass as the rain poured down the glass of the windows.

Inside, the car smelt of stale cigarettes. Gibson wound down his window slightly to allow the stink to escape. The smell of exhaust fumes flooded in to replace the other odour.

'You shouldn't have spoken to that reporter, you know,' said Chandler.

Gibson opened his eyes slightly and regarded the DS with annoyance.

'Don't tell me how to handle the press, Chandler,' he said, irritably.

'She's good looking though,' the DS said, smiling. 'I wouldn't mind a crack at her.'

'How do you know she goes for older men?' Gibson said, quietly, a slight smile on his lips.

Chandler shot him an acid glance.

'Anyway, we've got more important things on hand than women,' the DI said. 'Did you get the forensic boys to go over the house after we left?'

'Before and after,' Chandler told him. He turned a corner and was forced to brake hard as two pedestrians stepped off the pavement a yard ahead.

'Get out the way,' the DS snarled as he drove past.

Gibson looked at his colleague and frowned disapprovingly.

'We'd better hope forensic find something this time,' Chandler said. 'The longer these killings go on the bolder the killer's likely to get.'

'And if he does he's more likely to make a mistake,' countered Gibson.

'You mean it's just a matter of how many more people have to die before we come up with some ideas?' Chandler said sardonically.

'Like I said, I'm not the only one on this bloody case,' Gibson reminded his colleague.

'No, but you're in charge.'

'That's right. I am,' the DI said flatly. 'And don't you forget it. If you worried about the case more and less about losing your promotion we might all be better off.'

Chandler brought the car to a halt and the DI pushed open the door, stepping out into the rain. His own car was parked on the wet tarmac close by.

'See you tomorrow,' he said perfunctorily, slamming the door behind him.

73

'Yeah,' hissed Chandler. 'See you.'

He watched his superior clamber into his own car and, deep inside, he felt his anger seething.

Gibson would have to learn that Chandler wasn't going to allow himself to be walked over.

Somehow he would learn.

Obsession

The blood which covered the road was already beginning to congeal. Solidifying beneath the rays of the sun.

The cat had managed to drag itself across the road despite the fact that the car which had hit it had crushed its back legs into pulp. As it crawled it left a trail of blood and pieces of mashed entrails behind until it finally found refuge in a shallow ditch by the roadside. It lay there helplessly, its body twitching as spasms of pain racked it mercilessly.

The child squatted a foot or so away watching the dying feline, running appraising eyes over the shattered body.

The cat had been penned in the back garden to prevent it from getting close to the main road, but somehow it had found a way out and had paid the price. The child watched as blood ran freely from the smashed lower body, gazing with fascination as intestines swelled and bulged from the torn stomach as if they were being pumped up from within. Here and there amongst the crimson mush, pieces of bone gleamed whitely.

The cat had been old, fat and bloated and now it looked as if its body had burst, such had been the impact of the car when it had been struck.

The child watched as half a dozen flies settled on the bleeding remains, feasting like so many gourmets on the reeking banquet. The cat made a low mewling sound and, as it did so, fresh blood ran from its mouth and nose. Its eyes were half-closed and the child realized that the animal was close to death. Did the cat know that it was dying? Did it realize that it was going to lie in this ditch until it stopped twitching and moved no more? The child wondered as it watched, eyes roving up and down the cat's body.

The cat's fur had been ginger but now it was covered by thick, matted gore which stuck to the coat like crimson glue.

The child moved a little closer, watching more intently as the cat continued to utter the low mewling sounds, lifting its head as if soliciting help, but even if it had been able to offer help, the child would not have done so for it watched the dying moments of the creature with fascination.

What kind of pain was it feeling? Could it feel the steaming coils of its own entrails attempting to break free of its torn belly like bloated, bloodied snakes?

The cat's head flopped backwards for a moment and it lay still, only the scarcely perceptible movement of its chest showing that it still lived.

The child reached behind it and found a long branch, fallen from one of the trees that overhung the ditch. Gently, the child prodded the cat with the small branch, watching for any more signs of movement. The animal miaowed loudly, a sound of pain which the child recognized. It discarded the branch for a moment, watching the animal writhing in agony. More flies had joined their companions, some of them actually wandering inside the cat's riven body. The child looked on in wonderment, trying to count the black shapes against the vivid red of the cat's blood.

The movement of the cat's chest was slowing, its final breaths coming in shallower inhalations, as if the mere act of breathing was causing pain.

The child moved a little closer, listening to the rasping sounds that were receding into liquid gurgles.

Blood spilled more copiously from the cat's mouth and its body began to quiver uncontrollably, its forepaws jerking as if suspended by invisible wires. Then its entire body seemed to shudder and its head flopped backwards.

The child watched for any further signs of movement, and when none were forthcoming it reached for the stick again and jabbed gently at the cat's head.

It didn't move.

The child reached out and touched the intestines which bulged from the hideous tear in the animal's belly. They were still warm. The coppery odour of blood was strong in the air and the child inspected the gore which coated its hand, sniffing it slowly before looking once more at the dead animal.

One of the flies had crawled inside its blood-filled mouth.

The child looked on, mesmerized.

Fourteen

Frank Miller splashed his face with cold water then stood up, studying his reflection in the mirror. He watched the droplets of moisture dripping from his chin for a second then reached for the towel and dried himself.

'I can't condone your decision, Mr Miller,' said George Cook, watching as Miller ran a hand through his hair. 'As I told you before, if there is any adverse reaction I won't take responsibility.'

'I realize that,' Miller said, pulling on his jeans. As he pulled the dark sweatshirt over his head he noticed several small burn marks, no bigger than pin-heads. They were the result of the sparks from the exploding squibs which had blinded him. He smoothed his hair once more and ran a hand over his heavily stubbled cheeks, listening to the whiskers rasp beneath his fingers.

'I really want to thank you and your staff for what you've done for me, Doctor,' Miller said.

Cook sighed.

'You could show your thanks by staying here under observation for another two weeks,' the surgeon said.

Miller smiled.

'Nice try,' he said, crossing to the wardrobe and his jacket. From one pocket he withdrew an instamatic camera. 'I never go anywhere without it,' he said, his tone softening slightly. 'Look, I know this may sound ridiculous but I was wondering if you'd mind if I took a couple of pictures. You could call it force of habit.'

'You're the celebrity, Mr Miller,' Cook said, smiling. 'It's me who should be taking photos of you.'

The door opened and Nurse Brennan entered.

'Perfect timing,' said Miller, handing her the camera. 'Can you take a picture of Dr Cook and me together, please?'

The nurse nodded and smiled as Miller showed her how to work the camera, then he and the surgeon stood side by side as she focused. Miller winced slightly as the flash went off but he hid his discomfort well and asked Cook to repeat the procedure. Miller snaked his arm around the nurse's waist, smiling as she coloured slightly. The flash glowed once more and Miller took a photo of the surgeon and nurse. That task done he pocketed the camera and pulled on his jacket.

'You promise me that you'll be back in a week for a check-up?' Cook said. 'It could be vital. And if you have any pain or adverse reaction before then you must return immediately. For your own sake.'

Miller smiled and nodded. He stood before the doctor and extended a hand which the surgeon shook warmly.

'Thanks again,' Miller said, then he turned and kissed the nurse lightly on the cheek, watching as she turned a shade of scarlet.

'I'll walk with you to the main doors,' Cook said.

'There's no need.'

'It's hospital rules,' the surgeon said. 'At least do *one* thing you're told.'

Miller nodded and followed the surgeon out of the room.

They rode the lift to the ground floor, Miller resisting the urge to rub his eye as it blurred slightly, but as the doors slid open he could see clearly once more.

As the two men walked slowly up the long, polished corridor which led to the main doors Miller saw two interns hurrying through to casualty, one pushing a gurney, the other carrying two packs of blood for a transfusion. A nurse scuttled behind them.

Outside, the sound of sirens filled the air.

The electronic signal pinned to Cook's lapel began screeching and the doctor sighed.

'I think I've got work to do,' he said, extending his right

hand. Miller gripped it firmly then turned to watch as the surgeon sprinted off back down the corridor. Miller stood alone by the main doors for a moment then stepped out into the sunlight.

He almost shouted aloud in pain as the hot rays hit him. He shielded his eyes and sucked in a painful breath, staggered by the agony which throbbed in his skull. It fell as if someone were trying to pull his eyes free of their sockets with red-hot pincers. He stepped back hurriedly into the welcoming coolness of the entry-way. To his right were three public phones. Miller crossed to one and called a taxi to take him home.

He decided to wait for it inside.

By the time he got home the sun had been swallowed up by rolling banks of cloud drifting in from the west. Miller screwed up his eyes against the natural light but there was no more pain. He fumbled for his key and let himself in, standing in the stillness of the hall for long moments. There was a pile of mail lying on the mat at his feet but he ignored it, walking through into the sitting room instead. He crossed to the drinks cabinet and took out a large glass which he half filled with Haig. He swallowed a sizeable mouthful, wincing as the liquid burned his throat and stomach but then he smiled and held the glass before him.

'Welcome home,' he chuckled.

With his free hand he reached for the nearby phone, jammed the receiver between his ear and shoulder and jabbed out a number. He heard the drone of the ringing tone then a woman's voice at the other end.

'I'd like to speak to Phillip Dickinson,' Miller told her.

Mr Dickinson was busy on the set, he was informed.

'Tell him Frank Miller called. I'll be back at work tomorrow.'

She thanked him for calling and hung up.

Miller poured more whisky into his glass then walked out of the sitting room down a short corridor to another door. He unlocked it and walked in.

It was dark inside the room, the curtains still firmly closed, but Miller stood with his back to the door for a moment, enjoying the enveloping gloom. Finally he reached up and slapped on the light.

The banks of fluorescents in the ceiling sputtered into life bathing the room in a cold white glow.

To his right was a large desk, beyond it stood endless banks of filing cabinets.

Propped up in a metal dish on the closest of these was a severed head.

Miller looked across at the blood-spattered object and smiled.

Fifteen

The corpse was naked.

It sat in a straight-backed chair in one corner of the room, head tilted back slightly to expose the savage gash which had almost parted the head from its body. Blood had poured down the chest and stomach to the ravaged lower body.

Between the legs of the corpse, jutting out like a bloated erection, was a thick worm-like object, sickly white in colour but covered in blood too. Near the head of the object were what looked like two tiny arms, the fingers twisted into hooked claws. Like some kind of bloodless, deformed tadpole, the creature had its mouth open to reveal a row of sharp teeth, pieces of flesh stuck between them from where it had eaten its way free of the host body.

Miller studied the body with justifiable pride. It had been one of the most audacious and effective pieces of work he'd ever undertaken. It had been used in a film he'd worked on almost two years earlier called *Intruder*. When the picture had been released in the States there had been some talk of cutting the scene in which the creature tore its way free of its host while he was making love to his wife. It was then, according to the script, to have disappeared into her vagina where it created similar bloody havoc, but this latter part of the scene was eventually shelved. Even so, due to the other nauseating effects Miller had contrived the picture received an X rating in the US and, consequently, died a death at the box office. But Miller was still pleased with the way his effects had turned out. He gazed admiringly at the body for a moment longer then glanced across at another occupant of the room.

It was a woman.

The flesh of her face had been peeled off to reveal a network of muscles and tendons beneath. One eye was missing, dangling half-way down her cheek by the optic nerve. Her mouth was open to reveal the remains of a tongue, severed by a knife. The same knife which had been used to flay her so expertly.

Close to her was a badly burned body.

A severed leg, maggots attached to the stump, stood in a corner like some kind of umbrella stand.

Beside it lay the torso of a man, thick tentacles hanging from the place where his legs should have been. Gripped in those tentacles was the pulped and bloodied body of a child.

Miller smiled as he looked at that particular creation. Each of the tentacles had been worked by a combination of hydraulics and wires and it had taken himself and a team of six other technicians over a week to complete a shot which appeared on screen for less than eight seconds. To this day, when he watched the film, Miller could not see the wires, even though he knew where each one had been. It was another scene he was justifiably proud of.

Seated in another chair was a man with a gaping head wound. Miller had made the head of the replica hollow then filled it with steak, stage blood and sheep's brains. When the time came for the 'victim' to be shot in the head the actor responsible had merely fired a real shotgun blast at the top half of the dummy and half the head had been torn away. After filming had been completed, Miller had brought the dummy home. It now sat staring back at him with one blank, glassy eye.

The effects man sat down at his desk and looked around his workroom. He had converted the study himself shortly after moving into the house. Initially it had been used as a darkroom when he worked as a photographer. It still retained a double sink and the smell of developer hung in the air, mingling with the ever-present odour of rubber. Latex was one of the more popular materials for creating prosthetic effects and Miller had found that it was easy to work with as well as being durable. Some of the monstrosities which shared the room with him looked as fresh as the day they'd been constructed. Miller smiled to himself, remembering how an interviewer from a film magazine had called him a modern day Doctor Frankenstein, surrounding himself with his creations.

As well as the whole replicas there were numerous heads, eyes, skulls and limbs dotted around the room. All had been used in films on which he'd worked. On his desk lay several sketches of the make-up he'd devised for the *Astro-cannibals* and also a number of photos both of the finished product and also make-up in more experimental stages. Miller flipped through the sketches and photos as he seated himself behind the desk, his attention gradually drawn to the wall opposite him.

On it was a huge notice-board and completely covering it were more photos. Only these were not of Miller's creations. They were a legacy of his days as a police and press photographer. Colour and monochrome reminders of the horrors which he had viewed and preserved over the years.

The blood-spattered remains of a pram which had been hit by a drunken driver, the pulverized mess which had been its occupant wedged beneath the car's front wheel. Miller could still remember taking it, the horrified mother screaming behind him. Cars slowing down to get a glimpse of the accident. The blood running into a drain.

Click.

A woman gang-raped by four men and then tied up with electrical flex before a broken bottle was jammed into her vagina.

Click.

Two victims of a gangland reprisal killing, their teeth torn out with pliers before they were both strangled with cheese-wire.

Click.

The suicide who'd decided to take a businessman with him onto the electrified tracks at Knightsbridge.

Click.

A man who'd decided to be a hero and foil an armed post-office raider, lying in the gutter with his genitals blown off, his hands buried deep in the hole where his legs met.

Click. Click. Click.

Miller took another sip of his drink and glanced across at the filing cabinets. They were crammed full of photos too. A storehouse of pain and misery all immortalized by his camera. Laminated horror which he referred to often. But the sights were filed away in a much more complex cabinet too. The memory bank which was his mind. Each vile, repulsive sight gouged across his mind like a scab, never to be erased. Behind him the clock ticked loudly, its rhythmic refrain amplified by the silence inside the room.

Miller sat at his desk, the tumbler of whisky cradled in his hand. He blinked as he felt a slight gnawing pain in his left eye and a second later his vision faltered. It was like looking through a piece of gauze. Miller cursed and rubbed his eyes, gasping in pain as he did so, but when he'd finished his sight was clear again. He downed what was left in the glass and got to his feet, crossing to the bank of filing cabinets. Sliding the closest one open he reached in and pulled out a bottle of Haig. It was already half empty, a testament to his previous visits. He unscrewed the cap and poured a large measure. Then he looked across the room at his monstrous creations and raised the glass in salute.

It was the strident ringing of the phone which woke him.

Miller sat up sharply, a little too sharply, his head throbbing immediately. He managed to glance at his watch before snatching up the receiver.

It was 4.36 p.m.

'Hello. Frank Miller,' he said, massaging the bridge of his nose between his thumb and forefinger.

No answer.

'Hello,' he said, wearily.

Low breathing on the other end.

'You picked the wrong house for an obscene phone call,' he snapped, preparing to slam the phone down.

'Miller.'

The sound of his own name prevented that simple act of retaliation. He pushed the receiver gently against his ear once more.

'Miller, can you hear me?' the voice asked and he knew it instantly.

'What the fuck do *you* want?' Miller said angrily. 'I told you at the hospital not to contact me here. If I need you I'll call you.'

'Just wanted to check that you're back home,' said the voice.

'Get off the line,' he said through clenched teeth.

'See you soon,' said the voice and Miller thought he heard a low chuckle before the line went dead. He slammed the receiver down, pushing the phone away from him as if it had been contaminated. He just sat staring at it.

As if he were afraid it might ring again.

Sixteen

Miller stood in his workroom bathed only in the sickly red light positioned over the work-bench in the corner.

Water was running from the taps of both sinks, washing the developer from the photos he'd removed from his camera. Miller watched as the images formed more clearly and he carefully hung the photos up to dry, smiling as he saw the one of himself and Nurse Brennan. He peered up at the one of Doctor Cook and the nurse.

Miller's smile faded slightly as he studied the picture more closely.

At first he thought that his eyes were playing tricks on him.

He blinked but the photo did not change.

A fault in the film, he thought. It had to be some kind of fault in the film.

Miller checked the photo of himself and Doctor Cook.

Then re-checked it.

In both pictures there appeared to be a faint, almost luminescent outline around the figure of the doctor. As if his body were giving off some kind of aura.

Miller held the photos up to the light and closed his right eye, squinting at the curious haze which surrounded every inch of the doctor's image.

It seemed even more pronounced. He exhaled deeply, a frown creasing his forehead.

He closed his left eye and looked again.

'What?' he murmured. The aura seemed to have disappeared. The photos looked normal.

He tried it again looking through the left eye.

The luminous outer-shadow re-appeared.

Miller chewed his bottom lip contemplatively, aware now that the aura only showed up when viewed through the transplanted eye. He shook his head, puzzled not only by his ability to see the peripheral glow which was apparently radiating from Cook's body, but by the other fact which bothered him.

What the hell was it?

Seventeen

A couple of hijackings, a terrorist bombing in Italy, ever-increasing unemployment and a batch of rapes, muggings and murders.

Just like any other day, thought Miller as he sat watching the news, his glass propped on one arm of the chair. His eyes felt gritty, as if someone had rubbed sand into them and he rubbed the delicate orbs cautiously. The bottle of Scotch beside him was three-quarters empty but Miller was still far from being drunk. In fact, he couldn't remember the last time he'd been really smashed. Perhaps that was something he should remedy now he thought, raising the glass to his lips.

The phone rang.

Miller froze for a moment, listening to the harsh tones. Then he turned in his chair and glanced across the darkened sitting room towards the table where the device was housed.

It was still ringing.

He jabbed the mute button on the remote and the newsreader was transformed into a soundless cipher.

Still the phone rang.

Miller got to his feet and crossed to it, sucking in an anxious breath as he allowed his hand to hover over the cradle.

Not twice in one night, surely, he thought uneasily.

He waited a moment longer then reached for the receiver.

The ringing stopped.

Miller sighed and looked down at the phone, his hand still poised over it.

He drew it away sharply as the strident tone began once more.

This time he snatched the receiver up and pressed it to his ear.

'Miller,' he said, quietly.

'Frank, about time. How are you feeling?' said Phillip Dickinson. 'I'm sorry to bother you so late, but I got your message about coming back to work and I thought I'd better tell you that there's been a change in the shooting schedule. I'm going to need some different props for tomorrow. I know it doesn't give you much time but there's nothing else I can do.'

'What do you need?' Miller asked.

'Well, we're doing the scene where the cannibals break into the orphanage,' said Dickinson.

Miller raised his eyebrows and chuckled to himself.

'It's scene forty-three in the shooting script, if you want to check it out,' the director continued. 'I need a severed arm. The rest of the effects specifications are in the script. I'm sorry it's such short notice, Frank.'

'No sweat,' said Miller, sipping his drink. 'I'll get on to it now.'

They said hasty goodbyes and Miller hung up.

He turned and headed for the hall, not bothering to switch off the TV. Finding a copy of the shooting script in his workroom, he flipped through it until he found the required scene. In the margin, written in red ink he read;

> SEVERED ARM
> DEAD BABY

Miller checked his watch. It was approaching 11.36 p.m.
He set to work.

1.58 a.m.

Miller ran his index finger slowly around the rim of his glass and looked at the object which lay before him on the work-bench.

The arm had been severed at the shoulder, pieces of bone showing through the pulped mass of flesh. Several deep gashes had also been gouged into it around the wrist. The fingers were splayed wide as if ready to grasp the first object that came within reach.

The effects man looked at his creation with pride. It certainly looked realistic. As good as anything you'd find in a casualty room he thought, chuckling.

The arm was made of rigid foam and covered in rubber to give flexibility. Miller had then sculpted the latex into shape, working quickly and expertly. It had then been baked and painted. The script had called for an articulated arm so that the hacked off appendage could crawl along the floor and grab an actor by the ankle, but with such little time to work in, Miller had been unable to add the hidden motors and mechanical attachments which would give the replica arm a life of its own. The moving arm shot should be relatively simple. An actor would merely put his arm through a hole in the floor, that arm would then be made up to match the fake arm and the action could commence from there. Miller had used the same technique numerous times with decapitations. A dummy head was hacked off then an actor merely put his head through a gap and stage blood and latex flesh were spread around his neck to give the appearance that the severed head was still alive. Simple, he thought, smiling.

He glanced at his watch. Miller re-filled his glass and looked again at his work. Then he looked across at the shooting script, his eyes scanning the crumpled page.

'The cannibals grab a baby and take it into the kitchen,' Miller read aloud, smiling slightly. 'There is a fight between one of them and the cook. The baby . . .' He allowed the sentence to trail off, shaking his head. Someone was actually paying out over four million dollars for shit like this. The film business never ceased to amaze him.

'The baby,' he said, quietly glancing at the red handwriting in the margin.

DEAD BABY

Miller scratched his head. More work? He took a long swallow from his glass then hurriedly re-filled it, his hands shaking slightly.

Miller looked at the phone close by him.

The ticking of the clock was deafening in the silence.

He closed his eyes for a moment as his vision blurred slightly.

When he opened them again he was gazing at the phone. He exhaled deeply and reached for the receiver, hesitating slightly before picking it up.

He held it to his ear, listening to the low monotone buzz for a moment.

He clenched his fist, trying to stop his hand shaking, then, slowly, he relaxed. It had done no good, his fingers still trembled.

Miller gritted his teeth then, finally, he dialled.

Eighteen

The room at New Scotland Yard which had been chosen for the press conference seemed far too small for the purpose.

Gibson counted at least thirty journalists crammed into the small carpeted room which was already hazy with the smoke of many cigarettes. Periodically a flash bulb would explode and the air was alive with the constant clicking of cameras and the murmur of expectant voices. The DI shuffled the sheaf of papers before him as if anxious to find something to do with his hands.

Next to him, seated at the table which took up half the width of the room, the coroner, Sam Loomis, was busily attempting to light his pipe. The older man had practically disappeared inside a fog of smoke and it looked to Gibson as if his colleague was close to combustion himself. His face was red and perspiration had formed in silvery droplets on his bald head.

Next to Loomis sat Lawrence Chapman, the Commissioner of Police. Chapman was a tall, almost painfully thin individual with pinched features and short grey hair. He hardly looked the imposing figure who controlled the City's police force virtually single-handed, but appearances were deceptive. Beneath his harassed look, Chapman was a veritable demon. As a detective, earlier in his career, he'd twice received commendations for bravery, and on the second occasion he'd also received a bullet from a .38 through the shoulder as a more permanent reminder of the hazards of the job.

Beyond him sat DS Chandler, who was picking his teeth with a broken match. He stopped as Chapman threw him an irritable glance.

Terri Warner stood close to the table looking at the four men, waiting for her chance. No TV cameras had been al.owed into the conference, which had been announced only the previous day. Considering the police apparently had very little to go on, she wondered why they'd gone to the bother of calling a meeting of this kind. As she saw Chapman rise to his feet she hoped she was about to learn the answer.

The commissioner banged hard on the table with the flat of his hand then sat down again, waiting for the babble of conversation to die away. Only the clicking of cameras continued.

'Ladies and Gentlemen, I'd like to get this over with as quickly as possible,' he said. 'After all, we all have jobs to do, don't we?' He smiled humourlessly. 'The reason you were called here is because there have been significant developments in the case we are currently working on. I hesitate to use the term mass murderer, but I can think of no better description. Anyway, I would like to hand you over to the detective in charge of the case.'

Chapman introduced Gibson and then sat back in his seat, hands clasped across his stomach.

The DI coughed self-consciously and looked at the swarm of expectant faces. He spotted Terri at the front and looked away from her.

'As you know, the killer has so far murdered six people,' Gibson began. 'And, up until now, we've not been able to find any clues either to motive or suspects.' He coughed again. 'Yesterday we arrested a suspect. Someone is now helping us with our enquiries.'

The relative silence in the room was suddenly replaced by a barrage of questions and murmurs of surprise, not least from Terri, who saw Gibson glance hastily towards Chapman who merely smiled thinly.

'I thought you had no leads,' said a reporter from the *Express*.

'Don't believe everything you read in the newspapers,' Gibson said, trying to smile at his own joke. 'There are still one or two loose ends we have to tie up, but we are confident that charges will be formally filed very soon.'

'How was this breakthrough made?' a voice near the back shouted.

'We discovered a link between the six victims,' Gibson said, looking down at his notes.

'Can you say what that link is?' Terri persisted.

'Not at present,' Gibson told her. 'All I can say is that we found a number of similarities in the killing methods.'

'What details can you give about the murderer?' Terri asked, noticing that Gibson was glancing towards Chapman once more.

The commissioner shook his head almost imperceptibly.

'None as yet,' Gibson said, wiping a bead of perspiration from his top lip.

'How long will it be before you can give any details?' asked the man from the *Express*.

'No comment,' Gibson said, flatly.

There was another clatter as dozens of cameras were fired off in one noisy barrage.

'Is it true that all the victims were mutilated?' the man standing next to Terri called. He had his notepad open and was scribbling hastily.

'No comment.'

'Was there any form of sexual interference with the female victims?' yelled a *Sun* reporter from the back of the room.

'No comment.'

'Can you give any details at all about the suspect?' Terri demanded, her eyes never leaving Gibson's face. 'Age, sex, background or anything like that?'

'I've already said no,' Gibson responded, his throat feeling dry. He reached for the glass of water before him and took a hefty swallow.

Terri glanced across and saw that Chapman was looking at her. She felt curiously uncomfortable beneath his gaze.

'Has a motive been established?' she persisted.

'No comment,' said Gibson, rather hastily.

'We'd rather not disclose any more details at present,' Chapman suddenly interjected. 'Suffice it to say that an arrest has been made and we'll release a full statement in due course.' He looked across at Gibson and the two men exchanged brief stares. 'That will be all for now,' shouted Chapman as the sound of cameras and the babble of questions grew into one vast crescendo. The press showed no sign of leaving. Only when the policemen rose to their feet and headed towards the door behind them did the reporters begin to file out.

Terri paused for a moment, looking at Gibson and Chapman as they left the room, both of them chatting animatedly. Then the door was closed and both disappeared from view. She sighed and shook her head slowly, her brow wrinkled into a frown.

'They'll never swallow it,' said Gibson anxiously, standing in the annexe behind the conference room.

'Of course they will,' snapped Chapman. 'I think you overestimate the intelligence of the press, Stuart. We told them we'd made an arrest and they believed us. By tomorrow it'll be front page headlines in every paper and main report on every news programme. As far as the press and public are concerned this killer is under arrest.'

'And what if someone finds out the truth?' said Gibson. 'What if they find out we're no closer to finding the bastard than we were after the first killing? What then?'

'It's our job to make sure they *don't* find out,' Chapman told him. 'This conference was set up to give us a little breathing space, you know that. We've got to find this maniac before he kills again.'

Gibson sighed and looked across briefly at Chandler.

In that split second, he was sure the Detective Sergeant was smiling.

Nineteen

They didn't fit.

No matter how many times she re-arranged the pieces in her mind, Terri Warner could not get the pieces of this particular jigsaw to fit.

Less than a week ago the police had been completely baffled by the series of murders, totally clueless. But now, suddenly, they had arrested a suspect. She shook her head slowly as she considered the revelation. No way, it just didn't fit. As the saying went, '*If it don't gel, it ain't aspic.*' This wasn't gelling. She brushed a strand of dark hair from her face, feeling the perspiration on her skin.

It was like an oven inside the car.

Terri glanced down at the broken heater which was blasting out hot air and decided that next time she had a spare moment she'd get it fixed. As the traffic ahead of her slowed up she wound down her side window.

A cloud of exhaust fumes promptly poured in and she hurriedly closed the window again. The heat, she decided, was preferable to the smell. Behind her, the driver of a black Porsche banged hard on his horn. Terri adjusted her rear-view mirror and glanced at the impatient motorist who was tapping his steering wheel agitatedly. He finally revved up his engine, swerved out into the road and shot past her as if he were on the starting grid at a Grand Prix.

Terri smiled to herself, catching a glimpse of her own reflection in the mirror. She clucked her tongue as she saw the beginnings of dark rings beneath her eyes. Too many late nights, what would mother say? she mused. Theresa Nicole

Warner, you should take more care of yourself. She could almost hear her mother's voice inside her head. Both her parents had objected strongly when she'd announced her intentions to leave home seven years earlier. They'd trotted out the usual string of clichés about London being a hotbed of vice and iniquity, with evil people just waiting to get their hands on a naive twenty-year-old girl. The fact that Terri had a job with a large advertising agency already lined up, as well as somewhere to live, didn't seem to hold much water as far as they were concerned. However, she would have been surprised if they hadn't protested and she'd suffered their well-intentioned paranoia happily enough until her mother had tried a new angle of attack. Two weeks before Terri was due to leave, her mother had lapsed into deep depression. A state which rapidly became tiresome, especially when she took to bringing out the old photo albums and complaining that she was losing her only daughter. At first Terri had tried to humour her but then the first barbs had begun to cut her.

'Since Eve died,' her mother had said one evening. 'You're all we've got. *She* wouldn't have wanted you to leave.'

The reference to her dead sister had affected Terri deeply, if only because it was the lowest and most painful ploy her mother had yet tried.

Eve had been a year older than Terri and mention of the other girl had struck a chord deep inside her. She'd died of spinal meningitis when she was twelve and Terri could remember being dressed in her finest clothes and forced to stand for hours on end gazing at the body of her sister which was on display in the sitting room of the house. To begin with she'd stood and wept but, as the ritual was repeated day in, day out, for almost a week, she had gradually come to look at her dead sister with feelings of bewilderment rather than grief. Her mother had even taken photos of the dead girl as she lay in her coffin. Those were included in the photo album as well.

With Eve's death all her parents' smothering love had been transferred to Terri, who grew up feeling suffocated. To this day she wondered how she had ever found the courage within herself to leave home.

But, although her mother had attempted the supreme piece of emotional blackmail towards the end, if anything it had only stiffened Terri's resolve to leave. Her father had done his part too, taking her on one side and reminding her how deeply hurt her mother was going to be by her departure. But even this two-pronged assault on her family loyalty had not dissuaded her. Though, even now, she felt she was entitled to hate them both a little bit for not having been at the station to see her off. In fact they hadn't even been in the country. The week she was to leave they'd conveniently decided to take a week's holiday.

Terri rang them as often as she thought necessary, to let them know how she was keeping and that she still had a job, hadn't yet been gang-raped by hordes of psychopaths and, no, she had no intention of returning home. The hotbed of vice and iniquity was treating her rather well. She hadn't thought it worth mentioning the three or four short-term relationships she'd gone through. They'd meant little to her, why bother her parents with them? Up until recently she had shared a flat in Bloomsbury with another girl, but she'd left a month or two ago to live with her boyfriend, leaving Terri with the flat and two lots of rent. But she coped, her job as TV reporter paid well, and since she began reporting on the murder case she'd been given a rise.

She'd joined the Independent Channel four years earlier as a secretary, worked her way up to become a researcher, then finally been given a break in front of the cameras. Her appearance had swayed the powers-that-be, for not only was she good at her job, she happened to be very attractive too. News always seemed more palatable when it was being presented by a pretty face. Even if that pretty face *was* giving details of the most savage and bizarre string of killings seen for many years.

Terri swung the Mini Clubman into the car park at the rear of the TV studios, found a parking space and drove in. She gathered her handbag from the passenger seat, locked the vehicle and strode across the tarmac towards the glass doors which fronted the entrance.

The figure stood impassively.

Watching her.

Twenty

Terri rode the lift to the fifth floor, smiling self-consciously at two plump cleaning ladies who gazed raptly at her, beaming inanely. The reporter could smell bleach in one of the women's buckets, its pungent odour filling the lift. The two women continued smiling at Terri until she got out at the appointed floor. She heard an excited muttering from behind her.

'It *is* her, the one who's reporting on those murders.'

'I knew it was. Terri something . . .'

The voices were lost as the doors slid shut. Terri made her way down the corridor, her high heels clicking on the recently polished floor. She passed framed photos of staff members, of newsreaders, presenters and the station's controllers. The fifth floor was given over almost entirely to news, while those below housed the nerve-centres for light entertainment, drama and documentaries. The building was vast, but after four years there Terri knew it like the back of her hand.

She turned a corner, exchanging brief greetings with a cameraman she knew then she came to a door marked NEWS EDITOR. Terri pushed it open and walked in.

She was greeted by the clattering of typewriter keys.

Paula Crane looked up and smiled as the reporter entered.

'Morning, Terri,' said the secretary in her broad Cockney accent. 'Bob's in his office,' she continued, inclining her head in the direction of the door behind her. 'Shall I bring you a cup of coffee through?'

'Please, Paula,' Terri said gratefully. 'Is he in a good mood?'

The phone rang and Paula reached for it, raising a hand to silence Terri momentarily.

100

'Hold up,' she said, raising the receiver.

'Good morning, Bob Johnson's office,' said Paula, her diction perfect, her accent now completely devoid of its East-End twang. 'No, I'm afraid Mr Johnson's busy at the moment. Can I get him to call you back? Thank you.' She put the phone down. 'Bleedin' hell, that phone's been going mad all morning,' she said, slipping back into her usual accent.

Terri laughed and walked through into her boss's office.

Bob Johnson was sitting at a computer console, punching keys, but he looked up as Terri entered.

'What about this?' he said, holding up a computer read-out. 'The latest ratings. Our programme is up by 50,000 since these killings started.' He pushed the read-out towards her. 'That's about 8,000 a victim, isn't it?' he chuckled humourlessly. 'If this nutcase keeps going we'll be bigger than *New at Ten*.'

'Great,' said Terri none too enthusiastically. 'Only if what I heard from New Scotland Yard is right then you'd better start looking for another story, Bob. They reckon they've arrested the murderer.'

Johnson looked round, his forehead wrinkling.

'That's not possible,' he said, quietly, smoothing his black hair back with the palm of one hand. 'They said they had no leads.'

'That's what I thought,' Terri told him.

Paula entered with two mugs of coffee and set them down on Johnson's desk. She took one look at the news editor and hurried out again. He looked at the ratings read-out a moment longer, then dropped it onto his desk.

'Tell me about it,' he said, sitting back in his seat as Terri described what had happened at the press conference less than an hour ago. Johnson listened intently, his eyes never leaving Terri although she was aware that his attention was wandering. For short periods he would pin her gaze to his, but most of the time he seemed to be inspecting the rest of her body.

He studied her finely-chiselled features and her slender neck, framed by that mane of brown hair, before allowing his stare to move to her breasts, the outline of her bra visible beneath her blouse. She had her legs crossed and Johnson looked longingly

101

at her denim-clad limbs wondering how soft the skin beneath the material was.

She sipped her coffee, aware that his gaze was still upon her, only slightly unsettled by his unmasked appreciation of her physical attributes.

Bob Johnson was a powerfully built individual who looked as though he might have been a boxer earlier in life. His face was almost square, his nose flattened against the pitted skin close to his deep-set eyes. He had a scar below his right ear which ran parallel with his jaw until it reached his chin. The shirt which he wore was open at the throat as if to allow his pendulous Adam's apple more room. His hands were broad, his fingers thick despite their length. Beneath his shirt Terri could see well-developed biceps, and his forearms were also thick, covered in black hair. He was, she guessed, five or six years older than herself, but no one seemed to know Johnson's exact age. He'd been the editor and programme director of *News Update* for nearly a decade. And in that time had made it one of the most successful independent news programmes on the air. He was treated with a mixture of respect and fear by his staff and it was a combination of emotions which Johnson was at pains to perpetuate amongst those below him. During his reign as director he had, to Terri's knowledge, sacked at least a dozen people and once, when a cameraman protested too vigorously, Johnson had laid the man out with a left hook.

Now he sat listening as she spoke, seemingly unwilling or unable to tear his gaze from her body.

Terri shuffled uncomfortably under his constant stare and drank some more of her coffee.

Johnson looked at her soft hands as she cradled the mug in her lap, her fingers clasped around the china. He felt the beginnings of an erection growing between his legs and sat forward, leaning on the desk.

'I don't get it,' he said, as Terri finished speaking. 'And the police said that they had a suspect in custody?'

She nodded.

Johnson got to his feet, crossed to his window and looked down into the car park below.

102

'They can't know,' he said, quietly, his eyes narrowing.

'What do we tell people?' Terri asked. 'The viewers will have to know something. We can't just pass over the story, all the other news programmes will run it and the daily papers are going to be full of it tomorrow. I got the impression that's what the police wanted.'

Johnson didn't answer, he merely shook his head then said again, 'They can't know.'

Terri gazed at his broad back for a moment longer then got to her feet. Johnson turned.

'We'll have to go with the story,' he said. 'Go into studio three, I want something recorded for the six o'clock bulletin.' He exhaled heavily, watching as she put the mug down.

Terri nodded and left.

Johnson waited a second then moved across to his desk and picked up the mug from which Terri had been drinking. He was breathing heavily as he lifted it to his face, trying to catch a hint of her perfume on it. He pressed it closer to his mouth then, closing his eyes, he sucked gently on the rim of the mug in the place where Terri had been drinking. His tongue flicked hungrily over the china, lapping back a dribble of his own saliva, wishing that it had been hers.

He gripped the mug tightly, his erection throbbing even more strongly.

Exploration

The child knew where to dig.

There was no need to switch on the torch.

Not yet.

Every now and then the small figure would pause and glance around at the house, fifteen or twenty yards up the garden, but there was neither sight nor sound of movement.

The spade sank easily into the wet earth and the child turned the clods with ease, making a small pile of dirt as it dug deeper. From the bushes a few feet away there was a rustling sound and the child paused, squinting through the darkness in an effort to detect the source of the noise. But there was nothing to be seen. The blackness of the night closed around the child like a cloak.

It continued digging until the rustling came again and, this time, the child dropped the spade and picked up the torch, flicking it on, sweeping the powerful beam back and forth.

A hedgehog ambled into view from beneath one of the hedges, saw the light then scuttled away again.

The child extinguished the torch and continued digging until finally the shovel brushed against something soft and pliant. Now was the time to use bare hands. Squatting beside the shallow hole, the child scraped the remaining clods away exposing a torn grey dustbin bag. The child slid a penknife from its pocket and moved closer to the bag, running the blade into the plastic, cutting it open.

An overpowering stench of decay burst forth like the odour wafting from a gangrenous wound. The child coughed but continued cutting the bag, holding the torch in the other hand, shining it on the remains of the mangled cat which had been buried five days earlier in this humble grave.

The carcass was alive with maggots.

Both eye sockets were seething with hundreds of wriggling white forms which twisted and undulated in the light from the torch. Worms, bloated and swollen like tumefied veins, slithered from the nostrils and ears of the dead animal while dozens more had found nourishment in the cavity of the cat's belly. The body seemed to be stuffed with parasites, their appetites for carrion more than satisfied by the feast.

The child prodded the cat's head with the torch, watching as several of the maggots fell into the grave, their bodies standing out in stark contrast to the blackness of the earth. Smaller wounds were filled with freshly hatched flies' eggs, the smaller maggots also busily feeding.

The child sat on the edge of the hole watching intently. So, this was death. Was this how everything placed in the earth ended up? Food for worms and maggots? Was this the fate of human beings who lay in their coffins like carefully prepared meals until the scavengers arrived? The child wondered what it would feel like to lie there in the darkness and to know that thousands of parasites were eating into each eye, into every cut and graze, slithering into each orifice.

Was there a Heaven or a Hell, or was this all that remained? Nothing beyond death except the complete physical destruction of the body. Food for carrion eaters.

The child shone the torch over the dead cat once more and sat staring. The maggots continued to feed.

Twenty-one

The axe must have weighed close to six pounds and the force of its downward arc almost caused Miller to overbalance. He hefted the lethal object before him and smiled thinly.

'You should have been a lumberjack,' Phillip Dickinson told him, peering through a wide-angled lens at the effects man. Miller blinked hard as he felt a slight twinge from his left eye, but the feeling of discomfort rapidly passed and he handed the axe to the waiting actor. Pat Sullivan took it, watching as Miller drank deeply from his hip flask before returning his attention to the business in hand.

Standing close by, attempting to smoke a cigarette, was Kevin Brady. But even that most simple of acts was made almost impossible by the heavy make-up which the actor wore. He'd already been encased in the latex for three hours and it was starting to feel as if someone were crushing his skull inside a vice. He fancied that he could feel his veins swelling up beneath the mask of rubber, threatening to burst if he wasn't soon released from his mobile prison.

Miller beckoned him across and undid the heavy coat which the actor wore. Beneath it, his right arm was strapped across his chest, hidden from view.

'I feel like Nelson,' he mumbled through the make-up.

Miller ignored the remark and reached up to adjust the network of thin rubber tubes which terminated at Brady's shoulder. It was through these that the fake blood was to be pumped.

Miller now turned to the table behind him and pulled the piece of cloth from the object beneath.

It was the arm which he'd laboured over the previous night.

Dickinson stepped from behind the camera to look at the imitation appendage, shaking his head in admiration at Miller's prosthetic skills.

As the effects man set about fastening the fake arm to a harness on Brady's shoulder, the director described how he intended shooting the scene.

It took less than five minutes.

Brady, one of the 'astro-cannibals' was to confront Sullivan in the ward of the orphanage and, during the fight, Brady's arm would be lopped off. Dickinson would hold on a one-shot of Sullivan raising and swinging the axe then cut to a shot of the arm apparently being struck by the blade and flying from the shoulder. This illusion was to be completed by carefully concealed wires attached to the arm which two assistants would pull, thereby tugging the fake arm free. Miller had also built three or four blood bags into the stump of the arm which would be detonated by remote-controlled squibs as the stump was exposed to the camera.

'Then we'll cut there,' Dickinson said, smiling. 'If you'll excuse the pun.'

Miller bent close to the arm, swiftly inspecting the squibs, a flicker of concern in his eyes as memories of the accident suddenly came flooding back.

'Set,' he said, stepping back.

'I appreciate you coming back to work so quick, Frank,' Dickinson told him as the cast and crew took up their positions.

Miller merely shrugged, wiping his left eye gently as his vision blurred slightly.

'And I'm sorry I had to call you last night, but these scene changes couldn't be avoided,' the director continued.

'No sweat,' the effects man told him, inspecting the control panel which he held in one hand. In the other he held his hip flask.

'All right,' bellowed Dickinson. 'Everybody ready? Cameras, do we have speed?'

A garbled chorus of affirmatives rumbled around the set.

'All right, turn over,' Dickinson shouted. He prodded Pat

Sullivan forward. 'Action.'

Sullivan approached Brady, who was hunched forward before the camera, arms dangling limply at his sides.

Miller looked on intently, glancing to one side to make sure that the wires attached to the fake arm were not visible. He took a swig from his hip flask, one eye on Sullivan the other on the two men who crouched out of shot to his right.

Sullivan raised the axe.

Brady ran at him.

The blade swung down, the sound slicing through the air as surely as the metal itself.

'Cut,' roared Dickinson and Sullivan stepped back a couple of paces, still gripping the axe. 'Now, camera two, I want a medium shot of Kevin as the arm comes off.'

The lights were dimmed once more, the cameras began to roll and Brady found himself acting alone, feigning agony as the axe supposedly sheared through his arm.

He heard the material of his jacket rip and, a second later, on a signal from Miller, the two assistants tugged hard on the concealed wires, jerking the fake arm free. As it hit the ground Miller pressed the appropriate button on his remote and the blood bags burst with a liquid squelch, spilling their sticky contents around the latex stump. More of the fake fluid spurted from the network of tubes attached to Brady's shoulder and, as instructed, he slapped his free hand to the bogus injury as the fluid ejaculated forth.

'Cut it,' shouted Dickinson and lights once more bathed the set. 'Beautiful,' he said, patting Miller on the shoulder. 'I just want to try the axe-swinging bit from a couple of different angles,' he said to Sullivan.

Miller retrieved the arm as if it were a long-lost treasure wrapping it in the towel on the table behind him.

'Call me when you're ready for the next scene,' he told Dickinson. 'I'll be in the make-up trailer.'

The director nodded and returned to setting up his cameras to re-shoot Sullivan's attack on the 'astro-cannibal'.

Miller wandered away from the set, taking another swig from his hip flask as he reached the door which led off the sound stage. He stepped out into the sunshine, shielding his eyes momentarily against the searing glare of the morning sun. From the back pocket of his jeans he pulled a pair of sunglasses which he slipped on, welcoming the slight respite which the darkened lenses brought him from the ferocity of the glare. He made his way across the car park, feeling the heat through the soles of his shoes as he crossed the tarmac. Still cradling the fake arm he fumbled for the key to the trailer and let himself in. It was cool inside and Miller welcomed the lower temperatures. He laid the arm carefully on a table and sat down on the sofa nearby. He took another sip from his flask then pushed the receptacle into his back pocket.

Beneath the table he glanced at a large black leather hold-all, tightly sealed. Even the zip was secured by a tiny padlock.

Miller could smell the leather as he inhaled.

He gazed at it for what seemed like an eternity then he pulled it towards him and searched for the tiny key which would unlock the fastener. That done he pocketed it and slowly pulled back the zip. It made a low rasping sound as he did so, opening like a metal-edged mouth to reveal its contents.

Inside, like the occupant of a flexible coffin, lay the perfectly-formed body of a baby less than eight months old.

Miller looked in at the motionless form, his own eyes drawn to the hypnotic stare of the small child which looked back blindly through eyes which were balls of glass.

He ran appraising eyes over the inanimate body then, carefully, he drew the zip closed once more.

Picking up the hold-all, Miller made his way back out of the trailer.

'You make sure you get this right first time, Phil?' the effects man said, glancing through the glass door of the microwave oven.

The baby lay curled up inside like the still-born product of some steel womb.

'It's incredible,' said Dickinson. 'So life-like.' He seemed mesmerized by the sight of the tiny creature.

Miller took a hefty swig from his hip flask and ignored the

compliment.

'Let's get on with it eh?' he said, closing the door, watching as the camera moved closer, the man behind it focusing on the occupant of the microwave.

'How are you going to work this, Frank?' Dickinson wanted to know. 'Is the model already wired up with squibs?' He indicated the baby.

Miller nodded almost imperceptibly.

'Just turn up the heat and watch,' he said, swigging from his flask once again. Then he stepped back beside the camera which was aimed at the microwave oven and its occupant like some massive telescopic sight.

'OK,' Dickinson said to the cameraman. 'Turn over.'

'Rolling,' the man said.

Dickinson reached for the temperature control dial on the microwave and, out of shot, he turned it.

Inside the steel coffin, the baby's skin seemed to glow a dull pink.

The director turned the control again.

200 watts.

The heat from the oven could now be felt by those standing within a foot or so of it.

300 watts.

Miller took another swig of whisky and watched as the baby's flesh turned a deeper shade of pink. The searing heat, he realized was working from the inside out.

400 watts.

Two extras, one of them a woman, stood mesmerized as the lifeless shape of the baby suddenly twitched as if it still retained some semblance of life.

500 watts.

Its skin was beginning to pucker now, and as Miller looked on more closely he noticed that the flesh was beginning to undulate almost imperceptibly, as if the internal organs, having disintegrated under the ferocity of the temperature inside the oven were now beginning to boil. The small body seemed to be quivering.

600 watts.

Miller waited.

The baby uncurled inside the oven.

One eye melted in the socket as the temperature soared to incredible levels.

700 watts.

Miller wondered how much longer it would take.

Ten seconds. Twenty.

The baby's body began to shudder even more violently as its skin finally turned a livid red. Its mouth opened as if it were screaming for help, but all that came forth was a foaming flux of dark-brown fluid and bubbling pus which gushed from its throbbing orifices as if it had been some gigantic boil squeezed and milked by invisible fingers.

There was a loud and nauseating plop as the entire body burst like a corpulent balloon, the whole figure exploding in a reeking liquescent welter of corruption. The steaming mess splattered the insides of the oven, and at least one of the watching crewmen turned away in revulsion. Miller kept his eyes on the oven and its churning contents, now reduced to fluid by the incredible heat.

He looked on impassively, not even aware that others were gazing at him.

Some in amazement.

Some in disgust.

The cameraman didn't wait for Dickinson's signal. He merely stopped rolling, his own stomach lurching violently.

'How the hell do you make it look so real?' asked one of the extras, his face pale.

'Trade secret,' Miller told him.

He drank deeply from his hip flask and watched the steam rising from the door of the oven.

The stench was vile.

'Trade secret,' the effects man whispered softly to himself.

Twenty-two

Miller pulled down both sun-visors inside the Granada, but the powerful rays still seemed to find a route to his eyes. He blinked hard, squinting through the dark glasses in an effort to diminish the effects of the blazing orb which hung in the sky above.

As he drove he massaged the bridge of his nose between his thumb and forefinger, trying to stroke away some of the pain which seemed to be building in the centre of his forehead. He glanced down at the dashboard clock and noticed that it was almost two-thirty. He was due at the hospital in another fifteen minutes for his check-up. Miller pressed a little harder on the accelerator, coaxing the car along the nearly deserted road with a little more urgency.

He would not return to work that afternoon he had decided. Dickinson had said that he was going to shoot some interiors and discuss the following day's shoot with his leading actors, so there was nothing for Miller to do anyway. After his visit to the hospital, he would drive home. Before leaving the studio he had cleaned up the microwave, scraping the remains of the baby from the walls of the metal coffin, scooping them into a black bag which he had since disposed of. Miller had declined any offers of help with the cleaning up, preferring to attend to the task himself. Dickinson had told him that he thought the realistic effect had been achieved by placing some kind of heat-sensitive charge inside the replica child which had been activated once a certain temperature was reached.

Miller had smiled thinly and shrugged, content to let the director believe whatever illusion he chose.

Miller wasn't about to tell him the truth.

112

He slowed down slightly as he came to a bend in the road, muttering under his breath as his vision began to cloud slightly. He drove on, screwing his eyes up briefly in an attempt to clear the mist from his vision. It had descended like a film of gauze wrapped tightly around his head.

He cursed under his breath, his foot easing on the right hand pedal.

'Come on, clear,' he muttered, blinking hard once more.

His eyesight returned quickly and with surprising clarity. Miller smiled and drove on, noticing that a large container-truck was approaching on the other side of the road. Even from a hundred yards away he could hear the roar of its engine as the eighteen-wheeler thundered towards him.

Darkness.

'Oh Jesus,' he gasped.

Sudden, total blackness enveloped him. He was blind.

Unable to see a hand in front of him.

The car skidded wildly as he wrestled with the wheel, aware that the juggernaut was powering towards him. It blasted out a warning on its horn but Miller could only struggle with the wheel, trying to get the car off the road, knowing that the lorry was drawing closer.

Should he hit the brakes?

If he did that he risked sending the car into a spin.

If he could guide it towards the roadside hedge, perhaps the privet would soften the impact.

Provided the lorry didn't flatten him first.

Behind his blank eyes thoughts flashed through his mind and he gripped the steering wheel in blind terror.

Then, suddenly, as quickly as it had vanished, the light returned.

He could see again.

See that the lorry was only yards from him.

See that the massive truck was about to hit the car.

Miller stepped on the accelerator and sent the Granada hurtling across the road into the roadside hedge.

The lorry swept past, missing the tail-end of the vehicle by inches and Miller heard the loud hiss of its air brakes as the

113

massive juggernaut juddered to a stop.

For his own part he stepped hard on the brake, crashing forward into the steering column, the impact winding him. He slumped back in his seat, noticing out of the corner of his eye that the lorry driver was running towards him.

The man reached the car and pulled open Miller's door.

'What the fuck is going on?' he hissed, some of the anger leaving his voice when he saw how pale Miller looked. 'You could have been killed.'

Miller didn't answer, he merely took off his dark glasses and gently rubbed his eyes.

'Are you all right?' the driver wanted to know.

Miller nodded.

'Do you want me to get an ambulance or something?'

The effects man shook his head.

'No,' he said, and as he spoke the lorry driver detected the hint of whisky on his breath.

'Have you been drinking?' he demanded.

'Not so you'd notice,' Miller said. 'Anyway, it wasn't that.'

'Fucking drinking and driving. It's bastards like you that get people killed,' the man rasped.

'I said it wasn't the drink,' Miller hissed, fixing the other man in a piercing stare. His own breath was still coming in short gasps and he found it hard to swallow. He closed his eyes for a moment, frightened to open them in case he'd suffered another loss of vision, but as he allowed his lids to gently part, the light flooded in.

'Are you sure you don't want an ambulance?' the driver persisted.

'I'm all right,' Miller told him, starting his engine again.

The lorry driver stepped back as Miller reversed back onto the road, then he watched as the Granada sped off. Shaking his head he watched it disappear around another bend in the road.

'Bloody maniac,' the driver muttered to himself as he trudged back to his cab.

Miller shook his head and touched two fingers to his left eye. It was throbbing like a sore thumb. Bastard. He swallowed hard, noticing that beads of perspiration had popped onto his

114

face. He wasn't sure if they were a product of the heat or his near miss with the lorry.

Or the realization that blindness could strike again without any warning.

He drove on.

Twenty-three

Doctor George Cook brought the Audi to a halt, switched off the engine and clambered out.

There had been more traffic on the road than he'd expected, the congestion not helped by the fact that a tractor had overturned about a mile down the road and he'd been sitting in a jam for over thirty minutes while someone went for help. His shirt was sticking to him and he shrugged his shoulders in an effort to loosen the clinging material. He decided that the first thing he'd do when he got inside his house was take a shower. There was plenty of time for him to wash and change before he returned to the hospital.

He set off up the gravel driveway, his feet crunching the stones as he walked. In a tree to his right birds were singing, sheltered from the sun by the broad leaves. A tall hedge flanked the driveway and on either side of it were immaculately kept lawns. He paid a man called Doug Walsh to look after the gardens. Cook certainly never had the time himself and his wife, Helen, wasn't the gardening type.

She ran a boutique in the nearby town, but over the past few months she had shown less and less interest in it and had suggested selling her share of the business to her colleague. Cook had asked her what she would do with herself without the shop to go to but she was adamant that she wanted to finish work. Fortunately his salary was more than enough to support both of them and to keep their two children at boarding school.

Cook brushed the back of his hand across his forehead, puffing as he saw that it was stained with perspiration. High above him the sky was cloudless, the only blemishes caused by the vapour trails of a couple of aircraft.

As he approached the front door of his house he glanced up at the ivy which clung to the building, making a mental note to tell the gardener to cut it down. Cook fumbled in his trouser pockets for his keys, looking around as he did so.

The door to the garage was open slightly.

Frowning, he dropped the front door key back into his pocket and wandered across to the garage door to close it. As he reached it he peered inside.

Helen's car was parked inside.

Cook's frown deepened.

She wouldn't be home from work yet, it wasn't even three o'clock. So what was the car doing there? He stepped into the garage, placing one hand on the bonnet as he did so. It was cool. The car obviously hadn't been used that afternoon. The doctor exhaled deeply, feeling a bead of perspiration trickle down his cheek, but he didn't wipe it away, he merely turned and headed for the door which connected the garage to the kitchen.

It was locked.

He hurriedly pulled out his key-ring again, selected the right key and stepped into the welcoming coolness of the kitchen. He stood in the silence, his ears alert for any sound of movement from within the house.

There was none.

He crossed to the kitchen door and then wandered through into the dining room which was also empty. As was the sitting room.

Perhaps the car had failed to start and Helen had taken a cab into work. He decided to phone the shop to check.

It was as he turned towards the phone that he noticed one of her shoes lying beside the sofa.

Cook swallowed hard and crossed to it.

As he picked it up he peered through the half-open hall door and saw the other one lying at the foot of the stairs.

The doctor moved through into the hall, still clutching the first shoe, pausing at the bottom step, looking up towards the top of the flight.

Slowly, he began to climb.

117

It was as he reached half-way that he heard the first of the sounds.

For a moment he froze as he heard a low rasping exhalation coming from above him but then, moving quickly but stealthily, he climbed the remaining steps until he reached the landing. Once there he stood motionless, leaning against the balustrade.

Listening.

The sound came again but with it came other noises. Soft, slithering sounds suddenly punctuated by a gasp which was unmistakably female.

Cook crossed to the bedroom on the left and stood on the threshold listening, peering through the crack between door and jamb.

His face darkened and he stepped into the room.

They were naked, both of them.

His wife lay on her back, both legs wrapped around the buttocks of Doug Walsh as he thrust smoothly in and out of her. So lost were they in their passion that neither heard or saw Cook standing there clutching his wife's shoe, looking on like some kind of voyeur. He glared at the couple through narrowed eyes, watching as the perspiration glistened on Walsh's back, his muscles tightening with each thrust. Every penetrative movement causing Helen Cook to writhe with renewed pleasure. She was clawing at his back and buttocks, trying to force his erection more deeply into her, trying to heighten what already appeared to be the considerable pleasure they were experiencing. Hers were the soft rasping moans which he'd heard. Walsh seemed to answer her with deeper grunts, each one coinciding with his forceful movements within her.

Cook froze, riveted by the tableau before him.

It seemed an eternity before he finally moved.

As Cook stepped forward, his wife's eyes snapped open and in that brief second she saw him. She opened her mouth in a mixture of surprise and fear but all that emerged from her moistened lips was a gasp which Walsh took to be a further indication of the pleasure she was feeling.

The next thing the younger man felt were strong hands on both of his ankles.

118

He shouted in surprise as Cook gripped him hard and tugged, pulling him off Helen, the force of the wrench sending him sprawling on the floor beside the bed. As he tried to get up, Cook, his face now contorted with rage, swung the shoe he'd been clutching at the younger man. The stiletto heel caught him on the shoulder, breaking the skin and drawing blood. Walsh tried to roll to one side but Cook was too fast for him and he drove a powerful kick into his side, knocking the wind from his adversary.

Helen was sitting up on the bed, her body sheathed in sweat, her nipples still erect from the recent attention lavished on them, her dark hair smeared across her face like sticky tendrils.

'Stop it,' she shouted as her husband seized Walsh by the hair and dragged him upright, jerking his head back. A moment later he drove a powerful left hook into the youth's face, the impact splitting his bottom lip. He fell backwards crashing into a dressing table.

'George, stop it, for God's sake,' Helen sobbed, watching helplessly as her husband dragged Walsh to his feet and punched him twice in the stomach. The youth went down heavily again, and as he rolled onto his back Cook kicked him hard between the legs. This time the younger man let out a high pitched shriek of pain and swiftly drew himself into a foetal position, clutching his throbbing crutch, but Cook hauled him upright and shoved him towards the bedroom door, then across the landing towards the stairs.

'Get out of here,' the doctor rasped, returning to the bedroom briefly to retrieve Walsh's clothes. He rolled them into a ball and hurled them down the steps, pushing Walsh after them. He staggered on the top stair, teetering dangerously for a moment until it seemed as if he would fall, but he clutched the banister and made his way down, one hand clutching his throbbing testicles.

'If I ever see you around here again,' Cook roared at him, 'I'll kill you.'

Walsh paused to pull on his jeans.

'Get out,' bellowed the doctor watching as the younger man staggered out of the front door.

119

From inside the bedroom Cook could hear his wife sobbing, repeating Walsh's name over and over again. He gripped the balustrade until his knuckles turned white, the veins at both temples pulsing angrily.

'Shut up,' he rasped at her, his breath coming in short gasps. He waited a moment longer then stormed down the stairs into the sitting room. There he pulled open the drinks cabinet and poured himself a large measure of brandy which he downed in one mighty swallow, the liquid burning its way into his stomach. He wiped his mouth with the back of his hand and poured himself another.

A minute or two later Helen appeared in the doorway, a dressing gown wrapped around her. She had wiped her face dry of perspiration but her make-up was smudged, almost washed away by her tears. She ran a quivering hand through her matted hair looking away as Cook glanced angrily at her.

He wanted to say something but he couldn't. Under the circumstances, silence was its own communicator.

'George . . .' Helen Cook began, taking a step towards him.

'Shut up, Helen,' he hissed. 'Don't say anything. Not a word.' He finished what was left in his glass and brought it down on the table with a force that threatened to shatter the delicate crystal.

Then, he turned and headed towards the kitchen and the garage beyond.

She screamed his name but Cook ignored her cries, his jaw clenched tightly, the knot of muscles at the side pulsing madly. He pushed his way through the garage door and out into the sunlight again. The heat met him like a wall and he recoiled for a second, sucking in deep lungfuls of air in an effort to calm down. He wanted to shout, to yell his anger loud but something inside him prevented it, and he stalked down the drive towards his car repeatedly clenching and unclenching his fists. He noticed that he'd taken the skin off two of his knuckles, doubtless when they'd made contact with Walsh's teeth. There was blood on the sleeve of his shirt. Flecks of crimson were soaking into the material.

Cook reached the waiting Audi and slid behind the wheel.

Somewhere in the back of his mind he searched for the reason which had brought him home in the first place. Had it been to look for some notes? To check something in one of his own reference books? He couldn't remember now. All that remained in his mind was the vision of Walsh and Helen locked in their glistening embrace. He could only guess at how many times before such meetings had taken place. How many previous couplings there had been. How many more betrayals.

Cook thumped the steering wheel angrily then he reached forward and twisted the key in the ignition. The engine purred into life and he drove off.

The heat suddenly seemed to be the least of his problems.

Doug Walsh watched the Audi pull away, his eyes narrowed to steely slits.

'Fucking bastard,' he muttered, flicking his tongue over the deep cleft in his bottom lip. He tasted blood and spat out of the open window of the Datsun. Seated behind the wheel in just his jeans he rubbed his side, looking down to see that a violet bruise was already beginning to form.

'Bastard,' he whispered once more.

When he looked up again the Audi was rounding a bend in the road ahead.

Walsh started the engine of his own car, stuck it into gear and drove away.

He kept a safe distance, ensuring that even if Cook should peer into his rear-view mirror, he would be unable to distinguish the face of the man following him.

Walsh gripped the steering wheel tighter and drove on.

121

Twenty-four

'Follow the light with your eyes.'

In the darkened room the words seemed to come from some intangible source. Miller obeyed nonetheless, watching as the pen-light was guided slowly back and forth by Doctor Simon Thompson.

'The pupillary reaction is good,' said Thompson, aiming the thin beam away from Miller's eyes then directly into each one in turn. 'Have you had any discomfort at all? Any reaction?'

Miller swallowed hard, remembering the attack of blindness he'd suffered only thirty minutes earlier. Then there had been the incident with Cook's photo. The aura . . .

'No reaction,' he lied.

Thompson gently pulled down the lower lid of Miller's left eye, inspecting the conjunctiva, satisfied with its bright red colour. He noticed too that there was a dense network of veins snaking up from the bottom of the eye. The tendril-like lines appeared to be swollen and Thompson peered at them intently.

'Are you sure you've had no pain from this eye?' he persisted.

'Look, I can still see,' Miller said. 'That's all that matters to me. I knew there could be problems but I was ready to take that chance.'

'You said you'd had no problems.'

'I'm fine, Doc. Right?' Miller repeated.

'You know that I was opposed to the operation in the beginning?' he said.

'No I didn't, but it wouldn't have made any difference to me,' Miller told him. 'I was the one who was blind, remember?'

'That eye that we transplanted. . .'

Miller cut him short.

'It worked. I cancelled the order for the white stick and besides, guide dogs eat too much,' the effects man said. 'I've got my sight and that's the only thing that counts.'

'It's *your* future, Mr Miller,' said Thompson crossing to the window and opening the curtains.

He didn't see Miller recoil slightly as the sunshine flooded through.

The doctor returned to his desk and it was Miller's turn to wander across to the window. He peered down into the car park.

'What would you have done, if there *had* been any adverse reaction with the transplanted eye?' he wanted to know.

'We'd have removed it,' Thompson told him, flatly.

Miller nodded almost imperceptibly, his eyes still fixed on the tarmac area below.

Geoge Cook brought the Audi to a halt in its appointed place in the hospital car park. He switched off the engine and sat back in his seat, eyes closed for a moment. The surgeon was thankful that he wasn't scheduled for any operations for the rest of the day. His mind was bursting with thoughts and ideas. Anger and recrimination. He looked down at his bloodied knuckles and flexed his fingers rhythmically.

Satisfied that Cook was still unaware of his presence, Doug Walsh guided his Datsun between two parked cars about seventy yards from the surgeon's vehicle. He kept his foot on the accelerator, revving the engine gently as he sat watching.

'I'd appreciate it if you could come back to us for another check-up in a fortnight, Mr Miller,' Thompson said, scribbling some notes on a piece of paper. 'Or, of course, if there are any problems with the eye before that.'

Miller seemed not to hear. His eyes were fixed on the figure of George Cook who he watched as the surgeon locked his car.

'Mr Miller,' Thompson repeated.

'I heard you,' Miller told him, his eyes never leaving Cook as the surgeon strode across the car park towards the main doors of the hospital.

'Now we'll see who's the fucking big-shot,' rasped Doug Walsh as he watched Cook set off across the car park. The younger man jammed the car in gear, gripped the steering wheel tightly and pressed down on the accelerator.

The Datsun shot forward like a bullet, speeding towards its appointed target.

Miller, ten floors up, could only stand and watch as the Datsun bore down on Cook.

And, despite the warmth in the room, he suddenly felt a chill run through him.

He guessed that the car must have been doing almost sixty when it hit Cook.

Twenty-five

George Cook barely had time to turn before the Datsun hit him.

He certainly never had the chance to see Doug Walsh hunched over the wheel, a demonic grin carved across his features.

The car smashed into him with sickening force, the impact flinging him into the air like a rag doll. His body twisted once then crashed down onto the roof of the car and skidded off. He hit the warm tarmac, unconsciousness already closing in around him, but before he blacked out he had time to see the Datsun screech to a halt a few yards away. He had time to see the smoke spinning from the back wheels as it reversed towards him with the same furious intent.

The rear offside wheel rolled over his head, crushing the skull with ease, transforming his face and most of his upper body to crimson porridge. Thick grey slicks of brain matter sprayed out from beneath the churning tyres and, as the car sped backwards, one of Cook's legs was also pulped, the foot nearly severed at the ankle. Blood began to spread in a wide pool around the pulverized surgeon who, fortunately, was beyond pain by the time Walsh drove over him a second time.

The car skidded on the blood but Walsh ensured that he manoeuvred the vehicle so that it rolled across the dead man's spine. There was a loud crack as the vertebrae were splintered and the body, which had been jerking madly suddenly ceased its frenzied movements.

By the time Walsh reversed over it again the corpse had been transformed into little more than a rag. Blood, shattered bone and a reeking spillage of bile and mashed internal organs had

125

now spread for several yards in all directions around the devastated form.

Tyre tracks of blood formed a ragged pattern about the scene.

And now the car park was filled with other sounds.

Shouts. Screams.

A woman fainted, crashing heavily to the ground as her young son stood mesmerized by the grisly tableau before him.

Somewhere inside the building an alarm bell was throbbing with its strident tone.

Ten floors up, Frank Miller looked down on the scene impassively.

Attracted by the noises from below, Thompson joined him, a look of horror crossing his face as he saw the blood and the remains of the dead man lying on the tarmac.

'It's Cook,' Miller told him, flatly.

'What happened?' Thompson wanted to know.

Miller told him briefly then the doctor turned and headed for the door.

'I wouldn't rush,' Miller said. 'They're going to need a bucket, not a stretcher to move him.'

Thompson hesitated a second longer then disappeared, leaving Miller alone in the room, gazing down on the frantic scene. The Datsun had stopped moving now and the effects man watched as two ambulancemen dragged Walsh from inside. He stepped in some of the spilled blood as he stumbled out but it didn't seem to bother him. He merely looked across at the mashed body of Cook and smiled. Miller heard him bellow something at the remains but from his high vantage point he couldn't make out the words. The effects man crossed to his jacket and pulled out the small instamatic camera, complete with telephoto lens, which he always carried. He took three shots of the gathering below him then slipped the camera back into his pocket again. Hooking a thumb inside the collar he slung it over his shoulder and walked out.

The images gradually gained clarity as Miller pulled the photos through the developer using a pair of plastic tongs. He dipped them in fixer then rinsed the residue off, laying the prints on the worktop beside the sink. The pictures of Cook's mashed body were remarkably clear.

Miller shook the last droplets of water from the first picture and studied it more closely, his eyes drawn to the human wreckage which had once been a man. On the left hand side of the picture, almost out of sight, Doug Walsh was standing looking at his dead victim, peering down at the damage he'd done.

Miller looked at the second photo. And the third.

He sighed and shook his head almost imperceptibly then he crossed to his desk and fumbled in the drawer for what he sought.

Seated silently in the chair to his right, the flayed woman watched him with unseeing eyes and Miller noticed his image reflected in those glass orbs as he passed her. The burn victim, his flesh hanging in charred strips, also looked on impassively as his creator busied himself searching the desk.

The effects man finally discovered what he wanted.

He pulled out the photos of himself and George Cook and laid them on the desk.

Miller looked at them carefully for a moment then he covered his left eye and gazed at them.

The images remained the same.

He covered the right eye.

The faint luminescent line around Cook appeared as it had before. As if some kind of vague light were seeping through his skin.

Miller traced the outline of the aura, repeating his actions on the other picture.

It was present there as well.

Miller sighed and shook his head, reaching for the glass of whisky he'd poured for himself. Eyes still riveted to the pictures he swallowed a mouthful of Scotch, feeling it burn its way to his stomach.

The question persisted.

What was the aura?

He'd photographed Cook less than a week earlier and now the man was dead.

127

Murdered.

He looked across at the first photo of the surgeon who was smiling happily for the camera. Then he glanced at the one he'd taken that afternoon. The dead doctor lying in a pool of his own blood, his body crushed virtually beyond recognition.

He studied them both, his attention returning every time to that curious phosphorescent glow which surrounded Cook.

He shook his head slowly.

Twenty-six

Detective Inspector Stuart Gibson sat back in his seat and rubbed his eyes. He kept them closed for long moments, as if he were hoping that when he opened them again the piles of notes spread out before him would have vanished. It wasn't to be, and Gibson reached wearily for the clipboard on which he'd been scribbling.

On one corner of his desk a photo of his wife and two children gazed at him but the picture seemed in danger of being pushed off the desk by the sheer volume of material which Gibson had laid out for perusal.

He read his notes aloud, his voice sounding flat in the confines of his office.

'Peter Manuel. Executed July 11th 1958. Manuel's trademark was the murders of entire families which he completed by shooting them in the head with a .38 calibre pistol whilst they slept.' Gibson reached for the mug of coffee teetering on a pile of manilla files. He took a sip, wincing when he discovered it was cold.

'Mark Forrester. Shot in the head while he slept. Murder weapon, .38 calibre pistol.'

The date next to the note was July 3rd, just two weeks ago.

Gibson ran one index finger around the rim of the mug and scanned his notes again.

John George Haigh – *The acid bath murderer. Executed August 6th 1948. Dissolved his victims in acid.*

There was a name written opposite that of Haigh, except that this one was a victim, not a killer.

Nicholas Blake – *Battered then attacked with sulphuric acid.*

129

Murdered 5th July this year.

And so it went on, the names of past killers cross-referenced to those of contemporary victims, the catalogue of atrocities written out in Gibson's efficient hand. Each one linked by a red arrow drawn in Biro.

DENIS NILSEN – *arrested February 9th 1983 for the murder, by strangulation, and dismemberment of 15 men.*

William Young – *murdered July 7th. Strangled then dismembered with a meat cleaver.*

JOHN REGINALD HALLIDAY CHRISTIE – *Hanged July 15th 1953 for the murder, by strangulation, of at least six women.*

Angela Grant – *murdered July 11th. Strangled.*

PATRICK DAVID MACKAY – *Arrested 23rd March 1975 for the murder of Father Anthony Crean whom he battered to death with an axe.*

Louise Turner – *murdered July 16th. Beaten to death with a length of lead piping.*

And finally, Gibson wrote:

PETER SUTCLIFFE – *The Yorkshire Ripper. Arrested January 2nd 1981. Second victim stabbed repeatedly in the stomach and genitals.*

Bernadette Evans – *murdered July 20th. Multiple stab wounds to the stomach and genitals.*

Gibson allowed his eyes to skim over what he'd written, convinced now of the links between the killings.

The murderer was imitating the killing methods of some of the most notorious men in criminal history.

The question was, *why?*

But more importantly, could he be stopped before he took his total to seven?

Twenty-seven

She moaned softly in his arms, feeling one of his hands slip inside her dressing gown. There his questing fingers touched her breast, coaxing the nipple to stiffness beneath his expert attentions. She snaked one hand around the back of his neck, drawing him closer as they kissed, her tongue darting into the moist wetness of his mouth. He responded hungrily, the first sign of an erection pressing against his jeans.

They broke apart hurriedly as the trailer was shaken by three loud bangs on the door.

'Shit,' snapped Lisa Richardson, hastily pulling the cord of her dressing gown tight around her waist. She turned away and sat beside the mirror close to her, inspecting her features. At thirty-five she was what is euphemistically described as 'well-preserved'. Fifteen years as one of the country's leading actresses had not manifested itself in the lines of concern which she had seen etched deeply into the faces of other women of her profession. Her body, too, retained that youthful appearance. She was tall, and a little heavy breasted, that fact accentuated by the slimness of her waist and hips. Her finely-shaped features were framed by shoulder-length brown hair which was pinned up, loose strands dangling over her forehead like silky tendrils. Eyes like chips of emerald still glinted with a hidden mischief.

But Lisa Richardson was at a difficult age for an actress. Too young to play character parts and a little too old for the 'dewy eyed innocent' which she had often played earlier in her career. Hence her appearance in films such as *Astro-cannibals*. It was her second film since the beginning of the year, the previous effort having been a third-rate action adventure which had failed miserably in both the States and Europe. She'd done a couple of TV shows in the States but her agent had persuaded her to take the part in this horror picture mainly for the money which, surprisingly enough, was good.

And the film had shown other benefits too.

She sat looking at one of them now.

Colin Robson was four years younger than Lisa, a powerfully-built man who enjoyed the position of responsibility which the post of assistant director gave him. He and Lisa had been lovers for the past six weeks and neither of them made much of an effort to disguise the fact. *He* was unattached and *her* husband was in America. Who the hell cared anyway?

Robson crossed to the trailer door, opened it and looked out to see Frank Miller standing there.

'Well, what a surprise,' said Miller sarcastically. 'Fancy seeing you here and all that.'

'What do you want, Frank?' said Robson, wearily.

'I want the charming Miss Richardson,' Miller told him, clutching a copy of the shooting script in his hand. 'As you're no doubt aware, she is due in front of the cameras this afternoon.' He smiled thinly. 'I suppose that's what you've been doing. Rehearsing.'

Robson stepped back to allow the effects man into the trailer, his eyes narrowing in anger as he looked at Miller's broad back.

'I need you in my trailer, please,' Miller said with as much politeness as he could muster. 'Some of the make-up is pretty complex and I've left my notes there.' He shrugged.

'I told Dickinson I wasn't going to wear that shit on my face,' Lisa said, irritably. 'I don't know why it's necessary.'

'Look, it's in the script, I get paid for creating make-up effects so, if you don't mind I'd like to do my job. On you,' Miller added, his eyes never leaving hers.

'Perhaps we ought to call Phil and check whether or not he really wants the full make-up,' Robson interjected.

Miller turned slightly, a hard edge to his voice when he spoke.

'What is this? A debating society?' he snapped. 'It's in the script. The scene requires make-up, I don't see why we're arguing.' He took a swig from his hip flask.

Lisa looked on distastefully.

Miller rounded on her once more, their eyes locking.

'I told Phil that I didn't want that make-up on,' the actress said.

'He never mentioned anything to me,' Miller informed her.

'I think Lisa's got a point,' Robson interrupted.

'What are you, assistant director or fucking script supervisor?' Miller rasped at the other man. 'I came here to do a job. Now, you either want to work or you want to stand around moaning all day.'

'You know, Miller, your attitude might be a little better if you didn't drink so much,' Robson said, indicating the hip flask.

'I don't tell you how to screw the lovely Lisa here,' Miller said acidly. 'So don't tell me about my drinking.'

Lisa coloured and was on her feet.

'Get Dickinson now, I'm not being spoken to by a make-up man this way. Who the hell do you think you are, Miller?' she demanded.

'Don't pull the "star" routine with me,' he said. 'You're not even a has-been. You're a never-was.'

'You bastard,' she hissed, taking a step towards him.

'Get out of here now, Miller,' Robson snarled.

'Are you going to make me?' Miller said defiantly. 'Come on, big shot. Impress your girlfriend.' There was a fury in Miller's voice which was matched by his actions. He snatched up a stool close by him and brandished it like a club. 'I'll kill you.'

'You're crazy,' said Robson, swallowing hard.

'You might just be right,' said Miller.

'Forget it, Colin,' Lisa said. 'You're right, he's crazy. What's more, he's not even very good at what he does. I've worked with better make-up men . . .'

She got no further.

With a roar of rage Miller hefted the stool before him, swung it back over his shoulder and hurled it towards the actress. She screamed and dropped to the floor as the object flew over her head, propelled by the force of Miller's anger. It struck her mirror which promptly exploded in a frenzy of pulverized glass. Long slivers shot out, one of them nicking her left arm, drawing

133

blood. Shards sprayed around the room like crystal shrapnel. Miller picked up one of the longer ones, ignoring the fact that the sharp edge had laid the palm of his hand open. Blood ran from the cut and dripped from his wrist and for brief seconds he could see his own distorted reflection in the length of mirror.

He moved the point slowly back and forth, first to Lisa then to Robson.

'You *are* mad,' said Robson, quietly, one eye on the wickedly gleaming tip of the shard.

'Call the police, Colin,' Lisa said, tearfully, her eyes fixed on Miller.

Robson didn't move, his eyes too were on the glass dagger.

Miller finally hurled it to the floor where it shattered into several dozen more tiny fragments. He pulled a handkerchief from his pocket and wrapped it around his gashed palm, then he turned and headed for the door of the trailer.

'You've never worked with anyone better than me,' he said, his voice low but full of anger. 'And you never will.'

With that he was gone.

Robson crossed to the door and locked it. He looked across at Lisa who had paled visibly. Despite the fact that she was shaking, Robson seemed reluctant to move across to her, as if he were frightened to leave the door. Perhaps fearing that Miller would return. He swallowed hard and wiped a droplet of perspiration from his forehead.

He found that his own hand was shaking.

Twenty-eight

The lift rose slowly, bumping to a halt at the fourth floor. As the doors slid open a red-faced man wearing a safari suit peered in and enquired if the lift was going down.

Ken Rogers smiled politely and shook his head, clutching the gift-wrapped box tightly to his chest as the doors closed once more. He leant back in one corner of the lift, watching as the lights above him lit up in numbered sequence as the car rose higher. It reached the ninth floor and he stepped out into the carpeted corridor, still holding the box beneath his arm.

It had arrived on his night porter's desk about five minutes earlier, appearing as if by magic. He'd nipped off to the toilet and, when he'd returned, the box had been waiting there. The card on it read: *Lisa Richardson*.

That was it. Just her name. No room number, nothing else. Ken had left his cocoa to cool and checked through the register to track down the recipient of the gift and he'd discovered that she was in room 926. As he approached the room he hefted the box before him, inspecting the pretty paper and the carefully tied bow. Someone had told him that the woman in 926 was an actress, so perhaps what he held was a gift of some kind. Maybe from a fan. But who the hell delivered gifts at 12.30 a.m.? He checked his watch against the nearby wall clock as he passed.

Not to worry, he told himself, he was paid to take care of the hotel and its guests from midnight onwards, and if that meant delivering packages then fair enough.

He rounded a corner and approached the door of 926.

Lisa Richardson switched off the shower and stepped out from behind the frosted glass partition. She wrapped one towel around her dripping hair and another around her body, drying her arms and legs swiftly. From the bedroom beyond there came the sound of the TV set. Lisa wandered into the room, adjusting the volume control as she passed. Her companion didn't speak, he merely smiled at her, watching as she sat down at the dressing table and began towelling her hair dry.

There was a knock on the door.

'I'll get it,' Lisa said, standing up, checking that the bath towel was held firmly in place. 'Did you call for anything from room service?' she asked, but her companion merely shook his head.

Lisa opened the door and found Ken standing there, clutching the parcel.

'Miss Richardson?' he said, taking the opportunity to run appraising eyes over her slim legs and the hint of cleavage visible despite the thick folds of the towel. 'This just arrived for you.' He held out the gift-wrapped package. 'I hope I'm not disturbing you?'

She shook her head and took the package from him, frowning when he hesitated, waiting for a tip. She finally said a curt 'good-night' and closed the door.

'Tight cow,' muttered Ken to the closed door. He turned and made his way back to the lift.

'Looks like I've got a secret admirer,' said Lisa, setting the box down on the dressing table. She inspected the card for a moment but her name was typed. No clues as far as handwriting was concerned. She set to work opening the package.

Her companion swung himself onto the edge of the bed, watching as she unfastened the large red bow then slid her nail beneath the rim of the box lid. It was like a large hat box and Lisa lifted the top excitedly, peering in with all the excited curiosity of a child at Christmas.

There was another slightly smaller box inside.

She lifted it out, noticing for the first time a strange fusty odour which made her recoil slightly. Nevertheless, she pushed the first box to one side and set to work opening the second.

It too was fastened by sellotape but Lisa again used her nail to break the seal. She lifted the lid.

The smell rose like a noxious cloud of gas but, despite that, driven by a morbid compulsion, Lisa reached for the object within.

She was acting instinctively now, her eyes bulging wide, her hands and arms moving as if they had a will of their own. Her mouth dropped open and she made a low croaking sound in the back of her throat.

In her hand she held the severed head of Colin Robson.

Blood dripped from the stump of the neck as the grisly object dangled by its hair, held by Lisa against her will. She stared into the sightless eyes, gazed at the blood which had spattered the face. The mouth was open in a soundless scream, matching her own horrified expression.

Finally, with a shriek of pure terror, she dropped the head which landed on the floor before her, its eyes gazing at her lifelessly.

She screamed again. And again. The sound gradually merging into one high-pitched caterwaul of revulsion and shock. Red fluid began to run from the neck across the dressing table, some of it dripping onto her bare legs and this brought fresh screams from her. Try as she might, she could not tear her horrified stare from the severed head of her lover.

From behind her, the man darted from the bed towards her, his own mouth agape. His own fear and bewilderment now threatening to overwhelm even his sanity.

Colin Robson stood shaking, looking at a mirror image of himself. Staring at the head which was a perfect replica of his own.

Lisa looked at the severed lump then up at Robson and the sight of the two of them sent her into fresh paroxysms of hysteria. She fell away from the dressing table and began crawling towards the bed, trying to wipe the blood from her legs.

Robson reached out and touched the head, feeling the skin, noting how cold it felt. Like frozen rubber.

Rubber.

Latex.

He gritted his teeth and lifted the head up, dropping it back into the box, ignoring the blood which splashed him as it dripped from the tendril-like veins of the neck.

Lisa was still screaming, her body now curled into a foetal position on the floor, the shrieks punctuated by sobs.

Robson looked at her, knowing that there was nothing he could do to comfort her at the moment. He gritted his teeth but his expression this time was one of rage, not horror.

He reached for the phone.

Twenty-nine

Frank Miller inspected his reflection in the bathroom mirror, running his fingers over the stubble on his cheeks. To hell with it, he thought, he wouldn't bother shaving. He splashed his face with cold water, trying to wash some of the sleep from his eyes. He'd slept heavily the previous night, which was unusual for him, now he watched the sink fill with water, studying his own distorted image which rippled on the surface.

He was just wearing jeans and trainers, and as he turned slightly he caught sight of the vicious scars which ran across his lumbar region, legacy of being too close to a football riot which he'd been photographing some years back. One of the thugs had come at him with a Stanley knife, slicing two deep gashes across his back, one of them narrowly missing a kidney. That same day Miller had seen a policeman beaten to death with bricks.

The photos were on the wall of his workroom.

The doorbell sounded and Miller glanced at his watch. He frowned. Eight o'clock in the morning. He wondered who could be calling so early.

Miller yanked the plug from the sink, hauled a sweatshirt over his head and made his way downstairs.

He opened the front door, smiling as he saw his visitor.

'It must be important,' Miller said, 'to bring you to my house at this time in the morning.'

Phillip Dickinson nodded and walked in, following Miller through into the sitting room.

'It *is* important,' the director said. 'It's about Lisa Richardson.'

139

Miller smiled thinly and began filling his hip flask from a bottle of Haig.

'What about her?'

'She's in a London hospital suffering from shock,' Dickinson said. 'And don't ask me what that's got to do with you, Frank. I know about what happened last night. About your little "prank".'

'She had it coming,' said Miller, harshly. 'Her and that toss-pot she's hanging around with. She insulted my work, Phil. Nobody does that and gets away with it. Well, now she knows *exactly* how good I am.'

'You're a fucking idiot,' rasped Dickinson.

Miller eyed him malevolently.

'Why couldn't you let it drop?' the director demanded. 'So what if you had a row with her? So what if she's sleeping with Robson? You were hired because of your effects skill not as a fucking morality guide. I've lost my leading actress because of you. You've put back the shoot for at least three days. Jesus, when I rang the hospital this morning they said they had her under sedation. She was practically raving when they took her in last night.'

'If you're waiting for an apology, you can forget it,' Miller said, his voice devoid of any remorse.

'This is more than just revenge, Frank,' Dickinson said. 'It's costing the company money. Every day lost is thousands of bucks down the drain.'

Miller continued filling the flask, trying to ensure that he didn't spill any of the precious fluid.

'Get another actress,' he said. 'The only scenes she had left were ones under make-up. Who the hell would know?'

'That's not the point,' the director snapped. 'I didn't come here to discuss how we could get round the problems of not having a leading actress.'

'So what *did* you come for?'

'I came to tell you that it might be a good idea if you stayed away from the set for a few days,' Dickinson informed him.

'You're firing me?'

'No, I'm asking you to stay away until things cool down.'

140

Miller took a swig from the whisky bottle, gripping it in one hand.

'This could cause a lot of problems, Frank. I don't know why you couldn't let it go. But no, not you. You always have to have the last word don't you?'

Miller nodded.

'And I'm going to have it now,' he said, his eyes narrowing. 'I'll stay away from the set for a few days. I won't put any more spokes in, Phil. But I'm surprised at you. I never thought you'd let some nothing actress and her boyfriend frighten you. Why didn't you tell *them* to stay away from the set for a few days?'

'*You're* the one who sent her into shock, Frank. I'm just trying to smooth things over.'

'Ever the diplomat eh, Phil?' Miller said. 'Right, you've said your piece, now get out.'

'It's that goddamn temper of yours . . .'

'I don't need a character reference. Just get out.'

'People are frightened of you, Frank,' Dickinson told him. 'You're bad news.'

Miller drew his arm back, the empty whisky bottle still clutched in his fist.

'Get out,' he roared and flung the bottle.

It whistled past Dickinson's head, struck the wall behind him and shattered, spraying glass in all directions.

The older man looked first at the wall where the bottle had struck, then at Miller who was still glaring at him through eyes which were now little more than steely slits. Without a word Dickinson turned, opened the front door and walked out.

Miller took a hefty swig from his hip flask, wiping his mouth with the back of his hand.

'In a state of shock,' he said, a smile beginning to spread across his face.

He chuckled to himself and headed towards his workroom.

Fascination

There were uniforms everywhere.

Policemen. Ambulancemen. Railwaymen.

The child watched the profusion of officials with interest as they swarmed around the edge of the platform close to the front of the train.

The driver had been helped from his cab and was sitting, white-faced, on one of the benches close by. Both hands were pressed to his forehead and he was shaking his head almost imperceptibly. The body lay on the track about twenty feet away and the child stood gazing at the mangled form, watching as two sweating ambulancemen tried to lift the smashed individual free of the lines.

Passengers had spilled from the halted tube train, some gathering on the platform like the child, others only too anxious to be away from the scene of horror. Policemen were doing their best to usher the gathering crowd in the direction of the exits but morbid curiosity had gripped them like some collective fever and each pushed forward in an effort to get a better view than their neighbour. People jostled one another, craning forward to peer at the destruction before them. The child squeezed between the legs of two tall men who were trying to catch sight of the blackened shape being lifted from the rails. The child heard words floating around inside the cavernous platform area. Words like suicide. The victim, a man in his thirties, had apparently waited a few feet from the tunnel entrance, then as the train emerged, had launched himself at it. The damage had been horrific but, unfortunately, not fatal. The man's face had been staved in and, after having been catapulted several feet down the tracks, he had lost one leg, severed at the knee, to the churning wheels of the train. An arm, the fingers still twitching spasmodically, lay near the edge of the platform, blood oozing from the severed arteries.

Someone close by had vomited and the bitter stench mingled with the acrid odour of ozone and seared flesh.

The child moved closer as the ambulancemen lifted the body up onto the platform edge, laying it carefully on a grey blanket which had been spread out by their companions.

Blood from the stump of the victim's leg rapidly began soaking into the thick material. The child watched in fascination as the crimson fluid ran from the remains of the limb.

The policemen were still trying to push the crowd back but few seemed to pay any attention to the men in blue.

The child stared intently at the body which lay on the blanket. At the pulped face, pieces of shattered jaw-bone visible through the torn flesh and muscle. At the blackened skin and the ragged extremities of the leg and arm wounds which dripped blood with a rhythmic pulsing.

The child looked on with fascination at the mangled body, catching the first hint of a more choking stench. The stench of excrement. The contorted face of the man twisted into an even more repulsive visage as he opened his mouth and gasped out something unintelligible. Then, as the child watched, he rolled onto his side and let out a loud moan. A sound torn raw and bloody from the base of his shattered spine. A sound which reverberated in the underground cavern and bounced off the walls of the gaping tunnel. It was a grunting noise, the pained wailing of some great primate in agony. A bellow of unendurable suffering which drummed in the child's ears as it looked on impassively.

Then the sound dissolved into a low grunt, a rumbling like that of a stuttering motor. One filled with blood.

The child watched as the body underwent one final spasm, then the rumbling sound was replaced by the liquid sound of soft excretion as the man's sphincter muscle finally gave out.

One of the watching ambulancemen pulled a blanket over the corpse. The crowd standing nearby began to disperse slowly but the child remained where it was, gazing at the shapeless bundle beneath the blanket. Finally a policeman motioned for the child to leave, but it turned away reluctantly, finally caught up in the mass exodus from the platform.

143

As it moved away, the child glanced round one final time to see the body being lifted onto a stretcher, and in that moment the sound which the dying man had uttered seemed to echo around the inside of the child's head like some kind of wailing lament.

The child smiled thinly and walked on.

Thirty

Terri Warner nudged the front door of the flat closed using her elbow, almost dropping the armful of library books which she carried. She moved through into the sitting room, dumping the heavy tomes on her desk near the window, then she reached across and pressed the 'rewind' button on the answerphone. While the cassette spun in reverse, Terri wandered into the kitchen and retrieved a can of coke from the fridge. She stared in at the food and sighed softly. She couldn't be bothered to cook now, she thought, pulling the ring on the can. There was plenty of frozen stuff in the freezer. Thank God for convenience food, she thought as she moved back into the sitting room.

Terri kicked off her shoes, massaging her aching feet with one hand, reaching for the 'play' button of the answerphone with the other. There was a high pitched bleep and the first message began:

'. . . I hate talking to these bloody machines,' the voice said and Terri smiled. 'Terri, this is Peter Landon. I don't know if you remember me? We met at the studios about a week ago.'

Terri nodded as she sipped her drink. She did remember him, a tall, well-built man about a year younger than herself. He had been working as a floor director on one of the light entertainment shows which were made in the same building that housed her office. She sat back, listening to the remainder of the message feeling a little sorry for the caller as he muttered on as if racing the thirty-second time-limit which the machine allowed.

'. . . I know we only met once but I was wondering if you might like a drink with me some time. I mean, I'd buy. Or perhaps even lunch, or dinner? If you had the time of course. If you'd like to ring me back I'll give you the number. I know we might bump into each other in the building but I'd better give you the number just to be on the safe side. These bloody machines have a time-limit don't they? Oh shit, sorry.' Terri was giggling by now as she listened to Landon's frantic babblings. 'Look, the number to ring . . .' There was another high pitched bleep. End of message. Terri shook her head and chuckled.

'Hi, Terri, it's Tina. How about coming over to my place on Thursday night. Joe's away for a week so I've only got the dog to talk to. Ring me.'

Another high-pitched bleep.

Tina Kennedy had worked with Terri as a researcher when she'd first joined the independent network but she'd left about a month earlier when she'd discovered she was pregnant. Terri reached for her handbag and pulled her diary out, flipping through the pages. Thursday was fine. She scribbled Tina's name in the appropriate space and made a note to call her back as soon as the messages had finished.

Another bleep.

'Terri, it's me again. Peter Landon.'

She smiled.

'The tape ran out before I had time to give you my number, so here it is.'

Terri dutifully wrote it down in the back of her diary. Landon had seemed like a nice enough man, a little shy, but that was a welcome change in the loud-mouthed, ego-laden world of TV. She took another sip of her drink and wondered if she'd ring him.

Another tone. Another message.

'The police don't know.'

Then silence.

The tape continued running but there were no more messages.

Terri looked at the machine, her brow creasing. She rewound the tape slightly and listened again.

The tone.

'The police don't know.'

She put down the can of coke and swung herself around so that she was facing the machine, her attention now riveted by those four words.

She listened again.

And again.

'The police don't know.'

Terri exhaled slowly.

The words were spoken slowly almost as if the caller was choosing each syllable with care, ensuring that the message would not be misheard.

But the voice.

She re-wound the tape.

Listened again.

'The police don't know.'

Terri lost count of the number of times she replayed the message until finally she switched off the machine and reached for the phone.

'The police don't know.'

Bob Johnson stroked his chin thoughtfully and looked first at the answerphone then at Terri. The news editor shifted in his seat as Terri rewound the tape yet again.

'You say you don't recognize the voice?' he said, his eyes never leaving hers.

Terri shook her head.

'With just four words it's not much to go on is it?' she said. 'Do you really think it could be the murderer?'

Johnson shuffled in his seat again and shrugged.

'Everyone knows that you're heavily involved with this case,' he told her. 'If the killer has seen you on TV it's possible he might try to contact you. It *has* been known before. A bloke called Peter Alphon contacted a journalist about the murder that James Hanratty supposedly committed in 1962. Alphon confessed to the killing after Hanratty had been hanged.'

Terri sighed.

'But we can't be sure it's the murderer,' she said. 'It's the first message I've had. What I'd like to know is, how did he get hold of my number? I'm ex-directory.' There was a long silence

147

during which Terri was aware that Johnson was constantly allowing his gaze to travel up and down her body, pausing at her crossed legs and rounded breasts. She began to feel slightly uncomfortable beneath his unrelenting gaze and got to her feet. She asked if he wanted another drink and he did. She poured him another whisky and returned to her seat opposite Johnson who peered at her over the rim of the glass.

'Perhaps I should ring the police,' she said, finally.

'No.'

Johnson sat forward almost spilling his drink.

'Leave the police out of it,' he urged. 'For now at any rate. Firstly, you don't know if it is the murderer, but if it is then perhaps he wants to make contact with you.' Johnson paused for a moment, watching the expression on Terri's face change from one of fear to one of curiosity. 'There could be one hell of a story here, Terri,' he told her. 'Don't fuck it up by calling in the police. And don't destroy that tape, whatever you do.' He motioned towards the cassette. 'Wait and see if he calls again. See what he says.'

She nodded slowly, unable to maintain eye contact with Johnson. Terri felt as if his gaze were boring through her, probing her soul, such was its intensity. After a moment or two she got to her feet and padded through to the bathroom.

Johnson watched her go, sipping slowly at his drink.

He heard the click as the bolt was slid across, then, unhurriedly, he crossed the room and picked up one of Terri's discarded shoes. Gripping it by its long heel he ran his index finger slowly around the inside of the shoe. A feeling of warmth began to spread around his groin, growing more intense as he repeated the procedure with the other shoe, this time bringing it close to his face, sniffing at the leather interior, rubbing the high heel rhythmically. His penis was throbbing now, straining against his trousers and, as he heard the toilet flush he replaced the shoe and walked across to the window, looking out over the street below, trying to hide the bulge between his legs.

Terri seated herself on the sofa once more and looked at Johnson's broad back, watching as he turned slightly, downing what was left in his glass in one mighty gulp. He asked if it was

148

all right to use the toilet and moved quickly from the sitting room, hiding his bulging erection from her.

Once inside the bathroom he bolted the door and stood with his back against it, his breath coming in short gasps, the raging fire in his groin now almost uncontrollable. He fumbled with the zip of his trousers, freeing his rampant organ, massaging the stiff shaft with one hand. He crossed to the lavatory itself, kneeling in front of the porcelain bowl, gazing down at the seat. He reached out with one hand and touched it, feeling the warmth on the plastic, now rapidly fading.

Beside his hand there were two or three tiny, tightly curled pubic hairs.

Johnson picked each one up as if it were a strand of precious silk then he wrapped them carefully in his handkerchief, the black curls standing out starkly against the whiteness of the material. It was as he stood looking at the dark curls that he felt the first drops of thick fluid dribble from the end of his penis. The sensation, pleasurable though it was, startled him and his reaction was sufficient to prevent a full outpouring of his desire. He wiped the end of his organ with a piece of toilet paper then pushed his stiff shaft back inside his trousers, taking several deep breaths before he finally flushed the toilet. That done he folded up his handkerchief and put it in his pocket.

Johnson splashed his face with cold water from the sink and wiped the excess away with his hands before drying them on a towel. Then he slid back the bolt on the door and walked back out, through to the sitting room.

'Let me know if he calls again,' he said, looking down at Terri, who held the tape in her hand. 'But don't get in touch with the police.'

Terri nodded and replaced the tape in the machine.

Johnson announced that he would have to leave and it was with something akin to relief that Terri got to her feet and walked with him to the door. He looked deep into her eyes, allowing his gaze to rest briefly on her breasts. Then he stepped out into the hall.

'Don't let anyone know about the call,' he repeated. 'No one.'

She watched as he turned and headed towards the lift. After a moment Terri closed her door and retreated back into the sitting room where she crossed to the answerphone as if drawn by some powerful magnet. Johnson could be right. If the killer did intend contacting her then she would have a superb story on her hands. What puzzled her at the moment was the voice. She ran the tape again.

'The police don't know.'

Terri shuddered slightly as she realized that there was something vaguely familiar in those words.

She couldn't be sure but she felt she knew that voice.

Thirty-one

The Granada skidded to a halt as Miller stepped a little too hard
on the brake. The vehicle narrowly avoided the rear bumper of
the car ahead but Miller seemed unconcerned by the possible
collision. He switched off his engine then sat back in his seat,
catching a glimpse of his reflection in the rear-view mirror.

His hair was uncombed, and even in the harsh glare of neon
spilling from the club nearby his face looked pale. Dark rings
beneath both his eyes made it look as if some mischievous child
had been drawing charcoal clouds on his lower lids. He rubbed
the left eye as it blurred momentarily. Then, muttering to
himself, he clambered out of the car and locked it.

The drive into Central London had been uneventful. Not
much traffic and, fortunately for him, no vigilant policemen to
notice that he'd sometimes exceeded the speed limit by five or
ten miles an hour. Just as well they hadn't stopped him, Miller
thought, catching a whiff of his own whisky-sodden breath. He
was drunk and he knew it. What did he care? He could still walk
straight, still speak coherently. Still drive. When he passed out,
that was when he'd know he'd had enough. He glanced at his
watch. Almost 10.30. London's Soho was a blur of neon. A
kaleidoscope of colour and sound. Music blasted from the
doorways of clubs, here and there Miller heard shouts and
laughter from a pub across the street. Men and women, in
couples or alone, wandered past, some content merely to
glimpse the tableau of activity, others more intent on joining it.
Many were doing business.

At the entrance to the club Miller passed a doorman who was
busily picking the head from a bulging spot on his chin. He

151

afforded the effects man only a fleeting glance, his attention fixed on the small sore which he was now squeezing between thick fingers. Miller pushed his way through the curtain of plastic strips which served as a doorway and walked into the club.

The club was in semi-darkness, its denizens huddled in corners as if afraid to emerge into the subdued twilight within the room. There was a green strip-light above the bar which gave it the appearance of being covered in mould, but apart from that meagre glow of illumination the only brightly-lit spot was the stage. Miller paused and glanced across at it, leaning against a chair to support himself for a moment.

The stage was little more than a raised platform about twelve feet square. On it two girls were dancing slowly, moving with as much elegance as a couple of drunks. Their choreography left much to be desired, Miller thought, watching as they clumsily danced around each other. The first of them was dressed in a shiny black basque which barely covered her ample breasts. Her legs were sheathed in thigh-length boots. She wore nothing else.

Miller watched as her companion, a black girl with closely cropped hair and a muscular frame, shrugged herself out of the long cape which she wore, exposing her nakedness. The two girls kissed, the contrast in the colours of their skin rapidly lost as the stage was bathed in red light. Then blue, then green. All the colours of the rainbow lit the scene as a crackling p.a. system carried forth a roaring singer's voice and the screech of guitars. A deafening accompaniment to an act which was anything but tender in its execution.

By the time Miller reached the bar the black girl was on her knees before her partner, lips and tongue pressed urgently to the offered vagina.

'. . . *Thrills in the night, far from the light, passion taking over* . . .' roared from the p.a. Miller smiled thinly and managed to attract the attention of the barman who ambled over, his face expressionless. Miller ordered a large Scotch.

As he sat drinking he glanced around the inside of the club, peering at those who frequented it, some looking as if they used it as a refuge. There was a man sitting at the far end of the bar, slumped across the counter, his head in a puddle of spilt beer. Every time he exhaled bubbles formed in the liquid.

At the table to his right three men sat, all in their mid-forties, all of them staring raptly at the stage where both girls were now naked and were busy inserting a selection of dildos and vibrators into each other. The music seemed to grow louder, a growing crescendo which matched the mounting excitement of the performers. They were either acting or very close friends, Miller couldn't figure out which.

In another corner of the club, barely visible beneath the subdued lighting, a couple were kissing feverishly and Miller noticed that the man's hand was well and truly hidden beneath the short skirt which his companion wore. He watched the woman wriggling on her seat as the man's fingers probed between her legs.

Close by them sat a man on his own, his attention divided between the events on stage and those happening much nearer to him. Miller watched as a young woman approached him, seating herself on the chair beside the punter. Miller saw the girl smile and put her hand on the man's leg, but he seemed to shrink away from her. The girl's smile faded but she persevered a moment longer before finally getting to her feet. She tottered somewhat uncertainly on three-inch heels, towards the bar. Towards Miller.

She sat on the bar stool beside him and smiled her practised smile at him.

'My name's Penny,' she informed him, fluffing up her permed hair with both hands. 'I haven't seen you in here before.'

Miller caught a slight Welsh twang in her accent, although it was difficult to hear anything above the pounding music.

'We've both missed a treat then, haven't we?' he replied. Then, draining what was left in his glass he ordered another.

The girl regarded him warily for a moment then her well-rehearsed grin returned once more to lips which carried a cold sore at one corner. She was in her late teens Miller guessed. Heavily made-up. However, the thick layer of foundation she wore was unable to disguise the spots and craters on her cheeks.

False eyelashes curled out from her lids like marauding spiders. She licked habitually at the cold sore before she spoke again.

'Are you going to buy me a drink?' she wanted to know.

Miller looked briefly at her, features distorted by the phosphorescent green glow of the strip light. Her face was drawn and the look in her eyes reminded him of a predatory animal.

'Buy your own,' he said, flatly.

'If it's too noisy for you here you can always come back to my flat,' Penny told him. 'It's not far from here.'

'You want me to buy more than a drink then?'

'That's up to you,' Penny said, raising one eyebrow and smiling. The gesture was all the more repellent because of its artificiality. Miller felt as if that cold sore was winking at him. She flicked her tongue over it once more.

The effects man moved a little closer to her and her smile broadened.

'Do you know what I'd really like?' he began, forced to shout over the thundering rock music.

Penny looked hopeful.

'I'd like you to find some other mug. Leave me alone, will you?'

She frowned as if his words hadn't registered, then she slid from the bar stool and teetered away, her eyes narrowed as she cast him a derisory glance. Miller watched as she approached a balding man in a leather jacket who had just entered the club. In no time she was sitting on his knee. Miller shook his head and finished his drink.

12.36 p.m.

Miller pushed the glass back across the counter and got to his feet, steadying himself against the stool for a second. As he began walking he found that he could accomplish the action with surprising ease and dexterity considering the amount of alcohol he'd consumed in the last forty-five minutes.

Miller glanced at the stage as he made for the exit and noticed that two new girls had taken over. Both were dressed as nurses, one of them lying spreadeagled on a torn leather couch while the other did her best to insert a stethoscope into her companion's vagina.

'Doctor, Doctor' came thundering out of the crackling p.a. system.

As he reached the exit, Miller caught sight of Penny sitting happily on the lap of her customer. The man was sweating profusely, his face only inches from her breasts. Every now and then he would touch the tempting globes only to receive a mock rebuke from the girl. She shot Miller a triumphant glance as he passed. He smiled to himself. Penny had succeeded in the first part of her task, he thought. The pleasure would be short once the business had been done. The predator had hold of its prey.

As he stepped out onto the pavement the smell hit him like a putrid fist. The smell of vomit spilled in the gutter mingled with the ever-present odour of exhaust fumes. Close to his car two men were trying to pull their drunken companion to his feet as he sat heaving mightily in the direction of a drain that was already blocked. All three of them were drunk.

Miller fumbled for his car keys, opened the door and slid behind the steering wheel. He pushed the key into the ignition but didn't turn it. Instead he reached across and pulled something from the glove compartment of the car.

Checking that the camera was loaded, Miller raised it to his right eye and squinted through the view-finder, sighting it on the trio of drunks nearby.

Click.

He chuckled to himself as he thought how unusual it was to be taking photos of living subjects rather than the wasted, bloated or butchered corpses which had been his models for so many years. He saw two men leaving the club.

Click.

A woman walked past and stopped to speak to the club's doorman.

Click.

Miller sighed, smelling his own alcohol-tainted breath inside the car. He took more photos, recorded more of the gutter life which emerged every night like nocturnal prowlers. London was a city of changing moods, inhabited by two different sets of people. Those that did their living during the daylight hours and those who thrived at night. And now was their time.

Miller felt a curious affinity with those who frequented the darker hours. He belonged, he had come to realize over the years, with darkness. Darkness of the mind and the soul.

He looked up and saw Penny emerging from the club, her customer following meekly behind.

Click.

Miller took another shot of her then watched as she and her companion disappeared around the corner.

Miller blinked hard, trying to clear his head as much as his vision. He rubbed his face with one hand, then placed the camera on the passenger seat and started his engine. The Granada burst into life and Miller spun the wheel, guiding it out into the road. As he reached the corner of the street he peered to his right and left and caught sight of Penny and her guest as they entered a tall, three-storey house. Miller drove past, noticing that several windows in the building were lit. Each room, he presumed, had been converted into some form of bed-sit. He slowed down as he passed the building, running appraising eyes over it, wondering which room Penny was in.

The clock on the dashboard glowed 1.09 a.m.

Thirty-two

Paint was peeling off the walls like leprous flesh. Huge soft slivers of yellow which Penny knew she would have to cover somehow.

The flat had always been damp and now the dark stains were beginning to return on the skirting boards and in the cracks of the ceiling. Like gangrene in an open wound the damp seemed to creep insidiously into every crevice in the paintwork. Penny had decorated the place herself shortly after moving in two years before. Prior to that she'd been living in a squat in Wapping with two other girls. It had been one of them who'd persuaded her to go on the game. Penny hadn't liked the idea much to begin with, but as she realized how much money there was to be made out of it, the prospect of spending most of her time being pawed and mauled by strangers didn't seem quite so repellent. She'd had the odd weirdo in her time but never anyone into violence. There'd been one punter who'd asked her to kick him repeatedly in the arse but, when she'd dissolved into fits of laughter he'd refused to pay her. Bastard. That had happened when she was sixteen, a year after she'd first arrived from Cardiff. Now, three years older and wiser, she felt that she could handle anything.

The punter tonight had been easy. He'd asked for a blow job but Penny had refused. In the beginning she would have agreed but what with all this shit like AIDS about, she, like so many other girls she knew, refused to give blow jobs now. And, even for a straight fuck they insisted that the punter wore a rubber. Some worked without, but she didn't intend taking any more risks than she had to.

She'd satisfied her customer easily. He'd been so worked up by the time she'd pulled his pants off that he'd shot his load as she knelt between his legs. Her long bleached hair had brushed the end of his penis and he'd spurted copiously into her crowning glory.

Now she smiled to herself as she stood over the sink, waiting for it to fill, anxious to wash the dried semen from her hair. She tested the water temperature with her fingertips then retrieved some shampoo from the cabinet above. She switched on the portable radio propped up on the bath beside her and bent forward over the sink, using a plastic cup to scoop water over her hair. She began to sing along with the tune on the radio.

For those who know how, slipping a lock is a simple exercise, especially when the lock is old and needs replacing.

The figure that stood outside the door of Penny Steele's flat found that the task was easier than expected.

The door opened a fraction, the intruder slipped inside and hurriedly closed it once more.

From the bathroom came the sound of splashing water and music. And singing.

The intruder stood motionless at the front door for a moment longer, then advanced slowly into the flat, eyes never leaving the door of the bathroom. The figure trod stealthily, silently. Expertly.

Moving quietly, the intruder glided into the small kitchen. Past the stained cooker which still bore an unwashed saucepan. Past the cracked sink to the drawers.

There was a selection of knives inside.

Penny soaked her hair thoroughly then applied the shampoo, still happily singing along to the radio. She stopped abruptly as the sound faded. Batteries must be running low she reasoned, and shook her radio irritably. It crackled, burst into life again then faded just as rapidly.

A floorboard creaked.

Penny tried to rub the soap from her eyes with her fingers but it made them sting even more and she had to reach for the towel.

158

Hair dripping she stood by the sink, listening.

There was a sudden rattle of sound as the radio started up again and she glared at it a moment longer before bending over the sink once more.

The sound of splashing water and music blotted out all other noises.

Even the sound of footsteps outside the bathroom door.

The intruder paused, peering through the gap in the door. Aware that the sounds of approach had been masked by the water and radio. Now the figure put one hand gently on the door and eased it open a fraction more.

Penny Steele was wearing a thin cotton house-coat, worn at the elbows. Her head was bowed over the sink as if in prayer, her fingers moved slowly and carefully through her hair, massaging the shampoo into every strand.

The figure watched, gripping the largest of the two knives tightly, edging forward an inch or two towards the threshold of the bathroom.

Penny reached for the plastic cup to rinse the shampoo away.

The radio crackled loudly. Almost like a warning.

Then the intruder pushed the door hard.

It swung back on its hinges and banged gently against the wall causing Penny to look up, but soap ran into her eyes again, momentarily blinding her. All she saw was a dark shape before her attacker was upon her.

She opened her mouth to scream, both shocked and frightened by the sudden intrusion, but the sound came out as a strangled gasp as she saw the vicious glint of the first knife.

Penny tried to wipe her eyes so that she could see the attacker, so that she might have some chance of defending herself. Her wet hair flapped around her like dead snakes as she shook her head, then suddenly her assailant lunged forward.

The knife was fully eight inches long and it was wielded with fearsome power.

As the prostitute put up a hand to deflect the blow the blade sheared through her index finger above the knuckle and severed the digit before hacking a bloody swathe through her palm.

Blood began pumping from the ragged wound and the finger fell to the floor.

The second knife powered into her stomach to the left of her navel. The impact winded her and she felt as if she'd been punched with a steel fist. A sudden excruciating pain filled her lower body, and through it all she could feel the coldness of the steel being twisted inside her as the attacker pressed forward, finally knocking her over.

The second blade swept down again, missing Penny's outstretched hand, scything into her shoulder at the point of neck and clavicle. Blood erupted from the wound, spraying over the cracked white tiles on the bathroom wall.

Still unable to see because of the shampoo in her eyes, Penny began to moan loudly, desperate to escape this ferocious onslaught. It was useless. Both knives were brought down simultaneously. The smaller of the two tore through her left breast, bisecting the nipple. The second and longer knife punctured her lung after scraping off a bone. There was a sound like a rapidly deflating tyre and a foul-smelling blast of air escaped via the yawning gash.

Penny tried to draw breath but the effort caused her acute pain. Air whistled coldly through the hole in her lung and she gasped frenziedly, trying to fill her lungs, attempting to ease the growing pressure which she felt inside her head. But the wound prevented her breathing properly and she flailed helplessly with her arms, her pain now tinged with terror as she realized that she was dying. Blood filled her mouth, the bitter taste making her heave, but still her attacker kept up the merciless assault.

With a strength born of desperation, Penny attempted to fight back, throwing herself at her assailant, hands reaching for the twin blades.

The act of self-defence was useless against such a powerful enemy. The intruder merely dodged Penny's despairing lunge, watching as she sprawled face down on the blood-splashed floor of the bathroom. She lay there gasping for breath, feeling her life-fluid draining from her through the cuts and lacerations which disfigured her body. Then finally she began to crawl, her eyes filled with tears of pain and fear, struggling to find the breath to scream. Every time she tried to breathe searing pain enveloped her. She coughed, feeling a torrent of vomit forcing its way up her windpipe, mingling with the blood which was already flowing freely from her open mouth.

The attacker stood silently, watching as Penny crawled away like a crippled child, listening as the air hissed through the sucking wound in the lung. With a deliberation that bordered on fascination, the killer walked slowly behind Penny as she dragged herself from the bathroom, almost straddling her, much as a parent follows its child as the child learns the first rudiments of walking.

The assailant paused a moment longer then suddenly reached down and gripped both of Penny's ankles, dragging her back bodily into the bathroom, rolling her over onto her back. A position she was used to.

The killer knelt between her legs, as if worshipping at a shrine.

Then, the knives descended again.

And again.

And again.

PART TWO

'You give me evil fantasies.
I want to get inside your mind.'

Judas Priest

'Madness need not be all breakdown. It
may also be breakthrough. It is potential
liberation and renewal as well as
enslavement and existential death.'

R.D. Laing

Thirty-three

How he ever got home Miller couldn't work out. He sat at the kitchen table staring at the kettle, waiting for it to boil, wondering how he'd managed to drive the fifteen or so miles from Soho to his house the previous night. What he also wanted to know was who had set the pneumatic drill hammering inside his skull. He cradled his head in his hands, fists pressed to his temples as if that would stop the thudding inside his head. He swallowed two aspirins dry, gagging at the bitter taste as one stuck in his throat.

The kettle began to boil. Miller got to his feet and made coffee. Some of it spilled onto the work-top but he merely wiped the bottom of the mug with his hand and sat down again. He sipped the steaming liquid, wincing as he burned his tongue. Miller cursed under his breath and exhaled wearily. He glanced at his watch and noticed that it was just after seven in the morning. Three or four birds were singing on the branches of the tree outside the window, their dawn chorus irritatingly loud. Miller closed his eyes and took another sip of his coffee. What's the best thing for a hangover? he asked himself. Drinking heavily the night before? Very funny. It wasn't the time for jokes, not even with himself. What the hell was he going to do to stop his skull cracking in pieces? He was sure that if the pounding got any worse his entire cranium would simply explode.

He hadn't been *that* drunk for many years. So drunk that he couldn't remember what time he'd got home or, more to the point, *how* he'd got home. He was amazed at his own instincts, flabbergasted that he hadn't managed to wrap the Granada

165

around a tree on the way back. He remembered nothing. Not the journey, not his arrival home. Nothing. He could vaguely recollect leaving the house the previous evening.

He recalled finishing two bottles of Haig, driving into Soho. Then, nothing.

It was as if his mind was a computer screen and some bastard had erased everything from midnight onwards.

His camera was lying on the table opposite him and the effects man glanced at it, noticing that the case was open. The cyclopean eye of the lens stared blindly at him and he caught a brief glimpse of his own reflection in the glass. It wasn't a pretty sight. After a moment or two Miller got to his feet and picked up the Nikon, noticing that the film was finished. Whatever he'd been doing the previous night, he realized, at least he had some kind of pictorial record of it. Perhaps if he developed the film it might jog something in his mind. Help him to remember what he'd been doing. He wished that there was such an easy remedy for stopping the pounding inside his head.

Miller picked up the camera and headed towards his workroom.

He heard footsteps outside the front door, and a moment later the daily paper was thrust through the letter box. It landed on the mat and Miller stooped to pick it up. He carried it through into the workroom with him, snapping on lights as he closed the door.

He put his coffee down on one of the workbenches, beside a severed hand, then he flicked off the lights once more and carefully removed the film from the camera, his progress lit only by the single red bulb over the double sink before him. He immersed the strip of celluloid in developer and moved it back and forth with a pair of plastic tongs. While he waited for the images to form on the acetate Miller flipped open the paper and glanced at the headline:

PROSTITUTE SAVAGELY MUTILATED AS REIGN OF TERROR CONTINUES

Miller quickly scanned the report, squinting in the dull light, rubbing his left eye once when the clarity of vision faltered slightly. There was a photograph of the dead girl at the top of the page. Police had not released details of her name but he seemed to recognize the long hair, the sallow features, the cold sore on the bottom lip.

Jesus Christ. The realization hit him like a sledgehammer.

He blinked hard, focusing more sharply on the image of the girl in the picture.

All around her he saw a faint, almost imperceptible glow. A barely visible luminosity which surrounded her like a halo.

Miller studied the picture long and hard then glanced at the photographs he himself had taken. He lifted them from the developer, swilled them through fixer, then rinsed them with the swiftly-flowing water from the tap.

He held up the first strip of film.

Three drunks, one of them half lying, half crouching beside a car. Two men leaving a club. A woman speaking to the doorman. Other nondescript images of London's underbelly, not soft and white but moulding and rotten, putrid with misery and corruption both of mind and body. He looked at another of the photos, his hand shaking.

It was a girl. She was leaving the club with a man but it was her face on which Miller concentrated his attention.

The long hair. The sallow features.

The cold sore on her bottom lip.

He looked from his own photo to the one in the paper and he knew that it was the same girl. And in both pictures she carried around her that barely perceptible glow. An outline of vague effulgence much like that given to saints in religious paintings. Only this girl was no saint.

Miller looked at the photos again, closing his left eye.

They appeared normal.

He closed the right eye.

The peripheral glow returned, shrouding the images.

The effects man put down the picture of the girl and hastily crossed to one of his filing cabinets. He withdrew a manilla envelope and pulled out two snapshots. They were both of Doctor George Cook. And they too bore the slight glow around the man's image.

The aura was present on the photos of both victims.
George Cook.
Penny Steele.
Both dead. Both murdered.
Both surrounded by that almost imperceptible aura.
Miller put down the photos and reached for the phone.

Thirty-four

'No way.'

Detective Inspector Stuart Gibson drained what was left in the pint pot and brought the receptacle down so hard on the bar top it almost shattered.

'There is no fucking way that you are getting a look at the files on this case,' the policeman said, forcefully.

Miller eyed his former colleague over the rim of his glass, sipping slowly at the whisky.

'Who'd know?' the effects man asked.

'*I'd* know,' Gibson protested. 'Christ, Frank, you're not even on the force any more. The commissioner would have my bollocks for earrings if he even knew I was talking to you about this case, let alone anything else.'

Miller ordered another round, watching as the DI lit up a cigarette.

'I thought you'd given up,' Miller said.

'I had.' He blew out a stream of smoke and coughed. 'I'm always going on at Chandler to stop smoking and now I'm at it again myself.' Mention of his partner's name seemed to coax a frown from the older man. 'He never lets me forget that I got the job he reckons *he* should have had. You know, sometimes I think the bastard enjoys seeing me come up against brick walls in this case.'

'So you're no nearer to cracking it?' Miller said conversationally.

'You know what it's like, Frank. Sometimes trails just dry up. There wasn't a trail to begin with in this case. Seven people murdered in the space of a month and yet we're no nearer now than we were after the first one. I've had the press calling all bloody morning, the commissioner's been on my back. I wouldn't mind only that phoney news conference was *his* idea. "Stall the media", he said.' The policeman took a hefty gulp of his beer. 'If it gets out that the press conference was a fake then they'll crucify us – well, me anyway. I stood there and told them that the killer had been arrested, and now there's another murder.'

'The victim wasn't named in the papers,' said Miller. 'Who was she?'

'That's classified, Frank.'

'Come on, Stuart, you're not talking to a reporter now. She was a pro. An expendable commodity, what the hell difference does a name make?'

'Why is it so important to you?' Gibson wanted to know.

Miller reached into the inside pocket of his jacket and pulled out two photos. He laid them both on the bar top before the DI who raised his eyes in surprise as he saw the picture of Penny Steele.

'Where did you take that?' he asked, lifting the photo up, inspecting it more closely.

'It was taken last night, it doesn't matter how or why?'

'It might matter,' Gibson said, eyeing Miller suspiciously. 'Who's the other bloke?' He looked at the picture of George Cook.

Miller explained who the surgeon was then laid the photos out again.

'He was murdered about a week ago, run down.'

'So where's the tie-up with the maniac who killed the tart and the other six victims?' Gibson asked.

Miller asked the policeman to look more closely at the photos, to look for anything unusual. He could see nothing.

'There's a kind of aura around both of them,' Miller explained. 'Like some sort of light, it looks as if it radiates from the bodies, forms a kind of halo around them.'

Gibson raised his eyebrows then looked at Miller's empty glass.

'How many of those have you had?' he wanted to know.

'Only *I* can see it,' said Miller. 'Both of those people had that aura around them and both were murdered. I think it was a warning. They didn't know they had it either but it marked them out as victims.'

'Oh come on, Frank,' Gibson said, incredulously. 'I know you like a drink but right now you sound as if you're totally pissed. Are you trying to tell me that you knew these people were going to be murdered?'

'I saw the aura around them but not until it was too late.'

Gibson shook his head.

'Well, I can't see anything. The photos look normal to me.'

'I told you, only I can see the aura. That's why I want to look at the files on the other victims, to see if I'm right. I have to see those files, Stuart.'

'And I told you, no way. What the hell do you think would happen if the commissioner found out? I'd be out on my ear, that's what.'

'And what happens if the press find out that you haven't got a clue who the killer is? That the conference was all bullshit to buy you time? The commissioner isn't going to be very pleased about that either is he?'

Gibson frowned.

'What are you saying?' he muttered, warily.

'That I want to look at those files,' Miller told him, flatly.

'And if I say no?'

Miller shrugged.

'Then I'm going to phone every newspaper and TV station I can and tell them that the press conference was a farce, that you still haven't got a clue who the murderer is.'

Gibson glared long and hard at his former colleague, his eyes narrowing to steely slits.

'That's blackmail,' he hissed. 'Blackmailing a police officer isn't a very good idea, Frank.'

'You'd never prove it,' Miller said smugly. 'Now, do I get to see the files?'

'No,' Gibson said, unhesitatingly.

Miller slid off the stool and made for the phone in the corner of the bar. He'd only taken two steps when Gibson shot out a

171

hand and grabbed him by the arm. Miller looked down at the DI, his face expressionless.

'Wait,' he snapped, his jaws clenched in anger. He released his grip on Miller's arm, watching as the effects man sat down once more. They locked stares for interminable seconds, Miller's face impassive. 'What good can it do? Seeing the files?'

'I need to see the photos of the victims taken *before* they were killed. If I'm right then they'll show the aura too,' the effects man said.

'What is this crap? This rubbish about an aura? What is it?'

'I don't know what it is. That's one of the things I want to find out. I want to understand it. I want to know why it only shows up on photos.' Miller sipped his drink. 'You're the only one with access to those files. Get them.' There was a hard edge to his words.

Gibson sucked in an angry breath.

'And if I don't you'll really go to the media?' he said.

Miller raised his eyebrows.

'You've known me long enough, Stuart,' he said, a slight smile on his lips.

The DI nodded and drained what was left in his glass.

'Yeah. Too long.'

Miller cupped one hand around the cigarette, trying to shield the lighter flame from the icy gusts of wind which periodically swept across the concrete expanse of the underground car park.

The huge subterranean chamber was practically empty of vehicles. Apart from his own Granada, which was parked near the exit, only three cars occupied spaces in the vast arena. The air stank of petrol, the floor was spattered with the dark stains of oil and grease. Close to the pillar against which Miller leant, someone had urinated. Pieces of paper, cartons from a hamburger takeaway and other litter were tossed and blown periodically by the wind as it raced across the underground cavern. Miller leant on the bonnet of his car and waited.

He checked his watch.

11.14 p.m.

From above he heard the sound of movement, the rumble as a

car approached the ramp which led to the bottom level. Miller smiled thinly as he saw Gibson's Astra heading towards him. As the policeman drew closer he flicked off his lights, seeing Miller only as a dark silhouette, illuminated by the cold white light of the fluorescents that lit the car park. The DI brought his own car to a halt about twenty yards away and clambered out. Miller could see that he was carrying a briefcase.

The sound of the policeman's footsteps echoed loudly as he strode towards Miller.

'You've got fifteen minutes,' Gibson said irritably, dumping the case on the bonnet of the Granada.

'I won't need that long,' Miller told him, slipping the catches. He looked inside at the seven manilla files which lay before him, each one marked with a name. Miller removed the first of them.

'I must want my head examined for this,' Gibson observed.

'Better fifteen minutes with me than a grilling by the press and the commissioner,' Miller murmured as he flipped open the first file.

'You really are a bastard, Frank,' his former colleague snarled, and Miller caught the genuine anger in his voice.

He glanced at the first of the files, flipping past the coroner's report, the investigating officer's account of the case, the witnesses' statements, until he found what he sought.

'Mark Forrester,' he read aloud. The photo showed the victim posing with a girl who Miller took to be his fiancée. Both were smiling in the monochrome print.

All around the outline of Forrester's body he saw the aura.

'It's there,' he whispered, reaching for the next file.

'What's there?' Gibson asked, glancing behind him every now and then, checking that they were indeed alone in the car park. The wind wailed mournfully along the ramps on either side of them.

'Nicholas Blake,' Miller read on the second file. He skipped past the photo of Blake's acid-splashed face and found a photo of the young man taken when he'd been in the army cadets.

The faint glow surrounded him too.

As it did Anthony Banks.

And Angela Grant.

173

The aura was more noticeable around some than others.

It surrounded Louise Turner.

The hellish glow radiated strongly from Bernadette Evans.

Miller reached the last file.

Penny Steele. The latest victim.

He knew, even without looking, that she would bear the mark. The photo in the file proved him right once more.

Every victim killed during the present spate of murders wore the aura like some kind of luminescent shroud.

The effects man dropped the last of the files into the case and handed it back to Gibson who looked surprised.

'And that's it?' the DI said. 'You just wanted to look at the photos?'

Miller nodded slowly, his mind in turmoil. He closed his eyes for a second but it seemed as if the images were planted in his mind, jostling for space with so many others. Portraits of living souls mingling with the memories of those hacked, shot, strangled. Maggot-infested images of death and corruption branded on his mind as if put there with a red hot iron. Never to be erased.

'I can *see* murder victims,' he said, quietly. 'By looking at someone's photo I can tell whether or not they're going to die violently. All murder victims have this aura.'

Gibson shook his head and snapped the clasps of the case shut.

'Before I thought you were drunk,' he said. 'Now I think you're off your head.'

'I can spot potential murder victims,' Miller insisted.

'So what are you going to do? Run round taking everyone's photograph?' He snatched up the case and turned. 'And I risked my position for you to tell me that?' The DI opened the door of the Astra and tossed the briefcase onto the passenger seat. He slid behind the wheel and started the engine which roared into life, the noise amplified by the cavernous subterranean car park.

'Go back to the booze, Frank,' Gibson shouted. 'It's where you belong.'

He jammed the car in gear and drove off, the tyres spinning momentarily on the concrete. Miller watched as the car disappeared up the exit ramp.

Miller stood alone in the darkened arena, collar turned up to protect him against the cold wind. He shuddered as he opened the door of his own car and slid behind the wheel. Even inside it felt cold.

The ability to pick out a murder victim. The thought carried with it a strange feeling of power, almost of life and death. *He* knew who would die.

What he didn't know was when and how.

He started his engine, suddenly anxious to be away from the semi-darkness of the underground car park.

Gibson didn't believe him. But Miller didn't care.

He knew someone who would be more than interested.

Thirty-five

He sat naked before the TV screen. Legs crossed, buddha-like, in a posture that was intended for repose yet every muscle in his body was tense and throbbing.

The spools of the video recorder purred quietly as images were regurgitated and he sat as if mesmerized by the figure before him.

Bob Johnson sucked in a deep breath through flared nostrils and gazed at the screen, watching the image of Terri Warner. He had the sound turned off, able only to see her, not to hear the words she spoke. But words were not his concern. His eyes flickered over her slim form, his gaze travelling from her face to her breasts then back again. The erection had grown harder and he allowed his right hand to envelope it, squeezing the flesh hard until he began a rhythmic pumping action. His breathing became heavier and he shuffled closer to the TV screen, still in his cross-legged position, hand now clamped firmly around his stiff shaft.

The picture on the video shifted, broke up momentarily then settled once again.

Terri appeared on the screen again, in different clothes. It was a different report. Different location. Recorded over two years ago. Johnson had all the interviews she'd done on tape, all the reports. Each one copied from the master tape which he had access to.

He gazed at her face, his own features tightening as the feeling of warmth spread across his belly and thighs. His hand began to move more rapidly. He watched her lips moving soundlessly, wondering what it would be like to feel his own against them, to

176

push his tongue into the welcoming wetness of her mouth. He began breathing through his mouth, the sound loud and rasping.

His body tensed, muscles swelling. Johnson was aware of the strength within his own body and that knowledge seemed to please him. His right hand continued to pump unfalteringly on his penis as he drew himself to his knees only inches from the screen.

Inches from her.

From that mouth.

That body.

'Terri,' he whispered her name softly, then with increasing volume, thrusting his hips towards the screen as the camera moved in for a close up of her face, her mouth opening and closing as if in slow motion.

He wanted to be inside that velvet cavern, to feel the softness of her tongue and lips.

He wanted to be.

He needed to be.

He would be.

With a final grunt of satisfaction he ejaculated copiously, the thick fluid spattering the TV screen, one long strand of it briefly connecting the end of his throbbing organ to the face of Terri Warner like some kind of fluid umbilicus.

They were joined.

She would be his.

Thirty-six

Miller took another swig from his hip flask and drummed slowly on the steering wheel with the fingers of his free hand. The effects man kept his eyes fixed on the doors of the building ahead of him, breaking his steady gaze only to look at the dashboard clock which told him it was approaching noon. He blinked hard to clear the fuzziness from his left eye then resumed his vigil.

He'd been there for over an hour with only the smell of his whisky and the inane ramblings of the radio for company. But now, finally, the one he sought emerged into the car park.

'At last,' murmured Miller, taking a final sip of whisky.

He watched as Terri Warner pushed open the double doors, then immediately looked up at the banks of dark cloud moving in from the west. Large spots of rain had already begun to fall, a portent of what was to come, and Terri quickened her pace as she headed for her car which was parked close to Miller's.

He waited until she was less than ten feet away then pushed open his own door and clambered out.

'It is Terri Warner isn't it?' he said, although it came out more as a statement than a question.

She nodded slowly, running appraising eyes over this newcomer. He didn't look like an autograph hunter, she mused. She smelt the whisky on his breath as he stepped closer and felt compelled to take a step back.

Miller extended his hand and introduced himself.

Terri shook the offered appendage, feeling the strength in his grip.

'I need to talk to you, Miss Warner,' he said. 'It's important.'

'I'm busy right now,' she said, still unsure of this man. 'Perhaps if you gave me a number I could call you . . .'

Miller interrupted her.

'It's about this series of killings,' he said. 'You could say we both have an interest in it.'

Terri frowned.

'In what way?'

'I've seen your reports, watched you on the TV,' he told her. 'You've made quite a name for yourself out of this case.'

'Look, I'm just doing my job. If you want to criticize –'

He cut her short once again. 'I don't want to criticize, I want to help,' he told her. 'I think I might have some information you may find interesting.'

The rain, which had been falling in isolated droplets, suddenly decided to begin lashing down.

'I didn't really want to stand here discussing all this,' Miller told her. 'There's a pub nearby. Follow me.' He slid behind the wheel and started his engine, swinging the Granada out of its parking spot. In his rear-view mirror he saw Terri start up her Mini and follow. Miller smiled. He flicked on his windscreen wipers, watching as the slim rubber arms struggled to brush away the torrent of rain which was pelting down furiously. He signalled left and Terri followed, her eyes on his tail-lights as he braked to avoid a pedestrian.

Who the hell was this man, she wondered? She knew his name but that was all. And what was his interest in the case? She shuddered involuntarily and, for reasons which she herself found inexplicable, she heard the voice on her answerphone echoing inside her head.

'*The police don't know.*'

Was there something familiar there? Questions tumbled through her mind, all without answers. The main one being, if she was so wary of this man why was she now following him? Curiosity could kill more than cats, she told herself. But, nevertheless, she followed.

Other eyes had seen her go.

Had seen her standing, speaking to Miller.

As he saw the two cars disappear into the main stream of traffic Bob Johnson clenched his fists angrily.

'Bitch,' he murmured.

Thirty-seven

The lounge bar of The Phoenix was crowded and noisy and it smelled of damp clothes. People had bolted into the pub with the sudden onslaught from above and now stood drinking and talking while their clothes dried on them. The carpeted floor was sodden and Miller fancied that he heard it squelching beneath his feet as he returned to the table where Terri sat waiting for him.

Two youths with short haircuts and paint-spattered denim jackets were talking loudly close to him, jostling one another around the fruit machine. The taller of the two bumped into Miller, almost causing him to spill the drinks he was carrying. The youth laughed until he saw the look which Miller shot him, his eyes blazing.

'Get out the fucking way,' Miller hissed, pushing past the youth, who suddenly seemed to have lost his bravado. He raised two fingers to Miller's back then returned to his antics with the fruit machine.

The effects man put down the drinks and slid into the seat opposite Terri.

She smiled thinly, still unsure of this man and even more unsure of why she had agreed to come to this place with him.

'I realize that you don't know me from Adam,' he said, sipping his drink. 'But I had to talk to you about these murders.'

'So talk, Mr Miller,' she said, reaching for her own glass.

'Frank,' he said. 'We don't have to be *that* formal.'

She nodded but didn't relax.

'I know that you must be wondering what the hell I'm up to.'

'It had crossed my mind,' Terri confessed.

181

'What I'm going to tell you might sound crazy. In fact, maybe it was me who made the mistake bringing you here.' He shook his head and downed a mouthful of whisky.

Miller had played his trump card. The bait was there.

'I think it might be a good idea if I left. I'm sorry,' he said.

'No, don't go,' Terri said, sitting forward. 'Let me hear what you've got to say.'

Miller hid his smile. She'd bitten. He had her hooked.

'You're wondering whether or not to trust me,' he said. 'Well, the feeling's mutual.'

Terri sighed.

'This is all very vague, Mr Miller,' she said. 'Sorry – *Frank.* How do I know what I can or can't be trusted with until you tell me what the hell it is you're going on about? If you're going to confess to these murders then maybe you should have picked one of the newspapers –'

He cut her short. 'Were you at a press conference at New Scotland Yard about ten days ago?' he asked.

She nodded.

'The police told you that they had arrested the murderer, and before you say anything, yes I know it was on TV and in all the papers so I'm not telling you anything you don't know. That entire conference was a sham.'

'I had my suspicions. How do you know?'

'Because the head of the investigation told me himself. The police still haven't got a clue who they're looking for.'

'Why would anyone from New Scotland Yard tell *you* something like that?'

'Let's just say I used my influence. I used to work for them. Detective Inspector Gibson and I are close friends. Or at least we used to be.'

'I still don't see your interest in the case,' Terri told him.

'The seven people who've been murdered were destined to be victims. I could see that when I looked at their photos.'

Terri frowned, not sure whether to laugh, get up and leave or continue listening.

'*Destined*?' she said. 'This is beginning to sound a little bit melodramatic.'

182

'Every murder victim gives off some kind of aura, I don't know what else to call it,' Miller said irritably, realizing that his revelations were indeed beginning to sound ridiculous, knowing that even should he show Terri the photos of Penny Steele and George Cook *she* would be unable to see the aura. 'I can see that aura. But only in photos.'

'Are you telling me you've seen pictures of the murder victims in this case?' she said, her interest suddenly rekindled. 'But they're supposed to be closed files. How the hell did you get access to them?'

'That's *my* business. Anyway, I'm talking about photos of the victims *before* they were killed. That's when the aura is present.'

Terri sipped her drink, regarding Miller over the rim. Finally she put down the glass, toying with the stem.

'Why me? Why choose me to tell your secrets to?' she wanted to know.

'Because I think I can trust you not to repeat them. If there's one thing in this world I hate it's having to trust someone, but you seemed like one of the better choices. Now, what do you know about these killings?'

'Why should I tell you?'

He shrugged.

'Don't tell me if you don't want to, I probably know more than you anyway. I thought we might be able to help each other. Maybe you were right though, perhaps I should go to a newspaper.' He got to his feet but Terri shot out a hand to restrain him.

'All the victims were murdered by different methods,' she said. 'You probably already know that much. But the most interesting thing is that the MO in every case has been copied from a case in the past. Whoever is doing the murders has more than a passing knowledge of criminal history. The latest victim was killed and mutilated in much the same way as the victims of Gordon Cummins. They called him the Ripper of the Blitz. He murdered four women in four days in 1942, two of them prostitutes. The latest victim was a prostitute.'

'How do you know all this?' Miller asked, his eyes never leaving hers.

'After the second murder I got a call from someone claiming he was a member of the murder squad investigating this particular case. He told me he had information for me, about the killings. I thought it was just some joker after publicity, but what he told me was too detailed to be known by an outsider. He's called after every murder since then. But I don't know his name or his position.'

'An informer inside Scotland Yard?' said Miller, stroking his chin, thoughtfully, Gibson's words floating back to him;

'*Sometimes I think Chandler enjoys seeing me come up against brick walls . . .*'

'You said whoever was doing the killings had more than a passing knowledge of criminal history?' he muttered.

Terri nodded.

Bent copper? Miller wondered. One with an axe to grind?

Chandler certainly fitted the bill.

There was a long silence finally broken by Terri.

'He called me,' she said, quietly. 'The killer. A few days ago. I didn't go to the police, I thought he might try and contact me again but so far he hasn't.'

'You think he might?' Miller wanted to know.

'Who knows? I can't even be sure it *was* the killer.' She shrugged. 'It might just be someone with a sick sense of humour.'

'Sick enough to kill seven people seven different ways,' Miller muttered. 'Why didn't you tell the police? They could have bugged your phone.'

'It wasn't my idea to keep the call a secret,' she confessed. 'The guy I work for, Bob Johnson, he thought it might make a good story if *I* could find the killer, contact him.'

'Even though it means risking your life?' Miller said, flatly.

'It's a chance I'm willing to take.' She drained what was left in her glass and pushed the empty receptacle away from her. Miller offered her another and, after a moment's hesitation, she agreed. She watched him as he made his way to the bar, wondering why she found this stranger so captivating. Was that the word to describe him? He was attractive, there was no denying that, but Terri sensed a darker side to him, a bitterness

184

which seemed to cling around him like a cloak. When he spoke there was a weariness in his voice usually reserved for men twice his age, as if he were tired of everything around him. His tone, at times, carried something akin to contempt for what he spoke of. Yet somewhere deep inside her she felt drawn to him, or at least to what he had to say and the way he said it. Her musings were interrupted as he returned.

'You seem to know a lot more about me than I know about you,' she said. 'I don't even know what you do for a living.'

Miller smiled thinly.

'I'm a prosthetic make-up artist and visual effects man with a film company that's shooting a picture about ten miles outside London.' He went on to explain briefly his spells as both press and police photographer.

'You must have seen some awful things,' she said, quietly.

'After a while you learn to respect it,' he said.

She looked at him quizzically.

'Death. You come to respect death. How it comes in so many different guises. Some of them inventive, some of them plain bloody stupid. But you also learn that there's no such thing as death with dignity.' He ran his index finger around the rim of his glass. 'I've seen it all. Bodies hanging from trees, lying on railway lines, packed in concrete. Decapitated, gutted, dismembered. Swollen, black, putrid, crawling with maggots.' His eyes were no longer on her but looking past, staring blankly at the back of the seat on which she sat. 'Men, women, kids, babies. Sometimes alone, sometimes in groups. All stinking with that smell of death. It smells like bad eggs and it never leaves you. It gets into your clothes. Your pores. It even gets into your mind.' He swallowed a sizeable gulp of whisky. 'It gets to be like an old friend after a time,' Miller concluded.

'Friends like that I can do without,' Terri told him, smiling. 'Look, this business about the aura around murder victims, how is it you can see it but no one else can?'

He explained about the accident. The operation. The eye transplant.

'I can't think of any other solution,' Miller told her. 'It has to be the eye because I can only see the aura through my left eye.'

'And only on photos?'

He nodded.

'What would *you* think if someone came to *you* claiming that they could spot potential murder victims by looking at their photos?'

'I'd probably tell them they were mad,' Miller replied.

'Journalists and media people are supposed to be hard-headed cynics,' Terri said. 'I must be even crazier for believing you.'

Miller's face showed only a flicker of emotion.

'But keep this to yourself,' he said. 'I said I didn't like trusting people. I took a chance with you. It might just pay off.'

They both drank.

'Are you going to wait and see if you hear from the murderer again?' he asked.

She shrugged.

'I might as well. The police seem powerless to do anything anyway. If only I could build up some kind of rapport with him . . .' She allowed the sentence to trail off. 'I know it's dangerous, but it might get him caught.'

'It also might get you killed,' said Miller flatly.

'I don't think that would bother Bob Johnson, as long as he got good ratings out of it. That's all he seems to care about. This case isn't about people being killed as far as he's concerned. It's about angles, getting people to watch the programme. I think he'll be disappointed when the police eventually catch this maniac.'

'*If* they do,' Miller said, quietly.

'You sound as if you have your doubts, Frank,' she observed, again feeling the power of his stare upon her, but this time not feeling so uncomfortable beneath it.

Miller didn't answer. He merely watched as she got to her feet and manoeuvred herself past the stools next to the table.

'I've got to go,' she told him. 'I've got to work to do.'

Miller got to his feet and shook hands with her. He thanked her for listening to him. She took a piece of paper from her handbag and scribbled her phone number on it. Miller did likewise with his own.

'I'll be in touch, Miss Warner,' he said.

186

'Terri,' she told him.

They locked stares for brief seconds then she was gone. Miller sat down and finished his drink, pushing the empty glass away. He looked at the piece of paper she'd given him before folding it up and sticking it inside his jacket pocket.

It nestled between the photos of George Cook and Penny Steele.

He had her phone number now.

He had a way of getting closer.

Thirty-eight

The rain which had been falling heavily all through the day showed no sign of stopping. Against the black backdrop of darkness, storm clouds moved in rolling banks until the city was shrouded by the oppressive swirling shapes. So thick were the clouds that even the wind seemed powerless to move them. They unfolded, emptying their load on the buildings below.

Like distant cannons, thunder rumbled in the canopy of grey and black, the ever-present roar punctuated occasionally by a whiplash crack of lightning.

Terri Warner muttered to herself as the picture on the TV screen broke up again due to the massive amount of static in the air. She jabbed the buttons of the remote control but every channel was the same. Only a patchwork of broken lines and fizzing white dots. The picture returned briefly, then there was another almighty crack of lightning and the screen went completely blank. Terri switched the set off and wandered into the kitchen to make herself a cup of coffee.

She had barely filled the kettle when the phone rang.

Terri padded back into the sitting room and picked up the receiver, glancing out of the open curtains at the electrical storm which was slicing open the clouds.

'Hello, Terri Warner,' she said, her eyes still on the explosion of celestial fireworks.

There was no answer. Only the hiss of static.

'Hello.'

At the other end the receiver was put down, the click strangely loud in the stillness of the flat. Terri shrugged and replaced the receiver.

She had reached the door to the kitchen when it rang again.

She turned and, once more, picked it up.

Again there was only silence at the other end.

Silence.

But something else.

Breathing?

She pressed the phone closer to her ear, trying to make out the low rasping noise which barely filtered through the crackling which distorted the line.

'Who is that?' she asked, trying to sound calm. 'I think you've got the wrong number.'

Terri suddenly thought of the answerphone. She fumbled to reach the 'record' button. Pressed it.

'Right number.'

The words startled her. So much so that she almost dropped the phone.

'Who is that?' she demanded, her own voice now sounding strained.

Outside there was a deafening clap of thunder.

'Talk to me,' she rasped, anger and fear now shaping her tone in equal measures.

'I'm watching.'

Terri tried to swallow but her throat felt as if someone had filled it with chalk. Yet through her fear she tried to find something familiar in that voice, tried to pick out anything discernible from the brief words.

'This phone is tapped,' she blurted. 'I had it done after the last time you called.'

Silence at the other end.

Breathing.

Or something like it.

The phone went dead.

She dropped it back on the cradle, stepping away from it as if it were some venomous reptile.

For what seemed like an eternity she stood there, watching the phone. Waiting for it to ring again.

Outside, the storm grew in fury.

Thirty-nine

The call had come at about seven thirty that morning, rousing Miller from his slumbers. He'd woken up to find himself sprawled across the desk in his workroom, a bottle of Haig standing half-empty at one corner. He'd taken the call, his senses still dulled from the previous night, not even recognizing the voice at the other end for long moments. Then, finally, the caller had identified himself. Phillip Dickinson. The director sounded almost apologetic for disturbing Miller but, he'd told him, he had good news for him.

They needed the effects man back at the shoot, Dickinson had told him. Miller had asked about the row with Lisa Richardson, the macabre practical joke.

Lisa had walked out on them, Dickinson had informed him. Colin Robson had been fired after a series of rows. Miller was needed again. They'd replaced Lisa with another actress.

Miller had listened to the developments with ill-disguised glee, and for a moment he'd thought about telling Dickinson to find himself another effects man but then thought better of it. Yes, he'd come back and yes, he'd be on the set by nine that morning.

As he pulled the Granada into the car park behind the sound stage Miller felt strangely elated. He was back where he belonged. Working. And if it was amidst blood and violence then so be it. At least *this* blood could be washed off at the end of the day.

He had already seen too much of the real stuff.

As he clambered out of his car he felt the spots of rain splattering his skin. The savagery of the storm the previous night had given way to a mournful cascade of rain which fell from a sky the colour of wet concrete. Miller glanced up at it as he made his way to the door of the sound stage. As he reached it he looked across at the make-up trailer. His own private kingdom.

He was home again.

'Like you said before, there's no problem with bringing in a new actress,' Phillip Dickinson said. 'In the remaining scenes she'll be in make-up anyway. Nobody will know the difference.'

Miller nodded and took a swig from his hip flask.

'I hope you haven't picked another prima donna to take that other stupid cow's place,' the effects man said.

'I'll introduce you,' the director said.

Miller sat gazing down at the sketches before him while Dickinson picked his way through the crowded canteen in search of the one he sought. He returned to the table a moment later, this time with a companion.

'Frank, this is Susan Lewis,' the director said and Miller turned to see the actress standing close by him. He stood up and shook hands with her, running appraising eyes over her slim form. She was in her late twenties, pretty, wearing no make-up. Her long black hair was uncombed and she ran a hand through it as Miller looked at her. She smiled warmly and he noticed how her face seemed to light up with the gesture.

'Frank Miller, our make-up and effects supervisor,' Dickinson announced.

'You've got no objections to wearing make-up I hope,' Miller said. 'Prosthetics I mean, nct eye-liner and lipstick.'

'I've worn it before. It doesn't bother me,' she told him.

Miller seemed uncharacteristically fascinated by her face. By her high cheekbones, the way her chin came to a smooth point.

'You look more like a model,' he told her. 'It seems a pity to cover up that face with latex.' He managed a grin.

'I would have been a model but I was too short,' she told him.

'You're very pretty,' he told her.

'That's about as close to a compliment as you're likely to get out of him,' Dickinson told the actress and she chuckled.

Miller smiled back at her. She was indeed a very pretty young woman.

'I wanted to shoot one of Susan's scenes this afternoon if possible, Frank,' the director told him. 'How long will the make-up take to apply?'

Miller shrugged.

'Two hours, maybe more. I'll need to take some photos and maybe even some facial casts before I start.'

'I'm ready when you are,' Susan told the effects man.

Miller took a swig from his hip flask. Then he led her out of the canteen and across the tarmac towards the make-up trailer.

'I heard that you didn't get on with Lisa Richardson,' Susan said.

'Does that bother you?'

'No, I just heard rumours.'

'Whatever you heard, it was probably right.'

'I also heard that you can be a bit of a bastard.'

Miller stopped as he reached the steps up to the trailer door. He looked at Susan and smiled.

'Is that true as well?' she persisted.

'You'll find out,' he told her. 'If people think I'm a bastard that's usually because they disagree with me. I'm an exception in the film business, I'm one of the few people who actually cares about what they do. I couldn't really give a toss what the film turns out like, that's Phil Dickinson's problem. All I'm interested in is that my effects look good.' He shrugged and opened the trailer door, ushering her in. Miller slapped on lights and motioned for Susan to be seated before the mirror in one corner of the trailer. Then, from a cupboard nearby, he retrieved a polaroid camera.

'I saw some of the work you did on this film, Phillip showed me some rushes,' Susan told him. 'I thought it was great.'

'The sycophantic approach, eh?' said Miller.

Her smile faded, to be replaced by an expression which combined anger and disappointment.

'It looks like the rumours were true,' she told him. 'You can be a bastard. I meant what I said, your work looked great.'

'Thanks for the vote of confidence.'

'Did Lisa Richardson leave because of you?'

'Does it matter?'

'I was just curious. You don't strike me as the easiest man in the world to work with.'

'We had our differences.' He checked the camera, satisfied that all was ready. 'Now, can you and I get down to work?' He snapped the first shot, pulling the picture free as the camera rolled it out. He laid it on the table to develop fully then took another shot from the left hand side. Another from the right.

The trio of prints began to darken, images started to form as Miller took another couple of pictures.

'Do you suffer from any skin allergies?' he asked, sounding more like a doctor. 'The make-up can sometimes affect people with sensitive skin.'

Susan shook her head.

'I learned at the beginning that you need thick skin in this business.' She smiled at her own joke.

Miller nodded and turned to look at the pictures. They were still developing. He picked one up and waved it in the air, trying to speed the drying process. The image was practically clear now.

Miller studied the print.

The face of Susan Lewis was surrounded by the aura.

Framed by the luminescent glow.

The effects man clenched his teeth, the knot of muscles at the side of his jaw throbbing powerfully.

'Are the pictures all right?' Susan asked, wondering why Miller had suddenly fallen silent.

'What?' he asked, abstractedly.

'The pictures.'

'Yeah, they're fine,' he lied, his eyes drawn to that rim of light which framed her face like a halo. For interminable seconds he stood gazing at the pictures then Miller turned and headed for the door of the trailer.

'What about the make-up?' Susan called.

'It'll wait,' Miller said.

Then he was gone.

There was a phone in the portakabin near the studio entrance.

Miller told the security man on duty that he needed to use it and the man stepped outside while Miller hastily jabbed out the number he needed. He tapped impatiently on the desk as he waited for the receiver to be picked up.

'New Scotland Yard,' said the voice at the other end.

'I want to speak to Stuart Gibson, he's on extension twenty-two,' Miller said then he waited once more, listening to a succession of pops and clicks as he was re-connected. The extension line was ringing.

And ringing.

'Come on,' Miller hissed.

He finally heard the click as the receiver was picked up.

'Detective Inspector Gibson's office,' the voice said.

Miller recognized the voice.

'Stuart, it's Frank Miller.'

There was a moment of silence then the policeman spoke, the iciness in his tone unmistakable.

'I think we said all we had to say to each other the other day.'

'This is important. You know I told you about the aura around potential murder victims? Well, I've seen it again.'

'Look, Frank why don't you find someone else to pester, I told you, I'm not interested.'

'You'll be interested when she's killed though, won't you?' Miller snapped.

'Who is this *she* you're talking about?'

Miller explained.

'I'm telling you, Stuart. The aura is there on the photos. Just like it was on the pictures of the other victims. She's going to be killed. I'd bet money on it.'

'Then maybe you should have rung Ladbrokes instead of me,' the DI said sarcastically. 'Look Frank, I'm busy. I've got enough to contend with now with *one* nutcase running round, don't add to my problems with more of your hare-brained ideas.'

'What's it going to take to convince you?' snarled Miller.

'More than the word of an alcoholic with an over-active imagination and bad eyesight,' snapped the policeman venomously. 'Now get off the line will you?'

'At least put a tail on her, watch her house or something,' he said angrily. 'You can't just dismiss what I've told you. She's going to be murdered, I'm telling you.'

'Goodbye, Frank,' said Gibson and put down the phone.

'Bastard!' roared Miller and hurled the receiver down. He barged out of the Portakabin, almost colliding with the security man who had heard the raised voices and was making his way back inside. He opened his mouth to speak but Miller had already set off back towards the make-up trailer. The security man shook his head and disappeared back inside the little hut.

As Miller made his way across the tarmac towards the trailer he saw Susan Lewis standing in the doorway waiting for him.

Miller shuddered involuntarily as he glanced at the actress, the vision of her face suffused with the aura still strong in his mind.

Could he be wrong about the strange light? Had the other killings been a mere coincidence? He doubted it, but he prayed that this time he *had* made a mistake.

The shooting went as planned.

Susan Lewis performed well beneath the grotesque prosthetic make-up which Miller had created for her. He had applied it carefully, almost lovingly. Like some insane plastic surgeon, shaping and carving the latex, creating something of horror from what was formerly beauty.

And all through shooting he stood by the camera watching the actress. He stood, sipping from his hip flask and he watched. Haunted by the thought of what he'd seen in the photos. Aware that she carried the aura around her like a beacon. But one that only he could see.

It was approaching seven-fifteen when Dickinson finally called a halt to the day's proceedings, muttering something about the camera crew and lighting riggers wanting overtime. Miller ignored the director's remarks and stood waiting for Susan Lewis to come off-set. She was unable to speak because of the constrictions of the make-up and Miller found that he himself had very little inclination to talk, so once back in the trailer, the make-up was removed in relative silence. She pulled the last few pieces off herself, peeling the latex away as if it were sloughed skin.

As she splashed her face with warm water from the basin in one corner of the trailer she was aware of Miller looking at her.

'Is something wrong?' Susan asked him.

Miller shook his head and took a swig from his hip flask.

The polaroids of Susan nestled inside his jacket pocket. Like silent warnings.

'How are you getting home?' he asked her.

'I don't live far from here, I'm driving,' she told him. 'It should only take me about thirty minutes.'

The effects man nodded slowly.

He told her what time he wanted her at the set the following morning in order to apply the make-up, then he watched as she left the caravan and wandered across the tarmac towards her waiting car. Miller chewed his bottom lip contemplatively, watching as she swung the vehicle out of its space. He waited a moment longer, then pulled the trailer door shut behind him, locked it and sprinted across to his own car. Miller started up the engine and flicked on his lights at half-beam. The approaching evening loomed dull and grey and he needed the extra light as he drove.

At first he thought he'd lost Susan Lewis, but as he swung the car out into the main road he caught sight of her car idling behind a slow-moving lorry. Miller slipped into the stream of traffic four cars behind.

She drove on.

He followed, one hand on the wheel, the other gripping the hip flask, his eyes never leaving Susan Lewis's car.

So, Gibson wouldn't put a tail on her, Miller thought. Well, fuck him. He'd seen the aura around her. He knew she was in danger.

If he had to sit watching her all night he would.

He drove on.

196

Forty

'Miserable bastard,' shouted Mike Hamilton as the car sped past him and disappeared around a bend in the road. He jabbed a 'V' sign into the air and muttered to himself, gazing into the darkness, waiting for the approach of another vehicle. Maybe a van or small truck would come by, he thought, guys like that were usually amenable to hitch-hikers, and Mike was getting sick of standing by the roadside with his thumb out like a mannequin, relying on the generosity of some passing motorist. He fumbled in his coat pocket and found a roll-up but he was out of matches. Maybe whoever picked him up would have a light. *If* anyone ever picked him up. He stepped back from the roadside and sat down on his rucksack, manoeuvring himself into a more comfortable position.

He glanced up at the dark sky, hoping that the rain would hold off until someone picked him up. His parents would be furious if they knew he was hitching. They'd given him fifty pounds when he left home in Hull two days earlier, more than enough to cover his train fare back from London.

They'd be even more furious if they knew he'd spent more than half the money on drugs. That was why he was reduced to hitching. He'd been smoking the stuff for ten years, ever since his fifteenth birthday party when during a pub crawl a couple of mates had offered him a joint. Where was the harm in it? he asked himself. He hadn't felt the need to move on to the hard stuff, although he'd seen plenty of others who had. He had his own little habit well under control. So well under control, in fact, that he planned to sell some of his stash when he got to London. The trip, ostensibly, had been to visit his older sister who'd left the North to marry two years ago, but Mike was beginning to wonder if he was ever going to get there, despite the fact that he was only twenty miles from the centre of the capital.

He shifted position on his rucksack. If it hadn't been for the ridiculously intolerant attitudes of his parents he would have been driven down from Hull in their car, but his father had vowed that he never wanted anything more to do with his only daughter. Not after she'd married a black man. As far as he was concerned he no longer had a daughter. He'd made a pretty good job of ignoring his half-caste grandson too. Mike felt sorry for his mother, but she hadn't the guts or the inclination to defy her husband and visit her only daughter. Besides, she'd shown as much resistance to the marriage as her husband. So, Mike was the only one who visited his sister, Shelly. He didn't care what colour her husband was. He'd always got on with Roy. If he'd been a six-headed Martian with a lisp Mike would have got on with him. Why create problems in life when they could be avoided, he had always thought. After a couple of joints, nothing really seemed *that* important anyway. He smiled to himself and looked up as another car came towards him, its headlights cutting through the darkness.

Mike got to his feet, thumb hooked in the familiar gesture.

The car sped past and he was left cursing once more.

He felt the first drops of rain and groaned aloud, pulling the hood of his parka up to protect himself from the imminent deluge. The trees and bushes at the roadside grew thickly so Mike retreated towards them, seeking the added shelter. If the worse came to the worst he could always sleep on the roadside, or in one of the fields beyond the boundary of trees and bushes. It wouldn't be the first time he'd slept with the sky for an eider-down. Every year after the rock gigs at Donington he slept on one of the nearby hillsides where the smoke from the fires still reached up into the blackness. He'd done the same at Reading five years earlier. But tonight, with the rain beginning to fall more heavily, he didn't fancy sleeping under the stars.

More headlights were approaching and, again, Mike stepped forward hopefully.

He smiled broadly as he saw the car slowing down. It came to a halt about twenty yards further up the road and he stood for long moments, as if waiting for it to reverse, watching the tail-lights glowing in the night. Then he snatched up his rucksack and ran after the stationary vehicle.

The door on the passenger side was pushed open for him and Mike slid gratefully into the seat, tossing his rucksack into the rear of the vehicle.

'Thanks,' he said, not yet looking at the driver. 'I've been out there for hours. I thought I was going to get soaked.' He slammed the door and turned. 'If you're going into London . . .'

He got no further.

There wasn't much room in the car but the driver found sufficient space to bring the hammer down with devastating force.

It struck Mike on the right temple, staving in part of his skull which shattered with a sickening crack.

Searing white hot pain shot through him and he fell back, nausea beginning to bubble in his belly. He slumped against the car door, one hand fumbling uselessly for the handle as he struggled to retain a grip on consciousness.

The hammer swung round once more, wielded with incredible power and expertise within the confines of the car.

The second blow broke Mike's lower jaw close to his left ear, tugging the mandible from its socket. He felt two teeth splinter inside his mouth and blood began to run down his throat. He choked on the crimson flow, only the pain keeping him conscious. Mike Hamilton slipped from the seat, lifting both hands in a reflex action to protect the top of his head.

The hammer swung down and crushed his right thumb as he lay, face buried in the passenger seat.

The blow to the back of his skull opened a small hole through which blood began to pump thickly, matting his hair together. His body shuddered violently as if he were very cold and, somewhere through the agonizing pain which filled his head, he was aware that the car was moving once more. How far it moved he didn't know, he was only barely clinging to consciousness as he sensed rather than saw the driver clamber out once the vehicle had finally stopped. His eyes were clouded with pain, the raging agony making it feel as if his head were on the point of bursting. He heard the passenger-side door open, felt arms dragging him from the car. Then he lay on wet earth, water running into his mouth to join the blood already spilling over his lips. His stomach contracted violently and he felt hot bile clawing its way up from his belly, filling his mouth for a second before oozing down his shattered chin. He moaned, the sudden racking movement causing even greater pain from his smashed jaw and holed skull.

Mike was dimly aware of being rolled over onto his back but the face of the driver who looked down at him was invisible in the gloom. Had the youth been in any state to notice he would have seen that the driver had guided the car off the main road onto a dirt track flanked by high hedges which completely concealed the vehicle from any eyes capable of penetrating the darkness from the main road.

They might as well have been down an empty mine shaft so total was the seclusion.

Mike moaned gutturally and tried to crawl away from the car, white lights dancing before his eyes, his head still throbbing with a pain unlike anything he'd ever known before. It felt as if someone was massaging boiling oil into his scalp and brain with iron fingers and he burbled incoherently as he crawled, his movements slow.

A kick was driven into his side and, once again, he rolled over onto his back, this time unable to move.

The rain had stopped but he felt liquid spattering him.

Thick reeking liquid.

It took him only a few seconds to realize that it was petrol.

Even through his pain he flapped helplessly at his assailant as more of the stinking fluid rained down on him, some of it filling his mouth, making him retch with even greater ferocity. More petrol trickled up his nostrils, the stench unbearable as he writhed around on his back like a fish out of water, terror now filtering through the haze of pain which covered him.

He was drenched, soaked from head to foot in the fuel.

All he could do was lie and watch as the match was struck.

The driver held it above him for agonizing seconds then flicked it.

The moment it hit Mike's body there was a dull *whoosh* as his clothes ignited.

He tried to scream as the flames ate away at his flesh, searing the hair from his scalp before devouring the soft, bloodied flesh beneath, lapping around the hole in his skull, sometimes probing blazing fingers into the puncture until Mike began to pray for death. Anything to end the excruciating agony. He tried to roll over, to extinguish the flames in the wet grass, but it was useless. He felt his blood boiling in his veins, pieces of blackened flesh fell from his hands like flaming slime. His body began to swell up as the fire enveloped it. Fire ate away at his genitals and legs and he found that he was trying to fight the flames with little more than blackened charred stumps where his hands had already been eaten away by the staggering heat.

He tried to scream but his broken jaw prevented even that final act. His eyes dissolved into bubbling mush and, briefly, he smelt the stench of his own incinerated flesh.

The driver of the car stood back, watching the blazing torch which had once been a man. Then quickly, but without undue haste, slipped back into the car, reversed down the dirt track onto the road and drove off.

It was another ten minutes before a passing car spotted the flames twenty or thirty yards off the road. Another thirty before the police arrived.

By that time, the body of Mike Hamilton resembled a spent match.

Forty-one

The blanket was pulled carefully over the blackened remains of Mike Hamilton, hiding the charred corpse from view. The acrid stench of burned flesh still hung in the air and DI Gibson waved a hand in front of his nose as if to dispel the noxious odour.

'How long's he been dead?' asked the policeman.

'It's impossible to say,' Loomis told him, wiping his hands on a piece of tissue. 'Until I've done the autopsy.' He looked down at the grass around the area where the body had been lying. 'It can't have been more than an hour, the poor sod was still warm. Very warm.'

'Any ID on him?' Gibson asked a uniformed man.

'If there was it went up in smoke, sir.'

'Just like *he* did,' Chandler interjected, sucking his teeth and nodding towards the incinerated body.

They all watched as it was lifted carefully into the back of the waiting ambulance. The blue lights were turning silently in the darkness.

'I want footprint casts made and casts of the wheel marks,' said Gibson, sucking on his cigarette. He glanced across at the group of newsmen and women standing behind a cordon of uniformed officers about twenty yards away. 'And I'd like to know where that fucking lot came from? We arrived half an hour ago and they turn up within five minutes. How did they know what had happened and where?' There was anger in his voice. 'If I didn't know better I'd say they'd been tipped off.' He cast a sideways glance at Chandler, who shrugged.

The policemen made their way down the dirt track towards the eager press who moved forward en masse in their efforts to reach the two detectives.

'Who is the victim?'

' . . . has identification been made yet?'

' . . . is it the same killer?'

Questions came drifting through the night and Gibson merely pulled up the collar of his coat and headed for the waiting car.

'No comment,' he called, loudly.

A TV camera was pushed close to him and the DI shoved it away angrily.

' . . . are you treating this as the latest in the series of murders?'

'No comment.'

'You said that you had the killer in custody,' said a fresh voice.

Gibson paused at this latest barb, searching for its source. He spotted Terri Warner almost immediately.

'At the press conference you said that a suspect was under arrest,' she said. 'And yet, two more murders have been committed since then.'

Gibson glared at her for a moment then walked on.

'When are you going to arrest the real killer?' Terri called after him.

'No comment,' Gibson shouted back without looking round.

She watched as the DI and his assistant slid into the Astra and pulled away.

'Some bastard tipped them off,' he said. 'I know it.'

'Maybe the same guy who rang us, the one who found the body,' Chandler offered.

Gibson shook his head.

'He was in a state of shock. He's hardly likely to have informed the media, is he?' There was a note of agitation in the DI's voice.

They rode a long way in silence then Chandler said, 'That's eight he's chalked up now.'

'Thanks for the reminder but I *can* count,' Gibson hissed.

'And still no closer to finding him,' Chandler chided.

'You're enjoying this aren't you?'

'I don't know what you're talking about.'

'*I'm* in charge of the investigation. If the bastard isn't caught it's me who gets it in the neck, from the Commissioner, the media and anyone else with an axe to grind.'

'That's one of the hazards of the job isn't it, Chief?' said Chandler. 'If you crack it you get the credit, if you mess up you get the sharp end of the stick. With position comes responsibility,' he said scornfully.

'I don't need *you* to tell me my responsibilities, Chandler. But *I'll* tell *you* something. If we don't catch him, and I go down, I'll make sure I take you with me. We're in this together, it doesn't matter that I'm in charge. You're on the case too, it's as much your problem as mine.'

'But I'm not in charge, am I?'

'No, that's right. And if I'm replaced do you think *you'll* be offered my position?'

Chandler didn't answer.

'Do you?' Gibson pressed.

'I should have had it in the beginning,' the DS said, venomously.

Gibson laughed humourlessly.

'That's it isn't it? That's been it all along. You don't want the killer caught, do you? Because as long as the bastard's free, the more people he kills, the more it discredits me.'

Chandler shot his superior an angry glance.

'You won't catch him,' he said with an air of conviction which annoyed Gibson.

'I'll get him. With or without your help. And like I said, if I don't, then I'll make sure *you* never get my position. We're in this together, Chandler. It's time we started working together. Before anyone else dies.'

The words hung ominously in the air. Like the smell of burned flesh.

Forty-two

Had he been wrong?

Miller drained the last drops from the hip flask and asked himself that question once more.

He'd followed Susan Lewis to the block of flats where she lived and he'd sat outside in his car all night. Drinking, watching.

Drinking.

Christ, he must have got through more than he'd first thought. Most of the early hours were a blur, scarcely remembered. He could recall dozing periodically, waking suddenly to gaze up at her window again, but other than that the hours between midnight and four a.m. were vague. Now he sat in the driveway of his own house looking down at the dashboard clock which told him it was almost five-thirty. Dawn had risen grey and dirty on the horizon, like a rancid floor cloth stretched across the sky. Miller sighed and swung himself out of the car, not even bothering to lock it.

He fumbled for his house keys and prepared to let himself in. He'd have the chance for a shower and a cup of coffee before he had to leave for the studio. He wondered if he should mention his vigil to Susan Lewis when he saw her. He thought better of it. She'd either laugh in his face or call the police. He grunted. Not that that would do her much good.

Maybe he *had* been wrong.

He found his key and inserted it in the lock.

The door swung back a few inches.

Miller froze momentarily, withdrawing the key as if he'd received an electric shock.

205

He pushed the door and stepped into the hall, looking round warily. The house was cloaked in silence, an almost conspiratorial solitude which wrapped itself around Miller like invisible mist. He turned briefly and checked the lock. It hadn't been forced. Whoever had entered the house had slipped it.

Whoever had entered had known what they were doing.

There was soil leading out of the hall and towards the stairs to his left. Miller followed the trail slowly, pausing at the bottom of the steps to glance up.

It was only at that moment he realized that whoever had broken in could well still be in the house.

The thought hit him like a sledgehammer and suddenly from his befuddled state his mind seemed to clear. His actions sharpened as he sensed danger.

He began climbing the stairs, quietly but quickly, his eyes never leaving the landing above him, only occasionally glancing at the closed doors which faced him. He stopped on the top step, listening for the slightest sounds of movement.

There was none.

He tried to control his breathing, to slow the pace of his heart which was thudding so loud in his chest he feared that the intruder might hear it.

If *he* was listening out for the intruder then the other was probably listening for *him*.

Miller moved more slowly across the landing, picking up a long, thin glass vase from a cabinet as he did so. At least now he had some kind of weapon.

He pushed open the first of the doors and looked into the room.

Empty.

The door of his own bedroom was ajar.

Miller paused on the threshold, taking a firmer grip on the vase.

He pushed the door, stepping into the room.

Empty.

He swallowed hard and backed out onto the landing again.

There was a noise from downstairs. Miller spun round and walked to the landing, peering over the banister down into the hall.

He listened intently, trying to pinpoint the location of the sound but only silence greeted him this time. He made for the stairs, his heart now thumping madly against his ribs.

As he reached the foot of the stairs he heard the sound again.

It came from his right. From the kitchen.

There was a large window in that room, perhaps the intruder was attempting to clamber out, to get away before Miller got to him. Miller quickly turned over the alternatives in his mind. Should he let the man go? Perhaps he should call the police now. Or tackle the intruder himself?

And yet there was something odd about the entire tableau. If the invader *was* a burglar then why was nothing missing. As far as Miller could see everything was still in its place.

He made his way towards the kitchen as silence descended again.

He was only a couple of feet from the door now, his hand extended towards the knob, the vase gripped more tightly in his fist.

Miller closed his hand around the knob and steadied himself.

He almost shouted aloud when it turned in his grip.

The door was pulled open, the effects man overbalancing, sprawling on the floor of the kitchen.

He dropped the vase, which shattered.

As he struggled to get up he heard a low guttural laugh and looked up to see the intruder standing before him.

'Jesus Christ,' murmured Miller, transfixed by the sight before him.

The intruder smiled.

'I've been waiting for you.'

Forty-three

'What the hell do you want?' Miller rasped angrily.

John Ryker leant back against one of the kitchen worktops, arms folded across his broad chest. The smile had faded from his face and he regarded Miller impassively. Ryker was in his early forties, a tall, powerfully-built man with jet-black hair untouched by even the hint of grey. It looked as if someone had carefully painted each strand of hair with pitch. His forehead was heavy and densely lined, its prominence making it look as though his eyes were little more than small holes punched into his face. His lips were thin, almost bloodless, slashed across his mouth like a thin wound. When he spoke his voice was low but full of menace, and Miller could sense the pent up aggression in each syllable. It was like talking to a human firework. The fuse was lit but he was never quite sure if Ryker was going to explode.

'That's not much of a greeting is it, Frank?' Ryker said. 'I mean, I did take the trouble to visit you in hospital, too. How are you feeling now?'

'Since when has my bloody health been any concern of yours?' Miller snapped, brushing past the bigger man and making for the sink. He spun the cold tap and filled a plastic beaker with water, downing it in two huge gulps.

'Not on the wagon are you?' Ryker asked. 'By the way, I helped myself to a drink when I arrived.' He chuckled. 'You've got some good old malt whisky in your drinks cabinet.'

'Look, Ryker, I told you never to come here. That was the understanding right from the beginning,' Miller said angrily.

'We've got business to discuss. You owe me money.'

'You were paid for the last job.'

Ryker shook his head.

'Yeah, but not enough.' The older man's tone darkened and he took a step towards Miller. 'Listen, I was nearly caught last time. I think some bastard saw me. I'm not going to carry on doing these "little jobs" for you for what you're paying me now, got it? If the law get hold of me they'll throw away the fucking key. Especially with my record.'

Ryker had been in and out of prison for most of his life. A two year stretch for assault, swiftly followed by another for GBH. Then, as he'd got older, he'd graduated to bigger things. His part in a raid on a post office in Lambeth had earned him six years in the Scrubs. Less than two months after his release he was inside again, this time for aggravated assault. He'd been ejected from a pub for harassing customers and had returned the following evening to vent his rage on the landlord with the aid of a baseball bat.

It was during that eighteen-month period that he'd first met Miller. At that time the effects man had been working for the police and he'd been called to Wormwood Scrubs to take photos of a prisoner who was in for child molesting. Somehow, three of the other inmates had managed to corner the man in the showers and had succeeded in first hanging him with nylon string then slicing off his penis with a razor-blade. He'd bled to death.

Ryker had supplied the razor blade.

Miller knew exactly what this big man was capable of and he swallowed hard as Ryker now advanced another step towards him.

'I think it might be an idea to lay off for a while,' said Miller. 'Either that or be more careful.'

'I didn't expect anyone to see me,' Ryker countered angrily. 'Anyway, what the hell do you care? You're only worried in case you go down with me. The prosecution would have a field day with a "celebrity" in the dock. It's in your interests to protect our little business enterprise, and you can protect it by paying me more fucking money.'

'I can't pay you now, I haven't got money on me. Not the amount you're asking for,' Miller told him.

'You haven't heard my new rates yet,' Ryker chuckled. Then, just as quickly, the smile vanished. 'For the next job I want five thousand.'

'No chance,' Miller said, defiantly.

Ryker crossed the room in two giant strides, one powerful hand grabbing Miller by the collar.

'Don't fuck around with me, Miller. Five grand for the next job.'

'And what if there isn't a "next job"?' Miller snarled, pulling away from the older man, his unease temporarily replaced by rage.

'You still owe me more for the last one, I told you, I was lucky to get away. Say two thousand and we'll call it square.'

'You can *say* two thousand but you won't get it,' Miller informed him.

Ryker stepped back, releasing his grip on the other man.

'Two thousand,' he repeated. 'In the next week.'

Miller didn't answer. They merely locked stares for what seemed like an age, then, finally, Ryker turned and headed for the door.

'I'll be in touch, Frank,' he said, smiling. 'You need me.'

Then he was gone.

Miller let out a deep breath, aware that he was trembling slightly.

'Bastard,' he murmured under his breath, the anger boiling within him, but part of that anger was because of his own stupidity. *He* had been the one who'd contacted Ryker in the first place, *he* had offered to pay the man for his services. Miller slammed his fist down on the worktop, realizing that Ryker was right.

If the police were to catch the older man then both he and Miller would be put away.

Something would have to be done.

Forty-four

He'd taken five photos of Susan Lewis on the set that day, discarding the polaroid for a Nikon. Now, as the hands of the clock crawled round to 9.36 p.m., Miller stood in the darkness of his workroom watching as the images gradually formed on the acetate. He swirled it through the developer, the pungent smell filling his nostrils.

With his free hand he held a bottle of Haig which he drank from occasionally, lifting the photos into the tray of fixer. Then, finally he rinsed them with water.

Miller closed his right eye and looked closely at the photos, studying each one in turn.

The aura was present on every one.

But stronger than before, more piercingly bright. It radiated a full inch from all around her face.

Miller rinsed his hands beneath the running tap then flicked on the light, gazing at the pictures. He hadn't mentioned the aura to Susan, nor his long vigil outside her flat the previous night. He had asked her if she lived alone and he'd been informed that she shared a flat with her boyfriend, an out of work actor. She'd been pleasantly surprised by his interest in her private life, if a little puzzled by his incessant questions about her relationship with her boyfriend. Did they row very often? Did it bother him that she was working and he wasn't? Did he ever get violent? Miller himself had finally clammed up, worried that Susan was going to ask why her private life was so important to him.

He looked at the photos once more, tracing the outline of the aura with his index finger.

The loud banging on the front door broke his concentration. He turned, putting down the whisky bottle, wiping his hands on a nearby towel as he headed out of the workroom towards the door, wondering who could be calling on him at this time in the evening. He slowed his pace as he reached the hall.

Could it be Ryker?

No, he reasoned. He wouldn't need to knock. If he wanted to get in he could slip one of the door or window locks.

The knocking continued.

Miller pulled the front door open, his eyes widening in surprise as he saw who his visitor was.

'I'm sorry to call on you so late,' Terri Warner apologized, 'but there's something I think you should know.'

Miller nodded, attempted a smile, then thought better of it. He beckoned her inside, motioned her through into the sitting room. Miller joined her, seating himself in a chair opposite where she sat. He offered her a drink which she accepted.

'I'm sorry if I'm interrupting, I know you're busy working on this film, but it's about the murder last night. You have heard?'

Miller sat forward in his chair.

'I haven't seen a paper today, or heard the radio,' he told her.

She explained about the murder of Mike Hamilton.

'Jesus,' Miller muttered as she gave him the details. 'Did your informant tip you off again?'

She nodded.

'Was the murder another copy-cat killing?' he wanted to know.

'Yes,' she told him. 'The victim was a hitch-hiker as far as anyone can tell. He was battered then burned, just like the victim of Alfred Arthur Rouse. He picked up a hitch-hiker and killed him for no apparent reason. Rouse was hanged in 1931.'

Miller shook his head.

'Why the imitations?' he mused. 'I know the different MOs make it more difficult for the police, but it seems so elaborate. And why more than one murderer? Why not stick to imitating just one killer?'

'Let's just hope he doesn't decide to have a crack at imitating Charles Whitman,' she said, cryptically, expanding when she

212

noticed Miller's vague expression. 'He was an American, obsessed with guns. He climbed to the top of a water tower one morning and shot eighteen people in ninety minutes.'

'Great,' said Miller humourlessly.

Terri rummaged in her handbag and pulled out the tape. She held it before her then tossed it to Miller, who caught it with one hand and looked at her, a puzzled frown on his face.

'Play it,' she told him.

He didn't argue but merely got to his feet, crossed to the stereo and slipped the cassette into the machine. Terri took a hefty swig from her glass as she listened to the messages yet again. Miller looked at her in bewilderment.

'It's the killer,' she told him as he re-wound the tape and played it once more.

'How can you be sure?' he asked.

She didn't like the note of scepticism in Miller's voice.

'The same way you can be sure that you've got the ability to see the aura around a murder victim,' she said challengingly.

Miller smiled thinly and ejected the tape.

'Do you recognize the voice?' he asked.

'There's something familiar about it . . .' She allowed the sentence to trail off.

'What have the police said?'

'I still haven't told them. My boss at the TV station wants me to try and keep in contact with the killer if possible. To let him keep phoning. He thinks he may try to meet me eventually.'

'And then what?' said Miller, tossing the tape back to her. 'Corpse number nine?'

'I don't know,' she said softly, slipping the cassette back into her handbag. There was a long silence finally broken by Terri. 'Look, I think I'd better go now,' she said, getting to her feet. 'I'm sorry if I disturbed you but I wanted you to hear that tape.'

The effects man nodded as he walked to the door with her. They exchanged brief farewells and he watched her as she walked across to her car.

He stood silhouetted in the doorway as she drove off.

But his were not the only eyes that watched.

213

Terri parked her car beside the lift entrance in the underground car park and allowed her head to loll back against the top of the driver's seat. She closed her eyes for a moment, listening to the sound of her engine dying away within the cavernous confines of the subterranean chamber, then she swung herself out of the car and locked it.

Her heels clicked loudly on the stained concrete of the car park, the sound echoing around her. She reached the lift and jabbed the call button watching as the numbers above her lit up and it descended from the ninth floor of the block. It stopped at eight. Again at six. Terri rubbed her eyes wearily as she waited in the oppressive silence.

From behind her she heard the sounds of movement.

Footsteps. Scraping on the concrete.

She spun round, her eyes searching the poorly-lit area for the source of the noise.

She saw nothing, only the white light of the fluorescents reflecting off the bonnets and roofs of parked cars.

The lift continued to descend.

Terri glanced up at the numbers again, feeling curiously vulnerable. Her heart was thudding hard against her ribs.

The lift was still making its tortuous way down.

Fourth floor.

Third.

She heard more movement. Closer to her this time.

Second floor.

She stood with her back to the lift doors, pressed against them, wondering who the hell was down in this gloomy chamber with her. Why they were so silent.

Why they were drawing closer.

First floor.

She could hear breathing, faint but guttural breathing, and she guessed that it must be coming from behind the stone pillar less than ten yards from her.

The lift had reached the ground floor.

She fixed her eyes on that pillar, watching for any sign of movement, her hands clenched into fists, nails digging into her palms.

Could it be some kids, she asked herself? Just trying to scare her. All part of the game.

The breathing slowed, the silence became unendurable.

She chanced a look at the lift indicator and the blasted thing was finally descending towards the basement, towards *her*.

Terri saw movement behind the pillar.

She stifled a moan of terror as a dark shape seemed to detach itself from the concrete and move into view.

She tried to make out the face but it was impossible.

The figure took a step towards her.

The lift doors suddenly slid open and she almost fell in, jabbing the button which would close them. Jabbing it so hard she nearly broke her nail.

The figure remained motionless, finally disappearing from sight as the lift door shut.

Terri let out a long sigh of relief and pushed the button for two floors above her own. If someone was watching her then she wasn't going to make life that easy for him.

Was her imagination running wild? she wondered.

She had seen the figure there. Why hadn't the newcomer approached her rather than skulk behind the pillar? Why, unless he didn't want to be seen.

She reached the floor and stepped out of the lift, hurried to the stairs and descended the two storeys to her flat. Her hands were shaking as she found her key and unlocked the door.

She stepped on the note.

It lay just inside the threshold.

Terri slapped on the lights, anxious to be surrounded by brightness again, then in the glow of the lamp she looked at the note.

It was on a piece of typing paper, folded in half, the letters cut carefully from a book. The letters weren't taken from a newspaper. The print was most definitely from a paperback, that much she could tell from the quality of the paper itself. Each small letter had been painstakingly cut out and stuck together on the sheet of A4.

i hAvE wàtcHEd yOu I wanT to MEeT yOU now

I WiLl conTaCT You AGain Do Not teLL thE pOLicE
I aM WatCHinG

She held the note before her, unable to prevent her hands trembling.

When the phone rang she almost shouted aloud.

For what seemed like an eternity she stood staring at it, finally crossing and picking up the receiver, trying to control the fear in her voice.

There was only silence at the other end.

'Who is this?' she snapped, her voice low.

Breathing. Softly.

'I know you're there you bastard,' she hissed. 'Talk to me.'

'Sleep well,' said the voice. Then a chuckle which raised the hairs on the back of her neck.

The line went dead.

Terri slammed the receiver down and backed away from it.

She sat down in the chair opposite the phone, her eyes never leaving it, one hand still gripping the note.

It was warm inside the flat but Terri felt as if she had been wrapped in a freezing blanket.

She looked at the note again.

And she waited for the phone to ring.

216

Forty-five

Susan Lewis leant back against the headboard, the shooting script held across her lap. As she did so, the sheet slipped from her upper body exposing her breasts. She made to replace it but a hand reached up from beside her and pulled the sheet down once more. Susan chuckled and glanced quickly at Steve Bailey, who was lying on his side looking up at her. He smiled and she sighed when she felt his free hand brush against her knee as it moved steadily higher, stroking the inside of her thigh.

She parted her legs slightly, allowing him easier access, squirming as his eager fingers finally came to rest in the softly curled hair between her legs. Susan didn't stop reading, although little of what she saw was registering now. All that she was aware of was the growing feeling of warmth between her legs, spreading up her body until, as Bailey began tracing the outline of her mound, she also felt her nipples stiffen in anticipation.

He continued his expert manipulations beneath the sheets, his own excitement growing, his penis stiffening as he felt the moistness between Susan's legs.

He knew where to touch her. And how. They had lived together for the past two years, ever since they'd met while making a low budget six-part series for the BBC. Since then, neither of them had been inundated with offers of work. Bailey himself had only managed to land parts in commercials and a walk-on part in the last series of *Minder*. His agent had found him work modelling clothes for catalogues, but it certainly wasn't the big time. Susan, on the other hand, had at least worked steadily albeit unspectacularly. A succession of small parts in series and films and now the part in *Astro-cannibals*. It was her money that was keeping them and that was something which Bailey didn't like. At thirty-one, three years older than Susan, he felt that it was about time *he* broke through. He wasn't asking for the lead in the next Spielberg movie. Not just yet anyway. But he deserved more than he was getting.

He brushed a strand of his long brown hair from his face then resumed his explorations beneath the sheets.

Susan lay back further, the script still gripped in both hands, allowing him to stroke her pubic hair with his index finger, pausing occasionally to glide along the outside of her swelling lips. She drew in a long breath as he disappeared beneath the sheets, his tongue flicking across her pelvic bone then down into the valley between her lips, anxious to taste her wetness.

She made a show of continuing to read, but as his lips fastened around her clitoris she finally gave up and surrendered to his attentions. She felt his tongue glide expertly over her distended lips, outlining each fold and crease, adding his own saliva to the slippery juices between her legs. He coaxed some of that moisture onto his fingertips, rubbing it softly into the tops of her thighs, trickling the slippery digits down her legs and back again until finally he began to probe at the pink mouth of her vagina, his tongue slipping inside for precious seconds before flicking up to gently lash her throbbing clitoris.

He clambered between her legs, rising before her, ready to slide his own rock-hard member into that beckoning cleft.

She shook her head and held his shoulders, keeping him away. Ensuring that he didn't penetrate her.

'Not tonight,' she whispered. 'Carry on doing what you were doing,' she sighed, leaning forward, licking some of her own juices from his lips.

Bailey looked disappointed and rolled from between her legs, laying on his back, his erection poking up at her. She squeezed his penis gently but he knocked her hand away.

'What's wrong, Steve?' she asked, recognizing the look of irritation on his face.

'*Not tonight*,' he said acidly, mimicking her soft plea. 'I'm surprised you've got time for anything these days, not since you started working on this film.' He picked up the script and glanced at it. 'It's a piece of shit, Sue.'

'It's work,' she protested. 'And one of us has got to earn some money.'

Bailey regarded her angrily for a moment.

'Why the hell are you studying the script, you don't have to speak anyway. When the film's released no one's even going to see your face. You'll be covered in make-up.'

'This part might not be much, but the director was saying that he's going back to the States as soon as he's finished to make another film and he's asked me to go over and audition for one of the leading parts.'

'Great,' said Bailey, irritably.

'I thought you'd be pleased for me. For both of us.'

'Why? So I can carry on lazing around while you pay the fucking bills. Do you know how that makes me feel, Sue?' he demanded.

'For Christ's sake, what does it matter as long as one of us is working? I didn't think all this macho bullshit bothered you, or do you think that you should be earning more because you're the man?' There was scorn in her words.

'So you're off to the States eh?' he said. 'For how long?'

'I don't know. It depends whether I get the part or not,' she told him.

'And if you do I'll be lucky if I see you again.'

'What's got into you?' she demanded. 'I tell you a piece of good news and you act like it's an announcement for a funeral. I didn't realize that you were so jealous.' She swung herself out of bed but Bailey caught her by the arm and pulled her back. She shook loose of his grip, angry when she saw the red marks on her forearm.

'I think it'd be a good idea if I slept in the spare room tonight,' she told him. 'I don't think there's enough room in bed for me *and* your ego.'

'Are you sure that the director only wants you to test for a part out there?' Bailey said.

'What's that supposed to mean?' she demanded.

'Well, a big star like you,' his voice was heavy with scorn.

'You're bound to be in demand.'

She shook her head and reached for the script.

'I think I'll come back when you're in a better mood, Steve,' Susan said, picking up the slim folder.

Bailey knocked it from her grasp, the pages scattering over both the floor and the bed.

'You idiot,' she snapped, retrieving some of them.

'Leave them,' he snarled, gripping her wrist hard.

She tried to pull away but he held firm, squeezing so tightly that she was afraid he would break her wrist.

'Get off me,' she yelled and lashed out at him, her nails raking his face, drawing blood as they gouged the flesh just below his right eye.

'You cow,' he hissed, seeing the crimson fluid on his finger-tips. He leapt off the bed and struck her hard across the face with the back of his hand, a blow which sent her reeling. As she fell to the floor of the bedroom, Bailey advanced upon her, fists clenched. She waited until he was within striking distance then lashed out with her bare foot, kicking him hard in the groin. He let out a strangled cry and clutched at his testicles, his rage now reaching even greater heights as she tried to scuttle from the room. He grabbed her by the hair, his hand slipping, ripping her dressing gown so that she too was naked.

He pulled her to the floor, pinning her beneath him.

'Get off,' she screamed and spat in his face but Bailey seemed not to notice. As the long streamer of sputum hung from his cheek like a mucoid tear he fastened his hands around her throat and squeezed.

Susan felt a twinge of fear as Bailey's thumbs gouged her windpipe and she beat even more frenziedly at his powerful arms, but the effort was useless. There was a rage in his eyes. Blind, uncontrollable rage which seemed to add strength to his grip. He straddled her, his erection sticking up between her breasts, his knees pinning her arms. Susan wanted to cry out but the vice-like grip around her throat prevented her doing so. She felt as if someone was pumping her head full of air, as if her skull was expanding and she fought to catch her breath, aware now of white stars dancing before her eyes.

Bailey raised her head a few inches then slammed it back down onto the ground, sending a fresh jolt of pain through her head. He repeated the action, never once loosening his hold on her throat. Susan struggled more forlornly now, making a last desperate attempt to push him off. If only she could weaken his hold for a second, get away from him, lock him in the bedroom. If only . . .

She felt waves of unconsciousness sweeping over her as he slammed her head down once more, and this time there was a dull crack as the impact broke bone. Susan knew that she was not going to be able to fight back now, the effort seemed too great, the pain too intense and Bailey still leered above her, his teeth clenched, lips drawn back in a snarl of rage.

She managed to pull one arm free, but Bailey hardly felt the blow she dealt him. The power, the life, was draining rapidly from her now.

She tasted blood in her mouth but didn't even realize that she'd bitten her tongue. The crimson fluid ran in a thin stream from one corner of her mouth as she gasped for air.

Her body began to spasm wildly and she groaned as the final shrouds of blackness began to envelop her. For in those final seconds she realized that she was dying. She tried to pray but soon all thoughts of God were forgotten. Only the fear remained. The awful certainty that in a moment or two she would be dead.

Bailey lifted her head once more, staring deep into her glazed eyes for endless seconds before smashing her head down with even greater force. A force which finally caused her to black out and which also opened a large gash at the back of her skull. Blood began to soak into the carpet and he loosened his hold on her throat as the muscular jerks grew in intensity. Her legs stiffened for precious seconds, the muscles bulging, toes twisted upwards, and he actually felt himself lifted by the sudden rigidity which filled her body. Then it merely collapsed and he heard the soft hiss as her sphincter muscle opened.

The pungent stench of excrement filled the air as Bailey finally released his grip on Susan Lewis. He stepped back, his eyes riveted to the body which lay before him like some kind of discarded mannequin.

For what seemed like an eternity he stared at it, then, with as much speed as he could muster, he began to gather up his clothes.

Forty-six

'Still no answer,' the girl shouted. 'Do you want me to keep trying?'

Phillip Dickinson looked across at his assistant and nodded.

'Give it another five minutes, then forget it,' he called back, glancing at his watch.

'It's nice to work with reliable people isn't it, Phil?' Miller said sarcastically.

'Fuck you, Frank, it's too early in the morning,' the director snapped irritably. 'She's probably on her way here now.' He looked at his watch again, wondering why Susan Lewis was almost an hour late arriving at the studio.

It was Miller who first noticed Detective Inspector Gibson as the policeman entered the sound stage, glancing around him at the sets. The effects man frowned and pocketed his hip flask, surprised by the appearance of the policeman. He saw a stage-hand approach the DI, saw Gibson flip open the slim leather wallet which carried his identification. The stage-hand nodded in the direction of Dickinson and stepped back.

As Gibson drew closer he and Miller exchanged glances and the effects man turned to move away.

'Stay, Frank,' Gibson said. 'I need to talk to you.'

Dickinson looked bemused as the DI finally introduced himself.

'What can I do for you?' the director asked.

Gibson told him about the murder of Susan Lewis.

'We picked up her boyfriend about two hours later,' the DI concluded. 'He confessed to it, told us everything that happened.'

Miller swallowed hard, his mind suddenly filled with the vision of those photos he'd taken of Susan Lewis. Of the aura.

Dickinson could only shake his head.

Gibson looked at Miller.

'I want to talk to you, Frank,' he said. 'In private.'

Miller motioned for the policeman to follow him and they walked together through the maze of props and cameras set up all around the sound stage. Technicians glanced at them as they passed. Miller finally led the policeman out of the studio towards the make-up trailer. He fumbled in his pocket for the keys as they walked.

'I thought you weren't bothered whether you ever saw me again,' he said.

'This isn't a social call, Frank,' Gibson told him. He jabbed a finger in the direction of a waiting Fiesta and Miller looked over to see DS Chandler scramble out of the vehicle. He was carrying an attaché case. As Miller opened the door of the trailer, he joined them.

'I could say I told you so,' Miller said smugly. 'About Susan Lewis. But I'll resist the temptation.'

'Very funny,' Gibson said, taking the case from Chandler. He flipped it open and Miller saw a pile of photos inside, some of them yellowed and curled at the corners. 'I want to know more about this so called aura around murder victims.'

'Why the sudden interest?' Miller demanded.

'Look, stop messing about and tell me what you know,' the DI hissed.

'I took some photos, you know that,' the effects man began. 'The three people I photographed all had a kind of aura around them when the prints were developed. All three have since been murdered. I think that I can spot potential murder victims from their photos.'

'This is bullshit,' said Chandler, shaking his head.

Gibson shot him an acid glance then returned his attention to Miller.

'That applies to *all* murder victims?' he asked. 'If you see the photos, you can pick them out?'

Miller nodded.

'Convince me,' said Gibson and dumped the pile of pictures on the table in front of him. 'There are twenty pictures there, some of them are murder victims, some aren't. All the photos were taken *before* the victims were killed. Go on, Frank. Impress me.' Gibson stepped back, watching as Miller picked up the first of the photos. He closed his right eye and scrutinized the print. It was a woman, late twenties, pretty. The photo was old.

'Victim,' he said unhesitatingly, his eye picking out the aura which surrounded her.

He began working his way through the pile.

A man in his fifties, balding, eyes deep-set.

'Victim,' Miller pronounced.

Another young woman.

He shook his head and placed the photo on a different pile before continuing.

An old photo. An older woman. She carried the aura.

'Victim.'

It took him less than five minutes to complete the task. There were five photos on the pile he had designated as victims.

'Well,' he said, sipping from his hip flask. 'Do I win a prize?'

'I still say this is bullshit,' Chandler interjected, his comment now directed at Gibson. 'He could have recognized the victims from books or newspaper articles.'

'Do you know any of them, Frank?' Gibson asked. 'Have you ever seen any of the faces before?'

Miller shook his head.

'Just tell me who they are?' he said.

Gibson sighed and held up the photos one at a time. As he did so, Miller saw the aura around each one again.

'Margery Gardner, murdered by Neville Heath in 1946. Jack McVittie, stabbed to death by Reggie Kray in 1967.' The list went on. 'Ruth Fuerst, murdered by John Christie in 1943.' And on. 'John Kilbride, victim of the Moors Murderers.' He held up the final picture. 'Donald Skepper, killed by The Black Panther in February 1974.' There was one last photo. One which the policeman had taken not from the attaché case but from his inside pocket. He handed it to Miller.

225

'Susan Lewis,' he said. 'Murdered last night.'

Miller drank from his hip flask, glancing again at the photos, each victim surrounded by that infernal aura.

'Now will you believe me?' he asked.

Gibson didn't answer, he merely gathered up the photos and put them back into the case which he then handed to Chandler.

'He guessed,' the DS said, scornfully.

'He was right,' Gibson snapped.

'You're more stupid than I thought if you believe that,' said the older man.

'Wait for me in the car,' Gibson told his assistant.

Chandler hesitated.

'Leave us alone.' The DI inclined his head towards the door. 'Go on.'

The DS left reluctantly, glaring first at Miller then his own superior.

'You're still no use to me, Frank, even if I do believe you. Jesus, if the commissioner thought that I believed what you'd told me he'd have me pounding a bloody beat again.'

The two men regarded each other in silence for long moments then Gibson finally spoke again.

'If you get any more information like this, about possible victims, let me know,' he said, wearily, heading for the trailer door.

'Can I give you some advice, Stuart?' Miller said. 'Watch Chandler.'

The DI nodded almost imperceptibly then left, closing the door behind him. Miller was left alone in the trailer.

Alone with just his thoughts.

And fears.

Forty-seven

He had taken the photograph from Terri's flat during his first visit, pocketing it while she was out of the room with all the speed and assurance of a thief.

The picture had been taken, Miller guessed, three or four years ago. Her hair was shorter, her face a little fatter. But the feature which remained constant was the almost hypnotic perfection of her eyes. Miller had studied those eyes. He had studied the entire photo carefully. For it was not Terri's beauty which had caused him to steal the photograph, it was his need to know the answer to a question which had plagued him since they met.

He had to know whether or not she carried the aura.

'I think it's time you told the police,' said Miller, holding the note before him.

Terri, legs curled beneath her on the sofa, merely looked at him as he sat forward in the chair, the whisky tumbler gripped in his free hand.

'I think he was here the other night when I got back from your house,' she told him, recounting the episode in the underground car park. Miller listened intently, his eyes never leaving Terri as she told him of the man in the shadows who had merely stood watching her in that forbidding subterranean chamber. Even in the comfort and light of her flat she felt a shiver of fear ripple up her spine at the recollection. Miller waited until she'd finished speaking then got to his feet and crossed to the large picture window in the sitting room. He looked out into the night, peering at lights which glimmered in other flats and houses nearby or at the headlights of vehicles below as they pierced the gloom. The sky was mottled grey with rain clouds, the odd drop pattering the glass as if to give warning of what was to come.

'He says he's watching you,' Miller muttered. 'That must mean he's pretty close.'

'Thanks for reassuring me,' Terri said.

'Or he's bluffing. He wants you to *think* that he's watching you.' He took a swig from his glass. 'Either way, I think you should call the police in. This has gone far enough.'

'My boss isn't going to be very pleased. It'll blow the story wide open.'

'Fuck him, it's not him who's being threatened.'

'That's the point, whoever is sending these messages *hasn't* threatened me. Not once. I think he *wants* to make contact. If I go to the police now then I'll lose him.'

'Or he'll take his story to another TV station or newspaper,' Miller said sarcastically. 'That's your real worry, isn't it? You're as concerned about ratings as your bloody boss. You've made a name for yourself reporting these murders and you don't want to blow your chances of wrapping up the story by frightening the killer off. It'll make a great headline though, Terri. "Woman reporter murdered by maniac she hoped to interview".' He shook his head.

'I suppose I could ask what business it was of yours if I want to risk my life for a story. Couldn't I?'

'You could also tell me to get out of your flat.'

She nodded.

'You're probably right, Frank,' she sighed. 'Maybe it *is* time that I called in the police, but I should tell my boss about the note. He has a right to know. He's the one who assigned me to this job in the first place.' She was already on her feet and heading for the phone. Miller watched as she dialled, then he returned to gazing out into the night.

Terri could get no answer at Bob Johnson's home number so she tried the studio. It was snatched up on the third ring.

'News Update, Bob Johnson speaking.'

'Bob, it's Terri. Listen.' She quickly relayed the news of what had happened and Miller listened idly as she spoke, his back to

228

her. Every now and then he would hear Johnson's raised voice on the other end of the line.

'I think it would be better if we let the police handle it from here,' Terri said.

'No way,' Johnson snapped. 'We agreed that you wouldn't involve the police.'

'Unless it was absolutely necessary,' she reminded him.

'But you said yourself that he hasn't made threats.'

'Look, Bob, the phone calls are bad enough but when it comes to finding notes pushed under my door . . .' She let the sentence trail off.

'The minute he gets an idea the police are on to him you can kiss the story goodbye,' Johnson snapped.

'Well, I'm going to have to take that chance. I've been discussing it with Frank and . . .'

Johnson cut her short, his voice low but seething with anger.

'Who?' he demanded. 'You've been talking about this to someone else?'

'It's a free country, Bob. I needed some advice.'

'What was wrong with asking me?' he demanded, and Terri moved the phone away from her ear slightly, surprised at the vehemence in his voice. 'Who the hell is Frank, anyway?' he demanded.

Terri frowned.

'Look, we were discussing the murderer, not my private life. What the hell does it matter who Frank is?'

Miller turned slightly at the mention of his name. He saw the anger on Terri's face, heard Johnson's voice, even louder now.

'Did *he* tell you to call the police?' Johnson demanded.

'No one *told* me. We were discussing it, and I think that it might be a good idea if they knew what was happening and what's been going on with the phone calls. They might be able to trace the voice. Voice-print it.'

There was an angry silence at the other end of the line. Terri was aware only of Johnson's breathing.

She was about to speak again when she heard his voice. Flat and cold as steel.

'Do it then,' he hissed. 'Do as your *friend* tells you.'

Terri stepped back in surprise as the receiver was slammed down. She looked across at Miller and shrugged.

'What is it with him?' Miller asked.

Terri could only shake her head. She seated herself once more, running the index finger of one hand around the rim of her glass.

Bob Johnson sat at his desk and glared at the phone, the knot of muscles at the side of his jaw pulsing angrily.

For what seemed like an eternity he remained in that position, fists clenched, his body shaking with suppressed rage. Then, with a roar of fury, he brought one fist crashing down on the desk top.

'Bitch,' he hissed. 'Fucking bitch.'

How dare she go to the police? They had agreed that the law were not to be involved. This was her story.

Their story.

No one must be allowed to come between Terri and this story.

No one must be allowed to come between him and Terri.

There must be no interference. No police. No outsiders.

He could not, *would* not, permit it.

Forty-eight

As he climbed into his car Miller had no idea he was being watched.

The effects man guided the Granada up the ramp, out of the underground car park.

The driver of the pursuing vehicle kept a respectable distance, eyes never leaving the Granada. As if joined by some invisible tow-rope, the two cars threaded their way through traffic.

It had been a couple of minutes after eleven when Miller finally left Terri's flat. The drive back to his own house, he estimated, would take less than thirty minutes. He pulled up at a set of traffic lights, tapping gently on the wheel as he waited for them to change to green.

Behind him, the other vehicle also waited.

The driver watched Miller's car, coaxing the following car into pursuit once more as Miller moved off.

As he drove, Miller thought back to his conversation with Gibson and the incident with the photos. It had been no accident that he'd recognized each victim, every one of them marked out by the glowing aura. He knew now that the ability was his alone. He grunted. Ability? Was that the word?

Gift, maybe? Or curse?

Was it some kind of second sight, he wondered? But then quickly dismissed his own idea. No, there was nothing psychic involved. The answer lay in celluloid, emulsion and his own transplanted eye. He could *see* the victims.

Behind him, the other car kept up its steady pursuit.

Miller was less than half a mile from his home when the vehicle that had been following him began to accelerate.

At first Miller thought that the car was going to overtake, and he slowed down to allow it free passage. However, he frowned when he realized that the driver had no intention of passing by. The car bumped Miller's Granada gently and stayed where it was.

'What the . . .' Miller hissed, glancing round at the other driver, but the blinding light from the pursuing vehicle's headlamps made it impossible to see inside the other car.

Miller could see the outline of a Capri but that was all.

The pursuing car accelerated and once again Miller felt the slight impact as his bumper was nudged.

'Bloody idiot,' he snarled and put his foot on the gas, pulling away from the other car. Whoever was driving was probably drunk, he reasoned. Either that or they'd mistaken him for someone else.

Miller drove on.

The Capri kept coming.

Just what was this clown playing at, Miller wondered, staring into his rear-view mirror. The other car was speeding up once more, swerving out from behind the Granada this time, pulling up alongside it.

Miller wound down his window, preparing to shout some abuse at the other driver, when the Capri suddenly swerved across the path of the Granada.

Miller slammed his foot down hard on the brake, the front wheels locking as the car skidded three or four yards. His seat-belt gripped him hard, flinging him back against his seat, knocking the wind from him. He sucked in a deep lungful of air, his head spinning.

The Capri was parked about ten yards ahead, its tail-lights winking impishly, as if challenging Miller to get out. He wasn't slow to rise to that challenge. He flung open his door and strode towards the other vehicle.

As he reached the Capri he saw the driver clamber out.

Miller froze, looking into the face of John Ryker.

The older man was smiling.

'I reckon I should have been a private eye,' he said. 'I've been following you for half an hour and you never twigged.'

'What do you want, Ryker?' the effects man snapped. 'I thought we'd said all we had to say to one another.'

A car sped past, its headlamps momentarily illuminating Ryker's features.

'I told you the other night, we've still got business to attend to. You owe me money. Two thousand quid, and I want it before the end of the week.'

'And I told you that's impossible,' Miller hissed, turning away.

He saw nothing.

He felt Ryker's strong hand grip his shoulder then, in the stillness of the night, he heard the familiar *swish-click* of a flick knife. Before he knew what was happening the point was pressed beneath his chin.

'Go on then, kill me,' Miller said, defiantly. 'That's not going to get you your money, is it?' He swallowed hard, feeling the point of the blade against his Adam's apple as he did so.

Ryker pressed harder.

'There are worse things I can do than kill you,' he said softly and released his grip.

Another car passed and the two men locked stares. Then all was darkness again.

Ryker began walking towards his car.

'There are worse things than death,' he said and chuckled.

The sound raised the hairs at the back of Miller's neck. He stood immobile as the older man slid behind the wheel of the Capri and started up the engine. He spun the wheel and screeched away past Miller, who watched the tail-lights of the car disappear into the night. He stood there a moment longer, massaging the soft skin beneath his chin, feeling the warm blood where the blade had nicked him.

He shuddered and clambered into his own car.

Another ten minutes and he was home.

In the gloom of his workroom, lit only by the red light, everything looked as though it had been soaked in blood.

The burn victim stared sightlessly at his creator.

On the walls, hundreds of dead eyes seemed to gleam from the photos which recorded their deaths. As Miller glanced at them he could see the aura around those who had met their ends at the hands of others.

Photos of George Cook and Penny Steele now hung there with the other celluloid nightmares.

There were three pictures of Susan Lewis.

Smiling. Attractive. Dead.

From a nearby drawer, Miller took the photo of Terri Warner.

He held it before him, closed his right eye, and gazed at it.

Forty-nine

'You found this note this morning?'

Detective Inspector Stuart Gibson held the piece of paper before him like an accusation, glancing first at Terri then at the words on the note.

As before, they had been cut from a book, each letter methodically attached to the A4 sheet.

I aM stILl watChINg i wiLL cONtaCt yOU sooN

The GAmE iS NeArlY oVeR I will CaLl yOu

No pOliCE

Gibson handed the note to Chandler who scanned it briefly and nodded.

'Did you call us as soon as you found it?' he asked Terri.

She nodded.

'Does anyone else know about it?' the Detective Sergeant persisted.

'Like who?' she snapped.

'Boyfriend. Lover . . .'

She cut him short. 'No one.'

Chandler looked at her warily for a moment then crossed the room to the phone. A man dressed in an immaculately-pressed blue suit had the device in pieces and was attaching a small microphone to the earpiece. Chandler watched the man at work.

'Why didn't you notify us earlier?' Gibson wanted to know. 'About the phone calls and the other note? We could have tapped your phone. We might even have caught the bastard by now.'

Terri ran a hand through her hair and padded through into the kitchen, Gibson followed, watching as she poured herself a cup of coffee. She offered him one and he joined her, pushing the kitchen door closed, shutting out Chandler and the surveillance man.

'I didn't want to get in touch with you,' Terri told the policeman. 'I probably wouldn't have done this time, but to be quite honest, I'm scared.'

Gibson sipped his coffee and looked at the TV reporter.

'Why do you think he picked you?' he asked. 'Out of all the newspaper and TV people he could have chosen. Why you?'

'That's what Frank Miller said . . .' Terri smiled humourlessly, but the expression faded rapidly as she saw the policeman's reaction.

'Do you know Frank Miller?' he asked suspiciously.

She nodded.

'How is he involved in this?' Gibson wanted to know.

'He approached *me*. You could say we exchanged ideas about this case.'

'How much does Miller know about the killings and what's been going on?'

Terri frowned, surprised at the harshness of tone in Gibson's voice.

'Does it really matter?' she asked. 'You ought to be grateful to him, if not for his prompting I probably wouldn't have got in touch with you. He advised me to call in the law.' She took a sip of her coffee. She went on to explain about the possibility of making a story out of the calls, of finally meeting the killer.

'That wouldn't be a good idea, Miss Warner,' Gibson told her. 'Just leave it in our hands now.'

'I'm not dropping this here,' Terri said defiantly. 'I called you lot in for protection, but I still intend meeting the killer.'

'Not a chance,' Gibson told her. 'I told you, this is our concern now. You take the calls if he rings again, but nothing more.'

Terri didn't answer.

'I'm going to set up a twenty-four-hour surveillance team around this building. If he comes anywhere near then we'll get him.' The DI took another swig of coffee, warming his hands around the mug.

'There's another thing,' he said. 'I'd like you to give us a spare key to your flat. If he should break in for any reason or try to leave any more messages I'd like one of my men on the spot. You don't have to agree to *that* stipulation of course.'

Terri shrugged, got to her feet and crossed to one of the kitchen cabinets. She opened it and produced a key from a small dish.

'My spare,' she told Gibson, handing him the object.

They both turned as there was a knock on the door.

Chandler walked in.

'Sorry to interrupt,' he said sarcastically. 'Surveillance are finished.'

Gibson got to his feet, following his assistant through into the sitting room.

'If he calls,' he told Terri, 'try and keep him on the line as long as possible so we can get a trace going. There'll be men nearby at all times.'

'I hope they're discreet,' she said, smiling.

Gibson nodded then he and his two colleagues left, the DI pausing momentarily at the door.

'There's nothing more you can do now,' he said. 'Just wait for him to call.'

Terri nodded and closed the door behind her. She stood against it for a moment then crossed to the large picture window in the sitting room and gazed out at the other flats and houses which surrounded her. She shuddered involuntarily, wondering if at this moment someone was out there.

Watching.

Waiting.

The lift descended slowly from the fifth floor on its way to the basement car park.

Chandler lit up a cigarette, the smoke wafting in Gibson's direction. The DI coughed and waved a hand in front of him.

'How many men are you putting on her?' Chandler asked.

'It depends how many I can spare,' Gibson told him, glancing up as the lift passed the second floor.

'What if you frighten the killer off?'

'It's going to take more than a couple of plain-clothes men to frighten *this* bugger off,' Gibson said. He turned to look at his colleague as the lift reached the basement. 'You did surveillance work for the Vice Squad, didn't you?'

'So?'

'So, I need an experienced man. You just got yourself a job, Chandler,' Gibson chuckled. He reached into his pocket and handed the DS the key to Terri's flat. 'In case she's not in when you need to get inside.'

Chandler looked at the key then closed his fist around it.

Fifty

The street was almost deserted.

The figure walked slowly along the carefully-tended path, past immaculately kept hedges and fences, the boundaries of gardens lovingly cared for. Apart from the car which the figure had clambered out of there were only two vehicles parked in the street. Neither attended.

It was almost 2.30 p.m. Another hour and the children would be leaving school. As it was, mothers were out and about taking advantage of the respite, shopping or chatting or perhaps even tending gardens that looked as if they'd been lifted straight from the pages of a magazine.

The figure glanced from side to side every now and then but saw only one other moving occupant of the street. A woman dressed in a blue jogging suit was pulling some weeds from the front of her carefully-tended hedge. She had her back to the figure.

She never saw the stranger pass her on the opposite side of the road.

The figure paused, glancing across at the woman for a few seconds, then continued, finally reaching the front of the house which it was looking for.

Frank Miller's house, like most of the other dwellings along the road, was protected from prying eyes by a high fence, but the gate was open and the figure slipped through, glancing back briefly to check that the woman in the blue jogging suit had not seen, but she was still preoccupied with her weeds. The figure approached the house unchallenged, noticing that the garage door was also open. There was no sign of Miller's car. He would be at the studio.

That was how it was meant to be.

The figure moved with disquieting ease and speed around the side of the house, finding shelter in the shadows cast by tall trees.

There, surrounded by the stillness, the figure stood gazing at the small window before it. The tree and fence acted as a perfect barrier from the prying eyes of any neighbours who might be at home, but the figure worked quickly and assuredly on the window, sliding a short-bladed knife between the frame and the jamb, working away expertly until the lock was broken. The window swung inwards a couple of inches and the figure hauled itself through the gap, pushing the glass partition back further until it was possible to slide right through.

Inside the house it was deathly silent.

Particles of dust twisted and fell in the thin shafts of light which had forced their way past the curtains. The figure got up and turned to the left, towards the sitting room. The door was open, the contents of the room exposed.

The figure stood in the doorway for a moment then advanced into the room, towards the standard lamp which stood behind one chair.

The intruder gripped the lamp by its wooden shaft, wielding it like a club, raising it into the air. It stood for a moment, then brought the lamp crashing down on top of the TV set, cracking the cabinet. The second blow shattered the screen and glass sprayed into the room. From the mantlepiece vases were sent flying into the air, one of them smashing against a wall, the other exploding into a dozen pieces before it even hit the ground. A mirror above the fireplace was brought down with a fearsome crash, huge shards of glass breaking away from the reflective oval.

The intruder turned, pushing over the sofa, kicking a small cabinet until the door came off. Bottles spilled out from within, each one then dutifully smashed. Liquor of all colours and varieties spilled across the carpet.

The figure overturned the two chairs in the room then tossed the standard lamp aside, watching as it crashed into the electric

240

fire. Satisfied with the destruction in the sitting room, the intruder headed for the kitchen.

There it pulled out drawers, scattering cutlery all over the floor. Plates were sent crashing to the ground until the lino resembled crazy paving. Glasses were swept from cabinets to shatter amidst the other debris. Once the cabinets were empty the intruder tugged on the doors, finally ripping them from their hinges, tossing the broken partitions about like matchwood.

The orgy of destruction continued upstairs.

Clothes were torn from hangers and shredded by the short-bladed knife. Pillows were ripped and slashed by the steel until feathers filled the air like snow. The bed itself was torn and gouged with a ferocity that made even the intruder pant heavily. The smell of sweat began to fill the air as the figure ventured downstairs again towards the one room which had so far escaped such awesomely destructive attention.

The intruder found the door of Miller's workroom locked but it was only a momentary inconvenience. The lock was picked with the blade and the figure kicked open the door, advancing into the room with an eagerness bordering on glee. As if it were drunk with its own ability to create damage, intoxicated by the ferocious rampage which it had enjoyed.

But now, inside the workroom, the intruder found that it was engulfed by new feelings.

The walls, bedecked with a legacy of death and suffering, seemed to close in on the intruder as surely as if they'd been pushed forward. The endless array of photos. The catalogue of black and white horror which decorated the room like some kind of vile wallpaper caused the figure to freeze. Mesmerized, the intruder looked slowly around.

Sightless eyes glared back accusingly.

The corpse with the head wound looked on impassively, mouth open in silent reproach.

The flayed woman sat immobile, body exposed to the gaze of this newcomer.

The burn victim, face a contorted blackened mess, looked on blindly with one gleaming eye.

241

The intruder crossed to the flayed woman and slowly reached out a hand to touch the synthetic flesh. It was as cold and clammy as death but the intruder moved an inquisitory hand further up the bloodied arm to the shoulder and then across to the breast. To the latex, prosthetic mound lined with fake veins and raw with nauseatingly realistic blood. The hand of the figure closed around that cold lump, savouring the feel of the imitation flesh.

The smell of latex was strong.

The intruder touched the hair, feeling the softness of the willowy strands even though they were nylon. Half of the rubber scalp was bald, burned black and hairless, modelled to perfection.

The breathing of the figure slowed as it moved away from the flayed woman to the burn victim, running shaking finger-tips over each twisted knot of fake flesh, every ragged scar and seared disfigurement.

Dear God, there was beauty in those abominations.

The intruder leaned close to the gunshot victim, pushing an index finger into the bullet hole itself, marvelling at the feel of the rubberized flesh. How cold yet pliant it felt.

How real.

The back of the head was open, the hair ripped away to expose what was meant to be the exit wound. And through that could be seen the greyish-red mess which represented the brain. This brain was hard rubber, yet it felt gloriously real. The intruder cupped the back of the model's head with one hand and gently toyed with the flaps of fake skin around the exit hole.

The severed head, propped up in a dish on top of a filing cabinet, looked on silently.

From the models, the intruder looked at the photos which covered the walls. The endless shots of death, pain and mutilation. A testament to the ultimate horror which faces everyone. Violent death.

Stabbings. Shootings. Burnings.

Every twisted deviation in human imagination was there, immortalized on shiny ten-by-eight.

Decapitation. Dismemberment. Evisceration.

The invention was endless.

But it was the figures which the intruder finally returned its attention to. Those life-size monuments to a mind on the verge of breakdown.

All thoughts of destruction passed from the mind of the intruder. These models were not to be destroyed.

The intruder moved close to the flayed woman again and stroked her bloodied cheek, enjoying the coldness of her artificial body.

Such beauty.

Fifty-one

The phone was about the only thing undamaged and Miller sat for what seemed like hours in the remains of his sitting room with the device cradled in his lap.

He had checked upstairs, checked the kitchen, and had found the terrible destruction everywhere except the workroom, but now he sat alone in the lounge, surrounded by debris, his face pale. Twice he raised the phone, ready to call the police, and twice he replaced the receiver, allowing himself a moment or two for thought.

The house was a shambles. Whoever had wrought the destruction had been thorough. The bastard. But why had they not wrecked the workroom? The question plagued Miller's mind. The things he valued most were in there, and yet it had remained untouched.

Almost.

He raised the receiver and punched out three nines, asking for the police when the voice at the other end enquired which service he required, but before he could give his name and address he pressed his fingers down on the cradle, cutting off the call. No, he told himself, this was no emergency. Besides, he wanted someone on the job he knew.

He jabbed out the digits which made up DI Stuart Gibson's number, waiting patiently for the phone to be picked up, gazing around at the wreckage in his sitting room. Finally, he heard Gibson's voice.

Miller told him what he had discovered, what had been done to his house. The extent of the damage.

Gibson said that he would be there as quickly as he could.

Miller hung up, then got to his feet and wandered down the corridor to his workroom, still puzzled that the intruder should have left his inner sanctum in such good order.

If it hadn't been for the fact that he knew he'd left the door locked, Miller might not even have known that anyone had been in there.

The rest of the house had been destroyed. Not ransacked, not searched. There had been no theft. Destruction had been the sole motive.

The effects man massaged his chin slowly.

But if that was so, why had the model of the flayed woman been taken?

'You're sure that's all that's gone?'

Gibson looked at his former colleague who was staring at the chair where the model had previously been sitting.

'There was seventy pounds upstairs in my bedroom,' Miller said. 'It wasn't touched. The figure was the only thing stolen.'

Around them, fingerprints men were busily dusting for any clues.

Miller wandered out of the room, back towards the lounge where more plain-clothes men were examining the wreckage, hoping to find even a strand of stray hair or a particle of material.

'I'd ask you to take a seat,' said Miller, 'but, as you can see, there aren't any.' He smiled thinly and took a swig from his hip flask.

'Can you think of anyone who might have done this, Frank?' Gibson wanted to know.

'No,' Miller lied, turning away from the DI. 'Look, Stuart, I don't care about the damage, I just want that mannequin back.'

'Why the hell is that so important. Your house is wrecked and all you're bothered about is some dummy.' He exhaled wearily. There was a long silence between the two men, finally broken by the policeman. 'How well do you know Terri Warner?'

Miller looked at Gibson warily.

'Do you know her as a friend? A boyfriend? A lover?' the DI persisted.

'What difference does it make *how* I know her? She's got

245

nothing to do with what happened here,' Miller said, gesturing around him.

'We've got her flat under surveillance and her phone's tapped. She said it was *you* who advised her to call us in.'

'That's right. I thought she needed protection. Whether your boys will be able to give it to her is another matter.'

'I've put Chandler on it. At least it keeps him out of *my* hair.' There was another long silence then the policeman continued. 'Do you know of anyone who might not want you to see her, Frank? I'm just wondering if whoever broke in here today was trying to warn you off. Maybe there's a boyfriend somewhere she hasn't told you about, somebody who fancies her and feels threatened by you.'

'You tell me, Stuart, you're the policeman. Like I said, I can live with this damage, but I want that fucking model found.' There was a hard edge to Miller's words that Gibson wasn't slow to pick up.

'What's so special about it?' he asked.

'All my work means a lot to me. The models that I keep here are particularly special.' He took another swig from his hip flask.

'I'd just like to know who would want to steal something like that,' Gibson said, bemused.

Miller didn't answer.

Fifty-two

DS Alan Chandler glanced at the clock on the dashboard and grunted irritably.

Nearly eight o'clock and still no sign of Terri Warner. He reached into his jacket pocket and pulled out a pack of Rothmans, lighting one. His companion, Sergeant Derek Grant, glanced across at his superior then returned his attention to the flats across the road. Grant was in his late thirties, on the thin side of slim, his closely-cropped hair making his head look a little too large. As he sat behind the wheel of the Astra he pulled absent mindedly at the hairs which sprouted from the large wart beneath his chin.

As if doubting the accuracy of the Astra's clock, Chandler looked at his own watch. It was almost eight. He muttered something under his breath. Either together or one at a time, he and Grant had been sitting watching the TV reporter's flat for the last eight hours. Every now and then they would drive to another position so as not to make it too obvious that they had the building under surveillance, but they always ensured that they could see at least one of the entrances. Every person who entered or left was noted at arrival and departure, but apart from the other residents of the small block few people had either visited or left.

Chandler chewed on his cigarette, winding down his window to allow some of the smoke to escape. Beside him he heard the slow, rhythmic breathing of his companion. They had exchanged scarcely a dozen words all day. Chandler knew why he had been assigned to this task. He knew that Gibson wanted him out of the way. But if Gibson thought that he was going to give up that easily then he was in for a shock. Eight killings and still his superior was no closer to pinning down the murderer. Chandler smiled. It could only be a matter of time before the DI was removed. He sucked hard on his cigarette and glanced up at the window of the flat once more. There were still no lights. No sign of movement. Where had she got to? He fumbled in his jacket pocket and pulled out the key to Terri's flat.

'Go and check it out,' he told Grant. 'See if there's been anyone about up there. She might even be back by now. She could have used the other entrance.'

Grant nodded and took the key.

Chandler watched as the tall sergeant made his way across the street to the building, disappearing through the main entrance. The DS waited a moment longer, then he too swung himself out of the car. He stretched, hearing his joints pop. The wind ruffled his hair and almost blew the cigarette from his mouth. He re-lit it then dug his hands in his pockets. To hell with this, he thought, he was going for a walk. He'd been sitting for most of the day, it was time he stretched his legs.

Sergeant Grant jabbed the '5' button and stepped into the lift as the doors slid open. He rode the car to the required floor, still holding the key to Terri's flat as he approached the door. He knocked twice, waiting, in case she had returned. But when he got no answer he gently inserted the key in the lock and turned it, easing the door open slowly. He called her name quietly as he entered. After all, he reasoned, she could be in the bath and not able to answer the door, but no, the flat was in darkness. The wind whistled loudly outside, rattling the windows in their frames. Grant thought about putting the light on but found that he could see adequately enough as he moved through the flat. He wandered around the sitting room, not quite sure what he was looking for. It was obvious that no one had broken into the flat, the door showed no sign of forced entry and it had still been securely locked when Grant entered.

He moved through into the kitchen.

A couple of mugs left in the sink to be washed up. But nothing out of place.

The sergeant moved back through the sitting room and checked the bathroom.

Outside, from the lobby, the lift began to rise.

First floor.

Second floor.

Grant pulled the cord which set the fluorescent in the bathroom flickering. He peered inside.

Third floor.

Fourth floor.

There was a short blue bathrobe hanging behind the door, still damp. Nothing else out of place. He decided to try the bedroom then make his way back down to the car.

The lift stopped at the fifth floor and the doors slid back silently, allowing the occupant to step out.

Grant decided to take his time returning to the car. He was certainly in no hurry to be back in Chandler's company. Grant had been on surveillance duty before. It was boring at the best of times, but this stint with Chandler was almost unbearable. He'd tried to make conversation with his superior, but the older man seemed uninterested in contact of any kind. Well, Grant decided, he was a policeman, not a public relations officer, if he didn't want to talk he didn't have to.

Grant never heard the footsteps outside the door of the flat.

He cast appraising eyes over the bedroom. At the nightdress which lay discarded on the duvet, the comb and brush on the bedside table along with a thick paperback.

The wardrobe door which was slightly ajar. The key lay on the carpet nearby.

Grant frowned and crossed to it wondering if Terri had merely forgotten to lock it or whether someone had indeed been inside the flat that day. Perhaps they had been searching for something in the wardrobe. The sergeant opened the door a little further and peered inside, squinting in the gloom.

The door of the flat opened and the newcomer slipped inside silently, crossing the sitting room to the kitchen, moving swiftly in the darkness.

Grant heard nothing, he was too engrossed in the contents of the wardrobe. He looked at the clothes which hung there, smelled the delicate scent of perfume on some of them. He opened the door a little wider.

The intruder gripped the skewer tightly and advanced stealthily back through the sitting room towards the bedroom.

A floorboard creaked.

Grant spun round, his heart beating a little faster. He stood in the silence a moment longer then turned back to the wardrobe, his eye caught by an object which lay in the bottom amongst the rows of shoes and boots. A small innocuous object but conspicuous by its presence. He bent to pick it up.

The intruder moved into the bedroom as silently as a panther stalking its prey, the skewer gripped in one fist, the other hand extended towards Grant's head.

The sergeant frowned as he looked at the cassette which he'd found in the bottom of the wardrobe. As he held it in his hand he noticed that there was a small cardboard box pushed into one corner of the unit. It was full of cassettes, some in their plastic cases, others loose.

Each one was marked with a number.

Grant drew one thumbnail across his forehead, his head tilted downward as if in prayer.

He was still in that position when the skewer was driven forward.

Powered with demonic force it pierced his left ear, the needle-sharp point searching out his brain as it was pushed deeper. His attacker's free hand clamped over his mouth, preventing him from uttering the cries of agony which he longed to give vent to. He struggled in the powerful grip, one hand grasping feebly for the steel prong which was embedded in his skull. He felt searing white-hot pain fill his head as the skewer was twisted madly, boring as deeply as if it had been attached to a drill bit. He felt blood oozing from his ear, running down the side of his neck to stain his shirt, and now his struggles became less frenzied. He uttered a low growl, deep in his throat, as the skewer was wrenched free, only to be rammed in again with even greater ferocity. Yet still there was surprisingly little blood. The second thrust, however, tore his ear lobe and more of the crimson fluid came from that fleshy bud than from his punctured brain. A mixture of glutinous clear fluid and watery blood dribbled from his ear. His body began to spasm uncontrollably as the skewer was driven in as far as the hook at its end. Seven inches of steel had transfixed the policeman's skull and the soft brain within.

His attacker stepped back, watching as he shuddered and writhed like an eel on a hot skillet, listening to the soft sputter as his body voided itself and the stench of excrement filled the room. Grant's eyelids fluttered wildly, flapping up and down with dizzying speed but the eyes behind them were already blind. Already beginning to glaze.

For what seemed like an eternity the intruder stood, watching fascinatedly as Grant died in agony, then the figure stepped over the prostrate body, picked up the cassette which Grant had been holding and tossed it back into the box.

That done, the figure turned and slipped out as easily as it had entered.

Terri Warner balanced the bag of groceries on the crook of one arm as she fumbled for her key with her free hand. She found it and pushed it into the lock.

The door swung open before she could turn the key.

Terri stepped back in surprise, almost dropping the carrier bag.

Should she enter? The darkness inside the flat looked forbidding. Maybe she should go back downstairs and fetch one of the men who were watching her. But when she'd pulled up a couple of minutes earlier she'd noticed that the Astra was empty. Neither of the policemen was in evidence.

Terri swallowed hard and reached inside the door, slapping on the light. She ventured inside a foot or two, aware of a pungent odour. A cloying stench which made her gag. She put down the groceries, trying to figure out where the smell was coming from. It took her just a few seconds to realize that its source was her bedroom. She paused for a moment, listening for any sounds of movement in the flat, but all she heard was the rushing of blood in her own ears.

She drew closer to the bedroom, pushing the door open.

'Oh God,' she murmured, gazing at the body of Sergeant

Grant, his eyes bulging wide as if registering his horror at his own sudden and painful death.

Terri took a step backwards, her eyes never leaving the corpse, her hand fumbling for the door knob, anxious to be out of the flat.

When she felt her hand touch flesh she turned and screamed.

Detective Sergeant Alan Chandler stood in the doorway, staring at her as she shrieked in horror, the sound reverberating off the walls.

It was then that the phone rang.

Fifty-three

'Don't speak. Just listen. I know this phone is bugged. I know the police are listening to this message and I know that they are watching. But so am I. I said that there were to be no police involved but you disobeyed. By the way, don't waste your time trying to trace this call. You won't be able to.

'Now listen to me. I want to meet the girl but I want to meet her alone. It's the girl that I want. Are you listening to me, Terri? It's you I want. You must meet me.

'I want Terri to go to the public phones at Hammersmith Tube station tomorrow night at ten o'clock. You'll be given instructions there on where to meet me. And remember, I'll be watching. The game is nearly over.

'I won't call again.'

Fifty-four

Commissioner Lawrence Chapman leaned forward and switched off the tape. A heavy silence descended, broken only by the occasional cough. DI Gibson rubbed his stomach self-consciously as he heard it rumble protestingly. A thin mist of cigarette smoke drifted lazily across the room adding to the claustrophobic atmosphere. It was as if the walls were gradually moving in, inch by inch, threatening to finally crush the large table which occupied the centre of the room.

Seated around it were Chapman, Gibson, Chandler, two other murder squad detectives and Sam Loomis. The balding pathologist was busy extracting particles of dirt from beneath his thumb-nail and seemed quite oblivious to what was happening around him. The policemen sat quietly, Gibson gritting his teeth as his stomach rumbled noisily once again. He glanced across at Chandler who was in the process of lighting up another cigarette.

'Has this been checked out?' Lawrence asked, holding up the cassette.

'The lab boys ran a voice-print on it. It doesn't match anything in our files,' Gibson told him. 'They did say that whoever made the tape had some knowledge of electronics and access to specialized equipment.'

Lawrence looked puzzled, his brow wrinkling.

'That message was recorded at half-speed then played back through some kind of distortion device.'

'What do you mean "played back",' Lawrence asked.

'When the message came through on Miss Warner's answer-phone we assumed it was the killer speaking directly, but it wasn't. He was playing a tape of his voice straight down the phone.'

'Well, it beats putting a hankie over the mouthpiece,' said Chandler flippantly.

Chapman shot him a warning glance.

'What I'd also like to know is why the killer wasn't seen either entering or leaving Miss Warner's flat,' he snapped. 'Chandler, you were supposed to be keeping a watch on the place.'

'It was impossible to cover both entrances at one time, sir,' the DS said, moving uncomfortably in his seat.

Gibson looked on with ill-concealed glee.

'Why did you go up to the flat when Sergeant Grant had already gone to investigate?'

'I thought that Grant was taking too long.'

'You left both entrances unguarded,' Chapman rasped.

'DI Gibson only assigned two of us to surveillance, sir,' Chandler countered, looking at his superior with a sly smirk.

'Why only two men, Gibson?'

'I felt that there was a danger the killer might break off contact if Miss Warner was being too heavily guarded or watched,' the DI said, glaring at Chandler for fleeting moments.

Chapman nodded, his eyes still on the cassette. 'So it was the same killer who murdered Sergeant Grant?' the commissioner said, looking this time at Loomis.

'I have no reason to suppose otherwise,' the pathologist told him. 'The killer was right-handed, that's consistent with the other victims, and what's more he was very careful. Grant was killed quickly, he died almost instantly but he was stabbed so the murderer didn't end up covered in blood. Inserting the skewer through the ear would have caused maximum damage but with minimum blood-loss, otherwise the killer would have been forced to leave the building drenched.'

'Bastard,' muttered one of the other detectives. 'I knew Grant, his wife was expecting a kiddie any time.'

Chapman ignored the remark, content to tap his nails on the table-top.

'I think we should let the girl make the rendezvous, sir,' said Gibson. 'Let her meet him.'

Chapman looked at the DI aghast.

'You're mad,' the older man said, flatly. 'He'll kill her.'

'It might be our only chance of catching him. She could be tailed.'

'You heard the message. He wants her alone.' The commissioner made a hopeless gesture with his hands.

'I'm not talking about our blokes tailing her,' the DI announced. 'She's pretty close to a guy called Frank Miller and she might feel safer if she was being tailed by someone she trusted. He used to work for the Yard as a photographer a couple of years back. I want Miller to do the tailing.'

Chandler grunted indignantly but Gibson ignored him and continued.

'We wire Miss Warner with a microphone so she can talk to Miller. We give *him* a two-way and he relays information to *us*. Miller follows *her*. We follow *him*.'

'Will Miller do it?' Chapman wanted to know.

'Yes, I already asked him.'

'That's two people's lives we're risking now, Gibson. This had better work, because I'll tell you now, if anything goes wrong I'm holding you responsible. Understood?'

The DI nodded.

'Does Miller know how to use a gun?' asked Chapman. 'If not, show him. It's best to be prepared for every eventuality. And I want the back-up team armed too.' He glanced at his watch. 'It's four o'clock now. We've got six hours before the killer contacts her again.'

The weapon felt surprisingly light in his hand as Miller hefted the Smith and Wesson .38 before him. He thumbed back the hammer, listening to the metallic click, watching as the cylinder revolved to bring a shell beneath the firing pin. He raised it towards the target, closing one eye, squinting down the foresight in an effort to draw a bead on the man-shaped figure. He pulled the trigger.

The .38 slammed back against the heel of his hand, the vibration travelling up his arm with a ferocity that hurt his shoulder. The bang was deafening and his nostrils were immediately assailed by the pungent odour of cordite. The bullet powered into the sandbags behind the target.

Beside him, Gibson chuckled.

'It's not like it is in films, Frank,' he said. 'These are real guns. Real noise and a hell of a recoil. Try steadying your firing hand with your free hand. And squeeze the trigger, don't jerk it.'

Miller braced himself and fired again.

The bullet missed again.

He squeezed the trigger once more.

'Aim for the broadest part of the body,' shouted Gibson above the roar of the pistol.

The next shot clipped the shoulder of the cut-out.

The fourth one hit the leg.

The fifth blasted a fist-sized hole in the stomach of the figure.

Miller squeezed again but the hammer slammed down on an empty chamber. He pushed the cylinder release, flipped it out and ejected the spent cartridge cases before re-loading.

'Remember, Frank, you're only to use that gun if you've absolutely no choice, we want him alive if possible. Only use it if you or Miss Warner are in danger, if your lives are threatened. You never know, he might even chicken out if he sees a gun.'

Miller raised his eyebrows.

'And he might have one of his own,' he replied, firing off another round at the target. It hit home in the chest area. So did the second shot. And the third.

Miller paused, his hand aching, his ears ringing.

'Just make sure I've got plenty of ammunition,' Miller said.

He fired off the remaining two rounds and re-loaded.

Twenty minutes later he was still there.

It was 5.39 p.m.

Fifty-five

Terri Warner lifted her arms as the surveillance man wound the piece of thin cable around her torso, apologizing whenever he got too close to her breasts. By the time he'd finished his face was bright red and he kept his gaze lowered as he attached the tiny microphone to the lapel of her jacket.

Sitting on the bed in the hotel room, Miller watched as the policeman completed his task then stepped back almost thankfully. He handed Miller an earpiece which the effects man pushed into position.

'Say something,' he instructed Terri.

'Like what?' she said and Miller grunted in pain, clapping one hand to his ear.

'That's enough,' he said, smiling thinly. 'I'm not deaf.'

'The microphone is very sensitive,' the surveillance man told them. 'It'll pick up a whisper. But it's only any good for about a quarter of a mile, any further than that and you'll break contact.'

They both nodded.

'Miller, you keep in touch with us using this,' Gibson said, handing him a compact Motorola two-way. 'As soon as Terri makes contact with the killer on the phone, as soon as he's given the location of the rendezvous, you let us know.'

Miller nodded.

'What sort of distance are we talking about with the two-way?' he asked.

'Three or four miles,' said the surveillance man.

'Reece will be in the car with us in case you have any problems,' Gibson said, indicating the other policeman who

258

turned red once more.

He looked at his watch.

9.06 p.m.

'Terri, it's my guess that he'll bounce you all round London to make sure you're not being tailed,' said the DI. 'From one location to the next. Just make sure you tell Miller everything the killer tells you.'

'I'm not stupid,' she said quietly.

'No, and neither is the bastard who's after you,' snapped the policeman. 'Miller, if by some chance you do lose her then let us know straightaway. There'll be cars standing by.'

Miller pulled the hip flask from his pocket and took a hefty swig.

'Before you ask, Stuart,' he said. 'I *do* need it.'

'I was going to ask if there was any to spare,' said the policeman wearily.

Miller grinned and handed him the flask, watching as he drank from it, wiping his mouth with the back of his hand. He handed it back. Miller, for his own part, pulled the .38 from his belt and checked that it was fully loaded.

'Remember,' Gibson said, 'it's only to be used if you've got no possible alternative.'

'It's not you who's going to be going up against him, Stuart,' Miller reminded his former colleague.

A heavy silence descended, broken by the DI.

'It's time we took our positions. You leave when you're ready. Just make sure you're at those phones at Hammersmith by ten.'

'I will,' Terri assured him. 'Maybe I should have my camera crew with me,' she added, her attempt at humour failing to lighten even her own spirits.

Gibson and Reece left them alone in the room.

'Maybe it ought to be me who has the gun?' Terri said.

'Why? You'll probably try to interview him, not shoot him,' Miller said sarcastically.

Terri exhaled deeply and wandered across to the window, looking out into the darkness.

'He's imitated the killing methods of eight other murderers,' she said. 'I wonder who he's thinking of copying next?'

259

'Whichever killer specialized in TV reporters, I should think.'

Terri laughed humourlessly.

'Perhaps I should get you to look at one of *my* photos,' she suggested, a trace of sarcasm in her voice. 'You can tell me whether or not he's going to kill me.'

Miller didn't answer.

Terri continued gazing out into the night.

Gibson slid into the passenger seat of the Astra and glanced across at Chandler who was puffing on a Rothmans.

'Don't lose him,' the DI said.

'Why, in case the killer gets the girl or you lose your job?' the DS answered, smiling crookedly.

'If I go down, Chandler,' Gibson hissed, 'I'll make bloody sure I take you with me.'

The DS took one last drag on his cigarette then ground it out in the ashtray. A plume of smoke rose mournfully to join the cloud which already filled the car.

In the back seat Reece was fiddling with the two-way, checking frequencies.

'We're ready,' he said. 'It's up to Miller and the girl now.'

In the hotel room Miller and Terri checked their watches. She fastened her jacket, ensuring that Miller could still hear her. He told her that he could hear her heart beating through the earpiece.

Miller watched her leave, waited five minutes then took the lift down to the ground floor, walked out and slid behind the wheel of his own car.

'Moving,' he said into the two-way, and swung the Granada out into traffic.

It was 9.37.

Fifty-six

The man glanced at her as he passed, slowing his pace slightly, but he continued walking, on towards the ticket machines.

Terri swallowed hard and looked first at her watch then at the row of phones before her. Two or three were broken, the shattered receiver of the one closest to her dangling by the cord. Litter was piled in the bottom of some booths, and a beer can, blown by the wind, rolled gently back and forth, the metallic rattle echoing around the virtually deserted entrance to the station.

The tiles on the floor were coated with filth. The place smelt like a urinal.

Terri shuffled her feet and waited, glancing at the pieces of paper which were stuck inside the black-painted canopies that covered each phone. Numbers to ring. Names. As if each booth were some kind of miniature bill board for people to advertise in.

Phone this number for a sensual massage, said one.

Fresh young model, another proclaimed.

She glanced at each one.

Black Dominatrix wants willing slaves, screamed a third, written in yellow ink.

There was a familiar rumble as, below her, a train pulled in.

Terri glanced at her watch again.

Almost ten o'clock.

Would he ring on time?

Which phone would ring?

She pulled up the collar of her jacket and waited.

Miller took another swig from his hip flask and pressed the earpiece more firmly into his ear. All he could hear was the low thudding of Terri's heart.

She had spoken briefly as she'd climbed out of her car, but that had been more than ten minutes ago. He hadn't heard a word since, only the rumbling and rustling as she moved, fastening and unfastening her jacket. He looked at the dashboard clock.

9.58.

The two-way beside him crackled loudly and Miller snatched it up.

'Any contact yet?'

He recognized the voice as Gibson's.

'Nothing,' he told the DI.

There was a long silence and Miller looked at the two-way, wondering if the policeman was going to speak again. Above him, traffic rumbled noisily over the flyover and he cursed as a plane went over, adding its own deafening sound to that of the cars and other vehicles which swept past him.

He heard something in the earpiece.

Terri's voice. Distant and crackling as if someone were screwing up a paper bag beside her.

'. . . which one he'll use.'

Miller tapped the earpiece, muttering angrily to himself when he found that some of her words were slipping away.

'. ... almost ten. I hope you can hear me, Frank . . . calling soon . . . this place . . . deserted.'

'Jesus Christ,' Miller hissed, snatching up the two-way. 'Gibson, come in. The bloody signal from the microphone is breaking up.'

'Can you still hear her?' the DI wanted to know.

'At the moment yes, just about.' He looked at the dashboard clock once more.

9.59.

Terri's voice came in again, hissing in his ear along with a rasp of static which made him wince, but at least it was clearer this time.

'I wish he'd hurry up and ring, I'm freezing,' she said.

Miller took another swig from his hip flask.

'Almost time,' Terri said again.

There was another crackle of static. Miller banged the wheel in fury.

Her voice sounded thin, broken up by the static.

10.00.

'Come on, come on,' he hissed, as the sound crackled even more loudly in his ear.

Silence.

He snatched up the two-way.

'Gibson, I've lost the signal,' he barked. 'I can't hear her.'

Fifty-seven

Miller was half-way out of the car when he heard Terri's voice again.

'Thank God,' he whispered, then into the two-way, 'She's transmitting again.'

He clambered back into his car and started the engine, listening to the instructions which were coming through the earpiece.

'He wants me to go to a place called Gateway Towers,' said Terri. 'It's in Shoreditch. It's a block of flats, it's been empty for about six months. I hope you're hearing me, Frank.'

'Loud and clear,' said Miller, guiding his car out into traffic.

'Have you got the destination yet?' Gibson asked.

Miller didn't answer.

'Can you hear me?' the DI repeated. 'Have you lost the signal again?'

Still Miller remained silent, more intent on trying to pick out Terri's car in the mêlée of traffic ahead of him. The tail-lights of other vehicles looked like so much neon in the darkness and he blinked hard to clear the hazy film which seemed to have settled over his left eye. The haziness cleared and he drove on.

'Miller.' Gibson's voice was more urgent now. 'Can you hear me?'

Finally he picked up the two-way.

'I hear you.'

'What the hell are you playing at? Couldn't you hear me?' Gibson rasped. 'Did she give you the location? Where is he going to meet her?'

Miller hesitated a second longer.

'The Band Stand in Kensington Gardens,' he said quickly, then switched off the radio.

In the pursuing Astra Gibson shook the two-way violently.

'Miller,' he shouted.

'He's turned it off,' said Reece.

Gibson gritted his teeth angrily.

'Why, for Christ's sake?' he snarled, then he reached across Chandler and grabbed the radio in the car. 'All units to Kensington Gardens, the Band Stand.'

'But we promised them no interference,' said Reece.

'This isn't a game any more,' snapped Gibson angrily. 'And I also want all units to be on the look-out for a dark brown Mini Clubman, registration number OVV 368P, and a silver-grey Ford Granada, registration number SHK 665Y. They're to be stopped on sight.' Gibson sat back in the passenger seat, his face set in an expression of determination. 'Now we'll see,' he muttered.

Miller tossed the two-way onto the back seat and drove on. As he did so, he pulled the .38 from his pocket and once more checked that all the chambers were full.

He drove on.

Bob Johnson had sat looking at the phone for what seemed like an eternity, a slight smile on his face, but now he got to his feet, pulled on his jacket and headed for the door. He guessed that the journey would take him about thirty minutes.

John Ryker had slammed the receiver down, almost snapping the object in half. He ran a scarred hand through his hair and paced back and forth agitatedly, the anger seething within him.

It was time to settle things once and for all.

He headed towards the door, picking up his car keys on the way.

The time had come.

Fifty-eight

The concrete and glass edifice of Gateway Towers thrust upwards into the night sky like an accusatory finger.

It was a derelict. A monument to high speed building and quick profits. The manufactured leviathan rose from the street below as if pushed from the bowels of the earth by some primeval force.

The deserted building stood in total darkness.

Terri brought the Mini to a halt and climbed out, fumbling on the back seat for the torch which she had remembered to bring. It was large and felt more like a truncheon, and the weight reassured her as she approached the main doors of the high-rise. The glass in the doors and windows as high as the fifth floor had been broken. Some of it lay on the pavement outside but most was inside the building. Covered by a layer of dust in which Terri fancifully thought she could have carved rather than written her name.

She pushed the front doors which swung back to admit her, swallowing her up. The blackness closed around her and with it came the stench of neglect and decay. Of urine and excrement. Of stale vomit. For if no council residents were allowed to live in the tower then it had become something of a sanctuary for the down-and-outs who lived in the area. It was their empty bottles and cans that littered the entrance.

Terri moved further into the hall, her footsteps muffled by the thick carpet of dust. It clung to her like filthy snow and she put a hand over her face in an effort to prevent the swirling dust from penetrating her nostrils too badly.

Spray-can Picassos had been busy on the vast canvas offered

266

by the block's walls. Drawings seemed to vie with one another in offensiveness. Graffiti, some scrawled on with charcoal, some painted on, offered various observations on life in the gutter:

MAGGIE IS A FUCKING BITCH
THE QUEEN IS DEAD

Terri moved towards the lift, the doors of which gaped open like a yawning mouth. She recoiled quickly as she saw a pile of excrement in one corner of the disused car.

To her right was a flight of stairs and it was these she began to climb, the torch beam cutting through the darkness, particles of dust twisting and swirling in the light. Here she moved more slowly, aware of how loud the sound of her high heels sounded in the oppressive silence. She took the stairs slowly, eyes focused ahead, ears alert for any sound of movement.

'I hope you can hear me, Frank,' she whispered. 'And I hope you're close. I'm almost at the landing to the first floor. No sign of anyone yet.'

She reached the landing and peered down the corridor which led to the now empty flats. All the doors were securely locked, and after trying the first five or six Terri decided to go up another floor. She turned a corner and found that the stairs were on her left this time. She shone the torch over them, advancing slowly.

Something moved above her.

On the floor above she heard movement and, for long seconds, froze.

'I think he's here,' she said softly, aware of her blood rushing in her ears, her heart pounding against her ribs. 'I'm going up to the next floor.'

As she began ascending, Terri thought how ridiculous the situation was. She was alone in the derelict building except for a man who had murdered nine people and now, instead of turning and running for her life, she was climbing higher to meet him. The logical move would have been to get out, but instead she continued to climb.

'I really hope you're close, Frank,' she whispered once more.

She reached the second landing.

'I'm on the second floor now,' she said. 'Ahead of me, two of the doors are open. I'm going on.'

Miller checked his speedometer and noticed that the needle was nudging forty-five, but he didn't slow up. He had heard every word uttered by Terri since she'd entered the derelict tower. He was less than five minutes drive from it now. He dared not slow up.

He didn't even notice the police car pull out behind him.

The driver of the pursuing vehicle peered through the darkness at the car, a frown creasing his forehead.

'Silver-grey Ford Granada,' he said to his colleague. 'What was that number we were told to watch for?'

His companion repeated the registration number.

'Christ, you'd better call in. I think we've found him.'

The two cars sped on.

'What the hell does he think he's playing at?' snarled Gibson to himself. 'Why did he tell us *this* location?'

He gripped the car radio tightly then flicked the transmitter switch.

'Are you sure it's the same car?' he asked the policeman.

The uniformed man repeated the registration number.

'What's he doing in Shoreditch?' Gibson said angrily. Then, into the radio: 'Look, you keep on his tail, don't lose him. There'll be more men there in a few minutes but you're not to apprehend the driver of that car. Is that understood?'

Gibson banged the dashboard angrily.

'I should have known,' he said quietly. 'Come on, Chandler, turn this car around and let's go, otherwise we're going to end up with two more bodies on our hands tonight.'

'Two?' said Reece, looking puzzled.

Gibson didn't answer. He allowed his own hand to move to the bulge inside his coat where the 9mm Browning Automatic nestled in its shoulder holster. He looked at his watch. It was 10.47.

Already he had the unshakeable feeling that they were too late.

Fifty-nine

The first of the doors opened easily, swinging back on hinges that hadn't tasted oil for many months. The high pitched squeal made Terri wince and she looked around anxiously, the torch beam cutting swathes through the impenetrable blackness.

She paused in the corridor for a moment then looked inside the room. Apart from a couple of empty cardboard boxes, it was empty. In fact, the building reminded her of a gigantic, futuristic crypt. Silent and forbidding, a home for shadows.

And perhaps something more tangible.

Ahead of her the second door opened a fraction and Terri froze, aiming the torch at the movement, trying to pick out shapes in the cold white light.

From beneath her she heard footsteps.

And now ahead of her she saw signs that the dust which coated the floor had been disturbed.

Someone had walked this corridor before her. And recently too.

She advanced cautiously towards the open door, feeling a chill breeze nipping at her face while below her silence descended again.

Terri reached the open door and pushed it, directing the torch inside.

A dark shape moved in one corner of the room and Terri barely stifled a gasp.

The cat hissed at her and dropped the mouse it had been holding in its jaws. With one leap it bounded up on to the window-sill, eyes glowing yellow in the light of the torch.

Terri let out a relieved breath and turned away from the door.

At the end of the corridor two firedoors led to another flight of steps which she knew would take her up to the third floor. She paused a moment, noticing that the dust was not disturbed ahead of her. In fact, she was so taken with this latest discovery, all other thoughts seemed to leave her mind. She directed the torch at the floor.

Behind her, another of the doors opened slowly.

Miller took the steps two at a time, stumbling twice in the enveloping blackness, cursing as he fell on the stone steps, but he picked himself up and ran on, the .38 now gripped in his fist as he hurtled towards the next flight. Towards Terri.

Terri moved ahead slowly, torch aimed ahead of her, unaware of the dark shape which was moving into the corridor behind her, moving away from the room as if detaching itself from the blackness. She heard no footsteps because the dust disguised them.

She heard only silence and the thudding of her own heart.

Until finally, she heard the voice.

'Terri.'

She spun round, torch dropping from her terrified fingers, shattering on the ground, but in that split second before the light went out she had seen the face of the man who now barred her way.

The face of the man whom she had expected to find in this place tonight.

Bob Johnson was smiling.

Sixty

In the darkness of the corridor, Johnson was almost invisible. The only light came from the open door of the room, illuminating his features as he moved towards her.

Terri took a step backwards.

'I've been waiting,' he told her.

She continued to back away, glancing past Johnson towards the head of the stairs beyond.

She heard the sound of footsteps.

Growing louder.

Johnson heard them too and his face twisted in anger.

'What's going on?' he rasped.

Terri said nothing but merely continued her retreat, moving slowly through the dust which stuck to her shoes and swirled around her feet like noxious fog.

Johnson's hands tightened into fists and he glared at Terri, the knot of muscles at the side of his jaw throbbing madly.

'We were meant to be alone here,' he hissed.

The sound of footsteps was growing in volume.

From below, the beam of a torch bounced across the wall in an erratic pattern as Miller drew nearer.

He reached the landing, gun in one hand, torch in the other.

'You fucking bitch,' snarled Johnson, looking first at Terri then at the advancing Miller. 'You set me up.'

'Kill him, Frank,' Terri screamed, throwing herself to the ground.

Johnson let out a roar of rage and lunged towards Terri, but Miller steadied himself and fired.

The shot sounded thunderous in the confines of the corridor, the noise reverberating around the deserted building as if it had been some kind of echo chamber. The muzzle-flash flared brilliant white, blinding Miller momentarily, but he squeezed the trigger once more, the .38 bucking wildly in his hand as it spat out its lethal load.

The second shot caught Johnson in the chest, to the right of his sternum.

The bullet shattered two ribs as it powered into him, tearing its way through a lung before exploding from his back, punching an exit hole the size of a fist. Blood and gobbets of lung tissue sprayed from the wound as Johnson went down, his life fluid spilling in a widening pool in the thick dust.

Terri screamed and rolled away from him as he shot out a hand in an attempt to grab her leg, forcing himself up onto his knees as Miller took aim a third time.

He hesitated, terrified of hitting Terri in the darkness but her screams of fear seemed to spur him on and he fired again.

His next shot hit Johnson squarely in the back, pulverizing a kidney and ripping away a sizeable piece of flesh. Blood spurted from the wound, and as he opened his mouth to shout his pain, Johnson tasted blood in his mouth. Seconds later it spilled over his lips. He fell forward, face down, his hands twitching spasmodically.

Miller lowered the revolver slowly and shone the torch over the prone body, allowing the beam to rest on the bloodied face. His eyes were open but already beginning to glaze over, particles of dust settling on the whites. A trickle of blood was running from his left nostril, like a crimson ribbon.

Miller edged his way around the body, extending a hand to help Terri to her feet. She grabbed him, almost knocking the gun from his grasp, and Miller heard her sobs as she clung to him. Without taking his eyes from Johnson's body, he supported her past the bullet-torn carcass towards the stairs. Looking back as he reached them, staring for long seconds at the body. Then, together, he and Terri began to descend.

Her sobs slowly subsided and she paused to wipe her face, wiping both tears and dirt away.

'Are you all right?' Miller asked, his hand aching from the

vicious recoil of the .38.

She nodded.

Outside they heard the sound of a police siren.

'How the hell did they find us?' Miller mused aloud, slipping the gun back into his pocket. He put his arm around Terri's shoulder and they walked the remaining few steps to the first floor landing.

Beneath them they heard the first of the policemen come crashing into the building.

Behind them, they were oblivious to the fact that Bob Johnson, his clothes soaked in blood, now stood watching.

For unbearable seconds he stood there, supported by the balustrade, his breath coming in wheezing gasps where the bullet had torn open his lung. But then he gritted his teeth, his eyes narrowing in rage, and with a roar of rage he launched himself at the couple.

It was as if Johnson had been fired from a catapult. He flew through the air, momentarily defying gravity, his blood-spattered body seemingly suspended on invisible wires until he crashed into them. Knocking them both to the ground.

The impact stunned Miller and he felt a jarring pain in his skull as his head was slammed against the concrete steps. Blood burst from the cut which opened on his forehead, and as he rolled over, reaching for the .38, he felt strong hands being fastened around his throat.

Despite his wounds, Johnson seemed to possess almost superhuman strength, and he dug his thumbs into Miller's throat, simultaneously banging the effects man's head against the concrete. Miller blinked hard as white light flashed before his eyes. He struggled to reach the gun and succeeded in pulling it free of his pocket but Johnson released his grip long enough to grab Miller's arm, shaking it until the revolver flew from his grasp and went skittering away down the stairs.

Terri, herself dazed from the attack, struggled after it, looking back to see that Miller was weakening rapidly.

She heard the police pounding up the stairs but her only concern was finding the gun.

In the gloom she fumbled about, her hand finally closing

273

around the pistol. Terri scurried back up the stairs, using both thumbs to pull back the hammer on the weapon, drawing closer to the insane tableau before her.

Johnson raised Miller's head a few inches from the ground then slammed it down with a force that threatened to split his skull. Blood was now spreading from beneath Miller's head and he felt sick, waves of unconsciousness now flooding over him. It felt as if someone was pumping his head full of air. He tried to breathe but the thick dust filled his nostrils and all the time those huge hands gripped his throat and squeezed.

Miller found himself looking up into the maniacal face of Johnson. It was a face that belonged to a madman. His features were twisted, spattered with blood, but, as Miller fought back as best he could, those features began to dissolve before him. He was blacking out.

He saw, through a red haze, Terri standing behind Johnson, the gun lowered, pointing at his head.

Then he was sure that it was all over. He felt his bowels loosen. Felt his senses slipping away from him.

Terri pressed the barrel of the revolver against the back of Johnson's head and fired.

The explosion was deafening.

From such close range the result was devastating.

The top of Johnson's head seemed to explode like a volcano, the portions of his skull propelled by the bullet rising into the air along with an eruption of blood and sticky brain matter. His mouth fell open and locked in that position, his eyes still open as if registering surprise that half of his head had been blown away. Fragments of bone and thick slicks of blood spattered the wall, mingling with the flux of brain to form a monstrous collage.

Beneath him, Miller was aware of the crimson mess showering his face, but it seemed not to bother him. He was too close to unconsciousness for that.

All he knew was that the vice-like grip on his throat suddenly eased as Johnson pitched forward, crashing to the ground on his face, revealing the hole in the back of his head. Miller could have fitted both fists inside it.

Terri dropped the pistol and lurched against the balustrade, peering down into the blackness to see two uniformed policemen charging towards her. They were speaking but she didn't hear the words.

Neither did Miller, he rolled onto his side, away from the corpse of Johnson. When he tried to swallow Miller felt agonizing pain in his throat and he massaged his Adam's apple with one bloodied hand. He smelt the stench of blood, of excrement. Dust filled his mouth and nostrils as he rolled onto his stomach but he was past caring.

He blacked out.

Sixty-one

'What motive did Johnson have for committing the murders?' said Miller, tentatively touching his bandaged scalp.

'How much did *you* know about him, Terri,' Gibson wanted to know.

She could only shrug.

The policeman exhaled deeply and rubbed his eyes. He glanced up at the wall clock.

It was almost 1.15 a.m.

'Maybe this isn't the time to start sifting through this mess,' he said, softly.

'The killer's dead, Stuart,' said Miller. 'Isn't that all that matters at the moment?'

'I'd like you both to come in tomorrow and make full statements,' Gibson said. 'How are you feeling, Frank?'

Miller touched his head again.

'I'm all right,' he said. 'Nothing a drink won't cure.'

He and Terri got up from the table where they'd been sitting and made for the door.

'You look like *you* could do with some sleep too,' Miller observed, looking at his former colleague.

Gibson shrugged and got to his feet, opening the door for them. He watched them walk down the corridor towards the lift then he turned back into the room and looked at Chandler. The DS was shuffling uncomfortably in his seat, unable to maintain eye-to-eye contact with his superior.

'It looks as if you'll have to wait a lot longer for my job now, doesn't it?' Gibson rasped. 'This case is wrapped up. All the angles and the motive might still be out of our reach at the

276

moment, but like Miller said, we've got our killer. Bad luck, Chandler.' The DI smiled and pushed the door open, motioning his colleague to leave. 'Now get out, before I kick you out.'

The DS got to his feet and hurried from the room.

Gibson crossed to the table and sat down once again, looking at the photos of Johnson, and of his victims.

So, it was over at last.

He almost smiled. Apart from the paperwork.

Miller swayed uncertainly as he stood beside his car, a sudden stab of pain from his injured skull causing him to suck in a sharp breath.

'Maybe I'd better drive,' said Terri, walking round to the driver's side of the Granada. She slid behind the wheel and unlocked the door, letting Miller inside. He allowed his head to loll backwards. She studied his profile for a second, noticing how drained of colour he looked. 'The doctor did say that you weren't to be left alone for the next twenty-four hours. Have you got a spare room?'

Miller smiled but didn't look at her.

'Thanks for the offer,' he said. Then, looking at her, 'There's something else I ought to thank you for too.'

Terri looked vague.

'You saved my life,' he told her. 'Johnson would have killed me too if you hadn't found that gun.'

She didn't answer but merely started the engine and swung the car out of its parking space. Despite the late hour, the streets were still relatively busy and Miller guessed that the trip home would take about thirty minutes.

'What will you do now?' he asked as she drove. 'About work? I mean, with Johnson gone . . .' The sentence trailed off.

'They'll be looking for someone to take his place,' Terri said.

'What about you?'

She shook her head.

'I don't think I'd want the job. I think I'll take a couple of months off, try to forget about it all. I know that won't be easy.' She almost smiled. 'Maybe I'll sell my story to the newspapers and retire on what they pay me.'

Miller didn't answer.

Terri looked across at him and noticed that his eyes were closed.

'Frank,' she called softly, reaching across to touch his hand.

Miller didn't wake up until they were five minutes from his home.

He stretched, his bones cracking loudly, then apologized for dozing off. It must have been the bang on the head, he reasoned. At least the nagging pain which had been gnawing at his skull seemed to have eased somewhat. Terri parked the car in the road and the two of them walked to the front door of the house. Miller found his keys and unlocked the door, slapping on the light as he entered the hall.

'Jesus Christ,' he gasped, staring at what confronted him.

Terri could not find the breath to scream, her eyes bulged madly in their sockets, riveted to the vision which greeted her.

Suspended in the middle of the hall, hanging from a thick rope which had been secured to the banister ballustrade, was the body of a woman.

She had been expertly and painstakingly flayed so that not one inch of skin remained to cover the network of muscles and bones beneath.

It took Miller just a second to realize that the bloodied figure was the one which had been stolen from his house two days earlier.

It was as Miller moved towards the model that John Ryker stepped into view.

He was carrying a large double-edged knife which glinted menacingly in the light.

Ryker smiled crookedly.

'Welcome home.'

Sixty-two

'Shut the door, Terri,' Miller said quietly, his eyes never leaving Ryker.

'Do as he says, Terri,' Ryker echoed, chuckling. He eyed the TV reporter approvingly. 'I've seen you before haven't I? On TV? Very nice.' Then he turned his attention back to Miller. 'I told you the other day that we had business to attend to but you wouldn't listen, would you?'

'It was you who wrecked my house?' said Miller but it sounded more like a statement than a question.

'Let's cut the bullshit, Miller, I want my money now,' Ryker snapped.

'And I told you before I haven't got it.'

The older man stepped forward, bringing the knife up.

Terri stepped closer to Miller.

'What money is he talking about?' she wanted to know.

'Money for services rendered,' Ryker said to her, without taking his eyes off Miller. 'Money for helping to make him one of the best effects men in the business, money for supplying him with props.' He chuckled and reached for the leg of the model. 'Money for risking my fucking neck.' Ryker pressed the knife into the thigh of the dangling model, cutting deeply from femur to kneecap. He prised the latex open as if he were a surgeon, then, using the razor-sharp point, he carved a large portion of the rubber skin away, revealing what lay beneath.

'Money for robbing graves,' Ryker snarled and tore open the model's leg.

Hidden beneath the latex but now visible was real human flesh.

It was pale and shrivelled but well preserved. It gave off little or no smell.

As Ryker spoke he carved away more of the prosthetic flesh.

Miller could only watch as more of the real body beneath was exposed.

'"I need a heart, Ryker,"' the older man mimicked, sardonically. '"Get me one, I'll pay you well. I need a baby, Ryker. Get me one. Get me a body, Ryker. Get me an arm, Ryker".'

He tore off a large piece of the latex, exposing the lower abdomen of the dangling corpse. The flesh was mottled blue and green in places and now both Miller and Terri detected a powerful smell of decay which had previously been masked by the fake flesh.

Ryker slashed wildly at the corpse, hacking off one of the fingers.

Terri moved to one side, edging slowly away from the door, her eyes never leaving Ryker as he hacked and slashed at the body.

'Get my money, Miller,' he snarled. 'Or I'll carve you up like this bloody dummy.' He looked at Terri. 'You *and* your girlfriend.'

Miller took advantage of the brief respite, and as Ryker turned to look at Terri he stepped forward, shoving the corpse as hard as he could.

The grisly object swung forward and slammed into Ryker who was knocked flying by the impact.

The knife fell from his hand and skidded across the floor.

He leapt for it, his hand reaching for the deadly blade, but Miller too reacted quickly and brought the heel of his shoe crashing down on the older man's outstretched fingers.

There was a loud crack as two of the digits were shattered and Ryker yelped in pain, rolling away, trying to get to his feet.

The body, propelled by Miller's push, continued to swing back and forth like a monstrous pendulum.

Miller ran at the older man, hitting him with his shoulder, the impact sending him hard into the wall.

Ryker grunted, winded by the collision, but he steadied himself against the nearby table, his hand closing around the tall glass vase which occupied its centre. Hefting the ornament before him like a club, he advanced, holding one side, wincing every time he sucked in a breath.

Still the corpse swung to and fro, each fresh movement bringing with it the stench of decay. The sightless eyes gazed at the tableau below indifferently.

'I'll kill you,' hissed Ryker and ran at Miller, bringing the vase down with bone-crushing force.

Miller moved, but not quickly enough.

The heavy piece of crystal struck his shoulder and he sucked in a painful breath as he felt his collar-bone snap. A white-hot pain enveloped his upper body and his left arm suddenly went numb. Every time he flexed his fingers it felt as if someone were sticking red hot needles into his flesh, but he rolled back, that injured arm reaching for the fallen knife.

Terri could only look on helplessly as Ryker hurled the vase down at Miller.

Miller instinctively raised his arm to shield his face and felt another horrendous impact on his forearm this time. The vase shattered, showering him with crystal splinters, some of which cut his face.

Ryker was upon him immediately, driving a powerful kick into his groin.

Miller doubled up, but as he did so his hand closed over the shaft of the knife and he sprang forward, driving the blade deep into Ryker's thigh.

The body-snatcher shrieked and clutched at the weapon, trying to tug it free, feeling it rasp against bone as he did.

From the amount of blood which erupted from the wound Miller was sure that he'd severed his attacker's femoral artery. A great red fountain burst from the torn leg, spattering Miller and the wall behind him. He drew his hands across his eyes to clear his view, seeing Terri approaching the stricken Ryker from behind clutching part of the broken vase.

She struck hard, driving the jagged edges into his face, watching as he fell backwards, still trying to wrench the knife from his thigh.

Terri stood watching as Miller rolled on top of Ryker,

reaching for the knife, using all his strength to rip it out. It came slowly, tearing muscle and sinew as it did so. But finally the glistening blade was free and Miller raised it above Ryker whose face was now a bloody ruin, pieces of glass still embedded in it. One lethal shard had gouged away part of his upper eyelid, and every time he blinked a sticky flux of vitreous fluid and crimson would spurt out.

Miller found his own vision was clouding. He was hesitating.

'Do it,' screamed Terri. 'Kill him.'

Miller grabbed Ryker by the chin, and with one powerful thrust buried the knife in his heart.

'Kill him,' Terri shrieked again, almost knocked flying by the body which still swung its steady path back and forth.

She stood mesmerized by the bloody spectacle before her, transfixed as Miller put all his weight behind the blade, pushing it deeper into his opponent's body, ignoring the gouts of blood which splashed him as the heart pumped madly, expelling its thick contents with the force of a high-pressure hose.

He felt Ryker's body jerking beneath him as he stabbed again. And again.

Miller rolled onto the floor beside the punctured body, his breath coming in great racking gasps, his nostrils filled with the overpowering coppery stench of blood and the more pungent odour of excrement. His shoulder was throbbing mightily and he winced as he prodded the broken bone.

Terri remained motionless, her gaze fixed on the body of Ryker, her eyes flicking backwards and forwards, taking in every detail.

'Terri, call the police,' Miller said, trying to raise himself up on one elbow.

She didn't answer.

Miller wondered if she might have gone into shock, but when he looked at her he felt a cold chill run along his spine. He felt as if someone had pumped ice into his veins.

Terri Warner was smiling.

She was kneeling beside the body of Ryker, a broad grin on her face and Miller noticed with disgust that she had dipped one index finger into the dead man's chest wound. She withdrew the dripping digit, ignoring the blood which ran up and stained her blouse.

She licked the crimson fluid with a slow movement of her tongue.

Miller felt sick.

Not only because of the pain he was feeling and the sight he had just witnessed but because, in that second, the realization struck him.

'Terri,' he whispered softly, struggling up onto his knees.

She merely looked at him, that insidious grin plastered across her features, her lips stained with blood. But it was her eyes which he found most disconcerting.

The unblinking stare which seemed to bore into him.

'You killed him,' she chuckled. 'It's easy isn't it?' She laughed and Miller felt the hairs at the back of his neck rise.

'You murdered the others,' he said. 'You killed those eight people.'

'Nine,' she corrected him. 'I killed that policeman in my flat too. He'd found the tapes.'

'I don't understand,' Miller said, transfixed by that blazing gaze.

'The messages on the answering machine,' she told him. 'I recorded them myself. That's why the police could never trace them. I put them in the machine myself. I recorded them all at the TV studios, Johnson let me have free run in there. He thought a lot of me.' She chuckled again.

'But how did you know that Johnson would be at the flats tonight?'

'Because *I* called him. *I* told him to be there. I knew he'd do it for me.'

'Oh Jesus,' Miller gasped softly. 'But why the killings?'

'You could never understand, Frank. No one can ever understand the fascination of death. I've had it ever since I was a child. In the beginning I was frightened of it but then I came to understand it. To love it. Its power. Its inevitability. Taking someone's life is probably the greatest power that anyone has. The ability to kill. The others had it too. Haigh, Manuel, Sutcliffe, Nilsen. All of them. I wanted to feel that power too, I

283

283

wanted to feel what they had felt when *they* killed.' She paused to look at Ryker's body. 'Haven't you ever wanted to kill someone? To see them die? To watch them die? No other reason, just to watch. That power is inside everyone. There's a piece of every person that's capable of killing, but they hide it, they push it away, hide it in the backs of their minds and pretend it doesn't exist. But it's there and it never goes away. That desire to kill someone, sometimes a person you know, is in every human being. How many times have you rowed with someone and felt like killing them? How many people hate their relatives enough to kill them? How many would murder their neighbours if they had the chance? When you find out that someone has been talking behind your back, don't you feel like doing something to them? Like I said, the power is in us all. It's just that most people deny that it's there because they're ashamed to admit it's there.'

Miller listened dumbly, his eyes never leaving Terri as she faced him across the body of Ryker. The corpse was the only thing between them.

And the knife was still embedded in its chest.

Waiting to be picked up.

'I can't call the police, Frank,' she told him. 'Not yet.'

'You're going to kill me?' he asked.

She smiled.

'When you stabbed Ryker, didn't you feel that sense of power? You *took* his life. It makes you like God, Frank, able to decide who will live and who will die.' Her expression suddenly hardened, and in that split second Miller saw her hand dart forward towards the knife.

He lashed out, his punch catching her full in the face, the impact knocking her onto her back. Blood ran from her broken nose and she moaned feebly as Miller crawled towards her, looking down at her face.

She smiled crookedly as she looked up at him and, with a roar of rage, Miller drove another blow into her bloodied visage, this time cracking her jaw.

The impact knocked her unconscious.

Miller sat back on his haunches, his breath coming in gasps.

His injured shoulder was still throbbing but he seemed oblivious to the pain. His attention was focused on Terri.

Above him, the swinging body had finally come to a halt. It twisted and turned silently on the rope.

Sixty-three

When the police arrived Miller was sitting in his lounge drinking.

He heard the banging at the front door but finished what was left in his glass before getting slowly to his feet.

On his way across the hall he stepped over the body of Ryker. The corpse was already stiff with rigor mortis, the spilled blood now congealed into a sticky crimson porridge.

Miller touched his injured shoulder and winced painfully, pausing a second before he opened the door.

The leading policeman blenched as he saw Ryker's body lying in its puddle of congealing gore, but his superior pushed past him followed by a couple of ambulancemen. As Miller made his way back to the sitting room he saw the uniformed men lifting the corpse onto a stretcher.

Miller offered the policeman a drink but he declined. Miller looked at the man appraisingly. He looked as tired as Miller felt and had to keep rubbing his eyes periodically.

'Were you alone in the house when the attack happened?' the policeman asked.

Miller nodded and re-filled his own glass.

'Did you know the man?'

'We'd met a couple of times,' Miller said wearily. 'We worked together once.' He downed a sizeable mouthful of whisky, feeling the amber fluid burn its way to his stomach.

The questions continued and Miller answered each one dutifully, watching in amusement as the officer in charge wrote down his answers almost verbatim.

'You say the attack took place about 1.30,' said the

policeman, looking at his watch. 'That's almost four hours ago. Why didn't you contact us sooner?'

Miller shrugged.

'I must have blacked out,' he said, rubbing his shoulder.

The policeman chewed the end of his pen for a moment then flipped his notebook shut.

'There's an ambulance waiting outside to take you to hospital. That shoulder needs seeing to.'

Miller smiled thinly and finished his drink.

'I might need to ask you some more questions,' the policeman said.

'No sweat. Ride in the ambulance with me,' Miller said, wandering into the hall. 'Just give me a minute, will you?'

'I'll wait for you outside,' the officer said and walked out.

Miller waited until he was out of the house then turned and headed down the short corridor towards his workroom. The key was in the door so he turned it and walked in, shutting it behind him.

The flayed woman was back in her place, fresh latex now covering the parts which Ryker had exposed.

The severed head in the tray on top of the filing cabinet stared blankly at him.

The burn victim looked on impassively.

The work had not taken as long as he'd expected and he looked on with pride.

Seated in the far corner of the room, her body completely encased in latex, was Terri Warner.

Miller had carried her to the workroom and then, quickly but expertly, he had stripped her and covered every square inch of her flesh with his own prosthetic creation. The face he had distorted to mask her real features. She now sported an assortment of boils and sores, all moulded from the liquid rubber with matchless skill.

He had blocked her nostrils and mouth with cotton wool while he worked, finally covering her face with a mask of rubber.

She had already suffocated before he got that far.

The knock on the door startled him and he stepped away,

allowing the newcomer to enter.

The policeman looked into the room, scanning each one of the grisly creations.

'One of the men outside said you were in films,' the officer said. 'Special effects isn't it?'

Miller nodded, watching as the policeman looked at the creations with something akin to admiration.

'How the hell do you make them look so real?' the man wanted to know.

Miller looked across at the body of Terri Warner and smiled.

'Trade secret,' he said quietly.

'He that is without sin among you, let him first cast a stone . . .'

Luke 8:7

'We all need scapegoats, someone else to blame for what we're really feeling. Anything, as long as we don't have to face the truth.'

Anon.